D1038062

THE DIAMOND KEEPER

Also by Jeannie Mobley

The Jewel Thief

THE
DIAMOND
KEEPER

Jeannie Mobley

VIKING

VIKING
An imprint of Penguin Random House LLC, New York

First published in the United States of America by Viking,
an imprint of Penguin Random House LLC, 2021

Copyright © 2021 by Jeannie Mobley

Penguin supports copyright. Copyright fuels creativity, encourages diverse voices, promotes
free speech, and creates a vibrant culture. Thank you for buying an authorized edition of this
book and for complying with copyright laws by not reproducing, scanning, or distributing
any part of it in any form without permission. You are supporting writers and allowing
Penguin to continue to publish books for every reader.

Viking & colophon are registered trademarks of Penguin Random House LLC.

Visit us online at penguinrandomhouse.com.

Library of Congress Cataloging-in-Publication Data is available.

Book manufactured in Canada

ISBN 9781984837448

1 3 5 7 9 10 8 6 4 2

FRI

Design by Opal Roengchai
Text set in LTC Deepdene

This is a work of historical fiction. Apart from the well-known actual people, events,
and locales that figure in the narrative, all names, characters, places, and incidents
are the products of the author's imagination or are used fictitiously. Any resemblance
to current events or locales, or to living persons, is entirely coincidental.

The publisher does not have any control over and does not assume any
responsibility for author or third-party websites or their content.

For Claudia, who, like Claudie, is a solid rock and
an inspiration in the toughest of times.

Jacques Lambert brought the revolution to us. The revolution and so much more. Tucked away as we were in our quiet little corner of Brittany, the violence might have overlooked us. We had no quarrel with our king or our priests. Our lives had gone on, comfortable and complacent, while far away, the mobs stormed the Bastille, the women of Paris marched on Versailles, and Louis XVI became a prisoner in his own palace. None of that had anything to do with us.

At least, not until Jacques Lambert forced it upon us.

Perhaps you are thinking I blame Jacques unfairly, shooting the messenger, as they say. Certainly, Mathilde accused me of that, but then, I knew things my sister did not.

Jacques was the messenger, I grant you. It's what brought him through our village in the first place, carrying the post from Paris to Rennes, and sometimes on to Brest. And it is true that when he stopped at my father's inn for a fresh horse, a hot meal, and a few kisses from my sister, he brought us news of all that was happening in Paris. It was from Jacques's tongue that we first heard of the armed peasants and the Universal Rights of Man. It was on Jacques's jaunty auburn head that we first saw the *bonne rouge*, the red knitted liberty cap that distinguished the revolutionaries who meant to build a new republic in France.

But do not spare him, just because he was the messenger. Because Jacques brought more than news to us, and what he brought, the Army of the Republic was sure to pursue.

To our destruction.

CHAPTER 1

September 1792

Though there were riots in the capital and empty harvests elsewhere in France, in our small corner of Brittany, September turned golden and ripe around us. Thick shocks of wheat stood in the fields waiting for threshing, and the apple trees drooped beneath the weight of the harvest. Everyone was busy from dawn until dusk. No one had time for revolution.

Still, when Jacques came galloping recklessly into our innyard, his mouth as full of gossip as his saddlebags were of mail, everyone flocked to him. The men were eager for news, the women for Jacques's wink and mischievous grin. All the unwed girls dreamed of joining him in the daring exploits he bragged of while they sat, doe-eyed, at his elbow.

Almost all the girls, that is; I was never taken in. I heard his stories—how could I not when it was my job to serve the drink to everyone who came to hear him?—but I wasn't fool enough to believe them. If all the girls in town were in love with Jacques, he was just as in love with himself.

Mathilde, however, was head over heels, after the fashion of fifteen-year-old girls with dreams too big for their villages. She could hear him coming from a mile off, and whatever chore she was doing would be shoddily finished, or more likely not finished at all. Once he arrived, all she would do was see to his comfort and fill her head with his boastful stories. My sister was too sweet and pretty by far, and too trusting, and I always breathed a sigh of relief when he galloped away, so she could get her head out of the clouds he put it in.

Mathilde had just begun the evening milking when he arrived that September day. At once, the heavy udders of our poor cows were forgotten. She rushed from the barn and into his arms, and he hoisted her up, spinning her once around before planting a daring kiss on her cheek.

I had been sweeping the yard, so I witnessed it all. Seeing me glowering at them, Jacques gave Mathilde an extra peck.

"How did the same man sire one daughter so sweet and another so sour?" he asked her, taking no care to prevent my hearing. After all, what did a few sharp barbs matter to a plain girl like me?

Mathilde giggled. "Claudie's not so sour," she said, turning her bright face toward me. "Claudie, will you finish the milking? Please? Someone has to get food and drink for our guest, and Cook will be busy getting supper ready." With that, she turned her full, flirtatious attention back to Jacques, not waiting for my answer. They entered the inn, Jacques already telling her of his adventures on the road, while I was left alone with his lathered horse and all the unfinished chores.

I tended to the tired horse first, then completed the milking. By the time I trudged inside, lugging buckets of milk in each hand, a small crowd of village girls had gathered and were hanging on Jacques's every word.

"I tell you, Paris has turned upside down! The king is a prisoner, and criminals rule the streets. The poor wear their poverty with the arrogance of lords, while the lords try to pass themselves off as paupers. Nothing is sacred—the churches have been stripped of their gold, the priests of their vows. Do you know, even the crown jewels have been stolen!"

A collective gasp issued from the girls—whether at the audacity of the crime or the glory of such jewels, I couldn't be sure.

"Weren't they guarded?" Mathilde asked.

"They were, but the thieves were clever," Jacques said, smiling as if he admired their cleverness almost as much as he admired his own. "They bought the service of the guards, or perhaps they were the guards themselves. A window was left unlocked, a door was unprotected, and the next thing you know, the jewels had vanished!"

"All of them?" Terese, the miller's daughter, asked, her eyes huge and round.

"All the important ones. The yellow Mazarin diamond, and the one they call the Mirror of Portugal, and the greatest prize of all— the Blue of the Crown, in which they say the mighty Sun King, Louis XIV, captured the sun."

"Imagine!" Mathilde said, her eyes shining. "The crown jewels! Some lucky girl is walking around Paris shining like the queen herself!"

"Don't be a fool!" I hadn't meant to snap, but the thought of Mathilde wishing to put herself in danger vexed me even more than Jacques. "They'd have your head for wearing such things. And any-way, they are stolen. Have you no morals?"

Mathilde's eyes narrowed and she opened her mouth to hurl her answer at me, but to my surprise, and hers as well, Jacques jumped in to defend me.

"Claudie is right, Mathilde. You could not wear those jewels in public. They are too grand. Why, they say the Blue of the Crown is the size of your palm, with a piece of the sun at its heart. Such a thing would be dangerous, would it not?"

"Well, what is the point in taking such a glorious thing if you cannot wear it?" Mathilde said, sounding a little sulky.

"Perhaps those who took it had another reason. Who knows? To fund their revolution, perhaps? To ransom the king?"

"To satisfy their own greed," I muttered, pouring a bucket of milk into the churn in the corner, another of Mathilde's jobs left undone.

"Well, I don't believe a thing of beauty should be hidden away," Mathilde said, pouting because Jacques had sided with me.

"Such a thing would be a death sentence on the streets of Paris just now," Jacques assured her. "They are teeming with the self-appointed armies of the revolution, with their clubs and knives, looking for anyone who might be trying to smuggle their wealth out of the city. 'It is the people's wealth!' they cry, and by 'the people' they mean any of them who can get their hands on it. They see a man astride a good horse, they swarm like ants to pull him from his seat. 'Liberté!' they cry, by which they mean they will liberate the poor sod from his money."

"Did that happen to you?" Mathilde asked, breathless.

"It did," Jacques answered, his eyes agleam with adventure. He had, of course, known she would ask and had only paused so that his audience could beg him for more. "There is naught to be gained from pulling me out of the saddle, a mere carrier of the post as I am, but tell that to the mindless rabble packing the streets, throwing bricks through shop windows and working themselves into a bloodthirsty rage. I rounded a corner, and there was the mob, pulling the furniture from a rich man's house, heaping it like so much splintered firewood in the street.

"Before I could turn and try a different route, they were upon me, grabbing my bridle and my saddlebags, scrabbling like rats at my boots." His hands grasped at the air, fingers curled into demonic claws to illustrate. Mathilde's hands went to her mouth.

I began plunging the paddle in the churn hard enough to drown out his words, but to no avail. He only raised his voice.

"It was only a matter of time till they unseated me," Jacques continued.

"How ever did you escape?" breathed Mathilde, her cheeks flushed prettily with the excitement of it all. Since childhood, flushing prettily had been one of Mathilde's greatest talents. When I flushed, I looked blotchy and ill, but a rush of blood to Mathilde's cheeks was as smooth and perfect as summer cream.

"I tell you, I didn't know if I would," he said, leaning in, drawing the girls toward him. "But with my free hand, I brandished this!" He pulled the knitted liberty cap from his head and waved it in the air above us all so that the tricolor ribbons of his revolutionary cockade fluttered.

"And then," he continued, the twinkle in his eye growing more mischievous, "I broke into song."

He leapt up onto a bench, swung the *bonne rouge* over his heart, and in a clear, confident baritone, began to belt out "*Ça Ira*," a favorite anthem of the Republic.

> "Ah! ça ira, ça ira, ça ira,
> Les aristocrates à la lanterne!
> Ah! ça ira, ça ira, ça ira,
> Les aristocrates on les pendra!"

Mathilde leapt to her feet and joined him in a chorus before falling back into giggles.

"Did that really work?" Terese asked, the only girl in the group bold enough to try to pull his attention away from Mathilde.

Jacques beamed down at her, his eyes still alight with his own resourcefulness. "It caught them off guard, I can tell you. I wrested myself free of their grasp and explained who I was, a messenger for the revolution itself. '*Vive la révolution!*' they cried at hearing this, and before all was said and done, they drank to my health with bottles of wine they had pulled from the cellars of the house."

At that point, he reached into the saddlebag he'd brought in with him and extracted a dark bottle. "And they sent me with one for the road!" he added triumphantly, holding the bottle aloft. "*Vive la révolution!*"

Mathilde clapped her hands in delight, then hurried to the bar and retrieved glasses, enough for everyone in the inn. Jacques pulled the cork from the bottle with his teeth and poured a trickle of the red-black wine into each one, and Mathilde passed them around. The miller's daughter accepted her glass with a titter of delight. Wine was a rare treat, Brittany being poorly suited to the cultivation of grapes.

As for me, I refused a glass, choosing instead to retreat to the kitchen, where I wouldn't have to stomach any more of Jacques's boasting. I hardly believed his story—there wasn't a scratch on him, after all. It was all bravado, intended to take in foolish country girls, but it wouldn't work on me.

The inn grew busier after supper, when the local men, finished with their work and eager for news, came to hear what Jacques could report. As they filled the room, he removed his *bonne rouge* and stuffed it into a saddlebag. I didn't know what he carried in those bags, or for whom, but he took seriously the requirement that he keep the contents of them safe at all times. The bags never left his sight.

"The Prussian army—the greatest in the world—has already crossed the northeastern border and is advancing. They mean to liberate Paris," Jacques told the local crowd. "The Duke of Brunswick is at their head, vowing vengeance if one hair on the king's head is harmed."

"They will take Paris, surely," Reynard the butcher said, with his usual unwarranted authority. Beside him, his son, Pierre, sat leering at Mathilde, who still hovered as near to Jacques as she could. "The so-called Army of the Republic is nothing more than a crowd of rabble."

"They've become more than that, I'm afraid," Jacques said, his expression grim. "The Parisians didn't take kindly to the duke's threat. Paris is awash in blood—thousands of prisoners, and the priests and bishops too."

Everyone sat in silence for a moment, agape at the horror. It was unimaginable how so much rage could be directed toward king and church. Our village priest, old Père François, was like a kind old *grand-père* to us. He'd christened every child, married every couple, and we all expected him to see us safely off to God when the time came.

"We cannot stand for this," someone muttered, and debate erupted across the room, quickly escalating to a dozen shouting, arguing voices that made it impossible for me to follow any thread of conversation as I carried trays of mugs and pitchers of cider in and out of the room.

The crowd stayed late drinking that night, but Jacques retired early to his room and rode out the next morning before sunrise. I was in the barn feeding the horses when he appeared and saddled his mount. He led it out into the yard, but I did not hear him gallop away. Instead, I heard a murmur of voices, and I knew Mathilde was with him.

I gave them a few minutes to themselves, but only a few. I didn't trust him alone with my sister for any length of time. Still, I didn't want to intrude unnecessarily, so I moved quietly to the doorway of the barn, where I could keep an eye on them.

He had led the horse to the mounting block but had not yet mounted. The reins dangled loosely from his hand as he wrapped Mathilde in an intimate embrace. For all that I suspected Jacques of using my sister, I was moved by the tenderness in his face as he leaned down toward her upturned lips.

"Take me with you," she said, her whole body pleading as she pressed against him.

He brushed his hand along her cheek. "Soon, *mamour*, but not today. Today, I must make haste. Great things are afoot. Dangerous things."

"I want to be part of all that, Jacques. Don't you see? I could help you."

"I know, but what of your family? They need you too."

Mathilde made a dismissive noise in her throat. "My family doesn't need me! And anyway, Claudie is better suited for tending a dreary inn. She can have it—I want a life of adventure!"

Her words stung like a slap. It was true, the dreary work to keep the inn running—stabling horses, washing bed linens, tending the cows, the cheeses and apple trees—did fall mainly to me. Papa kept the books and managed the cider press and drank with the men of the village every evening while Mathilde and I waited on them hand and foot. But I didn't do it because it suited me. I did it for my family, especially for my sister, who had only been three when our mother's escalating fits of religious ecstasy drew her to the cloister, leaving me, a girl of only seven, to fill her shoes.

Perhaps what stung most was that Mathilde was right. However I might feel about it, I was built for the work. I was sturdy and plain beside Mathilde's petite prettiness. My role would be to keep my father's house and business as long as he needed me. Mathilde might make a good marriage; several men in the village had their eye on her, and Papa had set aside a small sum for her dowry. But not for mine. He meant to keep me to run the inn until the day he died.

I turned back into the barn, the bitter taste of my fate on my tongue, but my heavy wooden clog banged against a bucket that clattered onto its side. At once, Mathilde sprang back from Jacques's embrace.

"Claudie?" Mathilde's sweet voice broke through my anger.

I turned again, trying to look as if I hadn't heard a thing, as if I was simply done with my work in the barn.

"Do you need anything for your journey, Monsieur Lambert?" I asked, my voice brassy with false cheer.

"Thank you, Mademoiselle Claudette, but I have all I need," he replied. He turned one last tender gaze toward Mathilde. "I must be off, though parting is a sorrow." He placed a lingering kiss on her cheek, then leapt blithely to the saddle.

"*Au revoir, mamour,*" he said with his usual cocky grin, and blew her a kiss.

She rushed to his side, holding aloft her finest handkerchief, one she'd spent hours embroidering while I scrubbed and ironed piles of linens. Now I knew why.

He took the dainty cloth, held it to his nose, and breathed in the sweet smell of lavender. "And I will have a fine gift for you upon my return," he promised as he tucked the handkerchief into his coat, over his heart. "A gift more marvelous than your wildest dreams." He winked, then spurred his horse and galloped away.

Mathilde sighed a long, dreamy sigh as she watched him. I turned and went into the kitchen, kicking off my dusty clogs by the door. She was still gazing after him when I returned a few minutes later with the milk buckets and egg basket. I thrust the basket into her hands.

"Did you hear, Claudie?" she said, hugging the basket to her chest, her eyes still fixed on the road in the direction he had gone. "A gift more marvelous than my wildest dreams. What do you suppose it could be?"

"Don't be a fool. All he's ever likely to bring you is trouble," I said, giving her a little push toward the henhouse. "We need eggs for breakfast."

"There's nothing foolish about true love," she said defensively. "Someday he will take me with him."

I gave a little bark of laughter. "He rides through a dozen little villages like ours every week. He's probably got a girl in every one who thinks the same thing."

"He would never!" she protested.

"You're much better off with Pierre. He will inherit his father's butcher shop and give you a comfortable home and meat at every meal."

She tossed her bountiful dark curls over her left shoulder, her usual gesture of defiance. "A comfortable home might be enough for you, Claudie, but I want more. I want love. I want to live in Paris. I want adventure!"

I rolled my eyes. "This is hardly the time to wish yourself off to Paris. Haven't you heard a word of the news Jacques brings? Or do you only have an ear for compliments and flattery?"

"Of course I've heard! I'm not stupid," she said, planting her hands on her hips. "But surely this will be the end of it. Don't you see? The Prussians will restore peace. The revolution will be over and things can go back to normal, and I can go to Paris and marry Jacques—"

"He has asked you to marry him?" I had been heading off to milk the cows before putting them out to pasture, but I turned back to my sister in concern.

Mathilde giggled. "Not in so many words," she said. I breathed a sigh of relief. "But we dream of a time when we can be together."

"*You* dream of such a time," I said. "You and every innkeeper's daughter on his route."

"Not everyone. Not you. But then again, you don't know how to dream, do you?" With that, she turned and flounced off to the hen-house.

I strode off to the milking, my lips pressed into a tight line. So what if I didn't dream? There was no point to it, not when I knew exactly what my future was to be. Why imagine impossible futures that would only serve to make real life duller and less satisfying than it already was? It seemed foolish at best, and at worst—considering we were our mother's daughters—it could be dangerous.

CHAPTER 2

Two days after Jacques's visit, Mathilde and I were in the orchard, bringing in the harvest. Papa had nearly an acre of apples. It would take us a week to pick them, working dawn to dusk, laboring until our necks were stiff and shoulders ached from looking up. Four times a day, we would pull the full cart back to the cider house, where Papa was manning the press. Our livelihood depended on putting up a supply of cider to see us through the year. The rest of France had their grapes and their famous wines. We Bretons had our cider.

Of course, I picked three bushels for every one Mathilde carried to the cart. A pretty girl has a duty to herself and others to allow herself to be wooed, after all. She was the one with prospects and with eager boys happy to oblige her. While I stripped branch after branch of apples, hauling my ladder from one tree to the next, I was accompanied by the soft prattle and giggles of my sister and whatever young man happened to be assisting her at any moment, meaning that neither of them was getting much done. More than once over the years I had asked Papa to find a task for her in the press, but he had always refused.

"It wouldn't be proper to send you into a field full of hired hands alone," he would insist. "And anyway, I need you to keep an eye on Mathilde." By which he meant he wanted to give Mathilde a chance to be paraded before the men of the village, shown for the choice morsel she was, but discreetly. Respectably. Under the watchful eye of her plain, matronly sister.

Papa was most hopeful of Pierre, the butcher's son. Such a match would not only mean a secure future for Mathilde but also a greater profit for the inn, securing our meat supply at a discount. Pierre was eager to comply and for three years now had volunteered to help us during the apple harvest, where he followed Mathilde like a smitten puppy. She gave him smiles and merry conversation, as she did all the boys, but she was careful not to favor him above the others.

"Who wants to marry a man who smells of blood and death?" she would say, wrinkling her petite nose at the thought whenever I made mention of it. Still, I tried to steer her gently toward the idea, treating him with kindness and encouraging him in the suit whenever I could. I knew, even if Mathilde did not, that in the end her fate would be Papa's decision, not hers. In that, at least, we were not so different, Mathilde and me. So, despite the lack of help, I was not entirely displeased when, while carrying my next full basket back to the cart, I saw her sitting on a branch, swinging her legs, and listening with a rapt expression to some tale being told to her by the butcher's ruddy son.

My bushel was the last that the cart would hold, so not wanting to disturb Pierre when he finally seemed to be making a bit of progress, I called over one of the hired hands to help me haul the cart to the cider house, which stood on the edge of the innyard, flanked by the stable on one side and the cheese shed on the other.

As we rounded the end of the stable, toiling and sweating under the weight of the cart, I was surprised to see a man on a huge horse in the innyard. It was only midmorning, an odd time for a traveler to arrive, but there he was, astride his mount and gazing impatiently around him as if expecting an attendant.

"A moment, monsieur!" I called.

He watched as we pulled the creaking cart to the door of the cider house and struggled to tip it up and dump the apples into the pile. It was almost more than the two of us could manage, but the visitor made no offer of assistance. He just watched us or, more specifically, watched me, while his horse rattled its harness impatiently. Perhaps he was surprised to see a girl doing such manly work. Perhaps he was wondering if I was female at all. I gritted my teeth and strained harder against the cart, meaning to show him my worth and squelch the part of me that wished he would make a gallant offer of help.

When the cart was empty, I sent the hired man back to the orchard and I turned to the traveler, reminding myself I had a duty to serve him courteously, as a customer.

The sun was behind him, casting him as a towering silhouette, and for a moment my breath caught as I had the impression of a knight of old atop a great charger. But as I stepped toward him across the yard, the inn blocked the sun and the idiotic idea faded. His steed was no charger, but one of the sturdy Breton draft horses common to the estates west of our village.

The man resembled his mount—large, well-muscled, and shaggy. I might have thought him a farmhand on his master's plow horse but for his commanding presence and the horse's fine tack—not rich, but of good quality and sturdy, for long hours on the road. I shaded my face with my hand to better see him as I gazed upward. His hair was dark, and his face well tanned. His eyes were fixed on me with a gaze so intense it bordered on indecent. Involuntarily, my hand rose to straighten my bodice.

"How can I help you, monsieur?" I said politely, trying to ignore the blush unexpectedly heating my cheeks. "Will you come inside for a hot meal and a rest?"

"I have no time to rest, madame," he said, and I flinched a little at his assumption that I was a married woman. Had my duties at the inn aged me so far beyond my nineteen years?

"I am looking for Jacques Lambert."

My eyebrows raised in surprise. I shook my head. "I am sorry, monsieur, but you have missed him by two days."

The heavy brows drew down, shadowing his gaze. "*Blast* him. Where has he gone?"

He went on staring at me as if Jacques's timing had something to do with me. Did he think I was hiding Jacques from him? The implication annoyed me, and when I spoke again, it was without quite as much politeness.

"As I said, he is not here. I believe his route generally takes him toward Rennes."

"I know his route," the man said, waving an impatient hand. "The point is, he was to rendezvous with me yesterday and he did not show up."

"That is hardly my concern," I said, surprising even myself. Something about this fellow was bringing out the sharp edge of my tongue that I could usually curb. If Papa heard me, I'd take a beating for using such a tone with a patron, yet here I was. "I can offer you food or rest, but that is all. I am hardly Jacques Lambert's keeper."

One eyebrow lifted in a sarcastic expression. "Aren't you? Well, that is a surprise," he said. "As for food, madame, I would be glad for some bread and cheese that I can eat in the saddle. And a cup of cider would not go amiss." He glanced around, his eyes coming to rest on the well. "May I water my horse?"

I gave a grudging nod, annoyed by his sarcasm, as if I needed to be reminded that no man would be interested in me. I would have liked to turn him away, but of course, we were an inn and could not afford to lose anyone's custom. "The bucket is by the well," I called over my shoulder as I walked back toward the inn.

I heard him dismount behind me. When I returned with the bread and cheese in one hand and a cup of cider in the other, his horse was slurping happily at the full trough. He stood beside it, twisting to stretch the muscles of his back and shoulders, which were considerable. Now that he was on the ground, I could see he was younger than he had seemed when he was towering imperiously over me. In fact, he was not much older than me, which made his address of *madame* all the more annoying.

He did not, however, seem any smaller for being on the ground beside me. To the contrary, as he raised the cup and gulped down its contents, his arms bulged against the worn woolen sleeves of his coat, and I realized just how massive he was. My eyes only came to the level of his broad chest. Over his heart, a linen patch had been sewn onto the dark brown wool with clumsy stitches. On the patch, the sacred heart was painted in bright red, and beneath it were three words. *Roi et Dieu.* King and God. Dangerous words to wear on your breast when the new Republic had sworn to do away with both.

He wiped his mouth on the back of his hand before returning the cup to me with another penetrating gaze.

"How about a few of those apples?" he asked, tipping his head toward the cider house.

I retrieved six apples from the pile. When I returned, I handed all but one to the man and, without asking, gave the last to his horse, of whom I had a higher opinion than the rider.

"Have you any children, madame?" he asked, watching me with a flicker of amusement.

"It's *mademoiselle*, actually," I said stiffly. "So, no, I have no children."

His eyebrows raised. "Really? I am astonished."

I didn't know what to make of that so only stood there, my mouth open but empty as he tucked the apples into his wide sash and swung up into his saddle as if he meant to leave.

"That will be three deniers, sir. For the food and drink. The apple for your horse was on the house."

"Hear that, Gideon?" he said, patting the huge beast on the neck. "You have made an ally." The horse shook its head playfully at the pat, and the man chuckled, then reached into his purse for a few coins. He leaned down and held them out to me.

When I stepped close to take them, he spoke again, not in French this time but in Brezhoneg, our local Breton language. We spoke it among ourselves in the village, but I always spoke French with travelers, as the road before our door was a thoroughfare to Paris and French better suited many of our guests.

"Lock up tight tonight," he said, his expression once again grim. "Sisters, brothers, servants—whoever you care for, keep them safe inside."

"Why?" I asked, keeping to Brezhoneg, my voice a little unsteady with alarm. "What is happening? What have you heard?"

He only held a finger to his lips in response, then straightened in the saddle.

"If you see Jacques Lambert, tell him I will wait as long as I can before I go on to Rennes."

"But you have not told me who you are," I pointed out.

"He will know," the man said, then, with a twitch of his reins, he turned the big horse's head and spurred it to a gallop before he'd even left the innyard.

CHAPTER 3

I returned to the orchard, but my mind was hardly on my work. I was thinking about the strange encounter and ominous warning. I was worried for my family, for our harvest, our inn, and even, against my better judgment, for Jacques Lambert.

In the midafternoon, I broke from the work in the orchard, retrieved Mathilde, and returned to the inn to prepare for our evening business. Though it had become unpredictable since the onset of the revolution, we usually had a coach or a few wagon and cart drivers that stopped for the night. Business always picked up in the harvest season, and there was the steady flow of locals too, more eager than ever to hear the news and debate what it would mean for us, though it seldom meant very much. Ours was the kind of quiet village where we kept to ourselves, relied on no one, and went unnoticed by the world around us.

The stranger's warning, though, had unsettled me. I said nothing about it to Mathilde, but she knew me too well to miss my dark mood.

"What is the matter with you, Claudie?" she demanded as we drew off the night's cider from the big casks in the cellar.

"There was a man . . ." I began, then paused, unsure how much I should tell her.

"Oh, Claudie! At last!" she squealed, glancing up at me. I could see the mischievous glint even in the dim light of the cellar.

"It's nothing like that!" I snapped, regretting my ill-timed pause that let her think I had a suitor.

"No? Then what is it?" she asked, her tone teasing.

"He was asking after Jacques Lambert," I said.

Her eyes widened at the mention of the name. "Is Jacques coming?"

I reached across and turned off the tap on her barrel before her bucket overflowed. "I don't know. This man seemed like trouble, Mathilde. He said we should lock our doors tonight."

Mathilde's delicate brow knitted. "Was it a threat?"

I shook my head. "More of a warning."

"Of what? What did he say would happen?"

All I could do was shrug and shake my head again. By now, our buckets were full, and I closed the tap on my cask, making sure it was tight and wouldn't drip. Papa would tan my hide if I wasted any cider.

"Oh, I do hope Jacques will come," Mathilde said, her voice full of longing. "He would know if there was danger. I always feel safe when he is here."

"You are hardly safe with Jacques," I scoffed, which made her scowl. "You should mind your reputation and turn your thoughts toward the suitors who can give you a secure future."

Mathilde let out a huff of annoyance. "Honestly, Claudie, you're like a mother hen, always pecking, pecking, pecking!" She picked up a bucket in either hand and stomped her way up the steep cellar steps, leaving me to follow with the remaining four buckets.

Jacques Lambert did not show his face in our inn that night. An assortment of cart drivers and traveling merchants made their way in for a hot supper and a bed. Around dusk, the bell in the courtyard rang, indicating that a coach or private carriage had arrived with passengers needing assistance. I stepped out with a lantern to see a fine black carriage, the doors scarred where a coat of arms had been pried from it. The curtains in the windows were drawn tight. From its direction, I assumed the carriage had come from Paris and was headed to Rennes.

The coachman glanced around nervously. Seeing me, he tipped his hat in greeting.

"Have you private rooms?" he asked.

"*Bien sûr*," I answered, glancing at the carriage door, curious as to who might be inside. I knew better than to ask.

The coachman hesitated. "A friend, Monsieur Lambert, recommended your inn," he said, looking at me expectantly, though I wasn't sure what he expected. Did he think I would blush at the mention of Jacques?

I gave a small, curt nod. "We know Monsieur Lambert. His friends are welcome here."

The coachman's face relaxed, and he jumped down from his high seat. I hurried to bring the stepping stool as the coachman opened the carriage door. Several road-weary faces peeked out. The first to emerge was a tall gentleman dressed in plain brown woolen breeches and a simply cut linen shirt. The clothes were common enough, but the sheen of fear in in his eyes and his stiff, straight bearing belied his nobility. He glanced around him at the empty innyard before extending a hand to help down a woman, presumably his wife, then two girls on the cusp of womanhood and a boy no more than eight. Behind them came a nurse carrying a baby. A final girl stepped out without the aid of his hand, as she carried baggage in each of her own. Only these last two had the bearing of common folk.

"Good evening, citizeness," each of them greeted me, the girls with a small curtsy.

"Good evening. Welcome," I answered over and over, hoping to put them at ease. I smiled to assure them, without saying so, that we had no complaint with their kind here.

"Have you a stable boy?" the coachman asked, glancing around expectantly.

I shook my head. "Not when the harvest has every spare set of hands in the fields," I said. "But I can do that."

He shook his head. "Attend the family, if you please."

"Well then, come inside when you are done. There's plenty of food, cider, and good cheer," I promised him.

"Mademoiselle," he said with a hand to my arm. He cast a glance toward the door. "Will they be safe here?"

I gave him a reassuring pat on the hand and nodded. "They are safer in Brittany than anywhere else in France, I daresay."

"But here," he said again, "there are no soldiers in your inn? No one who might . . ." He paused, debating how plainly he might speak.

"No one here would turn them in," I assured him quietly. "But should they need secrecy, we have a private enough room upstairs where they might take their supper away from the crowd."

He nodded, looking relieved. "That sets my mind at ease, mademoiselle. If you would convey them there now, it would be best. Rest assured, they are good people, and they can pay."

"Of course, monsieur," I said, and I led the family to the kitchen door, where they could enter and climb the servants' stairs to the second-floor rooms, unseen from the common room.

"I have rooms ready, citizens," I assured them. The revolution's new address sounded strange and artificial. Here, so far from Paris and its revolutionary fervor, no one bothered with such things, but it seemed to set the family at ease.

I pushed open the door to the comfortable salon that had been my family's home before my mother left us. Technically, it still was, but we never used it anymore. We just sat in the common room for a few minutes in the evening after cleaning up, then trudged off to our beds, just like our customers. Relief flooded the faces of the mother and children when they stepped inside.

"Make yourselves comfortable," I said. "I will bring up your supper."

By the time I returned downstairs, another large crowd of local men had come in. It was shaping up to be a busier night than we'd had in some time. My father was at the bar filling cups and glancing around with an angry expression. When he saw me emerge from the staircase, he unleashed his tongue.

"Where have you been, you lazy girl?" he bellowed over the rising chatter, so everyone in the room could hear the reprimand. "We've got a full house, and you're upstairs lying about when there's work to be done?"

I quickened my pace to the bar, where a tray of filled cups was waiting. As I reached for the tray, he caught my wrist in a viselike grip. "If you're thinking of following in your mother's footsteps—"

"No, Papa, I wasn't! I was—"

He gave my arm a painful twist, and I gritted my teeth to keep from crying out. "You may think yourself all grown up, girl, but you're not too big for the switch. Just you remember that."

I might have told him of the large party safely settled upstairs. Of how I had acted quickly and cleverly to ease what might have been an uncomfortable and even dangerous situation, and how we could expect a lucrative payment for my quick thinking. But there was no point, not when he was in this mood. The best way to avoid the switching he was thinking about was to keep my eyes down and do my work, the picture of filial obedience. So, I just muttered, "Yes, Papa. I'm sorry, Papa," and took the tray of mugs.

Three trips between the bar and the tables and everyone had a drink. Then I was off to the kitchen to start portioning out food. The locals would go home for their supper, but our apple pickers and the cart drivers were hungry, not to mention the family upstairs.

Fearing my father's wrath, I began with the paying customers seated out front. Cook, our one paid employee in the inn, had wrung the necks of half a dozen chickens that morning and stewed up an enormous *pot-au-feu* that now bubbled and steamed enticingly over the fire. The smell made my mouth water as Cook hoisted the kettle off the hook and onto the table, where bowls and plates waited in stacks. As she began to dish up the meat and vegetables, I glanced around for Mathilde, but she was not there. My heart skipped a beat, remembering the stranger's warning, but before I could ask, she stepped in the back door carrying two wheels of cheese, and I relaxed.

I sent her out front with the first tray of plates. Her sweet, smiling face always cheered the crowd and placated my father in a way that

I never could. I was an asset to Papa as a dependable old plow horse might be; Mathilde was his sleek Thoroughbred he was proud to own.

Mathilde carried the tray out front cheerfully. By the time I carried a second tray from the kitchen, the room was loud with good cheer. Mathilde had set out all the plates of chicken and baskets of bread and now was moving through the crowd with a pitcher of cider in either hand, refilling the cups that were lifted toward her. More than once a hand reached out from a table to pat or pinch her bottom as she squeezed through. She bore it with gritted teeth, offering a smile if the pat came from a friend or a frown if it was a stranger or a man she didn't care for. Some nights, after we were abed, she complained that her backside was bruised from all the attention.

"If only they wouldn't pinch so hard!" she would sigh, rubbing a buttock. She never reprimanded a customer with more than a disapproving glance, not since the day that I had seen a man fondle her breast and had given the fellow a hard slap. Papa had seen it and had explained, while he beat me black and blue, that he would not have his business undermined by "the silly whims of stupid girls." I'd had a bruised face for a week. Mathilde had gotten a whipping too, but Papa had always been careful to leave her pretty face unblemished. He would not undermine his business.

Since then, Mathilde uncomplainingly put up with the pinches. Whenever I witnessed one and wanted to come to her defense, she reminded me, "They are more generous with their money if you let them enjoy themselves a little," parroting what Papa said whenever he witnessed a customer getting grabby.

As I carried a third tray of plates from the kitchen, I noticed the coachman had come in from the barn at last and was sitting by himself in a corner. He would not be alone for long. Once the locals spotted him and realized he had come from the city, they would be plying him for news. So, I hurried to serve the remaining carters waiting for their meal, then carried a loaf and cup of cider to him.

I bent low as I placed the loaf on the table, so I might speak quietly. "Your passengers are safe upstairs. Would you join them there, sir?"

He shook his head. "Thank you, mademoiselle, but I will keep my eyes open here. We are to meet a man named Jean—a man who transports grain. Do you know him?"

"Many wagons come through here, sir, but I don't know the drivers all by name." I pointed out the drivers where they ate, then returned to the kitchen, where I set aside portions of food for Papa, Mathilde, Cook, and me. I hoisted the pot with all that remained, put a large loaf on top of the lid, and carried it up the servants' stairs to the salon above. Balancing the pot against my hip, I knocked with my free hand. I waited a moment but heard only silence, so I lifted the latch and swung the door open.

"*Bonsoir!*" I called, keeping my voice low and gentle. "I've brought supper."

The family had spread out across the salon. The girl who had carried the bags, apparently a servant, had taken the children to the corner near the fireplace. The young boy had a beautiful book spread across his outstretched legs. Words ran down half the open pages while, across the bottom of the page, a maid in a white apron and overly large wooden clogs—the type we wore to work in the yard or the barn—was chasing geese, her cap flying off her head behind her.

It was a funny, foolish scene, but the boy was silent and solemn, and I doubted he was seeing the pages at all. Beside them, the two girls sat by the lamp with embroidery on their laps, but neither of them worked on their pieces. They were staring around themselves with dazed eyes, as if seeing a foreign country.

I set the pot on the table and began to spoon out the chicken, onions, carrots, and bits of pork fat onto plates. I wondered once again who they were, but I didn't ask. As I turned to leave, I noticed the nursemaid, a girl not much older than me, sitting on the floor in the far corner of the room, somewhat apart from the others. Her bodice was unlaced, and she held the baby to her bare breast. The child sucked greedily, as if he too had been deprived of his supper for too long. The family may have thought to disguise themselves, but the baby was still swaddled in blankets of snow-white linen, the edges trimmed with elegant and expensive lace. Nothing about the girl, however, spoke of nobility—neither her bearing nor her clothes nor the simple way she knotted her hair so that it would stay neatly contained beneath her cap. Whoever these people were, they were apparently rich enough to bring a nursemaid with them into exile. Most likely, they also carried all manner of jewels and coins sewn into their petticoats and tucked into hidden places in their bags.

Not that it mattered to me. I was all for liberty, fraternity, and equality, but I extended such ideals to include people such as these. They had never done me any harm, and I had no reason to harm them. So, I assured them once again of their safety and slipped away to leave them to their supper and their rest.

Downstairs, the common room had grown loud with revelry. The coachman had left his seat in the corner and insinuated himself among the other drivers, though I saw no special familiarity with any that would suggest he had found his Jean.

A few tables away, Mathilde stood, an empty pitcher in one hand, her other on the shoulder of Pierre, the butcher's son. She was laughing, and when Pierre caught her around the waist and pulled her to sit on his knee, she made no protest. Papa was watching with approval from the bar, where he was wiping cups and setting them out for the next round. I hurried to the nearest table and gathered up empty plates and silverware. When my arms were full, I carried them toward the kitchen. As I passed the bar, I heard a snippet of conversation between Reynard the butcher and my father.

"She'll have to work though," Reynard was saying. "I can't abide a lazy daughter-in-law, no matter how easy on the eyes she may be."

"Of course," Papa said. "I've taught my girls to work. But if she doesn't, a good switching will put her in the right frame of mind to stay off her backside."

They both laughed, but then Reynard noticed my disapproving glance. He glanced back at my father.

"You are lucky, Paul. Two daughters, but only one that needs a dowry," he said, meaning for me to hear. My punishment for eavesdropping.

Papa glanced at me and nodded. "Rest assured, *mon ami*, you are getting my better girl in Mathilde," he said. "I'd do better to keep her on hand and marry off that lazy one. But I've got to have someone here to run the inn, and your boy is so sweet on Mathilde, so I'll make the sacrifice, for your friendship."

I lowered my head and hurried into the kitchen. Such words from Papa shouldn't still sting, but they did.

Cook sat at the table, stripping the meat from a chicken leg with her teeth. "He doesn't mean it, *ma poule*," she said as I piled the dirty plates in the sink. Apparently, she'd heard the whole exchange through the open door. She shook her head. "He's just trying to seal a deal. You never tell someone they are getting inferior goods when you're trying to make a sale."

The thought of Papa selling my sister to such a man hardly made me feel better. I wiped the sweat from my brow and returned to the common room for another load of plates. Mathilde had extricated herself from Pierre's knee but was still chatting and flirting—and hadn't done a bit of work as far as I could tell.

I told myself I didn't care as I gathered up another load of plates. I told myself I didn't want a husband, especially not Pierre, the son of a prosperous butcher, who every girl in town would try to tempt from my arms. I looked at those arms—strong and sturdy, better for pressing apples or hauling plates to and from the kitchen than for wrapping around a husband. Not that I'd ever have the chance to find out.

The injustice of it flooded through me, but I forced it down and worked harder, desperate to prove my papa wrong. I loved my sister, I reminded myself. None of this was her fault. It wasn't her fault that she was born pretty and I plain, or that Maman had left or that Papa needed me to stay to run the inn.

I passed by Papa and the butcher once again, trying not to listen this time, but I couldn't help hearing.

"And how do I know she won't be afflicted like her mother?" Reynard asked.

"Of course she won't!" Papa snapped, his face reddening as it always did at mention of Maman's departure. "That was God's will, not the sort of thing that runs in families. I've never seen so much as a spark of religious fervor in my daughters."

There was truth enough in that, I thought as I continued on into the kitchen. I had been seven when Maman had left, and a year later, when I at last admitted she was never coming back, I threw away every rosary in the house. As for Mathilde, anyone could see she liked the attentions of men far too much to seek the cloister.

Cook was slicing apples and laying them out around wedges of the creamy white cheese my sister had brought from the cheese shed earlier. She slid two trays toward me wordlessly. I set down the stack of dirty plates and retraced my steps back to the tables with the cheese trays. Mathilde was once again filling cups, and Marc, the blacksmith, was settling in with his accordion to play a tune.

I set the largest tray of fruit and cheese in front of the cart drivers and the coachman. They were deep in conversation, indifferent to the revelry of the locals.

"Surely the worst is over," said a tall man to the coachman from Paris. "Now that the king is imprisoned, they will get on with building the new Republic."

The coachman shook his head. "Dangerous factions are on the rise. I doubt Danton can hold them at bay much longer."

"But surely he is victorious," the first man protested.

"If you could see Paris, you would not say so. Riots everywhere. Blood running in the streets." He gulped a mouthful of cider, and his next words came out in a growl that carried across the room. "The priests and bishops are the target now—hundreds being slaughtered like animals. I tell you, Paris is an abattoir."

The accordion faltered and stopped, and Marc turned his horrified face toward the coachman. Others too had heard, and even those who had not now turned to see what had interrupted their pleasure.

The coachman glanced around, his face going pale at all the eyes turned in his direction. He squeezed his lips shut. Across the room someone swore. Then someone else shouted a toast.

"*Roi et Dieu!*"

Around the room, there were angry shouts of agreement, and cups were raised in salute. I started. Was it a coincidence that I had only just read those words on the badge on the stranger's chest?

Marc on his accordion took up a new tune—a religious anthem that had been banned by the Legislative Assembly. Around the room, men leapt to their feet, holding their cups aloft and raising their voices in fervent song. When they finished, cries of "Long live the king!" shook the rafters.

I took the chaos as my chance to retreat to the kitchen and eat my own plate of chicken, too drained by the day's work and my father's insults to care about the harmless counterrevolution going on in the common room. I had only taken two bites before Mathilde arrived and joined me.

"So, you've decided to marry Pierre after all," I said.

Mathilde rolled her eyes. "Just because I let him flirt doesn't mean I'm going to marry him. Honestly, Claudie, you should try flirting a little more yourself. It makes the work far more pleasant."

I bristled, as she knew I would. She pretended to ignore my reaction. Nonchalant, she lifted a chicken wing to her mouth and picked daintily at the meat with her teeth.

"But you are going to marry him," I said. "I heard Papa and old Reynard. It's all arranged."

Mathilde gave a little shrug and went on eating. "Let them make their plans. It has nothing to do with me. I'm going to marry Jacques Lambert."

"Nothing to do with you? Don't you see, it has everything to do with you. Papa is ready to hand over the dowry."

"Let him. Jacques doesn't care about a dowry. We will be traveling, and a bag of coins would only slow us down."

"You and Jacques might not care about your dowry, but Papa does. Once he signs it over to the butcher, he will force you to marry. You won't have a choice."

Mathilde actually giggled at that. She licked the greasy sauce from her fingers, then leaned across the table to give me a kiss on the cheek.

"Good little Claudie. Has it ever in your life occurred to you not to do what Papa says you must? It's a whole new world out there. The king overthrown, the rights of man declared, and still, all you can imagine is a life of obedience to a father who's never cared one whit about you?"

I opened my mouth to argue but was interrupted by the clanging alarm of the church bell.

Mathilde and I stared at each other as the clamor rose, my mouth still open but empty of words.

The common room grew momentarily quiet too. Then there was a scramble as men grabbed their hats and hurried outside.

The warning of the man on the huge horse came back into my head. *Stay inside*, he had said, but of course, my bold, impetuous sister was out the door in an instant, and I chased after, determined to keep her safe.

The street grew crowded as neighbors tumbled out of every house, many in nightshirts and caps. Some already carried buckets, assuming an alarm from the church at this hour could only mean fire. Others, however, were fully dressed and booted and carried scythes, pitch-forks, and clubs. They made their way to the front of the crowd with more organization than one might expect of lowly farmers roused from their beds by an unexpected alarm.

I reached for Mathilde's hand, afraid of losing her in the crush. That's when I realized that she too was working her way forward with purpose, though we were unarmed and unprepared for what-ever lay ahead of us.

By the time we reached the square, we were near the front of the crowd. Here, torches brightened the night to full daylight. My feet faltered at the scene they illuminated.

A small troop of soldiers sat on their horses, their blue jackets crisp, their heads all adorned with red liberty caps. Each had a musket that glinted in the torchlight, and each musket was pointed at the gathering crowd. In the space between, three soldiers had dismounted and stood over our beloved priest, Père François, who swayed on hands and knees before them. His black cassock was torn at the shoul-der, and blood dripped from his nose.

"We know they came this way. A large party—the Marquis du Aubigny and his family. They are allies of the king and enemies of the revolution, escaped from their townhouse last night. Harboring them is an act of treason, punishable by death. Where are they, old man?"

My stomach turned over. I was the one harboring them—my family would be the ones punished for treason! And the beating Père François was taking was my fault. He couldn't possibly know of the fugitives I had taken in. I prayed his innocence could save him.

"I harbor no one in my church." Père François spoke boldly, though his voice was slurred as if his teeth were already broken. "But even if I did, who are you to defile the sanctuary granted by God?"

I winced at his defiant response, even as it earned him a hard kick in the ribs. He fell onto his side and curled into himself, coughing.

A cry of protest rose from the crowd, drawing the soldiers to attention, their fingers hovering on the triggers of their guns. I tried to draw back but was trapped by the crowd.

The captain of the troop rode a pace or two forward, bringing the hooves of his horse to within a few inches of our priest's head. Indifferent to the man's agony, he called out to the crowd.

"Citizens, it is a crime against France to help its enemies. Someone among you harbors traitors who would flee France with the wealth of her people. If any of you know where the marquis and his family are hidden, speak and you will be shown mercy."

There was a silence then, a long, pregnant silence, only broken by a cough from Père François and the clink of bridles as the horses, alert for battle, shifted. My heart was in my throat, strangling out any words I might have thought to say. What could I do? If I spoke, my family would surely be condemned, though they knew nothing of the refugees resting in our salon. I gripped Mathilde's hand tighter and prayed the captain's eyes would not alight on my guilty face.

"Citizens, return to your homes!" the captain called. "We will search this village from one end to the other, and when we find them—"

The captain never finished his threat. Somewhere high up and off to the left, where the apple orchards met the forested hills, a shot rang out. The captain jerked violently. His face registered shock, then he toppled from the saddle. With that, the front line of the crowd— the ones with pitchforks, scythes, and clubs—surged forward. The muskets fired in a great cloud of smoke. Women screamed. And I lost hold of Mathilde's hand.

CHAPTER 4

All was confusion. I called out for Mathilde, searching the crowd wildly, but all I could see through the haze of smoke was a shifting mass of men and horses, falling bodies and blood. I shouted her name, even as I ducked a blow from a soldier, who was swinging his spent musket like a club. A horse lunged past me. A neighbor staggered by, his head split and bleeding. I shouted again, then finally, I saw her. She was bent over Père François, helping him to his feet.

Without another thought, I rushed to her, and as I took the priest's other arm, we began to stagger toward the church. I prayed that in such a fray we might go unnoticed, but ten yards from the door of the church, a soldier drove his horse between us and sanctuary. I looked up, only to be confronted by the barrel of a revolver.

"Please," I begged, but my one word of supplication only drew his attention away from the priest. He pulled back the hammer with his thumb and turned the muzzle to point directly into my face. Me! A simple innkeeper's daughter, who had never cared one bit for politics, had never wanted to be part of revolution for either side. My mind was reeling. I was about to die. I couldn't think, I couldn't move. I just stared wide-eyed at the gun, even as the soldier's finger tightened around the trigger.

A chaos of hooves erupted as a gigantic Breton horse barreled into the soldier's mount. The smaller horse screamed and staggered, and the pistol ball whizzed over my head before the animal toppled. The hapless soldier slammed hard into the cobbled street, bellowing in pain as the horse rolled over him.

I looked up at our savior, meaning to thank him, but the words died on my tongue. Gone was the amusement I had seen in his face earlier that day in the innyard. He was scowling down at me, his eyes narrow and angry.

"By the saints, woman! I told you to stay inside!" he growled.

"You're ordering the saints around too now, are you?" I muttered, shifting my grip on the sagging priest.

"What, not a word of thanks? A smile for my trouble?" he said.

"Come on, Mathilde, let's get Père François inside," I said, point-edly ignoring him.

He gave a little snort of either laughter or indignation, I couldn't tell which. Then he spurred his horse away and back into the battle.

"Claudie—" Mathilde said, all curiosity.

I cut her off. This was no time to be explaining things, and any-way, I didn't know exactly how to explain it. "Hurry, Mathilde! Inside!"

With all the haste we could, we gained the steps, then the thresh-old, dragging our fainting priest between us.

The church was cool and dark inside. Others had sought its safety too, mostly women and their children who, like Mathilde and me, had come to the clanging of the bell, not expecting the violence it foretold. At once, gentle hands reached out to take up our burden and help Père François to the far reaches of the nave, where they might tend his wounds. I gladly released him to them, and in his place, I pressed my little sister into a tight embrace. "I thought I'd lost you!" I sobbed.

"Someone had to help our good priest," she said matter-of-factly, as if what she had done was an ordinary thing and our world wasn't falling to pieces just outside the church door.

I held her a moment longer, waiting for my fear to ease, but it did not. Instead, I remembered the words of the soldiers. They had accused the priest of harboring a noble family. A family I had sequestered away in our salon.

I pushed Mathilde away suddenly. "I have to get to the inn," I said.

"Claudie, no! It's not safe out there," Mathilde protested. Of course, she was right, but she didn't know of the family there. No one knew but me, and if these soldiers were hunting them, I had to get them away before they were caught and Papa was condemned.

Chaos still reigned in the square outside the front doors of the church, and several women were working to bar the door even as I spoke. But there was a small door off the right transept that led toward the priest's humble cottage and, I hoped, away from the fighting.

"Stay here," I ordered Mathilde, but of course she did not listen. She dogged my heels the length of the church and through the small chapel in the transept. The door was at the back, behind a painted screen depicting the holy family's flight to Egypt. I unlatched the door and swung it open cautiously. The garden outside was quiet, night moths fluttering peacefully among the priest's flowers, as if the battle before the church was a million miles away.

"Stay here!" I hissed at Mathilde again, then slipped out into the garden. Again, she came pattering along behind me.

The garden gate opened out into a narrow alley at the back, and after a glance to be sure it was safe, I hurried into it. There were a few people about—women running back to their homes to protect their children, men running toward the battle with whatever tools they could grab on the way. I ignored them all and bolted for the inn, cursing Mathilde, whose light steps paced easily along beside me.

"Who was that man?" she asked.

"Nobody," I gasped, panting harder than I needed to, hoping to deter any further questions. It seemed to work. She said nothing more all the way back to our home.

The innyard was deserted as we came bounding into it, but I could hear someone in the barn. I approached cautiously, taking up the hay fork by the front door, just in case. Inside, the coachman was leading his horses out of their stalls, making ready to leave.

"No, monsieur," I said, startling him. "You will need fresh horses tonight. Take those," I said, directing him to the stalls at the back, where the horses intended for the post were kept.

"*Merci*, mademoiselle," he breathed, his face full of gratitude.

"Are they ready to go?" I asked, tipping my head toward the inn.

"They are watching. They will come down when the coach is ready."

"Help him hitch up, Mathilde," I said, and for once, she complied.

I continued into the inn through the kitchen door. I gathered up the loaves that had been meant for our own supper, a dozen apples, and the last of the round of cheese in the kitchen and put them all in a flour sack, then I climbed the stairs. The door was barred, but I told them who I was and they opened it to me. The marquis stood at the window, a pistol in each hand and a musket on the table beside him. His jaw was clenched tight as his eyes scanned the growing darkness. The women were hurriedly stuffing clothes and toys into bags while the nurse huddled with the children, trying futilely to reassure them. The baby was wailing.

"Silence the child!" the marquis barked from his post at the window, only making the child wail louder, even as the nurse bounced and cooed and rubbed the baby's back.

"I've brought you some food for the journey. Take the road west from here, deeper into Brittany. Stay to the villages; you will find help," I said.

"Thank you," said the marquise in her perfect Parisian French, making a farce of her commoner's disguise.

"The carriage is ready," the marquis said from where he stood by the window.

I led them down the back stairs and out through the kitchen, in case anyone remained in the common room. I did not want them seen if I could help it.

Out in the innyard, the horses were snorting and shaking their harnesses.

Mathilde was holding open the carriage door. She helped the ladies in while the coachman and I loaded the baggage. The last child stepped inside, then the marquise stepped up to the door. She squeezed my hand in thanks, pressing some coins into my palm.

"I will pray for your safety," I promised her one last time. Then we closed the carriage door. The marquis took a seat beside the driver, his musket across his knees. The driver cracked the reins, and the carriage rolled out of the innyard, away from the fighting on the other end of town.

"Was that the Marquis du Aubigny?" Mathilde asked as we watched the carriage roll away.

I shrugged and turned my head to avoid meeting her eye. The less she knew the better, and anyway, they were gone now, thank goodness. "They didn't say who they were, and it's not for us to pry into the affairs of our guests."

Mathilde gave me a sidelong look, her eyebrows raised. "But you knew they were nobility," she said. "That's why you were hiding them."

"I wasn't hiding them!" I bristled. "They asked for a private room for the night, and I provided one, just as I would for anyone. We are an inn, are we not? Who am I to turn away the custom of good people with money to pay? We have to make a living."

Mathilde rolled her eyes. "Save it for the tribunal, Claudie. You were right to shelter them and smart to keep their presence a secret."

I bit my lip, looking back toward the center of town, where the bell tower of the church stood out against the glare of torches and the shroud of smoke, which I prayed was all due to the guns. If the soldiers had set fire to the buildings in the town square, it would spread fast through the thatched roofs of the village.

This was my fault. I had given shelter to the travelers, knowing perfectly well that it was illegal to harbor such fugitives. I hadn't asked if they were being pursued—hadn't thought about the consequences to my village. My family.

Mathilde gave a sharp pull on my sleeve. "Come on, Claudie, this is no time to lose your head. We should go clean the room, make sure there is no sign of them. I doubt the soldiers can make good on their threat now, but if they do search, we don't want them to find anything."

I nodded reflexively, and together we returned up the back stairs to the salon. The room showed the evidence of a hasty retreat, the cushions in disarray, plates of half-eaten food on the table, rumpled blankets on the beds. I brushed down the sheets, squared their corners, and remade the beds while Mathilde straightened the cushions and gathered dishes.

"We must go back to the square," Mathilde said when we had finished cleaning the room.

I shook my head. "It isn't safe. And anyway, what could we do?"

"We could help," she said, her eyes fierce. "We could help fight the soldiers. We could help the injured."

I kept shaking my head, more vehemently with each suggestion.

Mathilde stomped her foot, like she always did when she wasn't getting her way. "Don't be such a coward, Claudie! This is our village! These are our friends and neighbors. We have to go back. We have to help them."

Just then, Papa burst into the kitchen from the common room. "There you are!" he said. I wasn't sure if he was angry or relieved to find us, but his next words came out in a gruff command. "Never mind these dishes. Get buckets. There's a fire."

I wondered if he had yet left the inn—if he knew of the battle and what caused it. Had he watched, just now, as Mathilde and I sent the fugitives on their way?

I dared not ask as he thrust two cider buckets into my hands and pushed me toward the door. I grabbed another bucket and a kettle on my way out—everything that could hold water would be needed if there was fire in the village.

Outside, I smelled the unmistakable stench of burning thatch. We had been enjoying a fine, dry harvest season. Our roofs were surely tinder-dry. I could see smoke rising from the center of town, where the fighting was. Mathilde and Papa were already running in that direction, each carrying a bucket in each hand. I followed as fast as I could, the buckets and kettle banging against my legs.

By the time we returned to the square, the skirmish had mostly ended. The soldiers were in retreat, and the village men, who had attacked with such fierceness, were now moderating their pursuit, tapering off as the retreating soldiers reached the edge of town, like farmyard dogs that defend only to the edge of their territory. When we arrived in the square with our buckets, the fighting was two blocks away and the square was filled with the stunned and wounded remnants of the conflict. Opposite the church, the thatch of the tailor's shop was smoldering and a few still-sensible people in the square were shouting and pointing.

At once, Papa, Mathilde, and I ran with our buckets to the communal well in the center of the square. Mathilde began to draw the water and fill buckets while Papa and I rallied those who could to form a line to pass the buckets to the fire. Others showed up with more buckets and more hands.

The rest of the night passed in a blur of hard work, smoke, and blood. The fire was quelled before it could destroy the village, though the tailor's shop was destroyed and Reynard's butcher shop next door was badly damaged. When men or women staggered from the lines in exhaustion, they were sent to tend the wounded, who were gathered into the church, while those who had taken a rest took their places.

I did not relinquish my place easily. As more people had arrived, I had moved in beside Mathilde, drawing up water from the well, and I kept on, long after Mathilde and everyone else around me had been replaced. I worked on feverishly, determined to set right what my secret choice to harbor nobility had wrought.

The sky was beginning to grow gray with the approach of dawn when a pair of sturdy hands gripped my shoulders and moved me a step back from the well.

"But—" I protested as the bucket was firmly removed from my grasp.

"You're falling over!" the big Breton said, his voice harsh from smoke and exhaustion. "Give me that bucket and get yourself into the church, where you can be of use!"

"You!" I said, but wasn't able to finish the protest I had intended. He gave me a none-too-gentle push toward the church, and I had no choice but to stumble in that direction while he began to draw up water at twice the speed I'd been working.

Inside the church, the injured were laid out on the floor. Some were bandaged and resting peacefully. A few had wounds too severe to be made comfortable, and they moaned and cried. I looked around at them all in horror. They were neighbors and friends, people I had known my whole life. They were men and women who, just that afternoon, had been picking apples or threshing grain with an eye toward a cozy, uneventful winter. A future that would carry on with the same simple pleasures and hardships that had shaped village life for centuries and that none of us had ever thought would change. As I looked around me in the dim light of the church, at the wounded and the dead, at the weeping women and the children at their breasts, blissfully ignorant of the night's events, I knew that way of life was gone for us for good.

CHAPTER 5

For the next week, it seemed as if we were all sleepwalking—too stunned by our nightmare to do anything but shamble silently through our duties. We buried the dead—eight villagers and four soldiers—to subdued prayers and tears. We tended our wounded with hushed assurances they would recover. We returned to our work in the fields and in the evenings gathered for cider in the inn, but we did not know what to say to each other, or perhaps it would be more accurate to say we did not know how to say it.

This silence extended even to Mathilde, who rarely stopped talking. Her would-be butcher husband had been badly injured, less by the fight than by his own foolishness when he ran into the burning shop to save his possessions, only to collapse and have to be dragged out himself, burned and choking on smoke. Mathilde had dutifully dressed his wounds and once a day made the trek from our inn to his family's cottage with a bowl of soup or an apple tart to nourish his recovery, but I knew that she was secretly relieved by this turn of events that would forestall further plans for her marriage. Papa would not surrender her to a man who could not provide a living.

I too carried food and aid to my neighbors, though I had no beau to focus my attention on. I was sure that some of them must have known or guessed that the nobles had been sequestered at the inn, and that I had been the one to help them, but no one confronted me.

In fact, as the days passed, I began to notice that some of the villagers showed me a certain deference—a nod in passing here, a sly glance there. Gradually, I began to see it was the same handful of people, and as I thought back to the battle, I realized they were the ones who had seemed prepared for the soldiers—who had gone to the square armed and had pushed to the front of the crowd to confront the troops. This realization knotted in my stomach, and when I saw those men approaching in the street, I lowered my gaze and refused any conspiratorial eye contact. Whatever plans they had made or were now making, I wanted no part of them. I trudged through my days with a sick, gnawing dread in my gut, the same dread that was no doubt rendering all my neighbors mute. Our village had resisted the soldiers of the Republic. It would be reported in Paris that we had attacked them—even killed four of them. Such an act could not go unpunished by the Paris Commune, which had seized control of the government and showed no mercy to anyone who opposed them.

Our only hope was that they had their hands so full massacring the citizenry of Paris that they might not be able to send more troops to us. This, when at last we found our tongues again, was the central topic of debate at the inn in the evenings.

"I've got a cousin off near Redon," Armon said, to no one in particular. "Brings in a good harvest of buckwheat every year. Enough to keep his family comfortable with what they have to sell after they give the landlord his due. I might join him for a while. Maybe there's even a corner of land there I could till for myself."

"You're a free man," Papa protested. "What would you want with a landlord?"

Armon looked down into his cup and swirled the cider there, avoiding looking anyone in the eye. "It would be a living," he said. "This is hardly the time to go looking for work in a city."

"Then stay here!" Papa said, slamming a fist on the counter. "We haven't done anything wrong!"

"We defied and attacked the army," Jean Michel said. "They won't take that lightly."

"We defended our homes when we were falsely accused and attacked," Papa insisted.

I felt several eyes turn to me at this assertion, but I kept my head down and went on wiping cups and stacking them behind the bar, praying that no one could see the incriminating heat rising in my cheeks.

"Well, I'll be staying for a time," Reynard said, laying a hand on Papa's shoulder in support. "What choice do I have, with Pierre laid up?"

Papa refilled his cup in a show of solidarity. I slipped into the kitchen for another tray of cups before any more scrutiny could fall on me.

Mathilde was leaning over a kettle of beans that hung from the hook above the fire, tasting the broth from her big wooden spoon. Cook had a son in Rennes, and the day after the battle, she had packed a bag with her few belongings and set off to find him, leaving the cooking to us.

"It sounds like Armon will soon be gone," I told her, "so I suppose we will have to start baking all our own bread too."

She sighed and gave the pot a stir. "Cowards," she muttered.

"Or wise men," I said. "The army is sure to return. I think we'd be smart to leave."

"Well, I'm glad Papa is staying," she said, wiping her hands on her apron and coming to help me with the glasses. "If we left, I don't know how Jacques would find me."

Jacques Lambert was the least of our worries just then, but I didn't tell her that. There had been only peace between us since that terrible night, as if our secret effort to send the marquis and his family to safety had bound us more tightly together. I didn't want to do anything to compromise that, and I could see by the creases in her brow and the tightness of her expression that Jacques weighed heavily on her mind. He was overdue in his regular visit, and the large stranger's news—that Jacques hadn't turned up for their rendezvous—had her worried.

I had larger worries. Papa's insistence that we stay in the village seemed foolhardy, and my eyes and ears were on alert every minute for an approaching army. I was careful to always know where Mathilde was and to be aware of how we might flee should the need arise. Jacques Lambert could take care of himself. I had to take care of my sister, especially if Papa would not.

A little more than a week after the confrontation, we at last heard the familiar breakneck pounding of hooves that signaled Jacques's arrival. Mathilde and I were helping Papa at the cider press when we heard. Mathilde squealed and dropped her bucket of apples to rush out into the yard. I did not follow, but hurried to gather up the fruit that had rolled away from the bucket before Papa noticed. I paid little attention to the sounds coming from the yard until I heard Mathilde scream.

I dropped the bucket of apples again, not caring that they rolled in every direction, and I burst out into the yard. Papa had heard the scream too, and he was right behind me. At the corner of the inn, I froze in shock and horror.

Jacques was astride his fine mount, and he had pulled Mathilde up behind him, her arms gripping hard around his waist. All around them, mounted soldiers swarmed like flies as even more streamed in from the road. Absurdly, it occurred to me that I had been wrong about Jacques. He had finally made good his promise to take my sister with him. Then, with a sharp slap of horror, I realized the danger my sister was in. The soldiers circled around them, even as Jacques turned his horse this way and that, looking for an escape. At last, seeing none, he reined in and, though she resisted, lowered Mathilde back to the ground.

The circle of soldiers, now a complete and impenetrable wall, grew still. Papa and I were still too, frozen at the corner of the inn, just out of sight.

"Jacques Lambert! At last!" I didn't know which among the soldiers spoke, but I heard the triumph in his voice. "It is over! Surrender it now, and we will return you to Paris for a fair trial."

Jacques actually laughed at that, a sharp, clear sound over the shuffle of the horses. "A fair trial? In Paris? There is no such thing."

"Hand it over!" the soldier barked, impatient now.

"Friends," Jacques said, his expression all wide-eyed innocence, his tone placating. "I do not know what you think I have. I merely carry the post from Paris to Rennes."

He slid from the saddle to the ground. I could no longer see him amid the crush of horses, but I could still hear him.

"Search me if you wish. Search me and my horse; you will find nothing," he said, his voice as full of confidence as ever.

There was a general shifting among the soldiers now as they moved to do just that.

"He has no saddlebags," called out a new voice, perhaps the soldier who had moved to search the horse. This surprised me. I had never seen Jacques go anywhere without his saddlebags.

A soldier on the nearer side of the circle now dismounted, opening a narrow wedge in the crowd through which I could see Jacques facing him and pushing Mathilde farther away. I took a step forward at the sight of my sister, but only one. There was nothing I could do. The circle of soldiers was too strong.

The man who had dismounted approached Jacques until they were eye to eye. I could no longer see Jacques's face, but I could imagine the smug, cool arrogance he would be showing the soldier, even in the face of so much danger.

"Where is it?" I heard the soldier demand again.

I could not hear Jacques reply, but a moment later, Mathilde's scream shattered the air. The soldier turned, and I could see Jacques collapsed on the ground, my sister on her knees beside him. The soldier's bayonet glistened with blood.

"Search the inn," the soldier commanded. "This girl is obviously his conspirator!"

Another series of commands was barked out, and the soldiers leapt into action, dismounting and moving in groups of three or four to the barn, the cheese shed, the cider house, and the inn itself.

Papa and I had been huddled in the shadow of the inn, near the kitchen door, and we shrank back so as to go unseen. When a large contingent made for the front door of the inn, however, Papa swore and hurried inside through the kitchen door. I suppose he thought to reason with them or placate them with the offer of food or drink. I stayed where I was, watching as the soldiers scattered, until there was only a circle of restless horses and, in the middle of them, my sister, cradling her fallen lover's head to her breast and sobbing.

I ran to them, ignoring the horses, desperate to pull Mathilde away while the soldiers were distracted. It was our one chance to get away. She, of course, would not budge, not while Jacques still breathed.

I looked him over quickly. Blood was flowing freely from a single well-placed stab to his gut. I knew nothing of war or soldiers, but I'd seen enough hogs and goats slaughtered to know a flow of blood like that could not be sustained for long. And even if we could stanch the flow, we couldn't possibly move him. Though they were searching the inn and the barn, the soldiers were still all around us and would surely notice. There was nothing we could do for him—no way to protect him. Jacques Lambert was a dead man.

"Come on, Mathilde," I begged her urgently, pulling at her arm. "We have to get away from here."

"I won't leave him," she sobbed, shaking off my hand. "I won't leave you, Jacques."

He was gasping for breath, his eyes squeezed shut. One hand was bunching the cloth of his shirt over the wound as if trying to stanch it. The blood was welling between his fingers. At Mathilde's words, he opened his eyes and looked up into her face.

"Listen to your sister, Mathilde," he whispered. "Go."

She shook her head, leaning closer over him so that her tears fell on his face. "I won't," she said. "I want to be with you, Jacques."

"Go," he said again, his voice stronger. She was still shaking her head. He looked past her to me.

"Go to the woodcutter's hut, in the hills north of the orchard."

I nodded and swallowed the lump in my throat. Jacques Lambert had been no friend to me, but I would not deny a dying man such a simple request. Besides, the remote woodcutter's hut seemed as safe as anywhere just then. I glanced nervously around. The soldiers were still making a ruckus in the barn, but it wouldn't be long before they returned to us. This might be our only chance to flee.

He convulsed, his hand clutching tighter over his stomach. His mouth worked again, but it took a moment before words came through.

"Go to the hut, Mathilde," Jacques managed at last. "I need you . . . to carry out my mission."

I started to say we wanted no part of his mission, but Mathilde's headshaking suddenly switched to nods, and I held my tongue. "I will, *mamour*, I promise," she said, her hand caressing his cheek.

"My saddlebags . . . must be protected. Delivered."

"Delivered to whom?" Mathilde asked.

Before Jacques could answer, a shot rang out inside the inn. With horror, I remembered Papa rushing inside to confront the soldiers. I could stand still no longer. I grabbed Mathilde hard by the upper arm and hauled her to her feet, dumping Jacques's head unceremoniously off her lap and into the dust. She resisted, of course, but I no longer cared. I dragged her through the horses and past the barn, where I could hear the protests of our animals as the soldiers searched. I dragged her on, into the orchard.

We were only halfway through the apple trees, en route to the forest, when the dreaded smell of smoke reached us. I kept my eyes forward and quickened my steps. Mathilde was no longer fighting me, but she wasn't helping either. If I lessened my grip on her, she seemed likely to slow or even stop where she was, letting her despondence overcome her.

"Come on!" I hissed, the smell of smoke growing stronger and renewing my panic to get away.

She said nothing, only followed on leaden feet. This would never do. Any moment, the soldiers would notice our absence and come after us. In the forest, we stood some chance of escape, but here in the orchard, we were much too exposed. My back prickled with the fear of discovery.

"You promised him, Mathilde," I said fiercely. "You promised to finish his mission. We have to get to the hut before those soldiers."

As I had hoped, the idea of serving Jacques got her moving better than anything I asked of her could have, and soon she was running beside me on her own strength, though I still kept hold of her hand. I couldn't be sure she wouldn't bolt back to Jacques's side the first chance she got.

I did not stop running until we were well into the forest. It was late enough in the year that many leaves had fallen. Only ragtag clusters here and there still clung to branches, while more swirled in the air. Even so, the dense stands of trees and the thick underbrush concealed us more than the open orchard had, and the thick layer of fresh, bright leaves underfoot silenced our flight.

We ran until we came to an outcrop of stone, wild currants thick around its base. I knew the place—we had often come here over the years to pick the currants, and as children, Mathilde and I had discovered the secret alcove in the stone face where, if one was brave enough to push through the thorny branches, one could hide and giggle, eat the sour berries, and play truant from chores. Now I thought nothing of the thorns. Pushing Mathilde ahead of me, we pressed quickly through the tangle of branches into the dry, silent space beyond, and there we collapsed, breathing hard, hearts hammering in our chests.

Neither of us spoke while we caught our breath. Mathilde was still crying. She had been weeping the whole time, even as she ran, and her face was streaked with grimy tears and snot. I bit down hard on my lip, suddenly fighting back tears of my own.

"Mathilde," I said quietly, reaching out and putting a gentle hand on her arm. She jerked away and, for the first time, raised her eyes to mine. Despite her tears, her gaze was fierce with anger.

"You always hated him," she said.

"Mathilde—"

"You never wanted me to be happy!" A wail was rising again behind her words. "You couldn't stand it that someone loved me!"

"I'm sorry, Mathilde, but—"

She pushed me away, though there was hardly room in the small cave to do so. "But nothing! He needed me, Claudie! He needed me, and you pulled me away to leave him lying there in the dirt!"

"There was nothing you could do for him," I said.

"Yes, there was!"

"No, Mathilde!" I said, shouting over her, her accusations and her refusal to see sense raising my own hackles. "He was dying! There was nothing you could do."

"I could have held him," she said, and suddenly, her anger collapsed, leaving her limp. Fat tears spilled down her cheeks. "I could have kept him from dying alone." She began to shake all over, her breath coming in ragged sobs.

Just as suddenly as it had come, my anger dissolved too, and I took her in my arms, my sweet sister, and held her for as long as it took for her grief to purge her clean.

We stayed in the shelter of that rocky hill until the sun set. We heard no sound of pursuit, saw no sign of anyone else in the woods. At times, the scent of smoke was carried to us on the wind. I tried to keep my thoughts from Jacques, from Papa, from the shot I had heard just before I'd grabbed my sister and run, but as time ticked slowly by and the scuttling of little creatures in the underbrush made us rigid with fear, there was nothing else to fill our thoughts.

Twilight brought a chill, and I began to shiver. This shelter had been welcome when we had feared pursuit, but it would not keep us warm through the night. I took several deep breaths to ensure a calm voice, and I spoke.

"Do you know the woodcutter's hut, Mathilde? Do you think you can find the way in the dark?"

She glanced around her for a moment as if she had only just realized we were in the forest and needed to get her bearings. Slowly, she nodded. "It's to the west from here. Uphill and on the north bank of the stream."

"Come on, then. Let's get a start while there's still some light to set us in the right direction."

Once free of the thorny brambles, we set off uphill through the twilight. Around us, evening birds were singing and flitting in the branches, which gave me a little comfort. If a troop of soldiers was searching for us, surely the birds would take flight in alarm, or at least fall silent.

Beside me, Mathilde made her way confidently uphill. There was no hesitation in her step, and she did not pause to look around and assess her progress as I would have. In fact, her steady, brisk pace began to worry me.

"Wait a minute," I said at last, putting a hand on her arm to slow her.

She shook her head and kept walking. "The sooner we get there, the safer we'll be," she said flatly. "And the drier. It looks like rain."

"But we don't want to miss it in the dark," I said, looking nervously around. While I had a general sense of the direction we needed to go, I certainly didn't know the forest well enough to move so carelessly through it.

"I told you, Claudie, I can find it. It's this way."

Unless I wanted to force her, she wasn't going to slow her pace, so I let her lead, praying she wasn't getting us hopelessly lost. As the last of the light faded, we came to a narrow brook, its trickle across a stony bed melodic in the still night. We knelt and drank, scooping handfuls of the cool water greedily to our lips. When we were at last sated, Mathilde stood, and without hesitation, she gathered her skirts and leapt over the narrow stream, landing neatly on the opposite bank, even in the darkness. I was not so sure of my footing, but she reached a hand back to me. I took it and leapt across, grateful for the help and for the peace offering from my headstrong sister.

"Now we just continue along the creek until we come to it," she said.

She set off again, and I followed, admiration for her skill accompanied by a new suspicion. This confidence in her course suggested she had walked it in the dark before.

It was exactly as she said. We walked for another half hour, perhaps a little more. A steady drizzle set in, and Mathilde quickened her pace. The way grew steeper and the trees around us denser, but with the stream as our guide, we moved along certainly, only occasionally stumbling on the roots or stones made invisible by darkness and fallen leaves. At last, we rounded a final copse of beech trees and saw the dark outline of the cottage before us. We rushed inside, grateful for a door to close between us and the night.

CHAPTER 6

It was a tiny cottage, furnished with a narrow bed and a rickety table, but I could see Jacques had been here and had meant to return again, probably as soon as he had snatched Mathilde from my father's inn. A loaf of bread and a bottle of wine sat on the table, and the warm coals of a fire waited to be restored on the humble hearth. One more glance revealed Jacques's precious saddlebags, tossed into the corner. A shiver went through me. Jacques was never without them—never before now, anyway. Had he known soldiers were waiting for him on the road? Had he been so reckless to come for Mathilde knowing death was on his heels?

Whatever he had or hadn't known, one thing was clear: there was something in those bags that Jacques had died to protect. What could possibly have been worth his life? And what were we to do with it?

Mathilde collapsed weeping onto the bed, oblivious to the food, fire, or saddlebags.

"You should eat something," I said, turning my attention to the bread on the table. I found a knife, old and a little rusty, and I cut two slices from the loaf. She refused her slice but took a little of the wine. Then she turned her face to the wall and cried until she fell asleep.

Sleep did not come so easily to me. I did not have a lover's grief to drain me, only fear and worry filling me up. Was Papa dead? He must be—I had heard the shot, and surely the smoke had been the inn burning.

I tried to conjure up sorrow for Papa, but all I could feel was fear for Mathilde and me. Without the inn and without Papa, how would we survive?

I supposed Pierre would still marry Mathilde, but I had no such prospects. I had no dowry, and if the inn had been burned, no inheritance or means of survival. And there was the matter of the saddlebags. Even as I tried to sleep, I could feel their presence, waiting in the corner like a crouching wolf, ready to spring. I would have thrown a blanket over them to at least conceal them, but there were no blankets to spare, so I just tried to forget about them. When I slept at last, it was to nightmares of battle and fire, and always the saddlebags.

In the morning, I let Mathilde sleep while I took a bucket to the creek to fetch the water. It was a clear, bright morning, birds chirping in the trees. I sniffed the air but could only smell the tang of wet oak leaves underfoot. No smoke. A hopeful sign. Perhaps the inn had not burned. Perhaps I could return to find Papa safe and sound and life continuing as always in the village. The thought did little to untie the knot of worry within me.

Back in the hut, I lit a small fire and cut two more slices of the bread. After she woke, Mathilde ate a little, between fresh bursts of tears. I considered staying sequestered here for several days, until it felt safer to return, but we had little food, and the unknown of what had become of our village ate at us both, so I resolved to walk back and learn what I could. Mathilde wanted to come with me, but

I insisted she stay, and when I used Jacques's saddlebags as a reason, she agreed.

The way back was much easier by daylight, and I had no trouble retracing our steps of the night before. By late morning, I stood under the last sheltering trees, looking out across the orchard. Smoke hung in the valley, forming a choking haze among the apple trees, but I could see no sign that anything was still ablaze. Still, I stepped cautiously out of the forest.

There was an eerie silence. Even the birds had stopped singing, or maybe they had all flown. I strained my ears for any of the usual noises of the village—the blacksmith's hammer, the creak and clatter of cart wheels, barking dogs—but I could hear nothing. I told myself I was as yet too far away, but the cancer of fear in my stomach was growing so fast within me that I had to pause, pressing my hand against the smooth bark of an apple tree, trying to master myself enough to continue.

The fear of the unknown is often worse than the actual knowing, I reminded myself. After all, the smoke might be nothing more than a burnt haystack. The gunshot in the inn might have been a mere accident, nowhere near Papa. I squeezed my eyes shut. Papa. What if he had been hurt and had needed me? What if he was unharmed and had needed us to fight the fire, but we were nowhere to be found? If that was the case, he would be in a towering rage, and I'd be in for a beating.

It's better to know, I told myself again, and I forced my feet forward.

The smoke hung thick in the valley bottom, stinging my lungs and obscuring the view. I became disoriented as I moved through the bottom of the orchard. The inn, or at least the outbuildings of the cider house, cheese shed, and stables, should have been visible before me, but all I could see was the gray haze among the trees. My pace slowed as I glanced around in confusion. Was this someone else's orchard and I was lost? No, the trees were familiar, as was the cart track worn by the recent harvest. I took another step, and another. On the third step, I saw the burnt timbers, blackened earth, and smoldering mounds of thatch. It was all gone.

The same fear that had weighed down my steps only a moment before now propelled me forward. I ran into the yard, or what was left of it. The stone walls of the inn had collapsed, or been pulled down, leaving the innyard a jumbled mass of broken stone and splintered, charred wood. I could smell the stench of death from the mound that had been the stables. Jacques's horse lay dead in the courtyard, still saddled, a bullet hole through the blaze on its forehead, but I could see no sign of Jacques. For a moment, this gave me a glimmer of hope, but I quickly saw the futility of it. I did not think he could have survived the wound, but he was even less likely to survive an army that executed even his horse.

I turned back to the shell of the inn and approached it with trepidation.

"Papa?" I called, then wished I hadn't. My voice echoed obscenely through the ruins as if I, the living creature, was the abomination here.

I could still feel the heat from the jagged sections of standing wall. Cautiously, I looked in through the kitchen doorway. The roof and upper story had all collapsed, leaving an unrecognizable jumble of debris on the floor, still too hot to pick though.

I backed away. If Papa was in there, he hadn't survived. Still, there was a chance he'd gotten out or that some of our neighbors had come to help him. He might have spent the night with the miller or in the church.

I turned away from the ruins of our home and turned to the high street. At this hour, there would be someone about in the village square who could tell me what had happened after Mathilde and I had fled.

Only then did I realize the extent of the soldiers' revenge. The fire did not stop at the edge of the innyard. Every house and shop had been burned. I now saw that the rain I had cursed as bad luck in the night had been a gift from God. Without it, the fire surely would have spread to the forest that had sheltered us.

The fire, however, was not the worst of it. Dogs and horses had been slaughtered in the street. Some of our neighbors had been too, though most were not there. I prayed that they too were hiding in the forests. I did not look into the rubble of their homes to be sure. I could not bear to.

Pierre, the butcher's son and Mathilde's would-be husband, had been dragged into the street in his sickbed and lay sprawled beneath its shattered frame, staring vacantly at the sky. I closed my eyes and tried to picture him as the smiling boy he had been just a few weeks ago, but all I could see was his humiliating death, and the hard pain in my chest rose in a wail of despair. I stumbled past him to the village square, where I found Jacques at last. He'd been tied by the wrists to the public well and flogged. The torn flesh hung from his back, and his blood had congealed on the ground around his dangling knees. His *bonne rouge* had been placed carefully on his head afterward, the only unmaimed thing left in my village. Everything—everyone—I had ever known was dead. An enormous emptiness opened in my chest, threatening to swallow me up, just as it had swallowed my entire world. I collapsed sobbing and retching in the dust.

When the retching eased at last, it was replaced by a desperate urge to flee. I stumbled to my feet and back through the streets, but when I reached the innyard, I paused and forced myself to think. Mathilde and I could not stay here, that much was clear. There was no shelter for us, and anyway, I could not bring Mathilde back here to see the horror of Jacques's tortured body.

Perhaps we could stay for a time where we were, in the cot in the forest, but winter would soon be upon us, and we had neither food nor money. We might hunt or trap a few rabbits in the woods, but I knew we didn't have the means to feed ourselves.

Even if others had survived and returned to the valley, there would still be the problem of food for the winter. I gazed at the smoldering rubble that had been our cheese shed, and beside it, our ruined cider house. I walked slowly past both, but of course there was nothing salvageable. Not a single apple or wheel of cheese.

The root cellar had fared somewhat better, and I pulled a rope of onions, a handful of turnips, and a small sack of buckwheat flour from the collapse. Perhaps we might find more here in a few days, but I did not feel safe now, so I shouldered the sack and slipped away, back into the orchard. I scanned the ground as I crossed it, finding a few wormy apples to add to my bag. As I neared the forest, a movement off to my left startled me. Too late, I realized my danger and how careless I had been. How easy it would be for a soldier to simply wait, knowing I would return to the village, and capture me here.

Again, something rattled the underbrush, and in panic, I dropped the bag of turnips and ran to take cover behind a tree—a pointless effort if I had already been seen.

I snatched up a fallen branch, and holding it ready to strike, I peeked cautiously around the tree. The turnips had rolled from the bag and were scattered on the ground, which brought my imagined adversary from the underbrush. It was a nanny goat, trailing a length of singed rope. The rope was tangled with grass and twigs and held her back as she stretched her neck toward a turnip that had rolled from the bag.

I snatched up the turnip and the bag as the goat watched me, her eyes and ears nervous. She too had escaped the destruction of the village with only her life.

I scratched the beast's knobby forehead until she calmed, then gathered up the dragging rope, untangling it from the brambles. As I did so, I saw her heavy teats. She needed a milking—and the milk would be a welcome addition to my little hoard.

I coiled the rope into my hand, and she followed willingly, and as we walked together into the forest, I was glad of her company, one small stroke of good luck among all the bad.

Mathilde asked about Jacques at once when I arrived back at the cot. I answered carefully, wanting to spare her the cruelest details. I myself would be haunted by the vision of Jacques's mutilated corpse hanging from the well.

"And Papa?" she asked after a time, as if the daily fabric of our lives was a mere afterthought.

"Dead, I'm afraid," I said, and told her of the burnt inn. She said nothing, though I saw her eyes harden. Perhaps she was relieved to be out from under Papa's thumb, as I was.

"Jacques meant to marry me," she said after another moment, and the tears came again. I let her weep while I milked the goat and boiled two turnips. Perhaps I was weeping too, but tears would not feed us or keep us going.

"We cannot go back there," I said as we ate our supper of stale bread, boiled turnip, and goat's milk. "We must decide what we are going to do."

Mathilde sniffed. "We promised Jacques we would deliver the saddlebags."

"Deliver them to whom?" I asked.

Her eyebrows squeezed together as she thought, then she shook her head. "I don't know exactly. They are called the Legion."

"And where is this *legion*?" I asked with rising alarm that my little sister knew such secrets.

"All over," she said with a wave of her hand.

I narrowed my eyes in confusion. "But then, where are we to deliver the bags?"

Again, she shrugged.

I considered for a moment. Other than Mathilde, I knew of only two other associates of Jacques. One was the marquis's coachman, who had said they were friends. The other was the stranger on the giant horse who had warned us of the attack and who had saved my life in the battle, an act for which I could scarcely feel grateful since I blamed the whole incident on him.

Neither man had mentioned the saddlebags, but both men had been headed for Rennes.

"Rennes, I think," I said.

Mathilde's face brightened. "Yes! That's it!" she cried, snapping her fingers. "The Rooster of Rennes! That must be who they go to."

"Rooster?"

"That's what Jacques called him. I don't know anything more, but surely we can find him and deliver the bags."

"And what, exactly, is in the bags?" I asked, but received only a blank stare in answer, so I retrieved the bags from the corner. Mathilde gave a cry of dismayed protest.

"Please, Claudie, I can't!" she said, and flung herself down, sobbing, on the bed.

I waited until she was asleep, though it pained me, then I opened the bags and began pulling out the items within. First came the banal personal effects—a pipe and a pouch of tobacco, a warm scarf, a wedge of cheese wrapped in oilcloth. There was also a purse of coins that rattled promisingly. I tipped the contents onto the table to discover a handful of deniers as well as several coins that I recognized as English. I slipped the French coins into my pocket, sure that Jacques would have wanted them to see us safely to Rennes. The English coins I returned to the pouch.

There were also several packets of letters in the bag, tied in a length of twine and sealed with red wax. This, I knew, was the official post that Jacques was paid to deliver to cities and estates between Paris and Brest. I tucked the letters back into the saddlebag. Perhaps there would be a reward for delivering them to the postmaster in Rennes.

In the second saddlebag, I found a pretty linen handkerchief, its lace edge crumpled. I pulled it out with a lurch of my heart, remembering the day Mathilde had given it to him. I smoothed it on the table only to discover that the initials embroidered in the corner were PL. The handkerchief was not Mathilde's at all but belonged to some other woman. What was worse, I pulled a second then a third handkerchief from the bag. Each was delicate and lacy. Each bore a different set of initials. Anger flared in me on behalf of my sister. I had warned her of this for years, but deep down I had wanted to believe her innocent faith had been right. Cursing Jacques, I gathered the lovely handkerchiefs and threw them all into the fire. Mathilde would never know of them.

Another packet of letters and a pair of fine riding gloves brought me to the bottom of the second bag. I looked around at the bits and bobs I had pulled out, now spread across the table. It was so little, so ordinary. I could see nothing here that would have gotten Jacques killed.

I looked again at the bags, shook them out. Nothing. I gave a little sigh of relief, but I was disappointed too. Surely there had to be a reason Jacques had left them here when he came to fetch Mathilde.

I inspected the bags again. They were as they had always been— finely crafted leather bags, stitched with sturdy leather thongs and lined with brown linen. And yet I realized as I turned them in my hands that, while they looked well made, they were oddly unbalanced. I took one in each hand and hefted them. There was no doubt, the left bag outweighed the right.

I held the bags close to the lamp and examined the interiors. The left side had an awkwardly stitched section of lining at the bottom. I ran my fingers along it. There was something lumpy underneath. A prickle of excitement ran along my spine at the discovery, and I wasted no time. Using the dull kitchen knife, I slit the badly stitched seam. Soon, I had a hole large enough to reach two fingers inside, where I found two lumps of tightly wound fabric. I pulled the first from its hiding place and laid it on the table. My heart was thumping in my chest. I unwound the long strip of fabric faster and faster as I got closer to the secret inside. At last, a little satin bag studded with pearls and bearing a noble crest embroidered in silver and gold threads fell into my hand. I ran my finger over the crest—a lion and a red rose with a thorny stem. I was not familiar with the emblem, but that was no surprise. I knew nothing of the nobility.

I pulled the silk drawstring at the top of the bag and tipped it onto the table. A pair of pearl earrings and a fine pendant glistening with rubies clattered onto the tabletop. I caught my breath. I had seen such elegant necklaces at the throats of grand ladies passing through, but I had never touched one and certainly never imagined having such a thing in my possession. I picked up the necklace and held it to my throat, wishing I had a mirror and imagining myself as a fine lady.

"Where did you get that?"

I jumped and dropped the necklace. I hadn't heard Mathilde awaken or sit up on the bed, but I shouldn't have been surprised. The presence of a fine jewel pressed to my neck had roused her like a siren's call. She hurried to the table, picking up the necklace for herself.

I watched as she admired the sparkling jewel, tracing her fingers gently over the surface, and her face transformed, a flush of color coming to her pale, tearstained cheeks. She raised her eyes to mine.

"This was for me," she said. "He was bringing this to me."

It took me a moment to understand—to remember his words from their last parting, when he had spoken of something beautiful. My stomach dropped. "No, Mathilde . . ."

"He meant for me to have it," she insisted, raising it to her neck as I had done, but unlike me, she unfastened the clasp on the delicate chain and fastened it around her neck, a dreamy look on her face.

"Mathilde," I said again, trying to draw her back to reality. I held up the satin pouch. "It belongs to a nobleman. Look." I held the crest before her eyes, but she refused to look at it.

"It's mine," she said, drawing away from me, a hand over the necklace as if I might try to snatch it from her. "You heard him. He was bringing me something beautiful—he told me so."

"And yesterday he told you he needed you to complete his mission. What if taking these things to their rightful owner was that mission?"

She glanced around at the other things on the table and snatched up a packet of letters—not the ones with the red wax seal of the official post but the other packet, sealed with green wax. She waved this seal under my nose. "This was his mission. See? It is the symbol of the Legion. He wanted these papers delivered to Rennes. That is what we promised to do. They are fighting for the liberation of France."

I was taken aback at this. "You mean, they support the revolution? Jacques was in league with the soldiers who killed him?"

"Of course not!" she said. "Jacques only carried the *bonne rouge* to protect himself when he met soldiers."

"But you said—"

"The Legion *opposes* the new Republic," she explained. "They mean to restore the king. They want true liberty, equality, and brother-hood, not the tyranny the Republic has become."

The zeal in her voice surprised me. So too did the seal on the let-ters, as I suddenly realized I had seen it before, or something very like it. It was the sacred heart with an R&D emblazoned across it. *Roi et Dieu*, king and God, just as the big man on the Breton horse had been wearing on his chest when he stopped in our innyard.

"It is too dangerous, getting involved with this Legion," I said, as much to myself as to her.

"And what will become of Brittany if we don't? The Republic means to subjugate us, to take away our priests, commandeer our food for Paris, and destroy our way of life," she said, sounding as if she was reading from a script.

I searched her face. "Are you already part of this Legion?"

Her eyes slipped toward my scrutiny, then back to the pearl ear-rings on the table. "You've never been able to see beyond our little lives, have you?" she said. "You would have stayed under Papa's thumb forever, running his inn. You would have let him wed me to a butcher's son and be tethered forever to a dull existence. I'm not like you, Claudie. I want more out of my life. I was going to marry Jacques Lambert and leave with him."

"And fight against the revolution," I said. "Mathilde, you have no idea how dangerous this is."

"I have more idea than you," she shot back. "You plug your ears and bury your head in the sand every time Jacques comes to town with the news. You would just ignore it all and hope it goes away, but it won't, Claudie. The time is coming when we all have to take a stand."

"The time has already come," I said with a small shudder, horrible memories overcoming me. "Has it occurred to you that if Jacques hadn't thrown us into the thick of it, our village would still be un-harmed? We would be comfortable at home instead of hiding in this hut with no family or friends, no livelihood, nowhere to go."

"We have somewhere to go," she said. "We promised Jacques we would complete his mission. The Legion will be our new friends and family."

I wasn't sure I wanted new friends and family, at least not if they were part of this cause to defy the new government. But it was clear that we could not stay here. So, though I wanted nothing to do with this war against a war, I nodded. "Very well, we will go to Rennes," I said. "But you cannot wear those jewels along the way."

Again, her hand went to the necklace.

"Remember what Jacques said about the mobs in Paris?" She wouldn't listen to me, but I knew she couldn't deny what Jacques had said, especially not when she had just accused me of not taking heed. "Even a good horse was enough to get him attacked. What do you think will happen to us if you are seen wearing such a thing? It's bad enough that we are two girls unprotected."

She sighed and nodded. "Very well. I will make sure it is hidden before we set out."

I didn't argue. The necklace had at least revived her enough to get off the bed.

We got busy baking all the buckwheat flour into hard little cakes we could carry with us on our journey. For our supper that night Mathilde chopped and boiled the remaining turnips while I milked the goat and fetched the water.

I hadn't forgotten the other lump in the bottom of the saddle-bag, but I hadn't mentioned it to Mathilde either. I didn't want her laying claim to anything else from Jacques's possessions. It was dangerous enough for her to be walking around with the necklace in her pocket—at least I hoped she would keep it in her pocket.

I ate my meal in silence while Mathilde, finally pulled out of her grief by her fervor for Jacques's mission, speculated about the Legion—how we would live with them and all we could do to help them restore Brittany. I listened. I would need to know something about this Legion if we were to find them in Rennes. I had no intention of joining them, but perhaps they would give us a reward for completing Jacques's mission—perhaps enough for us to start over in life.

At last, the meal was cleared away, and Mathilde and I retired to bed, agreeing that we needed a good night's rest if we were to set out for Rennes in the morning. I lay still beside her for an hour until I was sure she was asleep. Then, carefully, I rose. I lit a candle in the banked coals of the fireplace and returned to the saddlebags, which were once again on the floor in the corner. I knelt and, very gently, opened the left bag, feeling my way to the bottom and the open seam in the lining. I slipped my fingers through, found the second bundle, and pulled it free.

Glancing at Mathilde to make sure she was still asleep, I settled the bundle in my lap and unwound its wrapping. At first, I was disappointed when a single hard lump fell into my lap. After the fine pearl-studded bag and elegant necklace, I had expected something ornate. This was something dark and hard and very plain. Or so it seemed until I lifted it from my skirt and the candlelight caught on it, flashed across its glassy surface, and scattered into a dozen dancing lights all around me. I gasped and closed my hands around the thing so that the room went dark again. What was it I held in my hands?

Cautiously, I uncurled my fingers and beheld not glass, but a stone.

No, not just a stone. A blue diamond, hard and smooth, cut into a dozen or more facets. I brought it close to the candle again, and again it flashed, but this time, I was not overcome with surprise, and I turned it, examined it. It sparked with fire, even while it was dark—a melding of sunlight and midnight spread across the palm of my hand.

I flipped it over, letting the candlelight shimmer over the facets at the center of the stone, a set of seven narrow rays radiating out from the center to form a sun. I gasped and closed my hand around it again, remembering how Jacques had boasted of the thieves' cleverness as if he had been there. This was the Blue of the Crown—the greatest diamond in the crown jewels of France—cut for the Sun King, Louis XIV, over a hundred years ago and worn by every monarch since. The greatest treasure in France—in my hand!

The necklace, I now realized, was nothing. The pearl earrings were mere trinkets next to this. This was what Jacques had been taking to his Legion in Rennes. This was what had gotten him killed. This was the mission he had thrust upon us.

My heart hammering in my chest, I wrapped the thing back in the rag that had encased it, blew out the candle, and got to my feet. I rushed outside and behind the cot to a small, rocky patch of ground. Taking up a pointed stick, I began to dig until I had a hole about a foot deep. I dropped the diamond into the hole and shoved the dirt back over it, then covered the whole thing with scattered rocks to hide it.

That done, I returned inside and slipped back under the thin blanket on the bed. I closed my eyes and willed my breathing and my heart to slow to their normal rate, trying to bring on sleep. It would not come, not when I could still feel the weight of the king's diamond in my hand. Behind my eyelids, it flashed and sparkled with the light of a single candle—what must it look like in full sunlight? Even the thought of it took my breath away.

I rolled over, tried to calm my mind. We had a long day ahead of us tomorrow, and no doubt for many days after. I wasn't sure how long it would take us to get to Rennes—would we have to walk the whole way? To sleep on the roadside? Or could we afford a coach and find inns for the nights? And even once we got there, what would we do then? I knew no one in Rennes. What if we couldn't find work or shelter? What would become of us then?

Our plan had been to find the Legion, deliver the packet of letters for Jacques, and retrieve a reward that would set us up in a new life.

Except the packet of letters was not what got Jacques killed and almost certainly not what his compatriots in Rennes were waiting for. Walking in with the letters and without the diamond would bring us no reward—more likely they would imprison and torture us to find the diamond. What would this Legion do to us if they thought we had stolen it? I had buried it behind the house because I thought it was too dangerous to take with us, but now it seemed just as dangerous to leave it behind.

I sat up in bed, gripped by uncertainty. Being caught with the diamond by soldiers was a death sentence, I was sure of that, but then, delivering the saddlebags to Rennes without the diamond might be too.

Perhaps if I once again sewed the diamond into the lining, just as I had found it, maybe then we could get it safely to Rennes. I rejected the idea as soon as I thought it. Jacques and his conspirators may have been clever enough to fool the guards and steal the diamond, but I didn't think much of the disguise. It had been easy for me to see the clumsy stitches in the lining and find the jewels, and I hadn't even known of them. Someone who was searching for them wouldn't have been fooled for a moment.

I got out of bed and relit the candle, then settled into the chair by the table and examined the saddlebags. I could not stitch up the lining so that the rent would be invisible. It had been too badly done before now. But, as I turned the saddlebags in my hands, I saw another possibility. The leather strap that went over the horse's flanks was two layers thick and slightly padded, and where it met each satchel, the satchel overlapped it so that the seam was not visible.

Taking up the knife, I slipped it under the leather thong that held the seam together, and with a little coaxing, I managed to work a stitch loose, then pull free the next stitches until I had a gap just wide enough for the diamond.

I paused then, poised on indecision. The diamond belonged to the king and, by extension, to all of France. What right did I have to take it with me? What right did this so-called Legion have to it? I had rolled my eyes and accused the thieves of nothing more than greed when Jacques had told his story. Now I wasn't so sure. A jewel like that could move nations—fund armies or sway foreign powers to rise to the aid of France. Perhaps it could even ransom the king, save his life and the lives of his imprisoned family.

The Army of the Republic was looking for it and had already killed Jacques for it. But Jacques was the sort who couldn't resist boasting of his exploits in every inn from Rennes to Paris. I was more careful. I would have the stone better hidden, and I knew how to keep my head down and my mouth shut—my father had pounded that lesson into me often enough.

I was not a brave person, nor did I have any wish to be part of this war. But Rennes was not too far away—perhaps a week of travel, or two if we had to walk all the way. There we could turn over the diamond, gather our reward, and I could take my sister off somewhere out of the way in Brittany, where the war would not find us again and we could live quietly until the revolution was over.

I took a deep breath, and on the strength it gave me, I hurried outside into the night. Clawing at the soft earth like a madwoman, I retrieved the diamond. I did not unwrap it or look at it again. I simply returned to the cabin and slid it into the gap I had made in the seam. Then, carefully, I adjusted the padding and restitched the wounded seam with the same leather thong until the disturbance to it was invisible. Only someone examining the saddlebags with a close and critical eye would notice it.

Vowing to keep anyone from that opportunity before we could make Rennes, I returned to the bed beside my sister and gathered in a few fitful hours of sleep before the sun rose and we were propelled on our journey, carrying the most dangerous item in France along with us.

CHAPTER 7

In the first light of dawn, we stripped the blankets from the bed and used them to bundle our food and the handful of useful items we could carry into slings. We put the saddlebags and their contents in one of the bundles as well, agreeing that it might be dangerous to be seen with them.

I hoisted the smaller sling onto Mathilde's back, then shouldered my own larger load. Taking the goat's rope in hand, we launched ourselves into the world. Neither of us knew what to expect—we had never left our village before now—but we cut northwest through the woods, hoping to intersect the road.

We had been walking for perhaps fifteen minutes before Mathilde spoke.

"The Rooster of Rennes," she mused. "What sort of man do you suppose calls himself a rooster?"

Unbidden, the image of the man on the big horse galloped into my thoughts. He had certainly been cocky enough. He had spoken Brezhoneg and had been an associate of Jacques, and just thinking of his condescension annoyed me all over again. Of course, he had saved my life during the battle, but that only made it worse.

"What *are* you thinking about?" Mathilde asked, her interruption pulling me out of my thoughts. "Honesty, you are blushing as red as a cock's comb."

I shook my head. "I am not," I said.

"You are."

"I'm only worried about how we will find this man. This Rooster." Even as I said the name, I could feel how well it fit him.

Apparently, Mathilde could too, because her eyes suddenly lit with recognition. "Oh! It's him, isn't it? It's your beau from the night of the battle."

"He's not my beau!" I snapped, my face burning hotter. "And we don't know anything about him. It might be him. It might not."

"You're in love with him!" Mathilde said. "This is perfect. Your charms will convince him to help us." I couldn't tell if she was serious or if she was mocking me.

It hardly mattered. We both knew I had no charms. I shifted my load and quickened my step.

"Oh, come on, Claudie," she said, hurrying to keep beside me. "You should at least try. It's easy. Smile, bat your lashes. Laugh at his jokes, whether they are funny or not."

"As if anyone would notice with you around to do the same," I muttered.

She giggled as if I were a man who had just told a humorless joke. "Well, then," she said, "I guess it will fall to me to charm yet again."

After that we walked on in silence, me glowering while she enjoyed her superiority. We cut downhill, skirting outcrops of stone and thickets of gorse that caught at our clothes and hair, no matter how we tried to avoid them. By midday, when we reached the road, we were scratched and cross. The track was narrow and ankle-deep in mud but mercifully free of brambles.

Still, I hesitated. Young trees and tangles of brush lined the verge, creating a thick hedge on either side. We would be trapped if soldiers came upon us. I glanced at Mathilde—sweet, pretty Mathilde—and I shuddered at the thought of what soldiers might do to her. But we could travel much faster on the road and might find shelter in a farmhouse or inn. So, we shared a bit of bread and Jacques's cheese, resting our legs for a few minutes. Then we once again gathered our burdens onto our backs and took to the road.

We walked for several hours before we encountered another traveler: a gruff old farmer, on foot like us, leading a mule loaded with sacks of grain.

"Good day, monsieur," I called out as we approached, nervous but trying to sound like I was not.

He muttered a greeting and gave a tip of his head.

"How far to the next village?" I asked.

He shook his head. "You'll find nothing at the next village, I'm afraid," he said.

"There's no inn there?" Mathilde said, and I could hear the quiver of disappointment in her voice.

"No inn, no nothing," he said in a low voice, barely more than a growl. "It's all been burned to the ground."

Mathilde and I stopped walking and glanced at each other.

"You'll find it's the same all along this road." He eyed the makeshift bundle on my back and our dust-streaked skirts. "Maybe you already knew that."

I barely heard him. I was wishing I could sink into the mud. Such a long road ahead of us and already there seemed no hope in going on.

"God keep you on your travels," he said as he moved away from us, but I didn't trust in God. Not after what he'd put us through so far.

We trudged on, but it was just as the farmer said—two burnt

villages before nightfall and no sign of any survivors. When the light grew dim and we were stumbling with weariness, we returned to the forest, hoping that for tonight, at least, nature would prove less cruel than man.

I milked the goat, then tethered her. We shared the milk and a hard buckwheat cake for our supper.

"What if there are no towns left, Claudie?" Mathilde said, after we'd eaten in silence and rolled ourselves in the blankets. It was full dark now, and we sat side by side, our backs against an old oak as if it were a shield. Around us, little creatures rustled through the fallen leaves, searching for acorns and sounding enormous when I tried to close my eyes. I had never slept outside, not like this, alone in the wild forest, far from home and protection. Mathilde's question had done nothing to comfort me.

"Of course there are towns left, Mathilde!" I snapped, then instantly regretted it. Mathilde sniffed and wiped her eyes with the corner of her blanket.

I put my arm around her and pulled her to me, though it meant releasing the blanket from around my own shoulders. When I spoke again, I made sure my tone was gentle. "The Army of the Republic has other things to do than to burn every town in Brittany. I'm sure the next town up the road will have a hot meal and a bed for us, and maybe a coach to take us on to Rennes."

She didn't respond, except to lean her head onto my shoulder. We fell asleep, propped against the giant tree, with only two thin blankets and what comfort we could give each other to keep the night at bay.

CHAPTER 8

The first light of dawn showed an ominous change in the weather. A misty chill hung in the air, and the faint odor of smoke drifted to us from the north. We were stiff from sleeping against the tree. The goat had entangled herself in the rope in the night and was nearly as cranky as I was, but she calmed some once I untangled her and extracted a bit of milk for our breakfast. It wasn't much, but it filled our bellies enough for a morning of walking.

"Come on," I said, swinging my burden onto my aching back. "Walking will loosen our muscles and warm us up."

Mathilde's heavy sigh jangled my nerves, but I said nothing.

An hour of trudging along the muddy road brought us to another burnt village. Unlike the villages of the day before, this place was not devoid of life, and a flicker of hope stirred in me. Villagers—mostly women and children—were digging through the blackened layers of wood, stone, and thatch, stacking piles of salvageable goods in the street. Pots, axes, spoons and knives, even some lumps of melted tin that might be sold to a traveling tinker sat in sad, filthy heaps. Some of the women looked up in suspicion as we approached.

Mathilde called a greeting in Brezhoneg, then asked what had happened.

The nearest woman wiped the back of a sooty hand across her forehead, streaking it with grime. "Soldiers," she said.

"But why?" I asked, seeing the utter exhaustion in the woman's face.

She coughed once. "Our priest has not signed the Civil Constitution of the Clergy," she explained. "Two days ago, they came for him. Called him a traitor to France."

"The monsters," Mathilde said, her cheeks blazing with anger. We all knew that "traitor to France" was a death sentence.

The woman's shoulders straightened a little. "We want nothing of their heresy or their revolution here. We fought to defend ourselves."

"How many were killed?" I asked, looking around at the women and children and their lack of men.

"We lost four men, but they lost six," she said.

Mathilde gave a satisfied nod. "They will learn not to bring their revolution here," she said. *"Roi et Dieu!"*

"Roi et Dieu!" the woman replied, the fierce pride reigniting in her eyes.

"But where are the rest of your men?" I asked.

"The men have gone to fight, Claudie," Mathilde said, as if I were a child and she had to explain the obvious. "To join the Legion. To defend Brittany."

The woman nodded. "The one they call the Rooster came through recruiting a fortnight ago, but with the harvest, no one could go. Of course, this changes everything."

"The Rooster of Rennes?" I said, alert to the name.

"That's what they call him. I don't know why. He looks more like a bull than a rooster." Several women nearby nodded.

"This Rooster," I started. "Does he have dark hair and beard? Rides a large Breton gelding with fine tack?"

"You know him!" the woman said, her expression brightening.

I nodded, not feeling bright at all. Was this one troublemaker responsible for the destruction of every village along this route? The pseudonym fit his strutting arrogance perfectly. Did he really think he was helping Brittany by bringing the wrath of the Army of the Republic down upon us? The thought set my blood ablaze.

Mathilde looked at me, her eyebrows raised, a teasing curl on her lips. I knew she was thinking of our conversation of the day before, once again mistaking my reaction to the man as infatuation. As if I were capable of such a thing. As if nineteen years of being snubbed, ignored, and trodden upon by men hadn't hardened me to something not only undesirable but incapable of desire.

Ignoring her look, I bid the villagers goodbye, filled our water-skins at their public well, and continued westward toward Rennes, Mathilde tagging along beside me, still smirking.

By nightfall, our backs ached, our feet bled, and Mathilde and the goat had both become stubborn and complaining. I was at my wits' end when, shortly before dark, we saw a small farmhouse, unscathed by the passage of the soldiers, a faint light flickering through the cracks in its shuttered windows.

We knocked at the door, but the inhabitants at first refused to open it, shouting that they wanted no trouble. I bartered the goat's evening milk for a night's shelter in their barn, and we went to sleep warm and dry, but hungry.

The next day the weather deteriorated, and for all of that day and the next two, we trudged the muddy road in an icy drizzle. There were few villages, and the countryside seemed largely deserted, as if war had stripped away all living souls. I willed my feet forward, though my traitorous heart faltered into despair.

Finally, on the fifth day, we came to a broad road and the town of Châteaubriant appeared before us, its massive old castle and elegant palace shining above the prosperous town like a miracle. We stopped, right there in the middle of the road, and stared up at it, our mouths open. Neither of us had left our village before, and though we had heard tales of cities and castles, we had never seen such grandeur as that now spread before us, offering rest and comfort.

Mathilde's hand found mine, and I squeezed it.

"A hot meal," she murmured.

"And a dry bed," I replied, and on those hopes, we found the strength to carry us forward into the town.

The houses and shops here were untouched by the conflicts that ravaged the countryside, but the town was crammed to bursting with refugees like us. We trudged past them, bedraggled and wet and grateful for the bag of coins from Jacques's saddlebags that would see us set up in an inn for the night rather than sleeping in the streets.

As it turned out, it was not easy to find a place to stay. The inns in the town were already filled with people, their common rooms abuzz with news of the marauding Army of the Republic, ready to sack and burn any village they thought opposed them.

"It's pillage, that's what it is," complained one innkeeper's wife. "The whole countryside being ravaged just for what they can steal and take for themselves." Still, despite her sympathy, she turned us away. "Every room's got four or five in it, when they're only meant for two," she said. "If we pack any more in, the whole place is likely to come down on us."

At last, we found a church that had opened its doors to beggars and travelers, and with Mathilde's charm, we secured a dry bit of floor near the fire to settle in for the night. As the light waned, two old shuffling nuns moved through the crowd, handing out crusts of bread and a ladleful of soup to anyone who had a cup or bowl to put it in.

I strained to see the faces of the sisters beneath their turned-up hoods, a wild hope filling me that I might see my mother's face. It wasn't until they passed and I saw that they were strangers that I realized I was not feeling disappointment but relief. Maman had left us years ago. God had called her, our village priest had said, forever destroying my belief in an all-loving God. It hadn't been so hard for Mathilde, a toddler, who remembered nothing of our mother. For me, a child of seven left motherless and forced to mother my sister, it had been the first and most painful rejection of my life. I had felt warm and carefree in the shelter of her love—or the love I thought she held for me. But then she had left without so much as a goodbye. What would I say to such a mother now?

Still, I could not take my eyes off the nuns. Was this what my mother's life had been since leaving us? Caring for strangers as she had once cared for her children? The thought squeezed my heart like a vise. How unlovable did a daughter have to be for a mother to prefer the drudgery of service to strangers over her?

Soon after the sisters left, we stretched out on the floor to sleep, along with the other travelers and homeless waifs who filled the church. Mathilde seemed quite comfortable, warm and dry at last, and was soon snoring softly, but I could not close my eyes. I had spent my whole life in inns listening to the noises of strangers through the thin walls, but this was altogether different. We were surrounded by strangers, more than one of whom had cast a hungry eye at my sister. And there was the matter of the secret diamond in the saddlebag. So, I lay awake, pinching myself whenever drowsiness came over me, keeping my eyes on what little I had left in the world.

The next morning, Mathilde and I set out to find passage to Rennes. Together, we walked to the center of town, where the coach embarked from a fine inn—much finer than we could have afforded, even if the city weren't full. As I expected, the fare was exorbitant.

"What are we to do?" Mathilde cried, wringing her hands. "I can't walk all the way to Rennes! I just can't!"

Nearby, I saw one of the coachmen, a handsome, blue-eyed fellow, watching her.

"Keep crying, Mathilde," I whispered with the tiniest nod toward the driver.

She took my meaning at once and began to weep in a display of deep sadness that in no way lessened her beauty.

In no time, the coachman had made his way over to us, offering Mathilde his handkerchief and asking what the trouble was. Mathilde, her thick lashes still glistening with tears, told the man of our troubles—troubles even I hadn't thought of—and of our need to get to Rennes, despite our lack of money.

"Mademoiselle, I'm sure we can manage a seat for you in the carriage," he said soothingly. "I will make them squeeze you in."

"But we need two seats." Mathilde sniffed. "My sister must go with me too."

The driver looked at me, a little surprised. Perhaps he had thought I was only sending her off to Rennes to meet family there. More likely, I had simply been invisible to him.

Mathilde looked at him from the tops of her big, tearful eyes. I wrung my hands for effect but didn't gaze at him like Mathilde did. From me, such a look was more likely to repel a man.

"Let me see what I can do," he said.

He crossed the square to the senior coachman, and the two of them talked, looking back from time to time at Mathilde and me. Mathilde kept up her display of despair, dabbing at her eyes with the handkerchief and letting her grief bring a pink glow to her face.

When the driver returned, it was with the good news that they would give us transportation to Rennes for what little money we had as long as we didn't have any baggage. And, of course, no goat.

I was a little sorry to say goodbye to the beast that had seen us through hard times, but one less stubborn creature to manage would be a relief, and the handful of coins she would fetch would serve us well in Rennes. By the time the coach was to depart, we had disposed of all but the saddlebags and their dangerous cargo, a blanket to bundle around them as a thin disguise. We shoved them under our seat when the coachman wasn't looking.

We were two of eight passengers in the coach, packing into the seats meant only for six. A stout townswoman and her skinny son squeezed in beside Mathilde and me, while across from us sat an old couple and two well-dressed men in black wool. Each man wore a tricolor cockade pinned to his lapel, advertising his support of the new Republic the revolution had established, the same Republic that had burned our village. A stormy silence filled the coach as they settled into their seats. I nudged the saddlebags farther under the seat with my foot and pretended not to notice the men leering at my sister.

Despite their presence, when the coach rolled out of the town, I gave in to my exhaustion and closed my eyes. I needed some rest, and the coach seemed as safe as anywhere we were likely to be.

I was jolted awake a few hours later when the coachman drew the horses up hard and the whole coach strained against the brake. An uneasy murmur ran through the passengers. Those with seats at the windows thrust their heads out, while others cowered back into their seats, murmuring fearfully about thieves on the road. I glanced at Mathilde, who had gone pale at the thought. Her foot was moving, no doubt pushing the saddlebags farther back. Not that that would matter if highwaymen pulled us from the coach and searched it. I swallowed hard, remembering the necklace my sister wore under her clothes and thinking of rough hands taking it from her—and searching for more.

"The road is blocked," said the old man opposite us, pulling his head in from the window. "There's an overturned carriage." I breathed a sigh of relief, along with all those around me. The coach came to a stop, and passengers scrambled out to see, Mathilde among them. I hesitated. The moment of privacy would give me a chance to better hide our possessions, but the thought of Mathilde outside, unprotected, pulled me from the coach.

A grand carriage lay on its side, halfway into the ditch. A door had been wrenched from its hinges and lay, along with a shattered wheel, upon the road. I froze at the sight, my blood rushing in my ears. Though the insignia had been pried from the doors, or perhaps because of the scar it left, I recognized the carriage.

Our fellow passengers had gathered at the edge of the road, looking at something in the ditch; their somber silence warned me of the horror. My steps faltered. This wasn't my war. I had already seen more atrocities than I could bear. But Mathilde was among the onlookers, her eyes wide and her face ashen. I was too late to spare her. I hurried to her, and despite myself, my eyes turned to the ditch.

The bodies lay sprawled in congealed blood, bloated from several days in the weather. The marquis's eyes had been picked by crows. His wife, the marquise, still gripped her children at her sides, where they had fallen together, their faces all but torn away by musket fire. A few feet away, the kind coachman had been hacked to pieces. I gripped Mathilde's arm, but I had no comfort for her. My throat was burning with bile as I looked on in horror.

"Was it highwaymen, do you think?" asked a woman in a hushed tone.

One of the young men with a tricolor cockade spoke. "The Army of the Republic, I should think," he said, his expression disdainful and his accent clearly Parisian. "Look at the coach. They were nobility. Enemies of the Republic."

The crowd eased uncomfortably away from them as his friend stepped to the marquis's body and removed the keys and seal that hung at his belt. He examined the seal. "Lion and rose," he said. He glanced around at the crowd, but no one said anything, and a few people shook their heads. The crest was not known to them.

I glanced away before our eyes could meet. I knew the crest. It adorned the silken pouch in the saddlebags. The necklace now secreted away somewhere on my sister belonged to the marquise who lay butchered at our feet.

As I stood rooted by the realization, Mathilde pulled from my grasp and fled the dreadful scene. I came to my senses and followed, afraid she was going to be sick. But rather than stumbling off to be ill, she made for the carriage. She flung the door open and reached inside even as I arrived at her elbow.

"That's the Marquis du Aubigny and his family," Mathilde said. "His whole family. Jacques was supposed to find them safe passage, and without him . . ." She was scrabbling around on the floor of the carriage. Too late I realized she was trying to get to something in the saddlebags. She had pulled the bundle out from under the seat and was pulling the blanket off before I could stop her.

"Mathilde—" I warned, reaching for the blanket.

"That's a shocking sight for a young lady. I do hope you are well?" said a deep voice behind us.

I spun to see one of the tall gentlemen who wore the tricolor. As if such a dandy had any idea of what we had seen, thanks to his Republic.

Then again, I doubted he was all that concerned about what we had seen. He was smiling past me to Mathilde, craning his neck to see what she'd pulled out from under the seat. I shifted to block his view and gave him a simpering smile.

"She came over dizzy, monsieur, but will be fine once she sits down."

I took Mathilde's elbow and tried to push her into the coach, even as she was turning back to see who addressed her so politely.

"May I offer my assistance?" the man said, his voice dripping with unctuous gallantry as he slipped closer. The saddlebags were still in plain view. I shifted again, the awkward country girl in the way of his gentlemanly effort. Mathilde, finally recognizing the danger, flipped the blanket back over the bag and turned a dazzling smile to the man. It had the desired effect, and while he was distracted, I pushed the saddlebags back under the seat.

"*Merci*, monsieur, but I am well enough with my sister to attend me," Mathilde said with a curtsy. She turned away from him to me, but there was no getting rid of him, and in the end, I climbed into the coach first, using my skirts to hide the bags, while the gentleman offered his hand to help Mathilde in after me. Once she was seated, she thanked him, and I pointed out that the elderly couple might need his assistance. Reluctantly, he turned away, and Mathilde squeezed my hand in relief.

"Do you think he saw?" she whispered.

I wasn't sure, but a deep sense of foreboding was settling over me as our fellow travelers returned to their seats and the coach started up again, inching its way around the wreckage.

"Enemies of the Republic," whispered one woman again as the dead appeared and disappeared through the window. All faces watched in silence as the scene slipped by and behind us, but as the coach regained speed, I felt the two Parisian men's eyes on my sister and me, with an interest they hadn't shown before.

I closed my eyes again and pretended to sleep, but I could not rest with the knot of worry tightening in my gut.

Innkeeper's daughter that I was, I knew the routine when the coach pulled into an innyard at noon. Those with money could enjoy a hot meal inside while the coachman changed horses. Those without could drink from the well and eat their own meager provisions in the shade of the stables. The elderly couple headed for the shade while our other companions made for the comfort of the inn.

I claimed poverty and insisted we stay in the coach, however much Mathilde glared at me.

"I'm hungry," she insisted.

"I don't trust those men," I whispered, nodding after the Parisians making their way toward the door.

"You don't trust anyone. We should go inside and enjoy our meal. They will only be more suspicious of us if they think we're avoiding them."

I shook my head. "We hardly look like we can afford a hot meal in an inn. And we should save what little we have for Rennes."

"What good will it do us in Rennes if we starve before we get there?" she grumbled. "Besides, the Rooster—"

"Very well!" I barked, interrupting her before her careless words fell on the wrong ears. "I will go inside and buy us a loaf, but you must wait here." She scowled, but she didn't follow me. I took a few coins from my purse, slipping the rest back inside my bodice, and hurried across the courtyard and into the inn.

It was much like my father's establishment—a two-story building of stone, the thatched roof drooping heavily over the eaves. Inside the door, the room was dim and noisy, a fire burning in a big hearth and several scarred wooden tables crowded with the passengers of our coach, a handful of farmhands, and other travelers, their coats and damp cloaks still draped over their shoulders. A warm, savory scent awakened a sense of home, and I breathed it in hungrily, along with all the yearning and pain in its wake. My resolve wavered, and for a moment I considered going back and bringing my sister inside for a meal. Then my eyes caught a flash of red in the corner. I stepped back into the shadow and peered harder. It was one of the Parisians, sitting at a table with two soldiers, the red epaulets on their coats standing out bright in the dim room. Their heads were together, and the Parisian was talking, his expression earnest.

An icy flood filled my belly. What could they be talking about other than Mathilde and me? Had the Parisian seen the saddlebags? Or did he just suspect we had known the marquis from Mathilde's reaction? It didn't really matter—if he brought soldiers to question or search us, we would be doomed. I slipped out of the inn as quietly as I could, and I rushed back to the coach.

"We have to go," I said, scrambling to pull Jacques's saddlebags from beneath the seat.

"Go?" Mathilde said, looking at me as if I were mad. "Go where? There's nowhere for us to go!"

She was right, of course, but it didn't matter. "We can't stay here. That man, he's bringing soldiers!" Even as I said it, I saw the inn door open and the three men step out, still in conversation, not yet looking our way.

I opened the far door so that the coach would hide us, at least momentarily, and I pushed Mathilde toward it. She didn't need further coaxing. She too had seen the uniforms on the soldiers and quickly slipped from the carriage, bending low so that we would not be seen.

I grabbed the saddlebags and followed across the yard and into a tangle of brush beside the road. Too late, we discovered that it was a bog and we were crouching ankle-deep in icy water, but the bushes at least had enough leaves still on them to shield us from view. We watched through the thin green shield as the soldiers climbed into the coach, then circled it, looking around. Seeing no sign of us, they turned to the elderly couple, and my heart sank. Surely they had seen our escape from where they sat on the edge of the well, slicing off bites of fresh cheese from a thick wedge. They spoke for a moment, then the old man gestured down the road, in the way we had come, and spoke loud enough for me to catch a few of his words—*run* and *back that way*. The old woman nodded her agreement.

The soldiers conferred with the Parisian for a moment, then mounted their horses and rode at a trot back the way the coach had come. The Parisian went back into the inn. The old woman glanced our direction, her eyes flashing defiance, before returning her attention to her cheese.

"Come on," I said, pulling Mathilde out of the bushes and up onto drier land. "They won't go far before they realize we didn't go that way."

We set out away from the road at a run, praying that no one would look our way. There were only farm fields here and none of the protective forests of home. We kept as low as we could, dodging between the standing shocks of harvested wheat, glad that they, at least, were standing and could be some cover if we heard hooves on the road behind us. We did not, so we ran on with no idea of where we were going. Our only thought was to get away from the road and the soldiers who now surely thought we were traitors to the Republic. If they caught us, I had no doubt we would meet the same fate as the marquis and his family.

We ran until our sides ached, until we could go no farther. A fresh drizzle had begun, spreading a cold but welcome veil behind us. We came to a scythed field with large stacks of hay. We had no need to speak. Without hesitation, we both ran for the nearest haystack and burrowed into it, sheltered from the rain. We stayed there all night.

I slept fitfully, stretched too thin to stay awake but too afraid to fall into a restful sleep. We had left our village with supplies and money enough to see us to Rennes. Now it was all gone. We were lost and alone, with soldiers looking for us and the dangerous cargo of Jacques's saddlebags ready to condemn us when they found us. How was I going to get Mathilde safely to Rennes now? How was I to keep her from giving up when I wanted to give up myself?

When I woke the next morning, I was alone. In a panic, I fought my way out of the damp hay and looked around for Mathilde. The rain of the previous evening was rising in wisps and strands of mist from the fields and hanging in a low bank over the marsh behind us. Mathilde was sitting in a patch of weak sunshine, holding Jacques's saddlebags in her lap. For a moment, I thought she had found the diamond, and my heart skipped a beat. When she looked up at me with her tearstained face, however, I could see only deep despair.

"I can't go on," she moaned.

I closed my eyes and sent up a small prayer to the Virgin for strength. It was exactly as I had feared. Somehow, I had to inspire Mathilde to action when I myself wanted to crawl back into the haystack and sleep for a hundred years.

"Nonsense!" I said brightly, sounding false even to myself. "We have come this far, and we had a good rest in Châteaubriant and on the coach. We will manage."

"I don't want to manage!" she screamed, her face suddenly scarlet with rage. She leapt to her feet, dumping the saddlebags on the ground, her fists tight at her sides.

"Mathilde—"

"No, Claudie! I am wet and cold and hungry, and God knows where we are! I can't walk another twenty miles!"

"Well, we can't stay here," I pointed out. So much for patience—or prayers.

"I should never have listened to you," she said. "Look what you've done to us!"

"What *I've* done?" I snapped. My voice rose. "You are the one who got involved with Jacques and his so-called Legion! If Jacques hadn't come for you, our home would still be standing and our father would still be alive. None of this would have happened!"

"Jacques was fighting *for* us!" she fired back. "He was fighting for all that's worth living for. And Jacques loved me!"

"Well, Jacques is dead, Mathilde, and you are the one who swore to complete his mission."

"How could you?" she howled, tears now streaming down her face. "You heartless monster!"

I took a deep breath and forced my voice back to a calmer register, hoping to inspire the same in my irrational sister. "If we walk north, we will be going in the right direction, and we are bound to come to a road or a cottage where they can help us. Perhaps we will find a farmer taking goods to market and he will let us ride in his cart."

"I'm not going," Mathilde said, every bit the petulant child.

"Well, what do you propose? Sitting in this haystack until we starve to death?"

"I'm going home. I'm going to bury Jacques, and I'm going to stay by his grave for the rest of my life," she said.

My fingers twitched with the urge to grab her and shake her.

"You've seen what the soldiers do. You saw what they did to the marquis. You saw what they did to that village. Do you think you will fare any better?"

"I don't care!" she shrieked, leaping to her feet, her fists clenched at her sides. "I just want to go home!"

With that, she stormed away, off toward the marsh, where the blackbirds had fallen silent. I could have gone after her, but I was too angry, and anyway, she would be back when she reached the marsh and discovered there was nowhere to get through in that direction.

I sat down to wait for her, leaning back against the haystack and letting the sun warm my tight muscles. I might as well rest as best I could while I waited for her; we had plenty of hard hours of walking ahead of us again. With that thought, I closed my eyes.

A mistake, as I did not see the soldiers until they were upon me.

CHAPTER 9

Rough hands hauled me to my feet, and I was face to face with a stocky, mustached soldier, his blue jacket flecked with bits of hay, his *bonne rouge* glowing brightly in the morning sun. Only when he commanded me to be silent did I realized I was screaming.

I clamped my mouth shut despite my panic and prayed Mathilde hadn't heard me. She, at least, had a chance to escape.

The man who gripped me was not alone. He dragged me away from the haystack while a second soldier bent and retrieved the saddlebags that had been at my side. The soldier held them aloft, a look of victory on his face. My thundering heart pounded harder than ever as he opened the first satchel, afraid of both what I knew he would find and what I hoped he would not.

"They're his, all right," the soldier said, holding aloft the bundle of post before he tossed it aside into the grass. He reached again and again into the bag. The marquis's pouch of jewels went into his pocket while the papers sealed with the sacred heart earned me a condemning glare. But the soldiers kept searching. They were looking for the diamond.

When everything had been removed from the saddlebags, the soldier turned them upside down and gave them a shake. Nothing more fell out. He plunged a hand inside again and discovered the repaired tear in the lining—Jacques's original hiding place. He tore it wide open and felt inside, but came away empty-handed. He turned the saddlebags in his hands one more time. I held my breath as his fingers slid over the diamond's hiding place. Finding nothing, he tossed the bags to the ground in frustration.

"There were two of them at the inn," he said to the man who held me.

Terror filled me, and my knees gave out. The man holding me stumbled, but, recovering, he jerked me upright.

"Where is she?" he growled, shaking me so that my head snapped back painfully. "Where?"

"I don't know," I managed to choke out. "We argued. She left."

He looked all around, then back at me. His partner gathered the reins of his horse and mounted, and for a moment, an irrational wave of relief swept through me, thinking they meant to leave. So, I was unprepared for the next hard shake and the question that followed.

"Which way did she go?"

I stared dumbly at the soldier while my mind raced. What should I do? I could lie and direct them the wrong way, but I suspected they would see through such a flimsy trick and would go the opposite direction from where I pointed them. But if I told the truth and they didn't suspect me of lying, they would easily catch up with Mathilde, who had disappeared off to the south.

Nervously, I let me eyes flicker off to the east, then let my expression harden as if I had just made up my mind, and I tilted my head to the west. "She went that way," I said, my voice shaking. The fear, at least, was not a pretense.

The soldier's eyes narrowed as he gripped me. "Think you're clever, don't you?" he said, just as I thought he might. He jerked his head eastward. "That way," he said to his companion.

The mounted man laughed, thinking they had outsmarted me, and he rode off into the morning sun as commanded.

"No!" I cried and struggled to help convince them they had been right and to mask my relief. The effort earned me a hard slap across the face. I stopped struggling and sucked the blood from my teeth, a skill my father had taught me.

"While we wait, you are going to answer a few questions," he hissed into my face.

"Please, sir, I don't know anything," I said, blinking hard and trying to force pretty tears onto my lashes as I'd seen Mathilde so often do. From the dangerous way his eyes narrowed, I could see I had not succeeded.

"How did you come by these saddlebags?"

"We found them," I said, which wasn't entirely a lie. It seemed best to stay as close to the truth as possible, but far enough away to deny any knowledge of what Jacques had been up to.

The soldier narrowed his eyes, and I felt his fingers tighten on my arms. "It's true!" I said quickly. "We found them in a woodcutter's cot near our village. Our father died, and we decided to go to Rennes, as we were all alone, and we stayed in the cottage and found them."

A quick movement of skirts caught my eye off to my left, and my heart nearly stopped. Why wasn't she running? Hiding? I fought the urge to shift my gaze or to wave her away. Instead, I kept talking, to keep the soldier's attention on me. "Truly, sir, we don't know who they belonged to. We needed to carry our things, that's why we took them. If they belong to you, sir, I'm very sorry. We meant no harm."

The soldier looked down at the scattered items at our feet, and his eyes landed on the sacred heart seal. He looked back at me.

"Then how do you explain these?" His hand shot to the back of my neck, which he squeezed so hard that the corners of my vision dimmed. He bent to pick up the papers, bending me with him so that my face was only a foot above the dirt. I fell to my knees and flailed with one hand in a way that I hoped waved Mathilde away. The soldier scooped up the letters and thrust them into my face.

"Royalist letters? Traitor!" he cried, and with a hard thrust, he shoved me face-first into the dirt, grit grinding painfully into my lips. I tried to roll away from him, but I was trapped by the haystack and so could do nothing to avoid his booted foot as it slammed into my stomach. Pain exploded through me. I struggled to draw a breath but could not. All I could do was to curl around the pain and hope it might shelter me from the next blow.

The next blow, however, did not come. Instead, there was a heavy grunt above me and then the whole man collapsed onto me.

I flailed frantically, kicking and heaving. He rolled slowly off me and lay still on the ground. I looked up to see Mathilde standing over me.

"Oh, Claudie! The way you screamed, I was afraid I was too late!"

I couldn't speak. I was still gasping from the kick to my gut. Mathilde helped me to my feet. I looked again at the soldier where he lay. The knife that had been in Jacques's bag was now embedded to the hilt in his back.

My mouth fell open. "You killed him!"

"Better him than you," she said. "Come on!" She scooped up the packet of papers and hurried for the soldier's horse, which was standing nearby, eating a hole into the haystack.

I hesitated, looking around at all that lay scattered across the ground.

"Never mind that, come on!" Mathilde said. She had already gathered the horse's reins in her hands and was preparing to mount.

I glanced at the saddlebags. I alone knew what was hidden inside
them, and where. If I left them, perhaps the remaining soldier would
not come after us, having what he had come for. We, at least, would
no longer by marked by them and would have a better chance of traveling undetected along the roads to Rennes.

But I saw again that great diamond, the way it had flashed in the
candlelight. The bright sun, like the glory of France, at its heart. If I
left it, it might be lost forever. If I left it, I would have nothing with
which to buy our future security when we did find this Rooster of
Rennes. And anyway, we had killed a soldier—that would give them
reason enough to keep hunting us.

I grabbed the saddlebags and our blanket. Then, grimacing, I
reached into the soldiers' coat and found his wallet. We would need
money in Rennes if we made it that far.

"Claudie!" Mathilde hissed. She had mounted and was reaching a
hand down to me. I hurried to her and struggled up behind her.

We were heavier than the beast was used to carrying, but we
didn't give it time to protest. As soon as we were both astride,
Mathilde dug her heels into the horse's sides and we were off at a
gallop, in the opposite direction from the one the other soldier had
gone. Mathilde bent low over the horse's neck while I, gripping her
from behind, pressed against her back. When we reached the road,
we spurred the horse until the poor beast was lathered and I feared
might give out. Only then did we slow to a walk.

"This will never do," Mathilde said. "That soldier will follow when he finds his friend, and he's not riding as we are, two together. He will catch us, and soon."

I nodded, but I wasn't sure what to do. The road passed through open farm fields and boggy fens. There was little or no cover, except the mists and drizzle that came and went. Even if we left the road, we would be easy to track and easy to spot.

"The next creek we pass, we must use it," Mathilde said. I wasn't sure what she meant, but I did not ask. I was still aching from the kick to my stomach and willing to let her make the decisions for now. When we came to a bridge with a rain-swollen brook swishing at its foundations, I followed her lead. We dismounted and found a way down to the water on a grassy bank where we left no tracks. We let the horse get a long drink of water before mounting again and urging the animal into the flow.

"The soldier will think we have kept to the road, and even if he doesn't, he won't find our tracks here," Mathilde explained. "We can ride downstream for a time before we continue on through the fields. Even if he realizes what we have done, he will have to guess which way we've gone. Upstream is toward Rennes, so he will guess that way. So, we will go downstream."

"Where did you come up with such a notion?" I asked.

"Jacques," she said. "He had many ways of eluding pursuit."

I didn't ask her how she knew this or what other pursuits he had told her about. At that moment, with death on our heels, I didn't want to know. I only wanted to get to safety. So, I held on while we rode down the stream, a hedge of small shrubs and trees closing in around us, quickly masking us from sight of the road. We continued this way for some time, the horse's hooves slipping now and then on wet stones. Eventually, we found ourselves once again in a wood, the banks of the stream starting to rise around us into a deeper valley. We nudged the animal up onto the bank, where we slid from its back and collapsed, exhausted, on the grass.

CHAPTER 10

We didn't rest for long, not then and not again for the next four days, though our bodies ached for sleep as we struggled in a haphazard northward line toward Rennes. We had stayed off of the road as much as possible, and in so doing had stretched what might have been a two-day journey into four that sent us through strangling thickets and wet marshes until we were bloody and caked in freezing mud. We had both fallen into a despairing gloom at times, but somehow we had struggled on.

At last, toward evening on the fourth day, we made out the dark mass of the city on the horizon, and our pace quickened. We came to one of the many roads converging on Rennes, awash with travelers with whom we could blend as we slipped into town.

Still, I didn't want to be seen riding in on a horse above our station. The animal was as muddy and tangled as we were, but it was still easy to see that he was a creature of value, and Mathilde and I were not. So, while Mathilde waited in a nearby church, I boarded the horse, paying the livery owner from the soldier's wallet. The man showed no surprise at the mount or at the quality of the saddle and bridle, but I left quickly anyway, winding my way back to Mathilde through crowds in case I was being followed.

Continuing into the city, we bought buckwheat galettes and a bit of salted meat from a street vendor, gobbling it all down while they still burned our fingers. The vendor took pity and gave us another small cake to share and directions to a respectable inn.

Filthy as we were, we had to show our money to the landlord before he would admit us to a room, but we were soon ensconced in it, and Mathilde talked the maid into an extra ewer of hot water. In no time, Mathilde was stripped to her shift, washing the mud from her arms and legs and enjoying the feel of a fresh flannel on her face. When she finished, I took my turn, and even though the water, what little she'd left me, had cooled, I didn't complain. After our days on the road, it felt like heaven.

We retired quickly to bed, too exhausted to care about anything but sleep, and yet, when I closed my eyes, I saw the Rooster of Rennes towering over me on his horse, the sun behind him. In the morning, I would be seeking him in the city, but how? We had come so far, and yet, when I thought of searching an entire city for a single man—a man I knew virtually nothing about—I felt small and powerless once again.

The next morning, Mathilde agreed to stay behind while I went looking for him. After all, I couldn't walk around the city carrying the saddlebags, knowing that the soldiers were looking for them, and we couldn't leave them behind unguarded in a rented room. I hoped I could find him quickly, as we only had enough money for one more night in the inn.

A thin, damp sunlight shone down into the cobbled streets as I set out. I walked through alleys and lanes, turning my eyes this way and that, trying to decide how I might find the help I needed. Everywhere, there seemed to be talk of politics. Even old women selling apples voiced opinions about the king's arrest or the royalist riots in the countryside. Broadsheets with blaring headlines were tacked to doors and streetlamps, grisly images of guillotined bodies or starving peasant children carrying their messages boldly for those who could not read them.

A tangle of arguing men spilled out of a tavern, shouting about the divine right of kings while, a few doors down, a knot of young bucks in red liberty caps debated the newer doctrine, the Universal Rights of Man. I rounded a corner and looked down a narrow alleyway. Men huddled around a charcoal brazier, their heads together in muttered conspiracies. I paused, watching them, and my heart quickened when I saw the flicker of red on a shirt and realized it was the sacred heart badge I had seen before. I hurried toward them, but when they saw me coming, they scattered into doorways and down side alleys, disappearing like so many feral cats.

"I am looking for the Rooster," I called out in Brezhoneg but was met by silence, and so there was nothing to do but move on.

I continued roaming the streets until sunset, but with no luck. No one had heard of the Rooster of Rennes, or at least, if they had, they weren't willing to admit it. I returned to the inn, where Mathilde was cranky and annoyed that I had spent my day seeing the city while she had been cooped up in the room. We ventured down into the common room to take our supper and paid the landlord for another night's stay with the last of our money. Tomorrow, if we didn't find the Rooster, either we would have to sell Mathilde's necklace, which I knew would be a fight, or we would be sleeping in a doorway somewhere.

The next morning, after a lengthy argument with Mathilde, I set out in a different direction. Again, I wandered for some time, finding no one promising to ask. Half-heartedly, I asked a few beggars, but they only held out a hand for a penny, which I did not have to give them. A greengrocer and a bookseller both looked at me like I was mad and shooed me away from their stalls when they saw I had no money to spend.

Midmorning, I found myself in a small square of modest shops. In the middle of the square, a traveling tinker had set up his grinding wheel and was doing a steady business, sharpening knives and scissors. A small crowd of chattering women stood around him, using their dull knives as an excuse to gather for a long chin-wag.

The familiarity of the scene warmed me. Apparently, things weren't that different in city and country. The women of our small village did the same thing. And if there was one place to learn news, it was from a bunch of gossiping women.

I hurried back to the inn, where I pilfered a dull knife from a dirty dish in the common room. Returning to the tinker, I mixed myself in among the women awaiting their turn. Several looked at me in curiosity. I smiled back at them, until finally one approached.

"And where did you come from?" she asked. I was taken aback. In my village it would have been a friendly question, born out of true curiosity. Here it had a defensive tone, as if I were an invader in their territory.

"I'm newly arrived in town," I said, keeping my voice and manner bright and friendly. "I come from a few days south of here."

"I thought so," said one of them, then she turned to the others. "I told you there was trouble brewing to the south."

I nodded. "You have heard of our troubles?" I asked, encouraged that the conversation was already turning in the direction I needed it to go.

"How could we not, with peasants streaming into the city day after day?" another woman grumbled. She looked me up and down with a sour expression. "Dirty, idle peasants filling the streets."

"I am not a peasant," I protested. "Nor am I idle. My father keeps a respectable inn." I could not deny the dirty part, even after our rudimentary bath two nights before, but I wasn't going to admit to them just how desperate and penniless we were.

"And yet you've come to Rennes looking for work?" asked a second woman, suspicious but perhaps a bit more willing to hear me out.

I took a deep breath. "I've come to Rennes," I said, leaning in to keep my words from being heard far and wide, "in search of the Rooster."

The women all looked at me with blank expressions for a long moment before several of them burst into laughter.

"You've come all this way looking for a rooster?" one of them crowed, a bit rooster-like herself in her glee. "What, have all the hens in your village stopped laying?"

"Oh no, look at that lovelorn look on her face. She's not looking for a rooster for her chickens!"

They all cackled wildly at that, while my face flushed red. I hurried away, their laughter still ringing in my ears. I had forgotten how big Rennes was. In my little village, everyone knew everyone else, but those women had no idea who I was looking for. How would I find a single man—a needle in this big haystack of a city?

A plain little church stood on one corner of the square, a few beggars lounging listlessly on its steps, and I joined them. Even from here, I could still see the women having a good laugh at my expense. I turned my gaze away from them and reminded myself of what I had in the saddlebags. They might think me an inferior peasant, but they had never held the king's diamond in their hands.

The king. *King and God*, that's what the badge the Rooster had worn on his shirt had declared. And I was sitting on the steps of a church. If anyone was likely to be on the Rooster's side, it would be the clergy, especially here in Rennes, where I had heard they had refused the Civil Constitution of the Clergy in defiance of the new government. They had as much to lose in this revolution as the nobles.

The heavy wooden doors creaked as I pushed them open. Inside, it was cool and dim, and I stood blinking until my eyes adjusted. Candles burned at the altar, but otherwise the space seemed still and empty.

"Hello?" I called. My voice echoed through the space as I waited. I was about to turn and leave when the door to the vestry creaked open and a balding priest stepped out, squinting at me with weak eyes.

"What is it, my child?" he asked.

"I am in need of help, Father," I said.

The priest gave a single nod and led the way to the confessional, where he stepped into his compartment and pulled the curtain shut.

I hesitated, thinking perhaps he had misunderstood my meaning. But deciding that what I had to say might best be said under the seal of confession, I followed him into the little booth. I knelt on the hard wooden step and crossed myself. What should I say? Certainly, I had plenty to confess, leaving Papa to his death and the lack of remorse I felt for doing so. But those sins would have to wait.

"My sister and I have come to Rennes after our village was destroyed and our father killed."

"Your father, he fought for the king?" the priest asked.

"My father wasn't political. He was just in the wrong place is all. But he was killed by the Army of the Republic."

"I will pray for his soul," the priest said.

"We are looking for a man they call the Rooster," I said, lowering my voice.

There was a hesitation on the other side of the screen. "I know nothing of roosters," the priest said, and my heart sank.

"But if I were looking for a rooster in the city, perhaps I would start at the tavern they call the Cock's Comb." The priest rose abruptly in a swirl of robes and left the confessional. Though I was trembling with my eagerness to follow this new clue, I stayed where I was while his footsteps echoed away across the stone floor. When at last I heard the vestry door close, I all but flew from the confessional and across the church.

I stepped out of the front door into the plaza just in time to see the arrival of a troop of soldiers, laughing as they swaggered through the square.

I stood perfectly still, fighting the urge to shrink backward into the shadows. One man's eyes grazed my face, but he turned away without recognition. They continued on, departing the square on the opposite side from where they had entered. All around me, people gradually began to return to their tasks, and I realized I wasn't the only one who had frozen in fear. Rennes, it seemed, was like a pile of dry kindling, and everyone was holding their breath, waiting for the spark.

My gut tightened at the thought, and I remembered Mathilde, alone and waiting for me in the rented room. I prayed she had stayed safely inside. With her impetuous nature, I could never be sure she would do the prudent thing, no matter how dire the consequences.

I hastened down the church steps to where a tinker sat at his cart, sharpening scissors on his grinding wheel.

"Excuse me, sir. I am looking for an establishment called the Cock's Comb. Do you know of it?"

He looked me up and down before he gave me directions—perhaps because the "establishment" was a tavern and not fit for a respectable girl, or perhaps because it was a secret meeting place of the Legion—I couldn't tell which. I thanked him and hurried away.

It wasn't far to the tavern, though the streets and alleys proved a formidable maze, the half-timbered upper stories of the buildings leaning over the streets until they nearly cut off the sky and any chance of navigating by the sun. How city folk managed to keep their bearings was a mystery. I took several wrong turns and had to backtrack when lanes led to dead ends or became so clogged by shanties built by refugees that I could not continue. I nearly laughed with relief when I finally turned onto a street and saw the sign ahead of me, a comical rooster with an enormous comb painted in the brightest scarlet.

Once that first wave of relief passed, however, my heart took up a faster pace in my chest. How was I to approach such a place?

Though I had worked in an inn all my life, this place felt entirely foreign to me, with none of the open, airy, good cheer of my father's establishment and without the protection of my father. The room was narrow and dark, with secretive, shadowed corners. Near the door, a group of grim-faced men played cards. I passed by them, pretending not to notice the eyes that followed me to the bar, not with the masculine hunger they would have shown Mathilde, but with heavy suspicion.

"Excuse me, sir," I addressed the barkeep in Brezhoneg. He was leaning idly against the counter and didn't rouse himself to serve me. I cleared my throat, mustering the courage to venture on, my voice trembling a little. "I was told to come here. I am looking for the Rooster."

Behind me, one of the card players laughed. "The Rooster?" he said in French. "And what would a plump little pullet like you want with a rooster?"

I ground my teeth at his insinuation. If I ever did find the rogue, I was going to have a word with him about his choice of pseudonym.

"Is he here?" I asked the barman, trying to ignore them.

He shrugged, still not bestirring himself from his lazy pose. "Don't know who you mean," he said.

I glared at this answer. Of course he knew who I meant. It was too much of a coincidence, given the name of this place, for the man not to be associated with it.

Behind me, one of the card players crowed while a second called out, "I will be your rooster, *ma poule.*"

Again, they erupted in raucous laughter and lewd suggestions, and my cheeks burned like a blacksmith's coals. Chairs were scraping on the floor as men got to their feet, and I knew that I could not stay much longer. If these men got their hands on me . . .

I turned back to the barkeep. "Tell him I must see him. I've a message—from Jacques Lambert."

I saw the widening of surprise in the barman's eyes, but I could not stay to see what he would do, not with the card players closing in on me. I bolted out of the tavern and away. I would have to return later to try again, hopefully to a more receptive barkeep now that I had dropped Jacques's name.

I ran until I was out of breath and thoroughly entangled in the city. It took me an hour and many wrong turns to find my way back. At last, and with a sigh of relief, I turned onto the right street and saw the inn where I had left my sister. I quickened my pace, my concern for her alone all this time rising above my other fears and worries.

Stepping through the front door, I was surprised to see the public room already busy, though it was only midday. Apparently, city inns did a substantial business all day long, unlike our little country inn that only served a midday meal when a coach stopped to change horses, something that had happened less and less with the disruption of revolution. Here, however, serving girls were bustling in and out of the kitchen with buckwheat galettes, plates of sausage, and bowls of eel stew. Mathilde, not sequestered in our room as she should have been, was sharing a table with a small party of country folk. They were chatting comfortably, a blue-eyed boy in the group making Mathilde dimple and laugh with his words.

I ground my teeth. She was supposed to be keeping herself—and the saddlebags with their precious contents—safe. She was supposed to be brokenhearted for her beloved Jacques too, so what was she doing here, flirting with a farm boy while I was out risking my life trying to secure us a future? Even now, soldiers might be searching the city for the girls who killed a man and stole his horse, and here she was, flaunting herself in public.

I strode to her table, trying hard to keep my anger in check to avoid any more of a scene. I bent to her ear and expressed my displeasure, but she brushed me away.

"Always worrying," she said as if we had nothing to worry about. Had she already forgotten the dead men in our wake: Jacques, our father, the soldier on the road? "We have to eat lunch, Claudie, and the galettes are delicious. Sit down, join us."

"I've already eaten," I lied through clenched teeth. "Come, Mathilde." Gripping her arm, I pulled her up from the table and away. She started to protest, but I gave her a look that froze the words in her mouth, at least until we were out of the public room and on the narrow staircase leading to the rooms above.

"Let go, you're hurting me!" she said, trying to twist her arm out of my grasp, though I had an iron grip on her. I pulled her along behind me without words until we reached the privacy of the landing. Then I rounded on her.

"How dare you!" I growled. "I left you in the room to guard our belongings. You promised me!"

"I was hungry," she whined, rubbing her arm as if I'd done her serious injury. "Besides, I'm still guarding the room. No one can get up here without going through the common room. I would see them if they tried."

"Did you see me come in?" I glared, knowing the answer before I asked the question.

She glared back. "So you would have me starve in our room? I don't know what it matters—we lost or sold most everything of value getting here. The only thing of value I still have is this." She pulled the ruby necklace out from under her bodice, letting the stones flash in the light.

"Put that away!" I glanced around, nervous that someone might have seen. The last thing we needed was to show anyone that she had such a valuable thing hanging around her neck.

She tucked the necklace back into its hiding place while giving me a resentful look. "You've been out all morning, seeing the city, meeting people, hearing all the latest news. I should get to do the same!" With that declaration, she spun and stomped back down the staircase to the lively public room below.

There was little point in going after her. Neither one of us was in the mood to be reasonable, so I let her go, and I hurried along the narrow passage to our room. I was relieved to find that she had at least locked the door, but inside our room, the window sash was thrown wide open. I crossed to it and looked out. It faced a dingy back alley, not visible from the street. Had Mathilde left it open for fresh air? Not likely, I realized, sniffing the sharp aroma of rotting garbage rising from the alley.

A chill ran down my spine, and I turned back to the room. Had thieves been here? Were they here still? I jumped in alarm at a movement, then realized it was only the breeze stirring the curtain. I glanced around the room, but nothing seemed to have been disturbed. Still, I needed to check, to make sure the saddlebags were still in their hiding place. Holding my breath, I bent and threw up the coverlet to peer under the bed. There they lay, safely stowed where I had left them. With a sigh of relief, I reached under the bed and pulled, but they did not come out. They seemed to be stuck on something.

Getting down on hands and knees, then flat on my stomach, I burrowed my head under the bedframe to see what was holding them back.

It was a large, hairy hand. Attached, to my dismay, to a large, hairy man, who was now face to face with me.

He grinned, exposing a row of gleaming white teeth in the dusty, shadowy underworld beneath the bed.

"*Bonjour*, mademoiselle," he said.

And even as I scrambled backward in alarm, banging my head on the bedframe, I realized he had at least taken care not to call me *madame* this time.

CHAPTER 11

The strangled sound that escaped me as I scrambled to my feet was not exactly a scream. It was more a confused protest of surprise and outrage, and it was utterly justified.

"Quiet down! Do you want to get us thrown out in the street?" he said, his words punctuated with bumps and grunts of his own as he extracted himself from the tight space between the bed and the far wall, where he had been hidden while he had fished under the bed for the bags.

By the time he finally got to his feet, my hands were firmly planted on my hips, and I was giving him what I hoped was a withering glare.

"I want to get *you* thrown out in the street," I said.

He did not wither. Instead, he gave a little snort of a laugh.

"What are you doing under my bed?" I demanded.

"The same thing as you, I'd imagine," he said, tipping his head toward where a corner of the saddlebags could be seen peeking out from the fringed edge of the coverlet. I refused to look. Instead, I stiffened my back.

"Hardly. I was not lurking with ill intent under a girl's bed," I said.

To my satisfaction, his eyes widened in horror, and at the edges of his beard, I could see color rising in his cheeks.

"Mademoiselle! You cannot think . . . I would not . . . I hadn't expected . . ." His flustered sputtering was so unlike his usual confident command that my annoyance gave way, at least a little, to amusement.

He must have seen the expression flit across my face because he stopped sputtering, and just as I had done a moment before, he straightened his spine.

"Ill intent? Mademoiselle, I am wounded," he said, his hand going to his heart. "I am here because I was invited."

"Were you?" I said, knowing perfectly well the answer.

"I was."

"And do you always enter through a window and hide in places where you are invited?" I asked, my eyebrows raised, waiting to see how he would talk himself out of such obvious guilt. He only smirked and raised his eyebrows in turn.

"You came to my tavern, announcing—in broad daylight, I might add—that you had something for me from Jacques Lambert. And as we are so well acquainted, I did not think you'd mind me retrieving it while you were out."

So he thought he could just take the saddlebags and leave me and my sister with nothing? Alone and friendless in the city? He would see that I was not so easily cast aside.

"We are not well acquainted, sir," I said, shifting closer to the saddlebags, so I might grab them first if the need arose. "You don't know me at all."

"No? Well then, allow me to introduce myself," he said, shifting toward the bed himself. My movement had not gone unnoticed.

"No need," I said with a dismissive wave of my hand. We would see how he liked being cast aside. "I know who you are."

He smirked. My attempt to insult him had amused him instead. I would have to try harder.

"Do you?" he said.

"You are called the Rooster of Rennes."

I was forming a cutting remark about the annoying qualities of roosters, but before I could say it, he dropped into an elaborate bow, his hand tracing curlicues in the air before him as if he were some grand duke and I a duchess.

"At your service, mademoiselle. And you, I believe, are the fair Mathilde Durand, comrade in arms, if Jacques was to be believed."

I gave a little snort at his mistake, and his shaggy eyebrows raised.

"Claudie Durand," I corrected him. "The fair Mathilde is my sister."

At that, his expression became incredulous. "Really?"

"You mock me, sir," I said through gritted teeth. I had almost been enjoying matching wits with him, but now I just felt like a fool. Of course, he was a man, and like all men had to point out my looks, or lack thereof. As if I didn't already know and needed reminding of my place.

"No, mademoiselle, I am only surprised that my colleague chose a foolish child over a capable woman such as yourself."

I hardly knew what to say to that. He seemed sincere, and yet the idea that he—or any man—would think me preferable to Mathilde was beyond comprehension.

"Well, he did," I said at last, after an awkward pause. "So, if you are looking for a comrade, you must speak to her. I want no part of your rebellion."

At that, his eyebrows dropped back into place, and the interest in his eyes dimmed. "That is a pity. You would be a great asset to our cause."

I shook my head. "My only cause is to ensure a safe future for my sister and me." I meant to continue, to negotiate a fair price in exchange for the saddlebags, but the friendliness had gone completely from his face, and when he interrupted me, there was no warmth in his tone either.

"Well then, if we have no business, perhaps you will give me what is mine, and I will be on my way. Let you get back to . . ." He shrugged, waving a vague hand. "To inspiring lewd suggestions in taverns."

I opened my mouth, then shut it against a surprising rush of fury—fury at what had happened in our village, at Jacques for involving Mathilde, at all of France for the madness of this revolution, and most of all, at having struggled to get to Rennes only to be mocked by this aggravating man. It was too much to be borne and far too much to swallow, and yet somehow, I swallowed it, knowing that if I did not make my case now, I was likely to never get another chance. I drew a deep breath, let it out slowly, and spoke.

"I am sorry," I said. "You frightened me, and I'm afraid we've gotten off on the wrong foot." Another breath. "As you can see, I am in something of a predicament. We've spent two long weeks on the road to come here, to find you."

"So I have heard," he said, an expression that might have been admiration coming into his eyes.

"You've heard?"

He shrugged. "Scattered reports. From south of Châteaubriant and from your unfortunate experience on the coach."

I thought back. "The old couple who sent the soldiers the wrong way?"

The Rooster smiled and nodded. "Your quick thinking saved you there, but we lost you. Had your sister not exposed you, the couple would have brought you to me. As it was, they could only help you escape and send word to me."

"So you've known of our plight all this time but did nothing to help us?"

"It might surprise you to learn, mademoiselle, that I have more to do than to rescue damsels in distress."

I bristled, but he continued. "Besides, the man I sent out to re-trieve you couldn't find you. He did find a rather unfortunate soldier who'd taken a knife in the back, from which he surmised that, in this case at least, the damsels didn't need rescuing."

"So you sat back and let us bring you what you wanted," I said, forcing the words out through teeth that wanted to clench hard.

He gave me a broad grin, either not noticing or not caring about my irritation. "And how well it worked," he said. "So now, if you will excuse me, I will collect it and be on my way."

His arrogant assumption that I would just hand over the saddle-bags that easily made me want to scratch his eyes out. Instead, I spoke calmly.

"Not quite yet," I said. "I believe we deserve something for our troubles."

He gave me an incredulous look. "Your troubles? Have you not no-ticed, mademoiselle, that all of France has troubles?"

"But not all of France has you to blame for them," I pointed out.

His eyebrows shot up. "Me?"

"You and Jacques Lambert," I said haughtily. "If not for you and your little revolt, my village would be standing and my father would be alive. I would not be here now with so few options that I would be asking a man such as you for help."

He was opening his mouth to reply, but he closed it again and tilted his head like a curious dog. "And what type of man is that?"

I hesitated, not because I lacked an answer—I had plenty of cutting words to throw at him—but a tiny voice in my mind was offering another answer: the type of man who preferred me to Mathilde.

Even the thought of such a thing was apparently enough to conjure her, for at that moment, Mathilde burst through the door, and I wished I had spoken. Because she looked at him with her large, round eyes, luminous with surprise, and I knew the voice was wrong. The Rooster smiled and gave a little bow, this time without a trace of mockery.

"You must be the fair Mathilde. *Enchanté*, mademoiselle," he said. She glowed, as she did with any compliment, and extended a hand, which he kissed, sending a little stab of jealousy through me that I couldn't quite explain. "I am the Rooster of Rennes, and I've been looking for you."

Her face transformed with pure joy. "The Rooster! Oh, Claudie! We are delivered."

"Indeed, mademoiselle. You have nothing to fear now that I have found you," he said, giving me a sidelong glance, as if to point out my own lack of appreciation for his arrival. Then his eyes turned back to Mathilde's, as men's eyes always did. "Jacques Lambert raved of your beauty, and yet, his words fell short."

Yes, the little voice had been very wrong indeed. Clearly, he had flattery for every occasion. How had I been fool enough to believe his praise?

Mathilde's face turned downward in sadness at the mention of Jacques, even as the compliment brought a pretty glow to her cheeks. "Jacques is gone. Murdered!" she said, choking a little on the words.

"I know," the Rooster said, his voice soft with sympathy. "He died for king and God, and his sacrifice will not be forgotten. Word reached me that he was dead and the saddlebags missing, and I despaired. But then I learned of two brave sisters bringing them to Rennes, and I rejoiced. And next thing you know, before my men can find the women on the road, I learn that one of them is asking all over town for me, with priests, tinkers, and barmen."

He paused and looked at me, and I felt my face go hot. "How did you . . ."

"The Legion has many eyes and many hands, mademoiselle."

I lifted my chin. "Then it won't be too hard for you to help us. Our home and livelihood are destroyed, and we've been through great danger to complete Jacques's mission. Give us fair payment, we will give you the saddlebags, and you'll be free of us."

"Don't be silly, Claudie," Mathilde said, stepping over to the bed and pulling the saddlebags out from beneath it. "We completed Jacques's mission for the cause, not because we expected a reward." To my horror, she handed the bags over to the Rooster.

"But—" I stammered, reaching for the bags, but the Rooster stepped back in one smooth step that turned into a bow.

"The Legion thanks you, mademoiselles. If we are successful, someday the king may thank you too. As for me, I wish you the best of luck. *Au revoir.*"

"But—" I said again, more desperately this time. He was out the door before I could say more.

For a long moment, Mathilde and I stared at each other. I couldn't believe what had just happened. I had imagined a negotiation, had spent wakeful nights on the road formulating what I would say to the man to secure our future. And just like that, in the blink of an eye, it had all gone wrong, and I had stood, staring stupidly and stuttering out *buts*, while he made off with everything we had risked our lives to bring to Rennes.

I yanked the door open and stormed out after him. He was already outside the inn when I reached the common room. I hurried through it, Mathilde still on my heels, and out into the street, just in time to see his mighty shoulders rounding a corner, his shaggy head rising above every other person around him.

I gathered my skirts and ran to catch him up.

"How dare you!" I said when I was finally on his heels and I knew he had to hear me. "You can't do this to us!"

He said nothing; in fact, he didn't acknowledge my presence at all. He kept marching along, his strides lengthening so that I had to jog every fourth step to keep pace.

"We risked our lives to bring that here. We deserve our reward."

Still nothing. His arrogance sped my steps so that I was in front of him, where he had to acknowledge me.

"If you don't give us what is ours, I will turn you over to the Army of the Republic!" I said, my voice now rising to a shrill screech.

Before I knew what was happening, he had turned and pushed me into the opening of an alley and up against the wall. I expected a hard slap—my father would have slapped me for speaking as I had—but instead, he rested his hand across my throat, not tight enough to hurt me or to even slow my breathing, but enough to warn me into silence. He drew his face down close to mine and hissed out his next words.

"If you don't keep it down, the Army of the Republic will have us all—is that what you want?" he growled. "Have you forgotten that the two of you killed a man? Me, they'll probably just execute, but I shudder to think what they will do with a pair of little dainties like you before you die."

My mouth had gone completely dry, and all I could do was stare.

"I like a woman with fire as much as the next man, but not enough to die for her. So come along if are going to, but shut your mouth until we get out of the street."

With that, he took his hand off my throat, turned, and began walking again at his brisk pace as if nothing had happened.

I stood against the wall for a long moment, catching my breath and willing some strength back into my knees. He was right, of course; I had been foolish and reckless and not myself at all. But I was still too angry to want to admit it.

Mathilde stood beside me, watching me with huge eyes. She had said or done nothing during the whole encounter, just stood staring in shock. I looked at her, then out into the street, at the Rooster's towering form disappearing in the crowd, hating every inch of those broad, well-muscled shoulders.

I pushed away from the wall, testing my legs to make sure they would hold me. When they did, I drew a deep breath. "Come on. We have to keep up with him if we want to know where he's going."

Mathilde's shocked expression transformed into a smirk that reminded me a bit too much of the Rooster. I narrowed my eyes, and because we were sisters, she knew exactly the question in my expression.

"He will be going to the hiding place of the Legion," she said.

"And what if he is?" I said. I didn't care if he was marching into hell itself—I had no intention of letting him get away.

"He's inviting us to join his cause by letting us follow him," she said, still smiling. "If we follow him into their hiding place, we are committing to their cause."

"Don't count on it," I grumbled. The only commitment I was making was to getting my due. And with that thought, I set out after the Rooster, thinking up a new, colorful curse for him with every step I took.

CHAPTER 12

I expected him to lead us back to the Cock's Comb, but he did not. Instead, we wound through a confusing array of narrow alleys, many choked with shanties built of sticks and rags, occupied by old men, blind beggars, and skinny women with babies. As we entered one such alley, someone crowed, and a gaggle of children appeared out of nowhere. Our mighty legionnaire paused to give each one a denier and a pat on the head. I could hardly believe he was the same man who, mere minutes before, had almost strangled me in a back alley. Not that he'd really come close, I grudgingly admitted to myself. His hands had been gentle, despite the threat in his words.

We crossed the river and continued past the old city walls into rutted dirt streets littered with garbage. The high half-timbered houses on either side leaned and bent as if they had chosen for themselves how they would stand, in defiance of their builders. At last, we came to a small, muddy yard behind the narrowest, most crooked building of them all. Several horses stood there, some being unsaddled and curried by stable boys, others standing patiently with their reins tied to the post, one hind foot cocked.

One boy leading a handsome sorrel saddle horse caught my eye. With a shock, I recognized the horse as the one we had taken from the soldier and that I had left, lathered and covered in mud, at a livery stable on the edge of town two nights before. I looked from the horse to the Rooster.

"The long fingers of the Legion?" I said.

"You learn quickly," he replied, then held the back door open and waved me inside like the gentleman I knew he wasn't.

The door opened directly onto a narrow staircase that climbed in a rickety line mirroring the crookedness of the overall construction of the building.

"All the way to the top," the Rooster directed from behind us. Mathilde scampered up the stairs, and I had little choice but to follow. At each landing a single door opened off the stairwell. On the fourth and top floor, she pushed open the door into a wide, comfortable room, the floorboards well-worn but smooth, an inviting fireplace on the opposite wall. I took three steps in, then turned, opening my mouth to resume my argument with the Rooster. I was met only by the door quickly swinging shut. The Rooster was gone.

"Oh, what a lovely room!" Mathilde said, looking around us. "It's much better than that other place."

"You can't think that we are staying here," I said, incredulous.

"Of course we are staying here," she said, looking at me as if she thought I was a simpleton. As if staying in the house of a dangerous revolutionary was the only logical thing for us to do. A dangerous revolutionary who gave pennies and pats on the head to hungry children in the street. Who had, at least for a moment, favored me over my sister. Which, on further reflection, just proved he was either a liar or a fool.

Mathilde cocked her head. "Honestly, I don't understand you sometimes, Claudie. We've traveled for days and through terrible danger to get here, you've been all around the city searching, and when we finally find exactly who we've been seeking the whole time, you are rude and insulting to him. You must apologize when we see him next."

"I was rude and insulting?"

"He likes you, Claudie. A little friendliness would go a long way," she said.

I stared in disbelief. "Did you fail to notice that he just took away everything we had?"

"Not everything. I still have this," she said, pulling the ruby pendant from beneath her dress and holding it up so that it sparkled in the light.

"And that he nearly strangled me in the street!"

She actually giggled at that. "He did not! And he's given us this fine room. Just look at these cushions!" she said, sinking onto a couch and hugging a large pillow to her.

"Don't get too comfortable," I grumbled, though I too was drawn in by the cozy room. I sat delicately on the opposite corner of the couch. The cushions were softer and more comfortable than any I had ever felt before. It seemed a miracle after our hard days of travel, and my resolve to resent the Legion quickly dissolved. I settled back with a sigh.

"We are only here until he gives us our due," I murmured, closing my eyes for just a moment.

The room was in twilight when I woke, alone. Frantically, I hurried to the door, fearing it might be locked. It wasn't, and I pulled it open. I stumbled hurriedly down the dark stairs, desperate to find my sister. Who knew what dangers a den of revolutionaries might hold for her?

At the ground level, the front door opened out into a wide, warm kitchen. Two huge kettles hung on the hooks at the fireplace, an aromatic steam still rising from them, though the fire was now banked. The big table in the center of the room sat heaped with dirty dishes, crusts of bread, and bones sucked clean of meat, apparently the leavings of a recent feast.

My stomach growled at the sight. I hadn't eaten anything since breakfast, but even so, I couldn't eat now, not when my sister was missing. I crossed the room to the door on the far wall, which stood slightly ajar, letting the murmur of voices and the warm, yellow light of lamps shine through from beyond. Through the gap, I could see a comfortable common room, not unlike my father's inn, furnished with long tables. A modest fire burned in the hearth. Men were seated at every table and standing along the walls. They were sturdy, working men for the most part, although some of the tables were occupied by skinny boys in tattered clothing, the likes of which I had seen in the alley where the Rooster had shown his kindness to the children. I suspected, from the mess in the kitchen, that these fellows had come for the victuals as much as any dedication to the cause, but then again, the dispossessed needed a cause as much as anybody.

As for that cause, it was being extoled enthusiastically by the Rooster, who stood by the fire, commanding the attention of the room. I hadn't meant to lurk behind the door eavesdropping, but having spotted him through the crack, I found myself transfixed. All those days on the road as I imagined searching for him in Rennes, I had thought of him as rough and uncouth, an opinion that had gone unchallenged when I found him robbing my room and followed him through the streets. Now, standing tall before the fire, the passionate rhetoric of loyalty and justice flowing smoothly from his lips, he seemed something else altogether. A great man, bold and brave. A hero of old, to vanquish evil. A wise philosopher king from the days of legend.

And it wasn't just me who felt it. When I finally wrestled my eyes away from him, I could see the same rapt attention, the same light of justice, in every face around the room. Listening to him, the ragged boys were seeing themselves becoming heroes too. The looks on their faces jolted me back to my senses. Had this man spoken to the men of my village? Incited them to attack that night, an act that no doubt seemed heroic at the time but in the end cost them everything when the soldiers returned? What right did this chanticleer have to sway the minds of impressionable folk to his cause?

I narrowed my eyes and looked back at the Rooster, ready to burst from the kitchen and oppose him. As my hand reached for the knob of the door, his reached for the person who sat beside him. "The last witness to the fate of our brother Jacques Lambert, who has risked a dangerous journey to bring us the news," he said. I froze where I was as Mathilde rose and faced the crowd.

"I was there when Jacques died," she said, her chin held high and her voice strong and clear in the quiet room. "I was beside him, and I've come to tell you what I saw, and what I saw after. The Army of the Republic didn't just kill the man I loved. They killed my father. They burned my village and all who could not escape it. Other villages too along the valley where we lived."

Her words were met by a murmur of outrage and commentary, but the Rooster held his hand up, and the room quieted. Mathilde then told our story, her lovely eyes shining with tears as she spoke of

Jacques and our father, of the burnt villages and frightened women digging through the remains.

"The farmers among you will know what it means to lose the stores now," she said. "The harvests were in, all tucked away in barns, cellars, attics. A year's work, wiped away. A year's sustenance gone, before the year has even begun. What is to become of those people now? How are they to make it through the winter? Where is the liberty, equality, and brotherhood in that?"

Shouts of support came from the crowd. From the looks on their faces, I suspected more than one man was considering proposing marriage to keep the wolf from my sister's lovely throat. But I was grinding my teeth in anger.

How dare he use Mathilde this way!

I burst through the door, ready to demand that he take his hand off my sister, for it had rested gently on her shoulder throughout her narration. My bursting, however, landed me amid a crowd of men surging forward to put coins into the hat that the Rooster had not so subtly swept from his head and turned up on the table. Thus, my dramatic entrance went entirely unnoticed. Instead of declaring my anger, grabbing my sister, and storming out in an impressive display, I was simply another body pressing forward, reinforcing the enthusiasm of the masses for the cause.

Mathilde, meanwhile, was beaming at the men around her, relishing the attention. I redoubled my efforts to reach her, employing a sharp elbow to the ribs or a heel to a foot when *excuse me* and *pardon me* did not work. At last, I broke from the crowd, gracelessly stumbling into an open space. I looked up to see the Rooster's eyes watching me with keen interest. The space between us was open, and two easy steps brought me up before him, where I meant to give him a piece of my mind.

Before I could speak, his big hand—the one that wasn't already clasping my sister's shoulder—clasped mine and turned me to face the crowd.

"Here she is, friends! The brave sister I told you of. The heroine of the battle! Claudie Durand, who single-handedly ensured the escape of the Marquis du Aubigny from the Army of the Republic, then returned into the fray to save the life of Père François, the village priest, who would have been murdered in cold blood but for this brave lady's quick thinking. Why, I myself stood by her side later that night as she fought on tirelessly to save her village from the flames set by the bloodthirsty Republicans. I ask you, men, if the fair maidens of our realm take so much upon themselves to see justice defended, will you not do the same?"

Another shout of approval went up at these words. Tankards were raised in salute, coins were tossed into the hat, and men lined up to sign their name to a lengthy paper on a nearby table.

I stood staring, dumbstruck. Never in my life had such a string of compliments been directed at me. In fact, I could have counted on one hand all the compliments men had given me over the years, and this barrage of praise had quite disarmed me. Of course, it was just empty flattery—propaganda for his cause—but I couldn't stop the warm glow spreading through me. I turned to look at Mathilde. She was beaming proudly back at me as if I were the fat hen that had just won her a blue ribbon at the fair.

"Oh, Claudie! Thank you for joining us," she said.

"I haven't joined anything," I grumbled, though the roar of the crowd drowned out the words beyond Mathilde and the Rooster, who was still towering over us, his hands on our shoulders.

He gave my shoulder an encouraging little squeeze. "Come now, Claudie, no need to spoil the moment with a fit of temper."

The warmth that had been spreading though me now turned to a rush of heat in my face. Why did this man insist on being so infuriating? But I bit my tongue and held back the many things I wanted to say. No point in proving him right about my temper. I stepped away from his hand, and he let it fall without resistance.

"You worried me when I woke and you were gone," I said to Mathilde, trying to steady my voice as if I weren't boiling over.

"Oh, Claudie, you don't have to worry about me now," Mathilde gushed. "Don't you see? We are safe here among the Legion. This is exactly where I need to be. Where we both need to be—serving the cause!"

She took my hand and pulled me onto a bench beside her. "Come, Claudie, you must be awfully hungry."

"Yes, someone get our heroine a plate of food," the Rooster crowed, and in no time, a bowl of mashed turnips, a heel of bread, and a tankard of cider appeared before me. It was hardly the fine meal that had left the mess in the kitchen, but I was hungry and grateful for something warm to put into my empty stomach, so I ate and left the revolutionary banter to others.

Gradually, the crowd thinned. Forgotten where I sat, I watched the Rooster. He seemed to be all things to all people. A man who needed courage got a confident clap on the shoulder or fierce words of encouragement. A fiery youth who seemed intent on burning down the provincial offices got a solemn word of warning. A cheerful neighbor got a joke and a hearty good-night, all with an air of sincerity and goodwill that left them feeling like his tried-and-true friend.

At last, there were only a handful of people remaining: kitchen boys sweeping the mud from the floor, a couple of older men tallying up the evening's takings, and the Rooster, who, upon seeing the last young farmer out into the night, returned to the table where Mathilde and I still sat and lowered himself onto the bench beside her.

Mathilde glanced at him, then at me with a meaningful look. "Well," she said with an exaggerated stretch and yawn, "it has been quite a day. I think I will be off to bed now. Good night, Monsieur Coq. Good night, Claudie." She gave me one last raised-eyebrow look and strode off.

The Rooster watched her go with a confused expression. "What was that about?" he said.

"She wants me to apologize to you," I said.

"Ah. Well, then, apology accepted," he said with offhanded magnanimity.

I fixed him with my sharpest gaze. "I haven't given it yet."

He shrugged. "I'm sure you mean to. A mere formality, really."

Despite myself, I almost laughed, but then I remembered my anger. So, I held my tongue and let the silence stretch long enough to make the lack of an apology within it quite loud.

"Well then, we've settled that," he said.

This time, a snort of laughter escaped me before I could stop it. He smiled, seemingly satisfied to have made me laugh. Then he grew more serious again.

"Now, let us address another matter," he said.

"The saddlebags," I said, sobering.

"The saddlebags."

I leaned across the table so that my words would not echo through the big room. "When Jacques knew he was dying, he asked us to complete his mission. To bring his saddlebags to you," I said.

"And we are grateful," he said.

"We did it for him, but also for us," I continued. "You must understand, we were left with nothing. No home, no family. Nothing."

"It is tragic, to be sure," he said, "but half of France could say the same. I cannot feed them all."

"Half of France has not done you the service we have," I persisted. "We brought you the saddlebags, just as Jacques asked."

"Did you, mademoiselle?" he said, looking me in the eyes, and suddenly his gaze was piercing. Piercing and green. I had not noticed those green eyes before now. "Just as Jacques asked?"

I squirmed a little and glanced away. "I don't know what you mean." My voice sounded weak, even to me.

"I think, perhaps, you brought me somewhat *less* than what Jacques asked."

So, he had searched the saddlebags for the diamond and found the torn lining—and the lack of a diamond within it—and been fooled. He had the diamond, but he thought I still had it. *This* was a bargaining chip I could use. This was how I was going to get the support I needed to start a new life.

I studied his face. What was the diamond worth to him? Enough to see us settled in a new inn, perhaps? Enough to ensure that Mathilde and I would be safe and able to support ourselves, or at least as safe as anyone could be in France in these troubled times?

I had done nothing to hide my calculations, and they had not gone unnoticed by that piercing look. I tried for innocence, glancing coyly up at him through my lashes as I had so often seen Mathilde do. "I don't know what you mean, sir."

"I very much doubt that," he scoffed. "And I should remind you of the danger. You are smart enough to understand, I think. You have already seen that there are those who would kill for—" He caught himself and closed his mouth before he could say it.

"For the saddlebags?" I offered, still smiling sweetly.

He scowled and leaned across the table to speak directly into my face. "You should consider the danger you are in, mademoiselle."

I leaned closer as well, so that the space between us was nearly gone. "But I am safe here, surely, with you to protect me."

He gave a little snort and rose from the bench. He began to walk away, but when he was directly behind me, he bent, so that his words came with a warm breath into my ear.

"Mademoiselle, has it not occurred to you that I may be the very danger that you are in?" With that, he walked away, leaving me alone in the room, with only the tingle running along my spine for company.

CHAPTER 13

We did not see the Rooster the next morning when we went down to breakfast. According to the handful of men in the common room, he was, like any good rooster, hard at work at sunrise, though they did not say what that work was. I was disappointed by his absence. I wanted to settle the matter of our reward. And if I am honest, I was eager to match wits with him again too. I looked forward to seeing the look on his face when I told him where the diamond was and he realized he had just paid me to get something that was already in his possession. But to have that chance, I would have to negotiate with him soon, before he thought to pull apart the saddlebags—if he hadn't already.

"We should be helping out here," Mathilde said through a mouthful of oat porridge, pulling me back from my thoughts. "Supporting the cause and earning our keep. Maybe we could help in the kitchen."

"Maybe we should find jobs in the city," I said, not wanting her to get too comfortable with the idea of staying here. The sooner we got our reward from the Rooster and left Rennes, the better, but we needed an alternative, just in case.

"Suit yourself," she said, carrying her empty bowl into the kitchen. A short time later, when I left, she was up to her elbows in dishwater.

I had thought, perhaps, that I might find work in an inn with all my experience helping Papa. Rennes, however, was crowded with rustics just like me, fleeing war and looking for work. So, after a day of grinding humiliation as I was shooed away—or worse, offered far less seemly ways to make a living—I returned to the Legion's quarters empty-handed.

Mathilde was still helping in the kitchen, so I climbed the stairs to our room, only to find it in disarray. The cushions had been pulled from the seats, and a thin layer of grime around the hearth indicated that someone had sifted through the ashes of the fire. So, they had searched our room, which meant they hadn't yet found the diamond. And if they hadn't yet found the diamond, there was still hope I could negotiate for a reward. A welcome thought indeed after my day of failures.

I returned downstairs and joined Mathilde in the kitchen, helping prepare and serve the evening meal. The common room filled once again with hungry men and boys. They filed in nervously in groups of two or three and were directed to take a seat. We handed out ample servings of mutton stew and brown bread, and as they set to eating, the Rooster appeared among them, greeting them, patting their backs, offering his condolences if they had lost a loved one or a living.

When the meal was almost over, he began his speech. This night he had a young boy to tell his tale of suffering at the hands of the Blue Army, as he called them. The sheet of paper was once again spread out on the table, and this, I realized as I watched the new men and boys flock to it, was the place to sign up for the Legion's army—an army that, when given the signal, would band together with émigrés returning from exile and overturn the revolution, restoring the king and returning Brittany to the way of life we had long enjoyed.

The Rooster paid me no attention through supper and the speech that followed. We served the food, then gathered the dirty plates and bowls and returned them to the kitchen. When the speeches were over and most of the men had gone home, Mathilde and I took bowls of stew for ourselves and returned to the common room to eat them. When the Rooster soon did the same, Mathilde gave him a bright smile and waved him over to join us. At once, she began to chatter cheerfully about her day and all the little tasks she had done in service to the cause.

He patted her hand where it rested on the table. "We are most grateful for your support, mademoiselle," he said, then his eyes flicked to me. "And for yours too, I assume."

"Oh, no," Mathilde said. "Claudie didn't help here today. She went around the city looking for a job."

He glanced my way with an arched eyebrow. "A job?"

"We must eat, monsieur," I said stiffly. "Since our father's inn was destroyed, we must find a source of income."

"I would have thought you'd already found one," he said, giving me a meaningful look.

I cocked my head and gave him a look of confusion—as if I had no idea that he was speaking of the diamond—and was satisfied to see a flicker of annoyance in his eyes.

Mathilde, comprehending none of the unspoken exchange, chimed in, "Oh, Claudie says she doesn't support the cause, that's why she went looking for work, but she didn't find a thing."

"I'm not so sure," the Rooster muttered, loud enough for me to hear but not loud enough to still Mathilde's tongue, which went right on, betraying my vulnerability to him. I would have kicked her if the Rooster's eyes hadn't still been locked on me.

"I told her there's plenty of work for us here," she prattled on. "If we set to it together, we could have this place shining in a day or two."

The Rooster's eyes still hadn't deviated so much as an inch from mine. "I do like things that shine," he said, lifting a spoonful of stew to his lips.

I could feel a bead of sweat forming between my shoulder blades, but I only blinked and held his stare. "For the right price, we would be happy to deliver all the shine you could ever want."

He choked on the stew, coughing and wiping his mouth on the back of his hand before he could continue. "So now we come to it. What, pray, is the right price?"

I gave him a cool smile. I had come here intent on as quick a res-olution as possible, but to my surprise, I was enjoying myself. I had never met a man willing to cross wits with me like this—Papa would have slapped me for my insolence. I was just calculating the answer that would best keep our negotiation going when Mathilde jumped in once again.

"Don't be ridiculous, Claudie! We are getting room and board, and this is a chance to help the Legion. We don't need more pay than that."

"Then we have a deal," the Rooster said before I could protest Mathilde's poor bargain. "It should keep you busy for a week at least. The place hasn't seen a proper cleaning in some time."

"Or ever," I muttered, looking around at the filth. "I have no desire to play scullery maid to a pack of wolves such as this."

He chuckled. "What, then? Would you prefer to take to a nunnery?"

How did he know of our mother to pick a taunt so cruel? I looked up at him, ready to unleash my anger, but of course I saw it was unwarranted. He did not know of Maman. How could he? I took a breath to ease the sting and let it out in a long-suffering sigh. "Very well, we will clean for our room and board, but our business is not finished, Monsieur—" I hesitated. It seemed silly calling him a rooster, like children at play. "What is your name? It is ridiculous to refer to a grown man as a barnyard animal."

He laughed. "Ridiculous, perhaps, but safe. If I tell you my name, what's to keep you from taking it right to the Republican Army?"

"You know the army is no friend of ours," I said, my heart icing over at the very suggestion.

"You haven't exactly declared your loyalty to me either," he said. A fair point, and one I didn't mean to amend.

"Oh, Claudie, never mind his name." Mathilde's offhanded dismissal surprised me. I had almost forgotten she was with us at the table. "It's a deal, sir. Now then"—she bounced up from the bench— "we should get a good night's sleep. We will have a full day's work tomorrow."

I hesitated, glancing between Mathilde and the Rooster. I wanted to stay and negotiate for the diamond, but what excuse could I make without making my sister suspicious?

"A word yet, Claudie," the Rooster said, saving me from the decision. With relief, I agreed to stay. Mathilde gave me one last questioning look but went off to bed without protest.

We were alone in the room, the Rooster and I. I glanced up into the intensity of his gaze and suddenly felt the weight of it. I had been enjoying the power of my secret, but now that we were alone, I was acutely aware of how strong he was and how alone I was in his headquarters. I waited warily for what he might say.

"I must ask what you know of Jacques's mission," he said, his tone cool but not threatening.

I kept a neutral expression on my face. "I did my best to stay out of Jacques's business," I said.

The Rooster laughed again, leaning back casually in his chair. "That's not the way he told it."

My hands clenched into fists at the thought of Jacques telling tales of his conquests and my name or Mathilde's coming into it.

"Jacques said that if it weren't for the vigilance of her sister, he would have had Mathilde long since."

I turned back to glare fiercely at him. "Is it wrong of me to protect my sister, sir?"

"A *hawk's eyes* is how he described it," he said good-naturedly. "And an uncanny sense of when and where to interrupt things that were meant to be secret . . ."

Of course that's what Jacques *would* say. "He could have ruined her reputation and any chance for a good future with his 'secrets,'" I said.

"My point is," he said, his amusement at having goaded me quite open on his face, "you *did* know Jacques's business. You worked to find him out. And if you listened at doors enough to always frustrate his romantic endeavors, then you may well have known other things."

I crossed my arms. "So you think I'm a spy? Is that it?"

His eyes grew sharper as they scrutinized my face. "Are you?"

"Of course not!" I wasn't sure if I should be amused or angry at his accusation.

"You have made no secret of your contempt for Jacques Lambert."

"Because he used my sister!" I exclaimed, incredulous.

"Or your contempt for me," he added.

I hesitated. "If you had never come to my village, I would still be safe at home," I said, repeating the objection I had told myself for days on the road. Despite the pain of the past month, *contempt* was too strong a word. I was not, however, in a mood to correct him.

"Mademoiselle, you are the one who sheltered the fugitives the Republicans came looking for," he pointed out.

"Because we ran an inn!" I explained. I refused to let him cast it as support for his cause. "I take no side in the wretched war!"

"But don't you see? We all must take sides," he said, his voice even. "Every act is an act of war in these times. When you took in the marquis and his family, you chose. Not just for yourself, but for your village."

I shook my head, not wanting that responsibility on myself. "You came even before the marquis," I pointed out. "You knew there would be a battle. You told me to lock my doors and hide inside."

"And had you locked your doors, the marquis would have gone on, the Republican Army at his heels, passing your village by. Mind you, I don't disapprove of you sheltering him. I am only sorry it brought you suffering."

I stayed as I was, arms crossed, glaring, trying to find the trick in his words. He spoke the truth, and yet somehow he had distorted it from what I believed to be true.

"But to the matter at hand," he said.

"There is a matter at hand?" I said, once again feigning innocence. He had bested my arguments blaming him for our fate, but he would not so easily get me to reveal the diamond.

"Jacques's business."

"You mean seducing my sister?" I said. If he wanted answers, he was going to have to work for them.

"His other business," he said, and I had to hide my pleasure at the hint of annoyance in his voice.

I shrugged. "I cannot help you there."

He leaned in closer, lowering his voice. "Did Jacques ever mention a jewel?"

A little chill went through me, but I suppressed it with an inno-cent wide-eyed look. Or at least I hoped it was innocent. "A jewel. Hmm. I remember he told us of the crown jewels being stolen." I waved the idea away with a breezy gesture. "Personally, I think he exaggerated the story."

I could see the flash of excitement in the Rooster's eyes, but I pre-tended not to. "What more did he say?"

I bit my lip and cocked my head as if I was trying to remember. I was enjoying myself enormously. "He said the king's diamonds are beautiful beyond imagining. That when the king wore them, he out-shone all the courts of Europe."

"And?"

I leaned across the table too. "And that just one of the diamonds would have been worth a king's ransom."

"Not a ransom," he said, "but perhaps a rescue. Enough to fund a war."

"That's what you are after, then? You think Jacques had one of the king's diamonds?"

He came to his feet suddenly, his frustration barely in check. "I think you know perfectly well what Jacques had," he said through gritted teeth. Then he calmed his tone, attempting to reason with me. "It's no use to you. Revealing it to anyone would only get you killed."

"Then I certainly can't reveal it to you," I said, then smiled and added, "*if* I knew where it was."

He ran his hand through his tangled curls, glowering, and I came to my feet too, ready to flee if I needed to. Were he my father, I would have already been nursing bruises. How far did I dare push this Rooster?

Before either of us spoke again, the front door opened, and a man in a heavy woolen traveling coat and muddy boots stepped into the room, accompanied by a boy and a priest. At the sight of them the Rooster's eyes widened in alarm. He drew back from me and gave a slight, stiff bow as if he were fighting the urge to bow properly and give away the status of the new arrival.

He glanced at me and said in a low voice, "We will continue this later." Then his attention returned to the arrivals and, with a sweep of his arm, he invited them to accompany him through the kitchen to the stairs. The men gave me a suspicious look as they passed.

I sat back on the bench, suddenly aware that my heart was racing, but not with fear. It was . . . I wasn't sure what it was. Excitement? Danger? I could feel it tingling through my limbs, making me eager for more.

I looked in the direction the Rooster and the new arrivals had gone. Whoever they were, and whatever had alarmed our host, was none of my business, but that didn't quell the sudden desire to know. I rose and crossed to the stairs, looking up them. I didn't know where they had gone—not exactly. The building was four stories tall, so they were somewhere on the second or third floor. I had no business looking for them. I had just assured the Rooster that I was not a spy, an assurance that would ring false if I were caught listening at a door. But curiosity was devouring my reason.

I began up the stairs—after all, our room was on the top floor, so I had no choice but to climb the stairs—my ears straining for any sound of them. On the second-floor landing, I listened at the door but heard nothing. I gave the door a little push and found it swung easily on its hinges. Beyond, I could just make out a long, dark corridor, doors opening off either side of it. Given that the building appeared to have been an inn before becoming the Rooster's roost, I guessed these were bedrooms, intended for paying guests and now housing his closest associates. I could hear no sound, nor could I see light under the doors of any of the rooms, so I let the door to the passageway swing shut and continued upward.

On the third floor, the door leading off was more substantial. If this was like our inn, this would be a larger set of apartments meant for the proprietor's family. I hesitated on the landing, knowing I should continue on up to the room he had given us but unable to force myself past this door without pressing an ear to it.

I probably can't hear anything anyway, I thought, trying to convince myself to move on, but even as I thought it, I noticed a sliver of light beneath the door. I meant to take a step toward the stairs, but instead, my feet turned toward that sliver of light. If I couldn't hear anything, there was no harm in listening, was there? With that thought, my resolve collapsed, and I pressed my ear to the door.

I might not have heard them, but their voices were raised in anger.

They were arguing, and as I pressed closer, at least some of their words came clear.

"We agreed on October," the Rooster was saying. "If we pull back now, we will lose our momentum. Half our force will go home for the winter and not return when there's spring planting to be done."

"It can't be helped," said a second voice, refined and Parisian, no doubt the man to whom the Rooster had bowed. A count or marquis in disguise, judging from his accent. "Without the Duke of Brunswick, we haven't a chance of taking Paris. I will not throw the forces we have against the Republican Army when they have no chance of victory."

"But what of the émigrés? Surely with their help—"

"Rousing men who have already fled to come back and fight won't be easy. They will not come back now that the Prussian army has retreated. They are not that brave," said a third voice, probably the priest.

"But the English," the Rooster's voice came out in a frustrated growl. "If we have the English army—"

"What progress have you made on that front?" asked the aristocrat. "Have Jacques's saddlebags been found?"

My stomach lurched, and I pressed my ear harder to the door.

"I have the saddlebags," the Rooster's voice said solemnly, "just not their contents."

I heard a thump and some rustling sounds and knelt to put my eye to the keyhole. After all, if I was this far in, I might as well go all the way. There was a table or desk opposite the door, and the saddlebags were on them in front of the aristocrat. He was examining the torn lining. I held my breath, wondering if he would notice the replaced stitches on the strap or the faint lump in the padding. Like those before him, his attention was drawn to the place where the diamond had been removed, and so he noticed nothing else. The man's expression was grim when he looked back up at the Rooster.

"This is most unfortunate," he said, his tone dark. "Is there no hope of recovering it? Vincent de Tinténiac has agreed to meet me in two weeks' time in Saint-Servan to sail for England."

England? Was this simply about another aristocrat's flight from France? What of the Rooster's cause? I felt strangely disappointed by the thought as I shifted closer to the door once again.

"Vincent de Tinténiac has joined us?" the Rooster asked. "That is good news. He was a fine admiral before the Republic did away with its officers."

"He has rallied other former officers to our cause," said the priest, "but what will be the use without the diamond—or without our forces here still ready to fight? We cannot ask them to fight without the English."

Ah! This wasn't a mere flight to England. They wanted the English to fight. I thought again of the size and weight of the diamond in my hand. Surely it would buy an army large enough to crush the new Republic.

"There is hope," the Rooster replied. "The saddlebags were brought to us by two sisters. I think the older girl knows more than she's telling me."

"And where is this sister?" demanded the aristocrat.

The Rooster chuckled. "Probably listening at the door, if I've judged her right."

They all turned to look at the door, and I pressed my thumb to the keyhole and held my breath, hoping they had seen or heard nothing. I wanted to flee, but I feared the slightest movement would be detected. "She's the one I was talking to when you arrived."

"Is she working for the Republic?"

"I don't think she's working for anyone. She wants reparations for her lost property in exchange for the diamond."

"Reparations," the priest scoffed. "Every peasant thinks they deserve reparations! I have lost five generations of wealth and yet ask for nothing!"

"Nothing but the English army," the Rooster said with the cool irony I had heard so often directed at me. I had to clamp a hand over my mouth to keep a snort of laughter from leaking out. "Don't worry, I think I can win her over."

"Win her over? This is not a courtship, Yannig!"

So the Rooster's name was Yannig. A little spike of victory filled me, at least until his companion spoke again.

"We need that diamond, and we need it soon," the aristocrat snarled. "Search her! Interrogate her! Make her talk!"

I pulled back from the door, my heart pounding as I remembered the Rooster's—Yannig's—huge hand at my throat. He could easily force the truth out of me if he wanted to. Sparring with him had felt like a game, but hard reality now slammed back into me. I had hidden a treasure from them—a treasure they were depending on for the success of their counterrevolution.

Yannig had been gentle with me, but he was a desperate man. His ambition to liberate the king and country would guide his hand at our next meeting, I was sure of it. What a fool I had been to think

I could bargain with him when he had the power, the means, and every reason in the world to simply wrest the information from me. This was war, and if I was not their ally, I was their enemy.

But England! They meant to take the diamond to England. Perhaps I had a chance after all, if I was quick and bold. I straightened my shoulders, took a firm grip on the doorknob, and threw open the door.

Or at least that's what I attempted to do, but the door was locked, and all I managed was to give it a good rattle. Then I knocked, though booted feet were already striding across the floor on the other side.

The door opened, and the Rooster towered before me, his expression transforming from surprise to amusement, and finally, to concern. That's when I realized the danger I had thrown myself into, revealing that I had been listening at the door. Would they kill me as a spy?

"Take me with you!" I blurted out.

His brow drew down in confusion. "Are you mad, woman?"

"I will tell you where the diamond is," I said, "if you promise to take me to England with you. Me and Mathilde. Away from the war here. That is the reward I ask."

Behind the Rooster, the aristocrat had come to his feet. The priest and the boy, who had been standing quietly by, rushed forward and grabbed hold of me. They may have been mere common folk, but they had the hard, merciless hands of soldiers, and my stomach lurched as they pulled me into the room while the Rooster closed and locked the door behind me. I was pulled forward to face the aristocrat. I could see from his narrow eyes, clamped jaw, and the way he was cracking his knuckles that he would not be granting me any rewards.

CHAPTER 14

"So," said the aristocrat, running a hard gaze over me as if he meant to see through to my soul. "You *were* listening at the door." He gave the Rooster a disapproving scowl. "If you knew this to be likely, why didn't you set a guard?"

The Rooster raised an eyebrow. "And lose the chance we have before us now?" he retorted. "Anyway, Claudie is not a spy."

"Your claim is rather remarkable, given that we just caught her spying."

Squaring my shoulders, I lifted my head. "I wasn't spying," I said. "I was going to my own bedroom, one floor up, when I overheard you. If you didn't want to be overheard, why didn't you lower your voices?"

The Rooster made a small noise in his throat; I wasn't sure if it was a warning or a suppressed laugh.

The aristocrat threw a glare at him before returning his eyes to me. "And how do we know you are telling the truth?"

"Because I know where the diamond is and can retrieve it for you quite easily."

"Can you now?" He rose from his seat behind the desk and approached me. There was a grim set to his lips that reminded me of my father. I would have drawn back from his approach, but I was still firmly pinioned by his two assistants. My stomach dropped, and I cursed my boldness. The Rooster had been easy to spar with and had not resorted to violence, but this man would.

"It's not yours to bargain with, mademoiselle," he said with quiet threat when he stood only a few inches from me.

"It's not yours either," I pointed out.

He raised a hand, and I closed my eyes, knowing all too well the pain that would follow.

Yet it did not come.

Cautiously, I eased my eyes back open.

The Rooster stood beside the aristocrat, gripping his raised wrist. "There is no need for that," he said. "She has already agreed to tell us where the stone is and knows we will be taking it to England. If she is a spy, the most dangerous thing we could do is to leave her here in France with that knowledge. What harm is there in taking her and her sister to England with us? We get the stone, we take them to England, drop them off in some isolated Cornish village far from London, and they are safely out of the way. Even if she does mean to run back to the Republic with the news, it will be too late."

"If she is a spy, we should do away with her now," the aristocrat said.

The Rooster gave an impatient snort. "If she is a spy, she is the worst spy I've ever seen, bursting in here and revealing herself. Honestly, man, think of it. Why make more enemies than we already have?"

The aristocrat slowly relaxed his arm. "We are asking for trouble taking women aboard ship."

"A foolish superstition!" Yannig said, sweeping the objection aside. "Just think. Transportation to England will cost us nothing.

It is a very advantageous offer and far more palatable than torturing a woman."

The aristocrat studied me for another long moment while my blood rushed so fast and hot through my head I felt dizzy. Still, I stood steady and met his eye. At last, he directed his men to let go of my arms.

"You seem to have won yourself a champion, mademoiselle," he said to me, before turning and pacing toward the desk. "Very well, you have your bargain." He turned again to face me. "Now, where is the diamond?"

"I will need a knife." I said.

The aristocrat snorted. "So now you are an assassin?" he said. "I don't think so."

"I cannot retrieve it without one," I said.

The Rooster stepped to my side and pulled the knife from his belt. "I will be your hands on the knife. Just tell me what to do," he said.

My knees trembled a little as I walked to the desk, where the saddle-bags still lay. I could see the aristocrat gritting his teeth. He did not like my approach, but he said nothing, and my confidence grew. The Rooster—Yannig—would keep me safe.

Lifting the saddlebags, I showed him the seam that I had replaced and directed him to cut the laces. His eyes widened with surprise.

"It was not well hidden in the lining," I explained. "I found it easily enough, and I wasn't even looking for it. I knew if I put it back there, it would be found by anyone who stopped us on the road."

"Clever," the Rooster said, and he slid the tip of his knife beneath the laces and slit them.

Once there was a gap in the seam, the aristocrat snatched the bags back from us and thrust his fingers inside. I saw his expression sharpen as his fingers brushed against the lump inside. All the men in the room drew close to the desk as he pulled it free and began to unwrap it. The air in the room grew so thick with anticipation that it was hard to breathe.

I had seen the stone only once before, in the dim light of the wood-cutter's cot. Even then, it had stolen my breath. But here, where a fire burned in the hearth and candles stood on the desk and mantel, it captured every spark and threw them in such a dazzling array along the walls and ceiling that it seemed I was inside a jewel myself.

No one spoke when the aristocrat tipped the stone out into his hand. No one even breathed. Not for a very long moment. Had I been a Republican spy, I could have made my escape and been halfway out of Rennes before they noticed, so enraptured were they by the king's great treasure.

The aristocrat held the stone out to the Rooster, who took it rev-erently and held it up to the light. "Imagine," he said softly, "I hold in my hand something Louis XIV held, and Louis XV after him, and then our current king. It has graced the fair neck of Marie Antoinette, and now, perhaps, it will save that neck from the guillotine."

Every eye in the room was still on the stone, but the Rooster's eyes strayed to me, and they were shining as brightly as the diamond. "Well done, Claudie."

He turned back to his companion. "You see? She will not be a lia-bility en route to England. She will be an asset."

The aristocrat gave the Rooster a skeptical look before turning a glare to me, though I had delivered the very thing he wanted most. "She better be," he grumbled. "The captain will have orders to let you off the ship the moment you cause trouble, whether or not there is any land in sight. Do I make myself clear?"

"Perfectly," I replied, trying to put as much ice in my words as he had put in his. It was not the most prudent response and might have led to more trouble, but the Rooster hurried to return the stone to the aristocrat and offered to escort me to my room. I did not object. I had what I wanted and had no desire to stay and hear anything of their plans. I wasn't a spy, but I wasn't a revolutionary either, I reminded myself, despite the exhilaration I had felt in Yannig's presence.

"Thank you," I said, once we were on the landing outside the room and the door was firmly closed behind us. "I don't know what they would have done to me if you hadn't been there."

"It's never advisable to eavesdrop on men such as ourselves, mademoiselle. You are lucky you had a strong position for bargaining."

I had meant to make a humble apology, but I bristled at this assertion. "It wasn't luck. I never would have stepped into the room if I hadn't had the diamond."

He gave a little chuckle. "You didn't have the diamond. We did. We've had it all along."

I couldn't help chuckling a little myself. "You did me a great service by not finding it. But truly, thank you for coming to my defense. Mathilde and I will be safer in England, I think. Here we have nothing. There we can start over again."

"Tell me," he said, and I could hear the amusement in his voice. "Do you speak English?"

A sudden ball of lead formed in my stomach. I hadn't thought of that.

He took one look at my expression and gave a bark of laughter.

"Does no one speak French in England?" I asked.

"Do not worry yourself," he said when he finished laughing at me. "We will take you to Cornwall. Cornish is much like Brezhoneg. You will not find it so hard to understand or to make yourselves understood."

By this time we were at my door and had paused to finish our conversation. We were standing quite close on the small landing, lit only by the single candle he had brought from the room below. In the candle's soft glow, I could see how young he was. Despite his blustering confidence and his command that made him seem older, his cheeks still held some of the roundness of youth. He wasn't much older than I, though I had mistaken him for older—just as he had me when we first met. The thought made me smile, and his eyebrows raised in question.

"You are not so much a rooster as a cockerel," I said. "I think I have mistaken your age."

Now his amusement matched my own. "Should I be insulted as you were, mademoiselle?"

"Youth has fewer advantages to a man than to a woman, I think," I said. "I doubt you would prefer me calling you Cockerel before your men."

"I think I will stay with Rooster before my men," he agreed. "But you may call me Yannig when we are in private."

Something warm awoke in my chest, and I suddenly found myself tongue-tied. I put my hand to the latch, preparing to push open the door, but there was one more thing I wanted to know, and my curiosity overcame my embarrassment.

"Yannig," I said, his name both foreign and familiar on my tongue, "why did you agree to take us to England? It would have been easier to leave us here."

He considered for a moment. "Maybe because I am a man of honor," he said. "It was a reasonable bargain, and I keep bargains where I can."

It was a fine answer, and yet something deflated inside me at his response.

He turned to make his way down the stairs, but at the edge of the landing, he looked back at me, his gaze holding on me long enough to sink into my soul.

"Or maybe," he said, "I am not ready to be rid of you just yet." With that, he disappeared down the steps.

CHAPTER 15

I woke the next morning to a new world, or perhaps as a new person in the world. Many days of hard travel lay before us, as they had before, and yet I did not tremble. The road no longer seemed like a vast and threatening unknown before me but rather a shining opportunity.

England! A land where we could make a new beginning, far from the revolution and counterrevolution, where we could run an inn of our own without the tyranny of a father or the shadow of a mother's abandonment. Of course, there were leagues of Brittany to cross, and then the perilous waters of the channel. Perhaps that should have paralyzed me with fear. But this time, we would not be alone. We would have Yannig at our side, a thought that might have annoyed me just a few days ago but now filled me with a pleasant anticipation. We would be amply protected in his company, and the hours would pass more quickly with his conversation.

Convincing Mathilde to start anew in England and leave the cause of the Legion behind would not be easy, so I decided to work at it a bit at a time. I told her Yannig had important work for the Legion there and had asked us to go along. With her usual naive enthusiasm, she did not question the flimsy story and eagerly prepared for our departure from Rennes. I would tell her the rest when we were in the boat and had no choice but go forward. I knew she would be angry, but it was for her own good. I hadn't decided whether I would even tell her of the diamond. It still seemed too dangerous a secret to share.

"You trust this cocky Rooster to get us safely across Brittany now?" she asked, her eyebrows high on her forehead and a little grin flitting across her face as she repeated to me my own insult from only a few days before.

Ignoring her expression, I nodded. "Whatever his character flaws, I don't doubt his prowess in battle," I said. "Don't forget, he has saved our lives once before. We will be safe in his hands."

"So it's as I expected then. You are in love with him," she said conclusively.

I felt my traitorous cheeks warm. I was not in love, and anyway, I was not the kind of girl men fell in love with, no matter what I thought of them. I pushed her away and stood to busy myself with preparations.

"He knows the road, and he's capable with musket and sword," I said. "If you want to call that love, go right ahead. My only interest is in getting to England safely."

She shrugged, still smirking. "You can make all the denials you want. I see it in your face. You, who have always spurned love—you have fallen head over heels!"

As usual, her careless words stung. I had never spurned love—I had been the one spurned, even by my own mother. But before I could formulate a protest, Mathilde had bounced on.

"So how do we get to England?" she asked.

I didn't know the answer to that, but we were to learn it soon. Only a few moments after we had settled at a table with our breakfasts, Yannig dropped into the seat beside me.

"It is four days of hard riding to the coast—are you equal to it?" he asked, sizing me up briefly, then turning a more critical eye to Mathilde's more delicate frame.

"Good morning to you too," I said, and scooped a large bite of gruel into my mouth. I saw no need for manners if he didn't.

He gave me a little roll of his eyes. "*Bonjour*, mademoiselle," he said with exaggerated politeness. "Now answer the question."

"We got here on our own, didn't we?" I sat up straighter, squaring my shoulders, meaning to look confident and self-reliant.

He gave a slight nod of acknowledgment, though there was still doubt in his eyes. "And you have experience with horses, do you?"

"I took care of them at the inn," I said, though I knew it was not what he meant.

"And we rode that soldier's horse," Mathilde pointed out.

"I'm glad to hear it," he said, a gleam in his eye that told me he was well aware of the challenge before us. "We will leave in the morning."

"So soon?" I said.

"Is that a problem?"

"No, of course not," I said, though I did think we'd have a few more days to prepare. "I only thought you might need more time arranging passage to England."

"We will rendezvous with our ship's captain nearer the coast," he said. "We will have adequate accommodations there if we must wait. With adequate chaperones, to keep things all very proper."

"Chaperones?" Mathilde asked.

Yannig rose, preparing to leave. "We will be lodging at an abbey."

My stomach clenched at this news. "An abbey?" I asked, my alarm too evident in my voice.

His eyes narrowed suspiciously. "You object to an abbey?"

I could guess what he was thinking; only supporters of the revolution had a quarrel with the church. I might trust him to get us to England, but he wasn't ready to extend that trust to me. Not completely.

"Of course not. It's just . . ." I hesitated again, not sure how much of our history I wanted to share with him. Mathilde, however, had no such reservations.

"Our mother lives in an abbey," she said, excited. "Maybe this is it, Claudie. Maybe we will meet her at last."

Yannig's eyebrows rose, and he looked from Mathilde to me for confirmation.

"She experienced religious ecstasies after Mathilde was born," I explained. "Père François declared them authentic, and she took the veil," I said.

He looked like he wanted to ask more. To hear the full story— how, when my mother had to choose between her children and God, she had left us, not even glancing back as the cart rolled away up the road.

"Can you tell me the name of this abbey near the coast?" I asked in a voice stiff with dread.

"The Abbey of Saint Canna," he said.

"That is not her abbey," I said. Mathilde looked crestfallen at this pronouncement, but I was filled with relief. True, I had spent hours imagining the conversations I would have should I meet my mother again. I had longed to ask her, to hear from her own lips, how she could have left us behind so easily. But now we were going to England. We were leaving Brittany, and I was just as happy to leave thoughts of her with it. We would start a new life in England. Maman, like Papa, was dead to us.

"Well then, that is settled," Yannig said, watching me closely. I knew he could read the relief in my face, and I was grateful he was willing to let the matter drop rather than pester me with questions. "We will leave at first light. Tell no one of our plans, do you understand?"

We assured him that we did, and he left us. We expected to see nothing more of him that day, but that evening, he summoned me to the same room where I had burst in on them the night before. I looked around nervously as I stepped in, worried that the aristocrat meant to interrogate me.

"You needn't worry. The marquis is gone. He is a busy man," Yannig said from his seat behind the desk—the same spot the aristocrat, apparently a marquis, had sat the day before.

"I need a favor from you," he said when I had stepped inside and closed the door. From behind the desk, he hoisted a set of saddlebags into view—not the fine, sturdy saddlebags that had belonged to Jacques Lambert but a beat-up, weathered set, long past its best days.

"Can you do with these what you did with Lambert's bags?" he asked, holding the bags out to me. "I cannot match your skill with a needle."

I took the bags and inspected them. "Such worn bags and already much mended," I observed. "Is the Army of the Republic still looking for Jacques's bags?"

"If they are, it will be no concern of ours, simple farmers that we are, riding to town for supplies."

"And anyway, we don't know anyone by that name," I said, taking up the needle and length of sturdy leather thong he offered me.

It was not hard to open the same seam I had in Jacques's bag and to disguise the diamond exactly as before. When I had finished and passed the bags back to Yannig, there was little sign I had done anything at all. He ran a finger over the new seam appreciatively. "It worked before. Let's hope it works again," he said, as much to himself as to me. I waited a moment, but he said nothing more, still admiring the bags as if he'd forgotten all about me. I rose from my seat and walked quietly to the door.

"Claudie."

I turned back, my heart thumping.

"Your mother. Do you know what abbey she is in?"

I nodded, my eyes on the floor. I was hoping, if I didn't look at him, I might keep all emotion from my face. "Bon Repos," I said. "Though Papa always said it was a cold, lifeless prison. Nothing *bon* about it."

"Bon Repos," he repeated. I looked up then, for there was a note of surprise in his voice.

"It's just—I know the place." He tilted his head, eyeing me curiously. "What is your mother's name?"

"Marie," I replied.

He shook his head. "She is not known to me."

"Do you know the place so well?" I asked. The abbey had never been more than just a name and a remote imagining to me. It had existed only in my imagination for so long, it seemed impossible that someone else would know it.

"I was schooled there," he said. "I thought I knew all the sisters."

"But . . ." I didn't know what else to say. I was sure Maman had gone to that abbey—it was the only name we'd ever been given.

"Many sisters take a new name when they take the veil," he said. "Perhaps it is so with her."

"Perhaps," I said, feeling a measure of bitterness that she had disavowed even the name she had shared with us.

"Would it give you pain or joy to see her now?" he asked in a tone so gentle I could hardly believe it came from such a big man.

I opened my mouth to answer, but I didn't know what to say. I had loved her once. She had been the center of my world. We had laughed and played while at our work, and I had thought she held me to her heart. Until she was gone, and I was alone with no one to comfort me. How could a mother do that to her child? Over the last twelve years I had felt nothing but anger.

I closed my mouth, then opened it again. "It doesn't matter, does it?" I said at last. "Since she is not at the Abbey of Saint Canna."

"No, I suppose it doesn't," he agreed, and bid me good night. And yet, I lay awake, long into the night, thinking of the mother I had lost and what had become of her.

Well before daylight the next morning, Yannig knocked on our door, eager to depart. We were dressed and ready. In the courtyard, three sturdy horses were saddled and waiting. In the still-dim morning light, I could see the beat-up saddlebags slung across the haunches of Yannig's enormous mount. The two saddle horses that stood beside it hardly looked its equal.

Yannig led the first horse to the mounting block and waved me over. I hesitated.

"If you want to travel with me, you are going to have to keep up."

"So you have said, but it seems we will be at a disadvantage," I replied, looking from the saddle horse to his mount.

He laughed. "Indeed. Gideon gives me an advantage. But I don't think you are quite ready for a warhorse, do you?"

I had to concede the point.

"It's just . . ."

"Of course, we have no sidesaddles for you to ride like the gentry, so I'm afraid you will have to ride like a soldier. That should get you ready for a warhorse in no time."

"Glad to hear it," I said. I stepped to the mounting block and made a leap for the saddle, giving him no chance to assist me. After all, I had told him I knew my way around horses, and I meant to prove it. I gathered the reins and moved the horse away from the mounting block so that Mathilde could use it. She accepted his assistance willingly, giving him the full force of her dimples as he held her stirrup and allowed her to put a hand on his shoulder to lift up into the saddle.

He mounted his own beast, then cut close to me as he rode toward the street. "You should come at the back. Put your sister in the middle. That is the safest place," he said.

I did as he said and rode through the morning trying to decide if he was being considerate of my concerns for my sister or if he simply

considered her more worth protecting. Either way, it meant no conversation, and the road quickly took on a dull monotony.

We spent the first night in a prosperous farmer's barn, cozy amid
the freshly gathered hay and the warmth of the animals. Yannig was
pleased with the day's progress but nervous about the farmer's news
of troops along the road, so in the morning, we turned from the main
road onto a muddy farm track.

"Fewer soldiers," he explained as Mathilde wrinkled her nose at
the greenish mud that stank of cows. Almost at once, her horse skid-
ded on the slick path. Unnerved, Mathilde gripped the reins tight.

"Give the beasts their heads, and they will find their footing,"
Yannig advised, showing us how to hold the reins loose and soft. We
both followed his advice, but Mathilde was soon clenching them
tight again.

"Softly, softly," Yannig said. "Look how Claudie's holding them."

Mathilde turned red and looked angrily at my loose grip on the
reins.

Warmed by the compliment, and perhaps a little by my rare superiority over my sister, I tapped my horse with my heels and followed
Yannig along the muddy track, letting Mathilde bring up the rear for
a change, her horse struggling through the mud against her restrict-
ing grip.

It was a short while after noon when we rounded a bend in the road
and saw what looked to be a farmer's cottage ahead of us, but with
the characteristic placard of an inn hanging by its door. Mathilde
saw it too, and for the first time all morning, her face brightened and
she nudged her horse a little faster, eager for a hot meal or a cup of
cider and a seat by a warm fire.

We were preparing to dismount in the yard when the innkeeper's wife appeared in the doorway, carrying the broom in both hands, like she was readying herself to shoo away bothersome cats. She relaxed when she saw us, but she shook her head.

"We've nothing to serve you," she called. "You'd best move on."

Mathilde's face sagged in a misery of disappointment. "We only want a meal and a bit of rest."

"We can pay," I added.

She bowed her head. "Soldiers took everything we have."

"Soldiers," Yannig repeated. He had only just swung down from the saddle, but he was back in it in an instant. "How long ago, madame?"

"An hour. Maybe less," she replied. "I thought you were them returning. Though why they'd return I don't know. They ate all they could and took the rest."

My hands grew cold where they gripped the reins. If all roads were swarming with them, how would we get to the coast?

"May God keep you, madame," Yannig said to the woman, turning his mount back the way we had come. Mathilde and I followed.

"What are you doing?" I asked. "There are soldiers this way too."

"A mile back we passed a crossroads," he said. "If they think we are making for the coast, they won't look for us on a road that goes west, into the hills."

"Won't that delay us?" Mathilde asked

"Not as much as capture," he said.

We turned west at the crossroads, into the low sun. With each step higher into the hills, my heart sank lower. How would we get to the coast, surrounded as we were with soldiers? As we climbed, the soil grew rockier and the track firmer. By sunset, we were deep in heavy forest, far from the gentle farmlands of the morning. As the sun dropped below the horizon, the air around us gathered in its wet chill to work upon our bones.

"We will have to sleep rough tonight, I'm afraid," Yannig said, looking around us. We had seen no one at all since we had been turned away from the inn, but he still led us as far from the road as we could get before darkness prevented us from going any farther.

Mathilde and I slid from the saddle, groaning with the ache of stiff muscles as our feet hit the ground. I pulled the blanket down with me and set off for the nearest patch of sheltered leaves.

"Your saddle, mademoiselle," Yannig said. "After all, that horse has done the work all day. He's surely more exhausted—and more deserving of rest—than you."

I staggered back to my mount, knowing he was right. How often had I taken care of the horses of weary travelers at the inn? But of course, there was no one to treat me as a weary traveler. I uncinched the saddle and pulled it from the beast's back, then removed the bit from its mouth and wiped its steaming flanks with the rag Yannig tossed to me.

He glanced at the horse Mathilde had ridden. I looked around too, only to see that Mathilde had bedded down in the prime spot I'd been aiming for while her mount stood patiently by, watching us unsaddle, its ears turned back in resignation.

I stepped to the animal and scratched its neck a moment, then unsaddled and groomed it as I had my own horse.

"You know what you are doing around a horse," Yannig commented, making me jump. I hadn't realized he was watching me.

"I haven't ridden much, but I've stabled many," I said.

"Is it always thus?" he asked, gesturing to where Mathilde slept.

A single nod was my only answer. I took little pride in my lot in life.

"Hmm," he said.

I threw him a sharp look. "What does that mean?"

"I cannot understand Jacques's choice is all," he said.

I gave a disbelieving little huff. "Have you no eyes in your head? Just look at her."

"I am looking," he said, though his eyes stayed glued to me, a most unusual sensation for someone who had always gone unseen when Mathilde was around. "I just don't see why he preferred a little flit like her. If I were him, I'd want someone more solid like you, Claudie."

Yes, solid. That was one word for it, I thought as I took in my dirty arms and hands, made strong by endless drudgery in Papa's inn. If he had meant to compliment me, he wasn't very good at it.

"Well, I hardly think Jacques was looking for someone to stable his horses when he chose Mathilde," I said.

"But as an ally," he persisted, not seeming to have noticed my failure to feel flattered by *solid,* "I would prefer you to her."

I gave the horse one last wipe across its withers and handed the rag back to him wordlessly. If he meant to woo me into an alliance, he was simply going to have to do better than *solid.*

When we had finished with the horses, Yannig built us shelters from brush and branches, and I scooped handfuls of dry leaves into them to shield us from the wet ground, although everything was so damp it hardly mattered.

I drifted off to sleep early but was awakened before long by my own shivering and the strange sounds of the forest. I sat up, listening. An owl screeched off to the left, then was answered, and answered again by other owls.

I had heard owls in the night around our own village but never more than a few lonely hoots. These woods seemed to be filled with owls, calling back and forth to each other, their positions moving through the trees all around us.

"Strange, is it not?" Yannig said, his voice a low rumble in the dark.

"What can it mean?" I whispered.

"How should I know? We roosters are not birds of the forest."

I considered his answer. "These owls," I said at last. "Will they attack a rooster?"

"Not tonight, I think," he said. "Now go back to sleep, mademoiselle. You are safe enough until morning."

When morning came, he was still sitting where he had been in the night, and I wondered if he had slept at all.

Mathilde had slept poorly and was exceptionally cross. She was no help as Yannig and I saddled the horses and scattered the evidence of our camp.

A heavy fog hid us from view as we set out, but by noon, it was giving way to rain, as the weather always seemed to do when we were traveling. We untied the blankets from behind our saddles and draped them over ourselves, looking like a series of disheartened mushrooms astride our unhappy horses.

We had trudged on for perhaps an hour when the single track gradually widened. We passed a farm, and the track widened again into a proper road. We all sat a little straighter in the saddle. We seemed to be returning to cultivated land, with the potential for shelter and food.

I was thinking of such comforts when Mathilde cried out and pointed.

"I think there's a crossroads ahead of us, and a building there," she said. "Perhaps an inn!"

She coaxed her horse to quicken its pace, and my nerves tightened. Leave it to Mathilde to rush in without a thought to what danger might await us. I pushed my own horse to a trot, eager to push in front of her, to shield her from whatever trouble her headlong rush might have raised.

"Claudie, wait," Yannig said, but I was already around her. I saw too late what he had seen—a large group of horses tied on the side of the inn. I was only beginning to comprehend what they must mean when a column of soldiers, at least six of them, issued from the front door.

I pulled back hard on the reins, wheeling my horse in the road. Mathilde, eyes wide, followed.

"Stay calm," Yannig said. "Don't look like you are running!" But Mathilde was already kicking her horse into a gallop.

"Claudie, don't!" Yannig hissed, trying to keep his voice low. I knew he was right. Running would only mark us as enemies. But Mathilde was in flight. I looked from Mathilde to him, caught between prudence and protecting my sister. My sister won out, and I spurred my horse after her.

A shout from the soldiers proved we'd been seen, and it was followed by a clear command.

"Stop, in the name of the revolution!"

CHAPTER 16

"Claudie!" Yannig barked, his tone both angry and disappointed, and my heart lurched. I hated having to take the foolish action, but what choice did I have? Mathilde had made my decision for me. She had apparently made Yannig's for him too because I could hear him thundering along behind us, his big horse catching up quickly. Strangely, as he rode, he gave the long-short-short call of an owl, like those that had filled the night, though less convincing. And though my ears were full of hoofbeats and the thundering of my heart, it seemed to me that an owl in the forest answered.

I had come up parallel with Mathilde now, and we hurtled along, neck and neck. We might have escaped our pursuers, but Mathilde's horse balked at a movement in the brush, a small thing until Mathilde yanked back hard on the reins in response, and her already skittish mount reared. Mathilde tumbled off like a rag doll, landing with a splat on the muddy road.

"Mathilde!" I shouted, reining in my horse. Behind me, Yannig swore.

Mathilde struggled to her feet. To my relief, she look unhurt. Her own horse had bolted the moment it was free of her, so I turned back and reached a hand for her. The soldiers were practically on top of us now. Yannig turned to face them, protecting us, a pistol in one hand and a sword in the other. Before I could get Mathilde up behind me on my horse, the soldiers were upon him.

His sword clashed with a soldier's while simultaneously, and without so much as a glance, he discharged the gun into the face of a second soldier bearing down on him. With a splatter of blood, the man slumped from the saddle. Four more soldiers were a few paces away. He would be desperately outnumbered in the blink of an eye.

"Run!" he shouted. I hesitated, even as Mathilde settled behind me and wrapped her arms around me so we could. How could I leave him to fight—to die—alone when it was our error that had brought this disaster upon us? But what could I do by staying? I had no weapon of my own.

"Claudie! Run!" he shouted again.

I spurred my horse off the road and into the trees. I was crashing through underbrush when a volley of shots went off all around me, so near I could see the flashes of the guns and smell the acrid powder smoke. Startled by the noise, my horse reared. I gripped it desperately to stay on its back. Mathilde, who was sitting behind the saddle, had no chance and once again toppled to the ground.

I was still hanging on for dear life when I realized someone had grabbed my horse's bridle and was speaking to it to calm it. A stranger, dressed all in drab greens and browns that blended with the woodland. He was leading the horse off, deeper into the woods, away from the road.

"Claudie!" Mathilde called.

I did the only thing I could think to do—I scrambled down from the beast and ran back for my sister. She was unhurt but trembling, tears streaming down her face. I followed her frightened gaze and saw the man standing over her, holding a gun. I would have fought him with my bare hands, but he grinned at us both.

"Be still and stay here," he said in Brezhoneg, and I saw the flash of red on his chest—the sacred heart of the Legion. I looked back the way we had come. Yannig was still surrounded by soldiers, but they were far fewer now, and he had been joined by three new men so that the battle was evenly matched. I looked again at the man with the gun. He was tamping powder into the barrel.

"Come on," I whispered to Mathilde, and bending low, we scurried deeper into the forest, taking shelter behind a broad oak near where our horse had been tied with a group of others. When the next volley of shots went off, it was behind us.

After a time, it grew quiet, the sounds of battle receding. Cautiously I peered around the tree but could see no one. Were they gone? Dead? Was it safe for us to move?

An owl hooted to my right, very close by, and I jumped in alarm. Within seconds, he was upon us—another man dressed as the first, in dull forest colors, cloaked and hooded in brown wool that hid his face. He gestured for us to get to our feet.

"Come quickly," he said in Brezhoneg.

I hesitated, searching the forest around us. I could see no one else. "Where is the Rooster?" I said.

"Quickly, it's not safe here," he said, and set off through the forest.

Mathilde and I looked at each other.

"We must find our friend," I said, and rather than follow, I turned back toward where the battle was.

At once the man was at my side again. He took my arm and pulled me away. "Now. The others will all join us at camp. You can meet him there."

He led us deeper into the forest. We were not on a road or even a trail, and yet he moved with certainty, as sure as if he were on a paved track. We had followed him for perhaps twenty minutes before he paused, holding a hand out to quiet us, and listened.

I heard nothing. He, however, cocked his head like a dog that could hear what we could not. Then he tilted his head back and hooted. An answering call came from the north, and with a satisfied nod, he began again. We followed him over a shallow rise and down a bank into a well-concealed encampment. Five or six small shelters made of twigs and brush blended into the landscape. In the midst of them, a thin thread of smoke rose from the coals of a fire, and a large pot hung from an iron tripod over it. A simple enclosure of logs and branches on the edge of the camp served to corral the horses.

The man who had escorted us directed us to one of the shelters. Mathilde collapsed onto the blanket within, but I sat in the doorway, fascinated by the men slipping in all around us. They seemed to be born out of the forest itself, materializing silently from its mists, moving with the swift, light steps of wild creatures, their clothing the colors of tree and shadow. Occasionally, the hoot of an owl came from the forest. Then someone in camp would reply in kind, and a few minutes later, another man would emerge from the dripping wood. Anxiously, I watched for a rooster among these owls, but though the population of the camp increased steadily, he did not arrive.

After some time, a mounted group arrived, breaking the stillness with the jingle of harnesses. They rode in, leading our horses and a few extras besides. I guessed they had belonged to soldiers who would no longer be needing them. I was relieved that Yannig's big Breton wasn't among them, and yet his absence seemed more and more ominous as the hour passed.

It was nearly noon when he finally arrived, and my relief would have pushed me to his side but for the heated words flying between him and his companion, a wiry fellow with a drooping mustache and a too-strong chin. He wore a wide-brimmed hat and a hairy goat-skin coat of the kind favored by the farmers of the mountains but his countenance was that of a commander, and one who disapproved of Yannig's views. Deciding I had enough adversity in my life, I stayed where I was, safely out of their line of sight.

From the other shelters and the margins of the wood, men emerged and gathered before the new arrivals. They did not array themselves in the straight formal lines of soldiers, but it was clear without those formalities that they were preparing for inspection by their leader.

Yannig had no interest in these troops. His eyes began searching the camp, and my heart leapt when I realized he was looking for me. I stepped forward from the shelter, glowing with happiness at his safe arrival. When his eyes landed on mine, however, his countenance darkened.

I hurried to him, my concern for his well-being outweighing my desire to avoid a fight. "Are you hurt?" I asked, my eyes roving over him for any sign of an injury. I could see none, though the blood on his clothes was unmistakable.

"I am fine, no thanks to you," he growled.

The reply brought me up short.

His words caught the attention of his mustached companion. "Have you no manners at all, Monsieur *Coq*? Can't you see that the lady is concerned for your well-being? And yet you have no thought at all for hers?"

The man dismounted from his horse and performed a short, stiff bow from the waist, his manner balanced between mockery and so-licitous good manners. "Welcome, mademoiselle. You are safe here," he said. "I trust you and your sister are well?"

"*Merci*, monsieur," I replied, surprised to be speaking French, as Yannig's men had always spoken Brezhoneg among themselves. I glanced toward Yannig. He was still scowling, so I turned all my attention back to my polite host. "My name is Claudie Durand," I said. "My sister and I are quite well and grateful for your help."

"*Enchanté*, mademoiselles," he said. "I am Jean Chouan, but you may call me La Chouette Hulotte, as I am known in these parts."

La Chouette Hulotte. The tawny owl.

"You are lucky we came along when we did," he continued.

I shook my head. "There was no luck in it, monsieur. You were watching us. I heard you through the night."

His eyebrows rose, and he glanced around at his men. "Heard us? We will have to be stealthier, men."

"You were stealthy enough. But there were too many owls for one night."

Despite his scowl, Yannig gave a little snort of laughter. "You have been outwitted by a girl, Monsieur Chouette Hulotte."

He laughed too. "Not outwitted, *mon ami*, just observed. We will be more careful in future. I do hope we did not alarm you, mademoiselle. We owls like to keep an eye on city birds, like this rooster, when he comes into our forest."

"So that is what you were doing? Keeping an eye on us?" I asked.

He gave Yannig a sly glance. "We are birds of a feather, the Rooster and I, but I try to know everything that goes on in my domain."

"I am glad you do," Mathilde said, appearing at my elbow. She

curtsied and gave him a bright smile. "You saved us from those soldiers. We are in your debt, monsieur."

Yannig returned to his scowl at the mention of a debt. "Where are
your horses?" he asked me.

I pointed across the camp to where a number of horses had been
gathered into the brush enclosure.

Yannig nodded, then turned back to the Chouette Hulotte. "Well,
we thank you for your assistance, sir, and now we will leave you to
your business and be on our way."

"Leave so soon? Monsieur Coq, you are our honored guest. You
must not rush away just yet," Jean Chouan said.

"But your men await you, sir," Yannig said, gesturing to the assembled men who still stood nearby, witnessing our conversation. "And
you must be away from here soon, before word of this skirmish makes
it back to other Republican forces in the area."

"Yes, we will be moving this camp before nightfall, but our business is not finished. You will stay until we have completed it, I think."

Yannig gave him an expression so dark, I took a step back from it.
"Are we your prisoners then?"

"You are my honored guests," the Chouette corrected. "Unless you
insist on making it otherwise."

Yannig clenched his teeth, but before he could speak, I stepped
forward and laid a hand on his booted leg where it rested in the
stirrup. "Thank you, Monsieur Chouette," I said, all humble gra-
ciousness. "We are most grateful for this rest. Come, Rooster. Let
me tend your wounds."

"I told you, woman, I am unhurt."

"I cannot rest until I am sure you are well," I insisted. "Come."

Still glaring, he dismounted and let one of the soldiers lead his horse away. I took his hand and gave a pull, and whether because he understood my effort to keep the peace or was simply too shocked by my forwardness to react, he followed obediently while our host stood by smirking.

"This is your doing," he muttered angrily to me. "We could be on our way if you had kept your head."

"It was Mathilde who ran ahead," I corrected him, "and she was the one who screamed."

"Mathilde is a silly child," he spat. "I expect such foolishness from her. I was counting on you to keep your head, not to run screeching, calling attention to yourself."

"I didn't screech!" I protested. "And I have a duty to my sister. To protect her."

I reached for his cheek, which, despite his insistence, was bleeding. He gripped my wrist and pulled me in, his intense eyes locking on to mine. "Don't put yourself at that kind of risk for anyone, Claudie," he said. "Not even your sister."

He held my arm a moment longer. Then he released me and stalked off in the opposite direction.

I did not see him again until our hosts were ready to break camp. Our horses were returned to us, and we mounted while, around us, men tore down the brush shelters and scattered the materials so that the small clearing looked no different from the rest of the forest.

A handful of men mounted, along with the Chouette and the three of us. The remainder of the men, a score or more, put on their dull-colored cloaks and melted away into the forest around us. Thus, as dusk settled into the branches, we set out. Yannig, Mathilde, and I rode at the center of the party, Yannig's expression like a thunder-cloud ready to burst. Clearly, he did not want to be riding with this troop, but even I could see, with the men moving unseen through the forest all around us, that it would be folly to resist.

We rode through the night, stopping at dawn in another hollow, sheltered from the world by the rise of the land around us and dense stands of ancient trees. I dismounted and stretched, my whole body stiff and sore. As they arrived, Chouan's men gathered the scattered logs and branches and transformed them into shelters. By the time I had unsaddled my mount and led it to the area where the horses were tied, the sun was lighting the upper branches of the trees on the hilltops around us, and I could think of nothing but sleep. When I was directed to a shelter, I didn't have to be told twice. I took my blanket and was asleep the instant I stretched out on the forest floor.

I woke abruptly to a large hand on my shoulder giving it a firm shake. I sat up and scrambled away.

"I am sorry, Claudie. I did not mean to alarm you," Yannig said. He had pulled his hands back and held them now in a gesture of peace. "I meant no harm."

I blushed and tried to get my heart to return to its usual pace. I didn't want him to think I feared him. My reaction had had nothing to do with him at all—it had come from my years with Papa, in which he had slapped, pinched, or pulled hair when he caught me wasting time.

"What is it?" I whispered, looking around. Mathilde was still snoring nearby. From the light coming in through the open doorway, it seemed to be midmorning, and all was quiet in the camp.

"Chouan wants to see us," he said.

"Chouan?" I said, still blinking the sleep away.

"Our gentlemanly host," he said, his voice full of irony but not the usual amusement that went with it. "He might have settled for questioning me, but it seems you showed yourself to be more agreeable."

"But isn't he your ally?" I asked as I untangled my skirts from my blanket. "They wear the sacred heart badge, the same as you."

"They oppose the revolution, to be sure," he said. "In that, they are allied with the Legion. But don't be fooled. Jean Chouan does as he pleases and follows no one's orders but his own."

"What does he want of us?" I asked, but something in me already knew.

Yannig gave me a look. My palms started to sweat as I followed him from the shelter.

At the center of the camp, we found a large canvas tent. Apparently, even creatures of the forest liked their comforts. Inside, a bottle and cups sat on a table, Jean Chouan seated beside it, waiting to receive us like a little king on his throne.

"Come, please, join me," he said, waving a magnanimous hand at several crates pulled up beside the table like chairs. While Chouan poured the dark wine into the cups, Yannig and I settled ourselves onto the crates. The wine was sharp and vinegary, and the bite of it on my tongue jolted me awake.

Chouan took a sip as well, then turned his eyes to Yannig. "*Mon ami.* I have heard the strangest rumors of late. Can it be true that Jacques Lambert is dead?"

Yannig only gave the smallest nod, but I started at the name. Chouan's eyes flicked at once to me.

"Ah, so he was known to you too, mademoiselle? Monsieur Coq told me you were merely farm girls and knew nothing of our cause, but now I think he has exaggerated."

"I am not a farm girl," I protested, then noticed Yannig's scowl. "Not exactly," I added more meekly. "Our father was an innkeeper in a small village to the east of Rennes."

"When I met you, you were harvesting apples," Yannig said.

"For cidermaking. I suppose everyone in our village was a farmer to some degree," I admitted, attempting to get us back on track. "It's all gone now. Burned by the Republican Army, monsieur. My sister and I escaped and made our way to Rennes. That is where we met the Rooster, and he agreed to help us get to the coast."

Chouan's eyebrows raised. "And what business do you have at the coast?"

Yannig's foot grazed against mine under the table to remind me I was not to tell our whole story to this man. As if I would be so foolish.

"We have a cousin in Saint-Servan who runs an inn," I said. "It is the only livelihood we know, and we had hoped he might provide us with work. The Rooster agreed to take us, for a fee."

Chouan looked at Yannig and then back at me, his eyebrows raised. "Ah. For a fee. And did you first pay this fee to Jacques Lambert?" he said.

"Jacques Lambert?" I asked with all the innocent confusion I could manage.

"I saw it in your face, mademoiselle. You cannot deny you knew him."

"I do not deny it," I said. "I knew Monsieur Lambert. But why would I have sought his help?"

"Because he carried nobles to the coast."

My mouth fell open. I could hardly believe anyone would mistake me for a lady. I was trying to decide how to play that part when he leaned in closer.

"Or perhaps you knew him more intimately. Jacques was reported to have many lovers."

I felt my face redden at the implication, but before I could form an answer, Yannig was on his feet.

"Chouan, you impugn the lady's honor!" he warned. "I demand an apology!"

"Come, come," Chouan said, smirking, waving him off. "We both know Lambert's reputation."

"That is no reason to cast doubt on hers! Your apology, or we are finished here."

The two men stared at each other, eyes narrowing, jaws tightening, until the air around us cracked with tension.

I came to my feet too. "Monsieurs, we are all friends here, are we not? Monsieur Coq, I thank you for your courtesy. I am sure Monsieur Chouette meant no harm."

I eased Yannig back down onto the crate. Then I turned to Chouan, still glaring from behind his table.

"Sir, I am neither of the things you suggest. But you have seen that we have not been fully honest with you. Please forgive our suspicious natures. These difficult times force all men as our enemies, though you came to our aid in our most desperate hour. You deserve an honest answer from us."

"Claudie—" Yannig said in warning. But I knew what I was doing.

Ignoring him, I plowed forward. "I did know Jacques Lambert, though not as a lover. Jacques had his pick of the girls and never had an eye for a girl such as me. But he recruited many in my village, women and men alike, to fight for the freedom of Brittany. That is how I knew him—as a compatriot. A leader among men. It was through Jacques that we knew to seek out the Rooster of Rennes when our father was killed and our village burned."

"I thought as much," Chouan said, throwing a smug, victorious glance at Yannig, who was glaring, jaw clenched, at me. "I had heard rumors of two farm girls completing Lambert's mission."

The label *farm girl* rankled once again, but I kept the annoyance from my face and nodded. "Jacques asked us with his dying breath to take his saddlebags to the Rooster." I leaned in and lowered my voice. "They carried valuable items for the cause."

"Claudie . . ." Yannig said, his voice moving from mere annoyance to alarm.

I turned to him at last. "There is no point in keeping quiet, Rooster. The man knows already. And he fights for the same cause we do. So tell him! Tell him what the letters said!"

Both men stared at me.

"Letters?" Chouan said at last.

I shrugged. "I cannot read, monsieur, or I would tell you myself. It was a thick packet of letters, no doubt full of secrets."

Chouan reached beneath his table and swung the beat-up saddle-bags Yannig carried onto the table before him. They landed with a thud that made Yannig flinch.

"Tell me, were these his saddlebags?" Chouan asked me.

"No, monsieur, those are the Rooster's," I said.

"No? Are you sure?" His smug expression slipped a little.

I nodded. "Jacques was a vain man. He never would have carried such worn bags. His were finely made and well cared for."

I paused a moment to let his disappointment settle, then added, "But the letters may be in there."

Chouan's stood and dumped the contents of Yannig's bags out onto the table. There were no letters, of course, but I feigned surprise at not seeing them.

Yannig sprang back up. "What is the meaning of this? What are you after, Chouan?"

"I think you know well enough what I'm after. What Lambert was rumored to have. Nothing happens in Brittany that does not reach my ears."

Yannig's face was turning purple with rage and indignation, but Chouan was not cowed.

"Come, mon ami. It is as your fair companion says: we are all fighting for the same cause."

"The same cause, but a different war," Yannig growled.

Chouan waved a dismissive hand. "You and your noble ideas of war," he said. "I'm fighting a poor man's war. But I assure you, with a little wealth, we could make our poor army as noble as any regiment you claim."

"I have no noble ideas of war, Chouan," Yannig said. "All war is ugly. But I will not throw men's lives away."

Chouan ignored Yannig's words as he spread our possessions across the table. When he did not find what he was looking for, he looked up at Yannig and at me.

"Perhaps I should search the women's belongings?" he said, his eyes on Yannig. There was a note of threat in his words. It was widely known that noblewomen fleeing the country sewed their jewels into their clothes. A search for such jewels would hardly be decent. Yannig took his meaning too, and a thick vein took up a quick rhythm in his neck.

Chouan picked up the saddlebags again, opening the pouches wide and running his hands around the interior. Unlike Jacques's finer bags, these were unlined and so afforded no hiding space inside them. But he was beginning to examine the seams.

"Perhaps he left the documents in Rennes," I offered. "Or perhaps in his satchel?" I said.

Yannig turned to stare at me, his mouth falling open. I could see a moment of confusion in his eyes, which I hoped Chouan would mistake for surprise at my betrayal. I hoped too that Yannig would catch on, before he ruined the ruse.

Chouan looked from Yannig to me, and his eyebrows rose. "His satchel?"

I nodded. "He has carried it slung across his chest since we left Rennes. I think he even sleeps with it, though I hardly care how he sleeps. My only business with him is to get my sister and me safely to the coast. I just assumed the documents were so valuable to him that he kept them that close."

"Indeed," Chouan said, his eyes still on Yannig, reading his reaction, which was growing more tooth-grittingly angry by the moment.

"And where is this satchel now?" Chouan asked Yannig, looking like a cat that had gotten into the cream.

Yannig ground his teeth for a long moment before muttering, "I don't know."

"Don't know?" Chouan chided. "Or won't tell?"

"The strap was cut in the fighting," Yannig said with a deep sigh, as if it pained him to reveal his secrets. To my relief, he had picked up on the deception perfectly. "I last saw it in the hand of a soldier who was galloping away along the road. You would not let me go after it, curse you"—he gave me a stern glance—"and so I fear it is halfway back to Paris by now."

"Is it possible that your men caught him?" I asked Chouan, allowing some alarm at this news. "Perhaps one of them recovered it—or it may be lying in the road or near the battle?"

Chouan considered for a moment. He gave the saddlebags another glance, then dropped them onto the table. "Return to your shelter and await my command," he said by way of dismissal, and he strode from the tent.

We stayed where we were a moment, listening to his retreat. "Good God, woman, but you had me scared for a moment," Yannig muttered at last.

I said nothing, unsure whether he meant to chastise or compliment me.

He stood and scooped his possessions back into his saddlebag, its precious contents still safely sewn into the seam. Finally, he glanced at me, and I could see the gleam of amusement in his eye.

"We should do as our host asks and return to our shelters. We are nothing if not obedient," he said in a tone so contrite it would have fooled a priest.

I almost laughed, but I held it in. It would hardly help our deception to be seen sharing a joke when a moment before it appeared that I had betrayed Yannig's deepest secret.

We left the tent and walked side by side back to the nearby shelters in the center of camp. As we walked, Yannig nodded toward where the animals were corralled. I could see his big Breton standing a few hands above the other horses. Jean Chouan was standing nearby, giving orders to two men who had saddled a pair of good animals and were ready to mount.

"It seems he is going looking for your lost bag," I said wryly.

"It could take them a day or two to search and report back," Yannig replied.

When we were back to my shelter, he gave a little bow and whispered. "If I were you, I would get some rest. In case we find ourselves traveling again tonight."

I nodded, now as eager to get away as he was. Once he was gone, I woke Mathilde and explained that we would be leaving in the night. We ate a meal with Chouan's men but otherwise kept to ourselves, claiming exhaustion. We had our handful of possessions ready to travel when Yannig whispered my name outside our door a few hours after nightfall.

The camp was so dark that I had to grip Yannig's coattail as we crept to the horse corral, Mathilde following with a handful of my skirt. Yannig had already removed our animals from the pen and had them saddled and bridled. We led them a short way from the camp, until we could mount and ride without being heard.

There was no road, but even in the dark, Yannig seemed to know where we were going. I was grateful that our horses were willing to follow his—otherwise Mathilde and I might have wandered aimlessly around the forest for days without getting anywhere. After a few hours dodging branches in the dark, we descended from the tree-clad hills and entered a more open country, dimly lit by starlight and the waning moon.

We took a few moments of rest in the shelter of a copse of birch trees, their trunks gleaming white in the moonlight. Yannig handed around chunks of bread and pieces of foul-smelling cheese.

"If you mean to elude capture, you shouldn't be eating this," I said, holding the cheese at arm's length. "They can probably smell this five miles away."

"Just eat it. You will need the strength," Yannig said, but I could hear amusement in his tone.

"It's strong, all right," Mathilde said, and she giggled. Yannig shushed her.

"Do you think Jean Chouan will come after us?" I asked.

"He won't need to. He has men loyal to him scattered all through the country. If he wants us caught, he only has to spread the word."

"And will he, do you think?"

Yannig shrugged. "I'd rather not find out. The sooner we make the Abbey of Bon Repos, the better."

I froze at the name, my gut tightening. "Bon Repos?" I choked.

"We are way off course now, and I am known at Bon Repos. They will shelter us as long as we need, should Chouan's men be looking for us." He paused a moment, then added in a quiet voice, "I am sorry, Claudie."

I said nothing more as we finished our meager meal. I was grateful for the dark to hide my expression from Mathilde, who hadn't recognized the name, having been too young to hear it when Papa banished any mention of Maman from the house. But I could still remember the first and last time he had spoken the words, spitting them out with bile and venom. *"Bon Repos? A living grave, more like. I hope she rots in it, the stupid bitch."*

Bon Repos. The name echoed through my mind as Yannig helped me up into the saddle. I was weary to the bone—cold and tired and aching from the rough days of travel. A beautiful rest should have sounded like the perfect end to our flight, full of peace and comfort. Instead, I was filled with an icy dread of facing again the mother who had abandoned me.

CHAPTER 17

We rested for only a few hours that night. Yannig wanted to be far from Jean Chouan before sunrise, a sentiment I shared. Between the Chouans and the Republicans, danger lurked now not only on the roads but also in the forests. The sooner we got to safety, even if it was in my mother's abbey, the better.

Our route climbed steadily through dark forests of ancient trees, their thick growth drawing in sinisterly around us. Under the spreading boughs, the chill of night scarcely lifted with the sun, and not a living thing seemed to stir around us. Midmorning, a birdcall in a nearby thicket caused Yannig to pause and call back. It seemed ridiculous, a grown man answering a bird, until a group of men armed with muskets, hayforks, and scythes emerged cautiously from the woods surrounding us. Yannig spoke to them in Brezhoneg, friendly but cautious. I held my breath and waited to see if they meant to apprehend us for Jean Chouan. It seemed, however, that any such orders had not yet reached this far. The men were eager to help us when they saw the badge on Yannig's cloak.

"Republican patrols are thick to the west of here," one told us, waving an arm in a vague arc off to the right.

How he could tell west from east in the thick forest I had no idea.

"And there are reports of clashes in the villages along the Bluvet Valley," another man added.

Yannig thanked them, and we set off again, our course leading slightly eastward from the arm sweep that demarked the location of the Army of the Republic.

By midday we were well into the hills that formed the knobby backbone of Brittany. Our mounts were heaving for air as we wound past jagged boulders and beneath grand ancient trees, their trunks thick with moss, their feet in perpetual shadow. There was no sound but the drip of fog off branches and the occasional passage of wings. When we spoke, it was in whispers, as if we had entered the great cathedral of nature, where human words were blasphemous.

The sun was at its zenith when we came out onto the bald crown of a mountain, like the tonsured scalp of a giant monk. A circle of weathered standing stones, the kind folks said were erected by the fairies in the mists of time, stood stark against the brooding sky. Despite the mist, we could see for some distance, rolling mountains reaching above the fog.

Yannig gave another birdcall, then waited, his head cocked. There was no answer.

His expression grew grave. "Come," he said in a low voice. "We should not make a target of ourselves." He was already steering his horse toward the shelter of the forest.

"But the man said the soldiers were the other way," Mathilde protested, stretching her arms to catch the sun.

"Do as he says, Mathilde," I snapped, urging my horse after the huge Breton.

As we rode back into the trees, the forest felt more sinister than ever. Yannig urged Gideon to a trot, and Mathilde and I began to fall behind, our smaller horses less sure of their footing on the rocky ground.

I was about to call to him to slow down when a horseman materi-
alized from the forest, squarely between me and Yannig. Even in the
murky light, I could plainly see that he wore the blue coat of a Republican soldier. Perhaps he was not aware of me following behind,
or perhaps he thought I posed no threat, because he was looking
toward Yannig, his back to me as he raised and steadied his pistol.

I shouted a warning, knowing even as I did that it was too late.
Yannig had no chance to react. I dug my heels into my mount and
lunged wildly forward, crashing into the soldier. His pistol shot
went off, the crack thunderous in the silent forest, and my heart
stopped. Was I too late? But as I looked toward Yannig, he did not
fall. Instead, he wheeled Gideon around, the beast more agile than
I had ever imagined such a large thing could be. I had succeeded in
throwing the soldier's aim off.

I turned my eyes back to the soldier. His hand was reaching for his
sword. In panic, I did the only thing I could. I lashed him across the
face with the ends of my reins, a blow that caught him so off guard
that he nearly lost his seat. By then, Yannig was bearing down on
him, sword already in hand. I thought we were safe until I looked
back over my shoulder and saw more soldiers streaming like ants from
the woods around us. We would be overwhelmed in seconds.

I turned back just as ragged peasants burst from the forest opposite, their pitchforks and scythes raised to meet the muskets and
bayonets of the soldiers. The two forces met with a shout and a clash
of weapons, and we were caught in the middle of a battle.

All around us, men and horses were screaming, guns firing. I turned
this way then that in confusion. A soldier grabbed for my horse's
bridle, but he met his end on the tines of a pitchfork. A toothless old

peasant grinned up at me as he pulled the pitchfork free, then moved to attack the next soldier. My stomach roiled, and I had to swallow the bile that rose in my throat.

I turned in the saddle, searching for Mathilde. She was struggling to control her horse and stay in her seat, a struggle that a nearby soldier had noticed and, judging by the sneer on his face, meant to take advantage of.

Suddenly, Yannig was abreast of me. "Mathilde!" I cried, pointing.

"Here!" He thrust the hilt of his saber into my hand before spurring his horse toward my sister.

Just like that, I was alone, with a flimsy blade I had never used and an onslaught of soldiers closing in on me. There was no time to think, only to act. I gripped the hilt with two hands and swung wildly, slashing and stabbing. I recoiled in horror as my blade bit deep into a man's arm, jolting against bone, but I dared not stop. I fought on, terrified that a bullet or blade would find me at any moment.

At the edge of my awareness, someone was calling out to me, but I didn't dare take my attention from combat, not until one of my wild swings finally clashed against the barrel of a musket, and I looked up into Yannig's face.

"Come on!" he shouted above the chaos, and turning his horse, he galloped into the trees. I spurred my own horse to follow. Mathilde sat behind Yannig on his horse, clinging to him for dear life.

We plunged away through the trees at a pace that took all my concentration and strength. I still expected a bullet or blade at any moment, but when Yannig finally reined in his mount and we slowed to a walk, the sound of the battle was far behind us.

"Well done, Claudie!" he said. Yannig's praise surprised me, and

I looked up into an expression of admiration that, for a moment, left me speechless. Then I remembered: I had just saved his life. His expression was merely gratitude.

He reached down and put his hand on Mathilde's, where she gripped him around his waist. A simple gesture that I wished, just for once, could be for me and not my sister.

"You're all right now, girl. You can let me breathe," he said.

"Is it over?" she squeaked in a voice so strangled by terror that I nearly wept. What was wrong with me, letting envy into my thoughts at a time like this?

"Probably not, but it's over for us. The Chouans will finish what they started," Yannig said.

Mathilde opened her eyes and slowly released her grip around Yannig's waist. "That man tried to kill you," she said, eyes wide. "He was going to shoot you in the back."

Yannig was gazing at me, a gleam of admiration in his eye. "He didn't know how formidable your sister can be."

Was that a compliment? "Formidable" was hardly something a man looked for in a woman, and yet that expression . . . Then again, it was easy to admire a woman who just saved your life.

"Claudie would make a fine soldier," Mathilde said.

"Claudie would make a terrible soldier," Yannig replied with a lighthearted grin. "She never follows orders!"

The two of them laughed together, and I seethed. Yannig was my friend, my compatriot. Hadn't we outsmarted the Chouans together? Hadn't I just saved his life? Yet here he was, sharing a horse and a joke with pretty Mathilde, who had caught his attention just like every other man she had ever known, while I, as usual, was left out.

"If we are going to make it to the abbey today, we can't sit here making sport, can we?" I said pointedly.

"Of course, you are right," he said. "The sooner we put distance between ourselves and whoever wins that battle, the better."

He looked down, scrutinizing my horse. "Can that beast of yours keep up?"

I rubbed the horse's neck. "I think so. I will try," I said.

He nodded and gave me another look of admiration, the kind that was usually reserved for my sister, but before I could grab hold of it and claim it for my own, he turned Gideon and broke into a gallop.

Long hours later, we looked down into a valley and saw the Abbey of Bon Repos. My mount and I had managed to keep to Yannig's grueling pace, but I could feel the beast's legs trembling as we paused. Mine shook as well, with the effort of staying in the saddle.

Relief surged through me at the sight of the twinkling lights and the thought of the safe shelter and warm meals they represented. But as we rode through the arched gateway and the towering stone buildings closed in around me, my chest tightened with thoughts of my mother. Was she still here?

My mind and heart stretched, feeling for something familiar in this unfamiliar place, searching for the bond between the hearts of a mother and child. I could feel nothing. Perhaps any such bond had been severed too completely when she had abandoned me and left me to care for my father and sister. For years, I had tried to imagine the place she had gone to, tried to picture the cloister she had chosen over us. I had asked Père François once, but Papa had overheard, and

I was not only denied my answer but given a thorough beating for my trouble.

Now I shivered as I looked around me. What would we find inside these walls? Was she waiting with open arms to embrace us, or would she turn away? And what would I do if I did find her? I was no longer the lonely, motherless child she had left me. What would facing her now do to me? I sent up a silent prayer that she was gone and I didn't have to find out.

I took a deep breath to steady myself and dismounted, keeping my expression carefully neutral. I didn't want to give anything away to Mathilde. She slid down from behind Yannig and stretched, looking around her with interest. She was only thinking of the warm bed and hot meal. I turned my mind to those thoughts as well.

Yannig dismounted too, just as a nun came hurrying from the great stone building to meet us. She was holding a lantern high, frowning at having to take in late arrivals, at least until her eyes landed on Yannig. Her face transformed into pure delight.

"Ah, it is you!" She turned back to the house and called, "Brother Yannig has come!"

At once, several other sisters appeared in the doorway, their faces bright. They streamed out into the courtyard, greeting Yannig, clucking and fussing over him like a whole flock of mother hens. Their excitement at seeing Yannig was so great that it took them a few moments to notice Mathilde and me, but when they did, they were not ungenerous. They led away our mounts and, taking us each by the arm, swept us into the warmth of their lodgings. Yannig was pulled off in one direction while Mathilde and I were courteously escorted to a small chamber in the dormitory. We were left with a candle, some clean flannels, and a ewer of warm water to wash. A few minutes later, a novice arrived with a stack of neatly folded garments, which she handed us before scurrying away, her sandals slapping lightly along the flagstone floor.

We had each been given one of the white woolen robes of the Cistercian order. Warm and clean, they should have been very welcome. Mathilde certainly wasted no time in removing her damp skirts, washing, and belting the voluminous folds of warm wool around herself. With a giggle, she pulled the old-fashioned wimple over her head and tucked her hands into the wide sleeves, taking on the pose of a solemn sister of the order. The sight gave me a pang deep inside. It was as if I beheld a vision of my mother.

"Well, go on, Claudie. Get changed, so we can go find our supper," she said.

I did not want to clothe myself in the garments of the very abbey that had taken Maman away from us, but my traitorous stomach grumbled. I, too, washed and wrapped the white wool around myself. Once I had tied the sash and slipped my feet into a nun's sandals, we ventured out into the corridor.

The novice waited at the end of the passageway, and she cheerfully led us to the great hall. Nearly a hundred sisters were already seated at long tables. A hundred pairs of eyes watched as we crossed the floor to the high table. Could one of those pairs of eyes belong to Maman? Did she recognize us, even now, from her seat in some hidden corner? I wanted to look around, to search for her, but we were being greeted by the abbess. She sat in an elaborately carved chair at the high table, the prioress at her left hand and Yannig installed on her right.

She was a tall, lean woman with strong hands and a large, star-tling disfigurement of mottled red-and-blue skin that stretched from her neck across her right cheek and disappeared at last where her forehead met her wimple. Even her eyelid, when she blinked, was the color of a fresh bruise, and her eye was streaked with bright red veins. The disfigurement had, no doubt, made her unmarriageable, and that had forced her into the cloister. The realization sent a chill through me. I too was an unmarriageable daughter, but that had not mattered as long as there had been a Papa and an inn that needed me and gave me a means of survival. But now . . .

I put the thought from my head and curtsied before the abbess, then took the offered seat beside Yannig.

He too had taken the opportunity to clean up, and when he gave me a small closed-lip smile in greeting, my heart faltered. Gone was the tangled mane that usually surrounded his face. He had tied his hair back neatly in a ribbon, and his beard was clipped short and even. He was dressed in a finely tailored frock coat and breeches that fitted him perfectly. When he rose to greet us, only his use of the Breton tongue marked him as the rough rebel we had traveled with and not a gentleman newly arrived from Paris.

If only I had met Yannig before the war, when there was still an inn that might have served as my dowry . . . I banished the surprising thought from my head, but not before it raised an unwanted color in my cheeks. What was I thinking? He was a revolutionary, and I was hardly some starry-eyed maiden.

He cocked his head, his eyes questioning my blush or possibly an expression I hadn't meant to have on my face.

"You look well," I stuttered, feeling the flush deepen.

He glanced down, looking a little sheepish. "They keep a few things on hand for me."

The prioress laughed. "Young Yannig grew up among us. He's like a son to many of us here."

At that, Yannig's face flushed too, very much like the young child of a bragging mother.

"You are an orphan?" I asked, realizing I knew nothing about his past.

"No. I am a lord's bastard," he said, and while there was no shame in his declaration, it stopped any further inquiries from me. I certainly wasn't one to judge.

A fine meal was brought in—roasted partridge, turnips and apples in butter, and warm loaves of brown bread—and I began to reflect as I bit into the tender meat that perhaps Maman's life had not been silent and bare after all. I had plenty of time to consider the idea. Yannig's attention was taken up by the abbess's eager conversation and as no one else was seated at our side of the high table, we had no one to converse with.

I took the opportunity to furtively scan the faces of the sisters before me, looking for any sign of my mother.

"You think she's here, don't you?" Mathilde surprised me with the words, whispered so close to my ear. I had thought I had hidden my thoughts from her, but she was my sister and had long experience reading me. There was no point denying it.

I shrugged and pulled my eyes from the sisters' faces. "I don't even know if this is her abbey," I lied. "And I haven't seen her, so maybe not."

The hopeful expression on Mathilde's face dropped a little, and I was sorry for my blunt words. Mathilde had never known Maman, and she was eager to meet her.

So I relented and gave her shoulder a small nudge. "I will keep looking, and if I see her, you will be the first to know," I assured her. Then I turned my attention back to my meal, the one place in the room I could be sure my mother was not.

The warm clothes and full belly had an overwhelming effect on my exhausted body. I only realized I had dozed off when one of the curates who had been serving the high table offered to guide us back to our room. I was glad to accept. I was ready to sleep and to let go of my fear of finding my mother here. I had glanced at nearly every face, and I had not seen her. Nor had we encountered anyone who had seen a resemblance in us or our name. At last, I could return to our room, fall into a comfortable bed, and sleep without fear or worry.

Mathilde, just as tired as I was, wound her arm through mine, and together, leaning on each other for support, we staggered toward the doorway behind our patient guide. We were nearly out of the room when a face in the back corner caught my eye and I froze, gaping.

I hadn't seen her in twelve years, and time had done its damage, but still I knew her at once. There, behind the wrinkles that age had added, behind the droop of once graceful eyelids, behind the gray pallor that veiled her once rosy cheeks, was my beautiful mother.

CHAPTER 18

Mathilde followed my gaze, and Maman, sensing eyes upon her, looked up. There was a moment without recognition—after all, she had last seen me as a child of seven and Mathilde as a toddler, but as I stared, a light of recognition came into her eyes. They widened and her mouth fell open before she looked quickly away.

"What is it? What's the matter?" our young escort asked.

"That woman," I said, nodding toward Maman, who was studiously keeping her face turned away from us.

The novice followed my gaze, then looked back at me.

"Never mind Sister Marie-Michel." The girl tapped her temple, her brow wrinkling in pity. "She suffers fits, you know, but she is harmless. Come now."

I tore my eyes away from our mother and followed the girl, scarcely seeing where I was going.

We had found Maman at last. Since I had heard we were bound for this abbey, I had been poised between hope and fear of meeting her. Now here she was, and the look that had come into her eyes when she realized who we were wasn't love or joy upon seeing us.

I had always coped with the loss of my mother by holding on to the belief that she still might love me. That her leaving, no matter how much it felt like it, had not been rejection. She had been called by God. Her violent ecstasies had been witnessed by our whole village. It was not a call that she could resist or deny. She had left us because she had to, not because she wanted to. That was the story I had clung to for years. But that look, when she'd realized who we were, had been one of horror. Dread. Fear. And I knew then that we, her children, were the last people she wanted to see. She had abandoned us with the desire to be rid of us for good.

The fine meal now churning in my gut, I followed the novice blindly to the chamber set aside for my sister and me. I stripped down to my shift, slipped under the covers, and turned my face to the wall.

Mathilde, however, had no desire to sleep or to let me sleep. She had been energized by the discovery. She paced the room, keeping up a steady monologue.

"It's her, Claudie! *Maman!*" she said, her eyes full of hope. "We must go to her, tell her who we are!"

"Enough, Mathilde!" I barked at last. "Let me sleep."

"How can you sleep at a time like this?" she demanded.

"Quite easily!" I replied. "Or have you forgotten? Some of us had to do battle and ride hard through the day and not just wrap our arms around a handsome man who could take care of us."

My back was still toward her, but I could feel her glare. She was, after all, my sister. "So you want to deny me the chance to meet Maman because you are jealous of Yannig and me? I saw the way you looked at us riding together, Claudie."

I gave a derisive laugh. "There is no *Yannig and you*, Mathilde," I said, the denial sliding from my tongue with more viciousness than I had intended. Or perhaps just more than I expected.

"Exactly," she said. "So why can't we meet our mother?" Her voice was trembling.

Feeling ashamed, I sat up and turned to face her. "We will meet

Maman in the morning, and we can talk to her for as long as you want," I assured her.

"You promise?" she said.

"I promise," I said, mild now. "In the morning."

She nodded and grew quiet, and I lay down again, but neither of us went to sleep for a long while. I wanted to, but when I closed my eyes, I saw again my sister's arms around Yannig, his hand resting on hers with gentle regard. And that look in my mother's eyes.

The look that told me once again that I was unworthy of love. Even from my own mother.

Mathilde woke me early the next morning, bouncing with excitement at the prospect of meeting our mother, indifferent to my dread. I watched my pretty sister comb out and braid her dark hair, then twist it becomingly around her head. I made no such effort. What was the point?

When she had finished her hair, she pinched some color into her cheeks, then turned her eager eyes to me.

"Come on, let's go find her," she said.

"Let's find breakfast first," I grumbled. Though my stomach rebelled at the idea of food, I hoped that these Cistercian sisters, with their vows of hard work and self-sufficiency, would put us to tasks that would keep us too busy to fulfill my promise. It wasn't just for myself that I wanted to delay the meeting. I was dreading the moment Mathilde's hopeful excitement was crushed by Maman's rejection.

My hope was to be in vain. As soon as we stepped from our room, we were sent to the abbess.

The abbess awaited us in her office, seated at a stout desk, ink-wells, pens, and paper arranged neatly around her and rows of books and scrolls on the shelves behind her. She was like a queen—or more accurately, a king—in command of her realm. Something in me stirred to see a woman in such a position of power—especially this woman who, just last night, I had thought of as a castoff from the world.

She rose from her desk when she saw us, her expression serious. She waved us to a hard wooden bench, then strode out from behind her desk as if she meant to chastise us for some misdeed or inap-propriate behavior. She scrutinized Mathilde's face, and I saw the recognition come into her eyes. The novice must have reported our interest in Sister Marie-Michel, and Mathilde's resemblance was un-mistakable.

"Tell me of your parentage," she said. "Who is your mother? Your father?"

"Our father ran an inn in a small village east of Châteaubriant. A place of little consequence in France. Our mother . . ." I paused and drew a breath.

"Our mother is here," Mathilde cut in. "Marie-Michel, you call her. We want to see her!"

The abbess's lips tightened. "This is most unexpected," she said, her tone curt. "Sister Marie-Michel has been with us for twelve years, and though she has often spoken of her babies when the melancholy is upon her, we thought they were lost in infancy. We would not have taken her in if we had known she had abandoned her children. Such a great sin—she must atone."

I opened my mouth to reply, but I found I did not know what to say. I had lived the last twelve years with pain and sorrow and even anger for my mother, and yet the idea that our coming here, our find-ing her at last, would bring punishment down upon her felt wrong.

"We want to see her," Mathilde demanded again, like a spoiled child used to getting her way, which was exactly what she was.

The abbess's eyebrows raised.

"Please," Mathilde added, only a little cowed.

"She is not well," the abbess said. It sounded more like a decree than just a statement of fact.

Mathilde sat up straighter, her face registering alarm. "Not well? What is wrong? If she is unwell, we must see her straightaway."

The abbess held up a hand to still Mathilde's panic. "She had a fit in the night."

"A fit?" Mathilde said, wringing her hands.

"An ecstasy," I explained to Mathilde. I could remember them— the frightening, rigid collapse; the rolling eyes; the wet, choking sounds in her throat. The memory made me queasy.

The abbess studied us for a moment. "How well do you remember your mother?"

"Not at all," Mathilde admitted. "I was only a baby when she left, barely three years old."

"And you?" She studied my face a moment, then nodded. "Yes, you remember, I think."

I nodded. "She was a good mother, before the ecstasies."

The abbess frowned. "A good mother does not leave her children."

"God called her," I said, choking on the words. How often had I railed against God for choosing Maman for his own and taking her from us?

The abbess shook her head. "She falls into fits. I cannot say that they are God's work."

"But she hears angels and sees the Virgin," Mathilde said, repeating the story our village had told for years. I said nothing, realizing for the first time that while I could remember the fits, I had never seen any evidence of angels. I had been with her the first time she'd fallen into a fit, not long after Mathilde was born. We had been in the barn, milking the cows, when she had collapsed, her body stiff and jerking. I had shrieked, bringing the stable boy running, and he had carried her inside and upstairs to her room. The priest had attended her while Papa raged in the kitchen about the spilled milk. When the priest emerged, he told Papa of her visions in front of all our assembled neighbors, who had come running to the inn as soon as the news came to them.

I could remember some of the weeks that followed as well, as Maman's episodes became more common and the whole town began to talk of the miraculous visitations. But I could not remember Maman ever speaking about them herself. Not once had she told me what the Virgin had said or how the angels had sung to her. She had only gone on about her work with me always at her heels, and when she thought Papa was not looking, she had held me to her and wept.

It came suddenly clear, a bright flash of memory I did not know was within me. My mother, with the swaddled baby Mathilde at her breast, holding me tight against her and sobbing. I had clung to her, afraid but not understanding. I still did not understand.

"Let us go see her," Mathilde pressed again.

The abbess was still watching me, no doubt trying to guess at my thoughts. With slow deliberation she turned from me to Mathilde.

"You can go to her, but she may have little to say to you just now. She had a fit in the night, and they leave her quite tired and weak. You mustn't tax her."

Mathilde burst into a radiant smile, and the abbess smiled back. It was impossible not to. But when the Holy Mother turned her eyes back to me, I could see the concern in them.

Mathilde threw open the door and stepped out. The novice still waited for us in the room beyond, and Mathilde instructed her, in a most imperious tone, to take us to Sister Marie-Michel's room. The girl gave the abbess a nervous glance but, upon receiving a nod of approval, obeyed. I stepped toward the door, but the abbess laid a hand on my arm.

"Your mother may be much changed, Claudie," she warned. "Be patient with her, as we are."

The dread that had weighed me down all morning intensified, but Mathilde was already hurrying along the corridor on the heels of our escort, and there was naught for me to do but follow.

CHAPTER 19

The tiny cell was lit by only a single candle and a tiny narrow slit high in the bare stone wall. The birdlike frame of Sister Marie-Michel stretched out on the small, stiff cot, asleep under a thin blanket. Her wimple and habit hung from a peg on the wall, and her short-cropped hair prickled out in gray tufts from her head. A memory came back to me, combing through her long shining tresses as she told me I would one day have such lovely hair. This fragile, aged creature was both the mother I remembered and a stranger to me.

Mathilde dropped to her knees beside the bed and laid her hand on Maman's where it rested atop the covers. Her eyes flickered open.

"Maman," Mathilde said, burying her head against the frail body. "Maman, it's Mathilde. Mathilde and Claudie."

Our mother stared blankly up at the ceiling, blinking, a slight confusion wrinkling her brow. At last, she turned her head, not looking at Mathilde but at me, still standing just inside the doorway.

"Claudie," she said. "My little Claudie." Whatever ravages had withered her frame and grayed her hair, her voice was unchanged, and a torrent of emotions flooded through me. I wanted to throw myself into her arms. I wanted to shout all the rejection and pain I had carried into her face. I wanted to weep and be told I was loved. Instead, I stood, cold as stone, while her eyes traced my face, trying to read me.

"And Mathilde," my sister said, raising her head to interpose it

between my mother and me. "I am here too, Maman. Remember me?
I was just a baby, but . . ."

Maman gave a tired sigh and closed her eyes again. "Yes, Mathilde.
Mathilde was my baby."

"I'm that baby, Maman," Mathilde insisted. "All grown up and
come back to you," Mathilde said.

The frail hand raised from the bed and smoothed over Mathilde's
hair, her eyes scanning the face leaning over her.

"My children," she said, her voice sleepy. "I dreamed you had
found me."

"No, Maman, it wasn't a dream," Mathilde said, gently shaking
her shoulder.

I pulled my sister back. "Remember what the abbess said. We
mustn't tax her."

Maman opened her eyes again and looked at us, her eyes traveling
from Mathilde's face to me, with my hand on my sister's shoulder.

"You've taken care of your sister, Claudie?"

"Yes, Maman," I said, wondering at how grown my voice sounded
when inside I was seven years old all over again.

"And your father?" she said.

"Yes," I said, choking on the words. "I have taken care of him too."

Her face grew anxious and she struggled to sit up. "He is here?"

Mathilde hurried to help her, then sat beside her on the bed, taking her hand and stroking it gently. It looked soft and unused, not the
hardworking, calloused hand of the abbess, but the delicate skin of
the convalescent.

"A month ago, our village was attacked," I said. "The inn was
burned, and Papa . . ." I paused, looking into her eyes, hoping she

would take my meaning without me having to say it, but her expression remained unchanged, and I was forced to continue. "Papa died, Maman. He died in the inn when it burned."

I had expected to see tears, but they did not form. Her eyes stopped searching and settled on my face, growing clear and alert for the first time.

"Paul is dead?" she said.

"That is why we had to leave our village. We are going to England to start over."

Mathilde gave me a sharp look. "To fight with the Legion!" she corrected me.

Maman seemed to hear none of this but instead repeated herself. "Paul is dead." The words came out in a sigh, all the tension in her frail body flowing out with the words. She closed her eyes again and leaned into Mathilde. After a moment, her breathing deepened into the nourishing breath of sleep.

I stared hard at her, confused. I had expected sadness when I told her of Papa's death. If anything, she had seemed relieved instead. Perhaps she was out of her wits and didn't understand.

Mathilde looked up at me, unsure of what to do. I took the weight of our mother into my arms as Mathilde stepped away, and we lowered her once again onto the bed. She stirred and settled in but did not wake, so we drew the blanket up over her and stepped away.

"We should let her rest, as the abbess said," I said, pulling my protesting sister back through the narrow door. "We will visit her again when she is feeling better."

"I don't understand," Mathilde said. "What is wrong with her?"

"You heard what the abbess said. She has had a—an ecstasy—in

the night, and she hasn't recovered from it. She will be better tomorrow."

"How can you be so calm about this?" Mathilde cried, shaking off
my hand. "It has been twelve years since you've seen her. Don't you
want to talk to her? Don't you even care?"

"Of course I care," I said, barely holding on to my patience. "But
as you say, Mathilde, it has been twelve years. What does one more
day matter? Let the poor woman recover her strength and then you
can ask her all the questions you like."

Mathilde strode off in a huff, leaving me to cross the cloister
alone. In truth, I was glad of her departure. I had my own thoughts
to contend with. Mathilde was not the only one who had dreamed of
seeing her mother again one day—but this day had been nothing like
the dream I had held on to. I had longed for years for someone to love
me, to take care of me as a mother should, but instead, I had found
one more person who needed taking care of. Was that all I was good
for? Plain, dull Claudie, pouring herself into taking care of everyone
around her, no one ever giving a thought to seeing her taken care of?
I sighed and closed my eyes for a moment, feeling too tired to take
another step.

"Ah, mademoiselle, you must keep your eyes open in these dangerous times."

Yannig had appeared beside me, seemingly out of nowhere. His
voice was pleasant, gently teasing, but I was in no mood. "It's all I do,
it seems," I said, opening my eyes and continuing on my way without
looking at him. "Look out for the needs of others."

"You are very good at it," Yannig replied, falling into step beside me. "If your eyes hadn't been open yesterday, I'd have taken a bullet in the back. It would have been a most ignoble death."

I turned to him, looking him squarely in the eyes. "You grew up here. Did you know Sister Marie-Michel was our mother?" I asked.

He was quiet for a long moment. "You said your mother had ecstasies, and Marie-Michel has never had visions with her fits, so I didn't put it together. At least not when you first asked me."

I sighed. "I suppose I should thank you."

"It is I who should be thanking you, for saving me yesterday. I cannot forget the look on your face when you lashed that soldier with your reins." His eyes unfocused a little as he remembered the moment, his expression one of amused satisfaction. "He underestimated you, to his peril." He looked down at me then, and the amusement melted away into something tender. He raised a hand and caressed my check. My breath caught in my throat, but I gave no protest, so he kept it there. Tentatively, I leaned into it. I didn't know what he meant by the gesture, but it felt good. Safe and warm.

"I underestimated you too," he said quietly. "I could use a woman like you at my side."

"Use me?" I pulled away from him and his warm touch. "*Use* me? I'm tired of being used!"

"Not used, Claudie," he replied, pulling back, his eyes wide in shock. "But use*ful*."

"Yes, useful," I spat out the bitter word. Why couldn't, just once, anyone want *me* and not just my labor? "Useful old Claudie. Take care of your sister, Claudie. Take care of your father, Claudie. Take care of the inn, take care of Yannig's revolution. Take care of everyone until the day you die, solid, *useful* Claudie!" And with that I stormed off across the sunny yard toward the dormitory, where I intended to close myself away for the rest of the day, where no one could *use* me.

My solitude, however, was short-lived, for Mathilde had been loitering in the courtyard and had witnessed my outburst. She followed me into our room.

"How could you be so unkind to Yannig?" she demanded. "He was trying to be nice to you. He was flirting with you."

"Was he?" I said, my tone sarcastic. "Tell me, Mathilde, is that what men whisper to you when they woo you? *Oh, Mathilde, you are so useful. Come feed the men in my army.*"

She threw her arms up and paced away from me. "Honestly, Claudie. It's not a bad thing to be useful. Men tell me I'm pretty and assume I don't have a brain in my head."

"Because you act like you don't when you are around them," I pointed out.

"You have to show them what they want to see. And if Yannig wants a useful woman instead of a pretty one, you could have him," she said, planting her hands on her hips and glaring. "Stop pushing him away."

As usual, her words stung without meaning to. "Go away, Mathilde," I said, exasperated. "Leave me in peace!" And with that, I flopped down on the bed and turned my face to the wall.

For once, Mathilde did as I asked, but her words echoed inside my head long after she was gone. What did she mean, I was pushing him away? Hadn't I saved his life? Hadn't I helped him escape Jean Chouan's camp? As I thought back, I remembered other awkward compliments and times I'd caught him gazing in my direction deep in thought. But surely that didn't mean he was flirting with me, and if I had scowled at him in response, it was only natural, wasn't it?

I closed my eyes and tried to make all my anger and uncertainty go away. I knew I should get up and offer my help to the abbey. After all, they were taking us in, feeding us, keeping us safe. I could be of use in the kitchen or the laundry. But I couldn't face another moment of being useful, and I couldn't bear the thought of encountering Yannig after the way I had just treated him. He had, after all, been trying to be kind. Deep down I knew that, and I knew he hadn't deserved all my pent-up rage at a world that saw me as nothing more than a workhorse.

Gradually, the room darkened around me, and the bell in the church rang for vespers. I could hear the sisters' doors open and close, hear their sandaled feet slapping along the corridor as they made their way to holy services. When at last the dormitory had grown quiet again, I rose, meaning to light a candle, but as I turned, I was startled by a woman standing silently in the open doorway of our cell, silhouetted against the dim lamplight in the corridor.

"Maman?" I said. It had been twelve years, and yet I knew that silhouette in a place deep inside me.

"May I come in?" Her voice no longer had the vague, dreamy quality it had had earlier. She seemed quite present now. She entered and sat on the foot of my bed while I lit a candle. Deep shadows encircled her eyes, but there was no other sign of her affliction.

We sat in silence for a long moment. I didn't want to look at her, but my traitorous eyes sought her out. There were tears on her face as she raised her hand to caress my cheek.

I leaned into her touch, the touch I had craved for so long, and before I knew it, I was in her arms, breathing in her smell, sobbing.

"There, there, my sweet girl," she crooned, rubbing my back. "My sweet Claudie. You've come back to me at last."

I pulled myself away from her, forcing down my tears, reminding myself of my anger. "We did not come back to you," I said, my voice flat. "We didn't even know you were here."

"Then God has brought you to me," she said.

I could feel my face tighten into an angry mask. I wasn't going to give God credit after all the injustice I had suffered on his account. "God took you away from us," I said.

She stroked my hair, much as she'd done for Mathilde earlier, and I nearly melted into her again. "You were just a little girl when I left," she said, "but even then, you were strong. I knew you would be all right."

I turned, glaring at her. "Did you? Was I?" How could I tell her what it had been like, taking care of the inn, my father, my sister, when I was but a child myself? How could I tell her of Papa's many beatings and cruel comments, of all the comfortless years without her? How could I tell her how badly I had wanted her? How badly I still wanted her, despite everything?

She looked down at her hands. "The fits started after Mathilde was born," she said.

"I know."

"You remember?" she said, looking up at me, hopeful. "And do you remember how they started?"

I shifted uncomfortably in my seat, pulling at my fingers to calm my racing mind. "I was with you when they started. We were in the milking barn."

She shook her head. "That wasn't the first."

I looked at her, surprised and wondering if she was still confused, but she returned a steady, clear gaze. "Do you recall the day your sister was born?"

I thought back again, reaching past the day in the barn to Mathilde's birth. I remembered it only in the vaguest of terms, like a nightmare. Cook keeping me in the kitchen with her while the maids ran in and out with kettles of boiling water, towels, and rags, hearing my mother's groans and shrieks of pain from the rooms overhead. Papa had stayed away that day, as was customary for a man when a woman was laboring in the house.

And yet he was in the memory. I remembered his voice mingling into the screaming. And Cook, seeing my fear, pulled me into her apron and sheltered me while she held the new baby, swaddled tight, near the fire for warmth. At some point, the priest was called and ran up the stairs.

The memory was all muddled, though. Why, if the baby was already born, washed, and swaddled, would Maman have still been screaming? And why the need for a priest? I had been afraid when I saw him, afraid that Maman was dying, even though Mathilde had been declared a strong, healthy baby. They were the tangled memories of childhood, and I couldn't make sense of them.

"Your father wanted a son," Maman said, cutting into my thoughts. "He hadn't been pleased with a daughter the first time, but I sheltered you. It would have been all right with Mathilde too, but hers was a long labor, and he stayed in the cider house all day. His temper was always worse when he had been drinking."

"Papa?" I said, struggling to understand. She was pointing out the puzzle pieces I'd had all my life but had never put together. "Papa was angry because Mathilde wasn't a boy?"

"I should have soothed him," she said with a sigh, rising up from the bed and pacing the room. "I knew how he was. I shouldn't have talked back."

I looked hard into her face now, remembering the bruises. How often had I seen her lovely face turned black and blue? How often had mine been injured by the same hand?

"Papa did this to you?"

"He was raging, breaking things. I should have stayed in bed, but I was afraid he'd hurt someone. Afraid for the servants, and the new baby, and for you," she said, sitting back down alongside me. "He picked up a chair to hurl against the wall, and I stepped in the way. They say it hit my head, but . . . I'm not good at remembering things. They slip away from me." She pulled back her wimple and traced her fingers through her short hair, and I now saw the long white scar, running like a seam from forehead to ear.

"They thought you were going to die," I said, finally putting the pieces together. "That's why they called the priest."

"The priest, yes, what was his name?"

"Père François."

"He saved my life, you know. He declared my fits as ecstasies, told the whole village of my visions. Is he still there in the village?"

I could hardly process her words, my mind still reeling from the details she'd just revealed. All that I had known my entire life, proven false by a single story. "Do you mean it was all a lie?" My heart was hammering with anger now, though I wasn't sure where to direct it.

She looked at me, her eyes desperate, for what I wasn't sure—my understanding? My forgiveness? I wasn't ready to give that just yet.

"Paul—your papa—would have killed me if I had stayed."

"And yet you left us with him." I wanted to scream. I wanted to cry. I wanted to reel back the last dozen years of my life and somehow make it all fair, but I could only sit, my hands balled into fists, paralyzed in my impotent rage.

"He had never raised a hand against you or your sister," she argued.

"He did later," I said through clenched teeth.

She was silent then for a long moment, looking down at her hands, ashamed. "I was sick," she finally said. "I could see no other way, and Père François knew they would take me in here if he only told them of my visions."

"Are they visions at all?"

Her face clouded. "Sometimes. I see things. I hear things. Sometimes I think they are angels. Sometimes they are lost children."

She raised a hand to my cheek again, and I could see all my longing mirrored in her tired, worn eyes. "And here you are, at last, and Paul gone. It is the miracle I have prayed for every day since I came here. Is that a sin?"

I didn't know if it was, so I stayed quiet.

She took my hand in hers. "Will you stay, Claudie?" she asked, her eyes searching my face hopefully. "Though we are cloistered, we are also free, not beholden to take care of a man, bear him children, cook and clean for him. It is a life of reflection, free from the constant demands of a family."

I felt the pull of her words, and she must have seen it, as her eyes searched my face a moment before she continued. "You are not destined to marry, I think. Your sister perhaps, but you . . ."

I rose suddenly to my feet on a wave of anger. "You don't know me," I said, stepping away from her. "You don't know anything about me!" And with that I strode from the room.

I did not know where I was going; I only knew what I was walking away from. I could see it now—all the years I had wasted thinking my lot in life was beyond my control. Thinking my destiny was sealed by my looks, my failures, my father's decisions.

No more. I did have a choice. I chose not to shrink from the world but to reach for what it offered me.

Suddenly, I stopped walking, aghast. Yannig's face danced in my memory, the warmth of his hand on my cheek once again. Had I just thrown away the very thing I wanted? Had I been offered love only to throw it away in a fit of pique? A rush of panic started my feet forward again. I had to find him, apologize, and pray that he would forgive me.

I found him in the courtyard of the abbey, his bulk standing out against the starry night sky. I paused, still under the dormitory porch, letting myself feel all the sensations that ran through me at the sight of him: the stirring in my gut, the eagerness speeding my heart, the smile pulling at my lips. I realized now, I had felt these things before, as I sparred with him over the diamond, as we had bluffed our way out of Jean Chouan's tent. I hadn't recognized it then for what it was. How had I missed it, I wondered, as it now set a glorious exhilaration through me.

I crossed the courtyard and stood beside him, suddenly embarrassed by my weeks of foolishness and my rudeness of the morning. Tentatively, I let my fingers graze his hand.

"I am sorry," he said, and I could hear the uncertainty in his voice.

"There's no need," I started, but he shook his head and turned to me.

"Claudie." He paused, and my heart paused with him. He drew in a breath as if he needed courage, and I almost laughed. I had seen him face foes with muskets, swords, pistols. What did he need of courage to talk to me?

"I have never met a woman like you," he said. "And I don't know how to tell you. I offend when I mean to compliment."

I chewed my lip for a moment, also getting up my courage. "I know I am not beautiful or charming, like my sister," I began, then stopped as he turned toward me.

"Not charming?" he scoffed, running a hand over his hair. "Claudie, it would take a hundred Mathildes to match you."

I wanted so badly to believe him. "Because I am useful?" I asked, fearful of the answer.

"Yes," he said, then just as quickly, "no. Because you are . . . you are . . ." He spread his hands out in a helpless gesture as he searched for the right word. "You are capable, and smart, and clever. I have never found more challenge—or pleasure—in debating anyone than I do with you. Claudie, you are the only woman I've ever met who could keep up with me, who could be beside me as a partner. God, Claudie, but you are driving me mad! I want you, but when I try to tell you, it all goes wrong."

"You . . . want me?" I said, my voice small and fearful.

He grasped my arms, and I looked up into his intense, bright eyes.

"I want you," he said. "Since the first day I met you. Since I took that bucket from your hands as you worked in the village square, I knew you were like no other woman I had met. And when you appeared in Rennes with the saddlebags, against all odds, I thought, *By God! A woman who can make her way in the world, who can best the Army of the Republic. That is the woman for me.*

"Even when you kept the diamond hidden, even when you declared no interest in our cause." He paused and chuckled. "Perhaps if you had handed the diamond over easily, or if you had given up when I walked away with the saddlebags, you would not have intrigued me so. And then when you burst in on our secret meeting with your audacious demands." He paused and ran his hand through his hair again. This time, it pulled loose from the tidy ribbon at the nape of his neck into the familiar mass of unruly curls around his face. "So much spine. So much fight! How could I want anyone else?"

I looked up at him, my eyes wide in wonder. With a trembling finger, I pushed the curls from his cheek. "I thought . . ." I paused and shook my head. How could I explain the past, and what did it matter? I had broken the tethers that had imprisoned me in that life. I would not look back. "Never mind what I thought. But, Yannig, are you sure? You have your cause, after all."

He leaned in, a devilish crinkle at the corners of his eyes. "Let me show you how sure I am," he said. Then he crushed his lips against mine, his massive arms cocooning me in an embrace. The kiss was fierce, full of passion and pent-up wanting. When he finally pulled back, he held me to him and I rested there, breathing hard, listening to the reassuring beat of his heart.

It was tempting to stay like that forever, but I had not come back to him to be coddled. He loved me because I was useful, and I had come back because that is what I wanted to be. It was not my lot in life to hide away in the shelter of a remote abbey like Maman. I was not meant to be tucked safely away, and I realized now that I didn't want to be.

I gave him one last squeeze, and then I pulled my head back from his chest and looked up into his eyes. "I want to help you," I said.

He searched my face, his expression hopeful but cautious. "It is about to come to war, Claudie," he said somberly. "Once we have the British navy at our back, we will move to liberate Paris and the king. I would not ask that of you for my sake. You must believe yourself in the cause."

"But I do," I said, with a conviction I hadn't expected but that came from my heart. "I'll admit, I didn't in the beginning. I wanted to be left alone—for the revolution to pass by without touching us. But that wasn't to be. The Army of the Republic burned our home, killed our father, destroyed our village. I told myself that I wanted no part in it, that I only wanted to get my sister to safety."

I paused, thinking again of my mother, of the abuse she had endured. Of how she had fled, only to live this half-life here, sequestered away from the world, still afraid. That was not what I wanted. I looked up into Yannig's face again.

"I am not going to shrink from the world," I vowed. "I will determine my own fate from here on, and I will start by swearing myself to your cause. For king and God!"

His face expanded in a smile so wide I could see his back teeth. "But what of England?" he said. "You told us where the diamond was in exchange for transport to England. You would be safe there, and you've earned your fare several times over."

"Yes, England," I said. "I will help you once we get there."

He shook his head. "Claudie," he said. "I'm not going to England. I'm staying here—to lead our soldiers. I will be marching on Paris."

"But—" I stared at him, my mouth open, trying to catch a breath, though the avalanche of my collapsing hope was suffocating me. "But the ship. The English navy. You said—"

"The Marquis de la Rouerie, whom you met in Rennes, will be meeting us in Saint-Servan and taking the diamond to England. He has the rank and the connections that will get him to the king or the parliament. My skill is in battle." He caressed my cheek, and I pressed into the strong, calloused palm, trying to hold back my tears of disappointment. "I am sorry," he said.

I drew a shaky breath. "Then I will stay with you. I will march and fight by your side."

He pulled me hard against him at that suggestion, as if he meant to keep me from even the harm of mentioning such a plan. "No, Claudie. You must go, and I will come to you when I can."

"But . . ." I said. It was the only protest I could make. It was too painful to speak the fear out loud—that he might never come. That I had found him, a man I could love and who loved me, but too late.

I let him hold me in silence then while my mind raced, searching for a solution. A way to stay with him or to keep him with me. To hold on to this fleeting moment when we were together and safe.

A commotion across the courtyard interrupted us. Regretfully, I pulled away from Yannig and turned to see the abbess running toward us, her voluminous robes flapping around her in her haste. She was holding aloft a lantern, and in its light I could see the fear in her eyes.

"Soldiers, Yannig!" she said. "At the main gate. You must go. Quickly!"

"Soldiers!" I said. "What do they want?"

She gave Yannig a dark look.

"What they have always wanted," Yannig said, "but they will not have it." Already he was hurrying toward his room to gather his things. "Quickly, get Mathilde. We must be gone before they get through the front gates."

I ran to my room. Maman had gone, and thankfully, Mathilde was there alone. She was in bed, but she turned when I rushed in. I grabbed her dress and tossed it to her.

"Quickly!" I whispered, gathering my own meager belongings as I spoke. "Soldiers at the main gate. We must flee."

She was quick to obey, but when I tried to pull her down the corridor toward the door to the courtyard where Yannig would be waiting for us, she pulled the other way.

"Maman!" she said. "We must take Maman with us!"

"We can't!" I said, pulling harder.

"We have to!"

I hesitated. I did not want to see Maman again, not after what I had learned. And fleeing with someone so ill could be a death sentence to all of us. Yet, Mathilde had pined for her mother too, and I could not deny her. Nor could I leave her here, knowing of the hatred the Republic held for the religious orders.

"We must hurry," I said, and together we ran through the corridors of the dormitory, Mathilde leading the way to Maman's chamber.

We found her there, reading her prayer book in the light of a single candle. Mathilde told her of the soldiers at the gate.

"You must dress and come with us!" Mathilde finished, pulling Maman's habit from a peg on the wall and tossing it to her where she sat on her bed.

Maman only stared at her.

"Hurry, Maman!" Mathilde urged again.

Slowly, Maman shook her head. "This is where I am safe."

"But Maman! Soldiers!" Mathilde all but shouted in her face.

Maman reached a hand to Mathlide's face, grazing her cheek with her bony fingers.

"This is where I belong. I do not want to go out in the world. But you may stay, my darlings." Her eyes roved upward from Mathilde and settled on me. "No," she said slowly. "No, this is not a place for you. You are of the world. You must go."

She dropped her hand from Mathilde, and seeing we would not budge her, I pulled at Mathilde's sleeve.

"Come, Mathilde. There is no time!" I insisted. "She will be well here. It is us they are after, not the nuns."

"We can't leave her," Mathilde insisted again.

"Mathilde!" I commanded in a voice so strong it shocked her into looking at me. "If you mean to fight for this cause, you must come. Now."

She hesitated a moment longer, then turned back to Maman and embraced her. "I will come back, Maman, I promise," she said. Then she pulled back with a resolute expression and stepped through the doorway, ready to leave.

I took one last look at the woman who had been my mother. Our eyes met, and she held my gaze for a moment before she spoke. "Go,

Claudie, with my love. Take care of your sister. I know you will be well in the world. Go, now."

I nodded, unable to speak, and I followed Mathilde out and down the corridor.

Yannig and the abbess waited impatiently for us just outside the dormitory. From the direction of the gatehouse, so close that it sent a shiver down my back, we could hear raised voices and the jingle and stamp of impatient horses. Without a light, we slipped in the opposite direction, cutting along a narrow passage of stone that led between the church and the dormitory, through the kitchen gardens, and along the back wall of the enclosure. In the moonlight, we could see the rows of vegetables and herbs in the kitchen gardens. Our nose led us to the stables, where a sister had already saddled our horses. She handed us each a Cistercian robe that we threw over ourselves. It was a thin disguise, but one we were willing to accept.

We led the horses out through the gardens and through an opening in the low wall of the close, praying as we went that the soldiers were all at the gate and not watching the back. We continued leading the horses until we were a hundred yards or more from the abbey, well into the darkness of the surrounding forests. Then Yannig helped Mathilde and me mount, and we were soon, once again, riding wildly through the night in a desperate escape, this time for the coastal village where a ship waited for England.

Where I would be parted forever from the first man to ever love me.

CHAPTER 20

A week later, in the murky light of dawn, I saw the sea for the first time. We stood on a hilltop, overlooking the fishing village of Saint-Servan, its small assemblage of boats pulled up on the muddy shore, while beyond the seething gray ocean disappeared into the mist. I shivered as I gazed at the swelling, shifting expanse of water. The flimsy wooden vessels drawn up on the beach did not look adequate to carry us out in all that vast swell. Perhaps I did not want to go to England after all, especially not if Yannig was to stay.

I glanced at him where he sat beside me on Gideon, surveying the scene below. I longed to reach out, to feel his touch. There had been precious little time to savor our newfound love since we had left the abbey. Though I had ached for him every minute, there had been only the briefest moments when we might share an embrace, a kiss, or even brush hands. We had ridden day and night, knowing that the army could not be far behind us, so we had to settle for stolen glances as we rode.

Twice, we had been delayed by the followers of Jean Chouan, who were everywhere in Brittany. Apparently, his orders to detain us had finally caught up with us. Once, we talked ourselves out of the encounter with information about the Republican troops in the area. Whatever Jean Chouan had told his followers about Yannig, it did not hold interest compared to the possibility of a nighttime ambush of their sworn enemy. Our second encounter had not gone as well, and we had been forced to fight men who should have been our allies. That encounter weighed heavily on Yannig's conscience.

Now we searched the scene below us, eager for the shelter of the village but wary of an ambush or an encamped army. Seeing no evidence of either, Yannig led the way down through the winding, sloping streets, to an inn only a few steps from the ocean, a low stone wall separating it from the muddy expanse of moorings. The air smelled of fish and an earthy, briny smell I couldn't identify.

The innkeeper greeted Yannig by name and ushered us upstairs to a room where I thought we would sleep. Instead, we were met by a stranger—a tall man with a powerful build, square jaw, and haughty expression. Yannig embraced him in greeting, then introduced him to us as Vincent de Tinténiac.

"Vincent was a lieutenant in the king's navy before the revolution decided they had no need of his kind." By this, I knew Yannig meant that Vincent was nobility, though I had already guessed as much from his manner. I gave him an appropriately respectful greeting.

"Pleased to meet you," Mathilde said with a dimpled smile that belied our exhaustion from the long ride.

"*Enchanté*, mademoiselle," Vincent de Tinténiac replied, kissing her hand. The gallant gesture brightened her expression, as Jacques's attentions once had. He turned then to Yannig. "Do you have it?"

"Have what?" Mathilde asked, cocking her head. When Yannig didn't answer, she looked to me. Neither of us answered her.

Yannig hoisted his battered saddlebags onto the table in the corner with a meaningful glance that told the lieutenant what he wanted to know. We all took seats around it, the lieutenant's eyes on the saddlebags and Yannig's on the street below through the small, diamond-paned window. The innkeeper, Henri, reappeared a few moments later with a tray of buckwheat galettes, salted herring, and a pitcher of creamy milk.

"Where is the marquis?" I asked while Mathilde wrapped the herring in the pancakes and handed them around.

Henri took the remaining seat at the table, frowning. "He has not arrived."

"Hasn't arrived?" I said, my voice rising with concern.

"Do not be alarmed," Henri said quickly. "He has not been captured. Only delayed."

"By our own alliance of fools," the lieutenant muttered, his tone as superior as his expression.

"The marquis was traveling among the chapters of the Legion, urging them not to disband. News of the Duke of Brunswick's retreat has hit some of them too hard," Henri explained, with an annoyed glance at the lieutenant. "Too many of our men are defecting to the ranks of the Chouans. It is taking the marquis more time to shore up their confidence than he anticipated."

"I have said it all along—we don't need the Prussians if we have the English," Vincent said. "The Marquis de la Rouerie should have let me negotiate with the English long ago."

"But we have not had what it takes to buy the English until now," Yannig said with an appreciative glance at me.

A hungry gleam came into Vincent's eyes. "May I see it?"

"See what?" Mathilde said, more pointedly than before. She was not going to be ignored.

"Not now, Mathilde," I said, which earned me a fierce scowl. "Later," I added in a whisper to appease her. "I promise."

"When can we expect the marquis?" Yannig asked the other men. "Is he on his way?"

Henri's brows drew down in deep concern, and he shook his head. "We aren't sure," he said. "The countryside is crawling with soldiers. If he has sent messages, they have not gotten through."

Mathilde pulled on my sleeve. "Not now!" I said again, annoyed, but she pointed out the window.

"Look!"

A troop of soldiers had come into view in the street. They were knocking door to door, making their way toward our inn.

Henri set his jaw. "I must attend the common room," he said, and disappeared out the door, shutting it very softly behind him.

"Are they looking for us, do you think?" Mathilde asked.

"Us and anyone like us," Yannig said.

The lieutenant glanced out the window, then stood.

"Let me take it," he said eagerly. "Admiral Howe is known to me. I can find the British fleet and buy their aid."

Yannig put his hand on the saddlebags and shook his head. "Admiral Howe is not enough," he said. "We require the approval of the English king and the parliament. We need the marquis!"

We all froze as we heard the banging on the door downstairs and the soldiers demanding entrance.

Vincent got to his feet. "We don't have the marquis, but we do have to get out of here," he said. "The tide is in our favor. Meeting those soldiers is not."

"I can't go," Yannig protested. "I am to lead the forces here."

The banging came at the door again, and this time we heard Henri call out for them to wait a moment, sounding as if he'd only just awakened.

We were all on our feet now.

Mathilde's eyes went wild. "We are trapped," she said, and I could hear the falter in her voice.

Yannig shook his head. "This is a smugglers' inn," he explained. He pushed the saddlebags into my hands. "You go for the boats; I will stay and fight."

"Don't be a fool," I said, pushing the bags back against his chest. "You can't escape them if you stay here. You will neither lead your army nor gain the aid of the British if you don't come along."

Vincent was already leading the way down the hall toward the servants' staircase at the back of the inn. I grabbed Yannig's sleeve and pulled, but his feet remained planted.

"Don't you see?" I hissed fiercely into his face. "You have to trade places with the marquis. There is nothing else to be done."

He set his jaw, but when I pressed him with the saddlebags again, he took them and followed me into the corridor.

The back stairs descended into the taproom, where Vincent opened a trapdoor into the cellar. We were just closing it behind us when we heard Henri open the front door.

In the darkness of the cellar, we groped our way to the back of the small room, where Vincent shifted a barrel. Behind it, we slipped into a pitch-black passage. We waited a moment while Vincent re-placed the barrel to hide the entrance. Then, each of us gripping the shoulder of the person in front, we shuffled down the sloping tunnel.

After a hundred feet, the floor of the tunnel grew muddy. Another dozen steps, and we were sloshing through water up to our ankles. Ahead of us, we could see a murky light and a small boat bobbing in the opening, the sea waiting beyond.

We climbed gracelessly into the boat, and Vincent took up the oars, directing the rest of us to lie still in the bottom, a difficult task as we were wedged in tighter than apples in the apple press.

The predawn mists had not lifted from the water, which gave us some cover as the tiny boat made its way across the small bay to where fishing boats were readying for a day at sea. Though it was early, the tide was starting to turn and fisherman were aboard their vessels, inspecting their nets and baiting their traps and lines.

We came abreast of the first ship in the harbor, and Vincent called up to the owner. An old fisherman, his gray beard spangled with mist, leaned over the gunwale to inspect us. He saluted when he recognized Vincent.

"My ship is across the bay, in the deeper water," Vincent explained. "We would be grateful for passage to it."

The fisherman took us aboard without question, giving Mathilde a blanket to wrap in and a comfortable seat out of the weather. He offered the same to me, but I would not take it. I was determined to stay at Yannig's side, to ensure that he boarded Vincent's ship with us. As it turned out, I had no trouble. Perhaps he had seen and accepted my reasoning, or perhaps he was as eager as me to have more time together. Whatever the reason, when the old fisherman brought his little boat out of the harbor and around the point and we came into view of the trading frigate commanded by Vincent de Tinténiac, the light of adventure came once again into Yannig's eyes.

"Well, Claudie," he said. "It would appear we are going to have to improvise."

I slipped my hand into his and squeezed it. "How can I help you?" I said.

He drew me into his arms, and I savored the warmth of him wrapped around me. "I only wish I knew," he said, his eyes on the horizon. "Without the marquis, it will be difficult to make the high connections we need."

I pressed myself into him, my ear against his heart. He had called me smart and clever, and I had never wished to be those things more than I did in that moment. But we were sailing for a strange land where I knew no one—where I didn't even speak the language—and my heart sank. If Yannig didn't know what to do, how would I?

Vincent was barking orders to his crew. He ordered us out of the way belowdecks, handing us a bucket with wry amusement.

Within a few minutes below, I understood why. When the ship cleared the bay and broke into the open ocean, it leapt and dropped and rolled, and so did our stomachs. We passed the bucket between us, even after we had lost all our breakfast into it.

Yannig looked green in the pale light, and I felt just as green. The ship lurched and the waves crashed against the hull in a continual onslaught. Ropes creaked, timbers groaned, and the barrels in the hold thumped against each other as they strained against their moorings.

"I think I'm going to die," Mathilde groaned, one hand pressed to her stomach while she reached for the bucket with the other.

"That's the beauty of the sea," Yannig said. "It either kills you or makes you wish you were dead." And with that and without waiting for the bucket, he bent forward and vomited.

Several hours out, the sea quieted, or at least it settled into a less pummeling roll, and I began to feel better. Yannig had gone above-decks, while I stayed below with my heaving sister, who was now curled into a limp ball. She had retched until there was nothing left, and even now, with a calmer sea, she couldn't lift her head without starting again. She lay perfectly still while I sat beside her, stroking her hair and trying to ignore the stink of vomit.

"Claudie," she said in a tiny voice.

"What is it?"

"What are we taking to England?"

I hesitated. I hadn't told her in all these weeks of travel. I had wanted to keep her safe—and I still did. But this was her cause. If I was honest, it always had been. Jacques had been her beloved, and she had embraced everything he stood for from the beginning. So, I drew a deep breath, and there, in the stinking darkness, I told her of the diamond, of its incredible beauty and the bright, shining hope it meant for the Legion. If only we could get it into the right hands in England.

"And whose hands are those?" she asked.

"The crown prince," I said, marveling at the words even as I said them. When Yannig had told me the plan, whispering it in the darkness when we stopped to rest in our flight from Bon Repos, it had seemed like a fairy tale, but now that we were on the sea, bound for England, I realized it was very real. I, a country innkeeper's daughter, was taking a king's diamond to the crown prince of England.

"Why not the king?" she asked. A smart question—a strategic question. From my fifteen-year-old sister, who giggled and blushed at handsome boys. My sister, who was a revolutionary in her pretty heart.

"Yannig says the prince is a collector of fine things, so he will be tempted by it. And he is deeply in debt, so the idea of getting it in exchange for sending the army and navy into the war, rather than having to come up with the cash to purchase it, will be just the enticement he needs," I said. "His father, the king, is eager to see him show an interest in governing and so will allow him to make such military decisions."

"It is a good plan," she said as she lay there, still not moving, though I could see that her mind, which I had so often taken for vacant, was busy thinking it all through. "But, Claudie, without a marquis or anyone else of title, how do we get to the prince?"

I had no answer for that. It hadn't been anyone's plan for Yannig and the marquis to change places. I did not know who Yannig knew who might help us. Perhaps Vincent de Tinténiac would? Perhaps someone we might meet in England?

"Never mind," Mathilde said. "You will find a way. You always do."

I wanted to hug my sister then for her confidence in me that, in that moment, I didn't share.

"We will find a way together," I said, still stroking her hair.

"I hope so," she murmured, sounding sleepy. "I want to be useful to the cause, like you."

I wiped the tears from my eyes and went on comforting her until she fell asleep.

***

Later, I stood on the deck, looking out over the vastness of the ocean. Nothing but water as far as the eye could see.

Yannig joined me and stood at my shoulder.

"Where is England?" I asked.

He pointed out vaguely ahead of us. "It will take us three days to make port in London if the weather holds," he said.

"Three days," I said, lifting my face, refreshed by the feel of the salt-heavy air on my face. "Poor Mathilde."

He pulled me tight against him, wrapping his arms around me, and we stood like that for a long time, feeling the wind, watching the waves. I could almost imagine us alone in the world, with no king to save, no prince to woo, no war spreading out ahead of us. I closed my eyes and pictured that life, Yannig and me, married, running an inn, raising children. I opened my eyes abruptly and shook the fantasy from my mind. There was no point in dreaming of such a future. Not with such danger ahead of us.

"What are you thinking?" he asked.

"I was wondering what England is like," I lied.

"Not so different from France," he assured me, "except they speak English."

"I don't speak English," I said, remembering how he'd assured me I could be understood in Cornwall, only for me to find myself bound for London.

"Never worry, *ma poulette*," he said. "The English nobility all speak French. They understand it to be a superior language."

"*Ma poulette?*" I repeated, pulling away and laughing at the pet name, *chicken*, that was usually reserved for little children. "Do you think me a baby?"

His eyes lit with mischief. "I would never mistake you for a child, *mademoiselle*," he said, emphasizing the word to remind me of his much earlier error, which seemed like an age ago now. "But if I am called Rooster, shouldn't you be my little chicken?"

I laughed and lifted my lips to be kissed. He obliged, and I decided, in the sweetness of that kiss, that those lips could call me whatever they wanted as long as they remained mine.

CHAPTER 21

We arrived on a crisp, clear day in early November. Mathilde and I could not believe our eyes. To us, Rennes had seemed like the big city, but it was nothing compared to London. Fine stone structures, three or four stories in height, lined every street—and not the rough-cut gray stone of my homeland but smooth edifices of a polished white granite that shone in the sun. Roofs of slate and copper, cobbled streets, towering statues in the squares, and more people, carriages, and chaos than I had ever seen in my life. Mathilde and I gawked out the windows of our conveyance like the country bumpkins we were, until Yannig admonished us not to make a spectacle of ourselves. I sat back beside him then so that my awed face might not be seen by the people we passed. Mathilde was too excited to take notice and stayed where she was.

We made our way to a townhouse in a neighborhood called Cheapside, though nothing about it seemed cheap. Sparklingly elegant townhouses packed in cheek by jowl against shops selling everything from cloth, ribbons, and buttons to cabinetry and heavy oaken furniture. Tailors, barbers, chandlers, and printers squeezed in amid vast stores bursting with commerce. All along the streets, women and children strolled, gazing in windows laden with goods, while men engaged in heated negotiations on the doorsteps of their establishments.

Amid all this business, we stepped down from our carriage before one of the smaller houses. It had been leased by a French expatriate family who supported our cause. They had successfully left France before the trouble and so had escaped with their wealth as well as their lives. Vincent introduced us as one would to an old friend, and we were welcomed by the family, Madame and Monsieur de Lavallée, their daughter, Marie-Louise, and a little boy of nine, who was the apple of his aging father's eye. The lady of the house, staunchly aristocratic in her towering powdered wig, was more pleased to welcome the handsome young naval officer than Mathilde and me in our tattered peasant garb, but she directed the servants to lead us to a well-appointed bedroom.

Marie-Louise, a pretty and exuberant girl of marriageable age, immediately took a liking to Mathilde and couldn't wait to turn her into a fine lady. Mathilde was, of course, most happy to oblige, and the two of them disappeared almost at once into the girl's room along with her lady's maid, to transform my sister.

We dined with the family on that first evening after our arrival, Yannig and me in our common clothes of brown wool and coarse spun linen, Vincent in the crisp uniform of the king's navy, looking quite dashing, even if that navy had been disbanded by the Republic. Mathilde appeared in the dining room beside Marie-Louise, wearing a silk gown the color of a robin's egg, her hair tied up a little clumsily in a matching blue ribbon and her face powdered and rouged.

I frowned at the sight of her. We had not come here to play dress-up like silly children, and if she thought she was going out in company, she was very much mistaken. She was far too young, too pretty, and too naive to throw herself into the power of smooth-speaking gentlemen likely to seduce and abandon her.

I was glowering at her across the table when Yannig leaned closer to me and spoke. "What is the matter, Claudie? Do you not find your sister rather beautiful tonight?"

"Yes, very beautiful," I agreed, annoyed that he had made such an observation.

"Then what?"

"What does she mean to do in such attire?" I said, incredulous. "Go to balls? Dance with wealthy gentlemen?"

Yannig's eyebrows raised at this idea, and he looked back at Mathilde with appraising eyes. "I believe it is our best chance," he said.

I turned to stare at him. "To do what, embarrass ourselves?"

Yannig laid a hand on my shoulder. "Well," he began. "I've been trying to think of a way to get the prince's attention."

I balked. "You mean to send Mathilde to the prince?" I said, my voice rising in alarm.

He shushed me. "Not the prince. But London society gossips," he said in hushed tones. "We can start by getting the attention of wealthy gentlemen, and she certainly has a talent for doing that."

"She's only fifteen!" I reminded him. "And she's never been to a ball, or in a city, or with real gentlemen before. It isn't safe. I won't allow it."

"I would never endanger your sister, Claudie. I only mean for her to catch a few eyes, start people talking. Let them know we are in town."

"But there are dozens of French émigrés in town, are there not?"

"There are, but there are not many who are rallying support for the Legion."

"And how, exactly, will they know that Mathilde is with the Legion?" I asked. "Do you mean for her to create another spectacle akin to your gatherings in Rennes?"

He smirked, remembering those evenings in Rennes and my impudent rage that had so amused him. "She will just have to dance and flirt and be charming, which comes perfectly natural to her. You can go along to chaperone if you wish."

I ignored this last dig and instead turned the conversation to him. "Why don't you go out and be seen—wouldn't that do more to alert people that you are in town?"

By now servants were bringing around courses of food, and Yannig paused while a maid ladled soup into our bowls. He seemed to be carefully formulating his response as he watched her.

"The thing is," he said when she finally moved on to the next person, "I have been, perhaps, too vocal in my past attempts to gain support. Another reason the Marquis was meant to come instead of me."

I narrowed my eyes and watched him innocently raise his spoon to his lips and sip the soup from it. "Too vocal. You mean you have offended."

"I might have been barred from a gentlemen's club or two in the city," he said, before taking a well-timed sip of his drink.

I raised my eyebrows. "And so you mean for Mathilde and me to do the same now in the ladies' clubs?"

He laughed. "There are no such things as ladies' clubs, Claudie."

I could feel my face redden with my mistake, but I would not withdraw from the debate. "You see? We know nothing about London society. We cannot hope to gain the prince's ear."

"Men do business in gentlemen's clubs, but ladies—especially pretty, young, unmarried ladies—go to balls. And of course, a ball wouldn't be a ball without the men there too, to dance with all those elegant young ladies. Madame de Lavallée and her daughter have vowed their help. Let them teach you and Mathilde to behave as ladies. Let them prepare you for the season."

"The season?" I had no idea what he meant. Where I came from, the only seasons of consequence were planting and harvesting, and those were past.

"The season," he said. "When all the gentry come into town from their country estates and all the unmarried ladies show themselves off for the young gentlemen."

Now I glared at him. "You mean you want Mathilde and me to catch husbands in London?!"

He laughed loudly enough to catch the eyes of several others around the table. "I mean for you and Mathilde to catch the attention of wealthy gentlemen. The kinds of gentlemen we need to open doors for us."

I glanced again at Mathilde. "As long as they aren't bedroom doors," I muttered.

He snorted. "I only mean the doors that have been slammed in my face in the past. Once those doors are open, I will take over, and there will be no risk for your sister at all."

It seemed like a flimsy plan, but as I had none better to offer, I agreed. The next day, I joined Mathilde and Marie-Louise, along with the Madame de Lavallée, and we began our education. Being a lady was going to take much more than fine clothes and an experienced maid to dress our hair, although that was a good start. I had never worn anything so delicate and soft against my skin as the dress Marie-Louise picked out for me, and even though it fit me poorly, I felt pretty as the graceful, flowing drape of fabric swished about me. At least until I looked in the mirror and saw the same old bland features and dull complexion.

Putting on the dresses was the easy part. We also spent hours learning how to walk in tiny, mincing steps, to hold our backs and shoulders so stiff that a book could sit perfectly balanced on our heads as we drank tea, and to dance several stiff dances that were far less interesting or fun than the country dances we had grown up with. We learned the most basic English, though we were assured that English gentlemen could all speak French. We learned to eat in tiny bites and sip our tea and wine so slowly we could hardly taste it.

Mathilde took to her lessons like a duck to water, though she was careless in the finer skills. She preferred the lessons on dancing and flirting with elegant gentlemen. She was eager to see London and to meet its inhabitants, and whenever she could, she ventured out arm in arm with her new companion, only to come back hours later, the lady's maid weighed down with Marie-Louise's packages of lace, ribbon, perfume, and pretty trinkets of cut glass meant to look like jewels. I did not join her, preferring to spend what little free time I had in Yannig's company, helping him in whatever way I could, enjoying the warmth of his arms in the rare moments we could steal for ourselves.

Two weeks before our first ball, seamstresses arrived at the house to take measurements for new gowns. They started with the lady of the house and her elegant daughter. When they were finished, they asked Mathilde and me to stand.

"But," I protested, looking at her ladyship, "we haven't the money to pay for them."

"Not to worry, my dear," the lady said. "It is the least we can do."

And so we were measured and, two weeks later, dressed in new gowns that fitted us perfectly, mine the color of ripe plums and Mathilde's the sweet pink of cherry blossoms. In a final test of our lessons, we descended the staircase in our finery while Yannig and the lieutenant watched from below. The gentlemen were finely attired as well, and I thought no man ever looked more dashing than Yannig, his beard trimmed, an ivory silk waistcoat and dark jacket highlighting his broad chest and square shoulders. The lieutenant once again wore the crisp dress uniform of the French Royal Navy, striking in his white pants and stockings, his blue coat flashing with silver buttons.

Mathilde descended the stairs first, her back stiff and her expression victorious, as if her dreams had all come true. From where I waited out of sight at the top, I could see the open admiration on the faces of Yannig and the lieutenant, and I felt my cheeks warm beneath their powder.

My one consolation for the evening would be that Mathilde looked so lovely that no one would notice me, which was, of course, the plan. I did not need to be seen. I just needed to keep an eye on my lovely sister, to help her avoid any missteps while the gentlemen of London flocked to her side and the ladies shopping for husbands cursed her arrival on the scene.

As Mathilde stepped off the bottom stair, the lieutenant came forward and bowed deeply before her, then offered her his arm as if she really was a fine lady. She laid her gloved hand gently on his arm and smiled up at him with all the confidence of one who had been born into this role.

I felt no such confidence. I was wishing I had gone down the stairs first. To have, just once, been admired by these men without the comparison being set by my sister before me. It was with that regret in my heart that I stepped out of the shadows onto the stairs, the deep folds of plum silk whispering around me, one gloved hand gently resting on the rail as Marie-Louise had shown. I was so nervous about this grand entrance that I was halfway down the stairs before I raised my eyes to the gentlemen at the foot of the banister.

Yannig's mouth hung open as he stared up at me, and my step faltered, wondering what was wrong with my appearance. My hand went to my hair, which was mounded unnaturally on my head and bound in bands of pearls, borrowed from the lady at Yannig's suggestion.

"Claudie," he said, my name a little choked, and I relaxed, hearing all the admiration in him.

With new confidence, I glided down the last steps to meet him.

He bowed and kissed my gloved hand. I hated that glove just then.

"You are magnificent, mademoiselle," he said. "You look . . . you look . . ." He shook his head, still searching for the right word.

"Beautiful!" the lieutenant called over his shoulder.

"Yes, of course. Beautiful. Regal. Enchanting," Yannig said. "We are here to meet and mingle with the British gentry, and it would be most inappropriate of me to claim your first dance, but I am sorely tempted," he said.

"Well, monsieur," I purred, feeling my new elegance in the glow of his admiring gaze, "you are lucky, as my dance card is empty at the moment. I will save you a place."

"Where are we going?" Mathilde asked as we climbed into the carriage alongside the lady and lord and Marie-Louise.

"We are starting out at Almack's Assembly Rooms," the lady explained. "It is an excellent place for you to be seen. Very prestigious for London society but not requiring an invitation like a private ball would. Those will come later, once you have made a good impression at the Assembly Rooms."

"So make a good impression," the lieutenant said, giving Mathilde a wink.

"How do we get in if we don't have an invitation?" Mathilde asked.

"You must have vouchers," Madame de Lavallée said, and she waved a handful of slips of paper in the air before her. "They are easy enough to obtain if you know the right people. I have been in London long enough to be established among the city's elite, and so they will be happy to welcome our beloved cousins, newly arrived from France."

Marie-Louise giggled and slipped her arm through Mathilde's. "I wish we were cousins. What fun we would have!" The two of them had become thick as thieves in the few short weeks we had been in the girl's house, and I felt a pang at the ease with which my sister had abandoned me and our upbringing.

I did not have long to dwell on it, as our carriage soon joined a long line of carriages. We disembarked amid crowds of well-dressed ladies and gentlemen before a stately, if somewhat plain, building of pale granite.

We climbed the stairs and entered into a grand foyer where four magnificent young ladies sat on fine chairs like queens on their thrones. Each of them wore elegant silk gowns and hairpieces replete with velvet and ostrich feathers, the height of fashion. The ladies and gentlemen entering Almack's were all bowing and curtsying before them as they handed over the vouchers. The four ladies inspected the vouchers, looked up and down at the new arrival's ensemble, and then gave a nod of approval that allowed the hopeful visitor to pass, or a tight-lipped shake of the head in disapproval that turned them away, despite the voucher they had presented.

"The patronesses of Almack's," Marie-Louise whispered to us. "If they don't like your clothes or if they have heard a nasty rumor about you that they disapprove of, they will bar your entrance."

"They believe themselves rather important, controlling the gates of Almack's Assembly Rooms," the lieutenant said with something of a sneer in his voice. He didn't seem to care for the English or their way of doing things. It seemed that their highest institutions were simply not up to his standards.

My hand tightened nervously on Yannig's arm.

He patted it gently. "You have nothing to worry about," he said. "No one could find fault with your appearance tonight."

Despite his assurances, I could feel my face stiffen into an awkward mask as we stood before a stiff, genteel lady, arrogant in her authority. Her gown of lavender silk rustled around her as she reached for our vouchers, examining them down her long nose.

"More Frenchmen," she said, a note of derision in her voice as she looked us up and down. "Honestly, is all of England to be overrun before this dreadful revolution is over?"

"Dreadful indeed," our hostess replied smoothly, showing no offense at her rude words. "As you know, my husband and I work tirelessly for the safe return of our countrymen to our own shores."

This idea either pleased the patroness or she wished to avoid any talk of politics, because she quickly added our vouchers to the growing pile on the little table beside her and looked toward the next gentleman in line, the only sign that we were free to pass.

The building may have been plain on the outside, but the interior was quite the opposite. The walls soared to a ceiling two stories above us. Beside one wall, a series of chairs was arrayed beneath an ornate balcony from which a dozen young ladies already surveyed the growing crowd below, whispering to each other behind their fans. The remaining walls were draped with fine velvet curtains with gold cords, tapestries portraying dancing nymphs, and gilded plaster-work that created the illusion of tall Greek columns holding aloft the painted ceiling.

Along the opposite wall, a raised platform had been erected, and a group of musicians sat upon it. I paused, transfixed by the sound. Sweeping, soaring melodies played by sweet, high violins, deep-throated horns, and resinous basses. I had never heard such a harmonious intermingling of sounds nor such elegant, richly flowing music. I closed my eyes and let it twine among my heartstrings like roses in a bower.

I could have stood there lost in that music forever, but Yannig gave my arm a tug. "We must keep moving. The dance is about to begin, and we are in the way!" he whispered.

I opened my eyes to see that the dance floor was growing full around us. If we did not mean to dance this first dance, we had to clear the floor. I tightened my grip on Yannig's arm, which felt like a life buoy in this crowded room of gentry, all chattering away in English, and we crossed to the side, where young ladies stood with their chaperones and young gentlemen gathered their courage to talk to the ladies.

Mathilde and Marie-Louise were already there, already being introduced to handsome young men.

"How do we meet the right people?" I whispered to Yannig. "How do we even know who the right people are in this crush of bodies?"

"In London society, everyone is the right person," Yannig said as we joined Mathilde and the lieutenant on the edge of the crowd and the dance began.

"Everyone?" I glanced around. "All these people know the prince?"

"Most of them do not. But the cream of London society comes here, and we will be seen," Yannig assured. "We can start people talking."

"Is that good?" Mathilde asked as she adjusted one long satin glove, an accessory not only fashionable but practical, as it would disguise our well-calloused hands.

"It's very good," the lieutenant replied. "The British like to make up every sort of story about a person before meeting him, you know."

"Well, it looks like you will have the chance to wag a few tongues," I said to Mathilde as two admiring young gentlemen approached, eager to be introduced to her and secure a dance. Marie-Louise was kept busy making introductions.

To my surprise, I too received a few requests for dances. I accepted them; after all, we were here to meet people and make contacts, but

I would have preferred to sit on the side with the other wallflowers. For years I had looked on while Mathilde got all the praise and attention, wishing to be noticed. Now I was being taken out onto the dance floor by strangers, and I cringed. What if I couldn't remember the steps to the dance or couldn't converse with my partner because he didn't speak French nor I English? And all the while, Yannig was scowling from the side as if he meant to duel any man who vied too openly for my attention.

Fortunately, the quadrilles that had become fashionable in London that season were similar to, though tamer than, the country dances we knew at our harvest festivals and Christmas celebrations, and I remembered most of the lessons Marie-Louise and her mother had given us. I got through the dances successfully, even learning a few trivialities about the English gentry and their attitudes about the French war. After each dance, I thanked the gentleman and escaped back to a corner, relieved to have successfully avoided catastrophe.

Yannig, of course, also claimed some dances and was a surprisingly graceful dancer, moving through the steps effortlessly while I had to concentrate on each one.

"Did the nuns teach you to dance so well?" I asked him as he expertly guided me across the floor.

He grinned. "A fellow never lacks for a partner in a nunnery."

I raised my eyebrows. "I did not think the sisters danced."

"I am a nobleman's bastard," he said. "There was always a chance I might be taken back into the gentry. I was educated for that possibility. Ironic now, isn't it?"

We turned and moved apart from each other. "Do I embarrass you, mentioning my parentage here?" he asked when we met again.

I laughed. "A nobleman's bastard is still well above my station. I should be grateful to be dancing with one so superior to me."

"Superior? Mademoiselle, I would not be interested in a woman who was not my equal."

We completed the dance, during which I proved that I was *not* his equal, at least not where dancing was concerned. Then we moved out of the crowd to a quiet corner, where we could observe the room. The crowd had grown larger through the evening, so that the space was now quite full of ladies and gentlemen, most of them of marriageable age and all of them seemingly eager to find a mate. Mathilde, with her good looks and penchant for flirtation, was in the thick of it, giggling and fluttering her fan, her expression enraptured while an eager gentleman expounded on something, his flailing gestures looking quite comical.

"It's something to behold, is it not?" Yannig said. "All the gentry come into town so the men can go to parliament and the daughters can find a husband."

"Not just the daughters," I observed. "Look at those young men. They are sizing up the girls as if they were racks of lamb in the market."

"Yes," Yannig agreed, "I think it would be fair to say Almack's is the meat market of the London season."

I chuckled at that. "At home, our fathers just made the decision for us, so flirtation was more just a bit of fun. Poor Mathilde, she knows the game, but here the rules have changed. I hope she doesn't get herself in trouble," I said. "Though perhaps there was an element of the meat market there too. Certainly more than one man in town wanted to sink his teeth into the tasty morsel that is my sister."

Beside me, a stranger gave a low throaty laugh, and I blushed. The lieutenant had told us that London society was filled with gossip-mongers; I should have been more careful.

Yannig turned at the sound of the laugh and his face lit in a broad grin. "Chevaliere d'Éon! A pleasure to see you!" he said. "Allow me to introduce Mademoiselle Claudie Durand."

I curtsied as deeply as I could. After all, someone with the title of chevaliere was deserving of a high level of respect. The woman looked me up and down with a sharp eye, then gave a small nod as if she felt no compulsion to return the courtesy I had shown her. Perhaps my common upbringing was that obvious to her, though something in her expression told me that she was not one to bow too readily to anyone.

She was a tall woman, much older than most of the sparkling young nobles in attendance. Her gown was elegant and expensive, but in keeping with her venerable age, austere and a little out of fashion. Not that I knew much about fashion.

"It is good to meet a fellow countrywoman," the chevaliere said to me in clear Parisian French. Her voice, like her laugh, was deep and buttery. "Tell me, mademoiselle, how long since you have left our motherland? Not long, I think."

"Only a few weeks, madame," I replied, feeling exposed. If she knew I was newly arrived, what else could she read in my face? I glanced around the room, but she took no notice of my interest in ending the conversation. In fact, she smiled in a way that suggested she knew I was uncomfortable and longing for escape, and she had no intention of allowing it.

"And tell me, for what purpose has the infamous Rooster of Rennes brought you to this meat market of London?" she asked.

I fought down the urge to turn to Yannig for help. There was a challenge in the woman's eyes, and I knew if I wanted to gain her respect, I had to answer for myself.

Keeping my eyes leveled on hers, I said, "As you know, madame chevaliere, the meat markets in France are all closed just now. The butchers, it seems, have all gone into politics."

Her eyes widened, then she burst into laughter.

"I think I like you, Mademoiselle Claudie Durand," she said, putting her arm through mine like an indulgent aunt. "I think you might be a tasty little morsel yourself, in your own way."

I was pleased to have gained her approval, but nervous too. If she was expecting more such witty responses, I was likely to disappoint.

"Now, d'Éon—" Yannig started to object, but she cut him off.

"Never you mind, my little cockerel. Your chick is safe with me." And with that, she pulled me away from him and began to walk with me around the room, away from the safety of Yannig's side. I gave him a panicked look over my shoulder, but he only shrugged and turned to a gentleman who was trying to engage him in conversation.

"Don't worry about your sister," the older woman said, glancing toward Mathilde, and I wondered how she knew about Mathilde when we'd only just been introduced. "She will find herself well attended. The English aristocracy quite enjoy a pretty face."

We made our way through the ballroom, the chevaliere pointing out various personages of high rank. I could scarcely keep track of the profusion of duchesses, earls, ladies, and barons, all with titles that connected them to places I knew nothing about. I curtsied until my knees ached, my English "a pleasure to meet you" growing smoother with each repetition, though my head swam.

"Honestly," I said as we walked away from our meeting with the fourth baron in short succession, "does everyone in England have a title?"

"Everyone worth knowing," she said with a gleam in her eye. "Did you think Yannig brought you all the way here just to introduce you to blacksmiths and fishermen?"

"Of course not," I said, feeling foolish. I was supposed to be masquerading as a gentlewoman, and yet I had given myself away in just a few minutes to this lady. A girl of gentle birth would think nothing of meeting her tenth baron, let alone her fourth.

"But of course, you have had a long journey and are tired," the chevaliere said. "Come, let us go to the supper rooms for some refreshment. In truth, it's not supper, only some dry cake and lemonade. I prefer a good port myself, but you will find that you could put everything the English know about good wine into a thimble. So lemonade will have to do." She pulled me along, parting the crowd like the prow of a battleship.

The supper room was somewhat smaller and less elaborately appointed than the ballroom. Long sideboards graced two walls, laden with treats—dainty cakes dusted with sugar; small, perfectly round biscuits for dunking in tea; slices of bread slathered with a thick, sweet butter. Pots of hot tea and a punch bowl filled with lemonade completed the spread. Ladies sat at the tables, plates of bread or cake before them, some conversing with gentlemen while others awaited their suitors, who were crowding around the drinks table to get tea or lemonade for them. I, myself, had never tried lemonade and was eager to taste it, despite my companion's disparaging remarks, but she put a hand to my arm as I stepped toward the drinks table.

"It is a lonely woman indeed who gets her own lemonade at Almack's," the chevaliere said. "A faux pas of that magnitude will be the talk of London for days."

"London must have very little to talk about," I said, looking longingly at the punch bowl as she directed me toward a table. My plate of cake looked quite dry and unappetizing without something to wash it down.

She laughed. "*Ma chérie*, how refreshing you are!" she said.

"Am I?"

"Indeed. As you will soon see, the English keep a tight lid on their thoughts and feelings, but you have seen through them after only a short acquaintance. I do appreciate a clever wit. Yes, I see why Yannig has chosen you for this mission."

My heart skipped a beat, and I went rigid. "Mission?" I repeated. "I do not know what you mean."

She gave a little chuckle and tapped the side of her nose. "My dear, the Rooster of Rennes does not come to London merely to enjoy the society."

I glanced around and gave her what I hoped was a sly smile. "Perhaps he is in the market for a rich English wife," I said.

"The Rooster?" she scoffed. "Mademoiselle Durand, if you are here to keep secrets, you must learn to tell a plausible lie. If there's one thing our friend has no interest in, it's a wife."

Try as I might, I couldn't keep the scowl from my face, and her eyebrows arched upward. "Oh, I see. You have set your cap at him, have you?" she said, making no effort to contain her amusement. "Well, don't say I didn't warn you."

"Madame," I said, swallowing. "I think you will find my sister Mathilde is the one with a mission. Yannig is merely doing us a favor."

"And what is your sister's mission?" she asked.

I glanced around. "The same as most ladies here, I think. To find a suitable husband."

"And by 'suitable,' you mean rich."

I shrugged. "Money can certainly make a man more handsome."

Her lips twitched, but she shook her head. "For women who would live by our wit, a husband can be rather constraining. You are such a woman, I think."

Again, I said nothing, only picked up a piece of cake and nibbled the edge, careful to keep the dusting of sugar from my gown.

She too took a bite of her cake. "I think," she said, glancing around, "that you are here to make connections. To meet the people who can open doors for you into the most elite of British society."

"The same could be said for everyone here tonight, could it not?" I asked, glancing around at the ladies blushing and listening to the boasts of young gentlemen. "Now tell me how to get some of that lemonade. I'm parched."

"Ah. Lemonade." She scanned the room, nodding at last to a tall gentleman in fawn-colored breeches and a green jacket who had just entered the supper room and was glancing around with a somewhat disinterested air.

"That man will get us our lemonade."

"You know him?"

"I believe I was introduced at some point, but that hardly matters. I am old and dull. When he glances this way, you will draw him in."

"Me?" I said, feeling my earlier nervousness rising once again. "There are far prettier girls in the room."

She shook her head, dismissing my objection. "He's bored. He wants someone to liven a dull evening of dancing with giggling half-wits. When he looks this way, meet his gaze with intelligence and curiosity. An air of mystery would be a nice touch too."

I had no clear idea of what she meant. I was hardly mysterious. But I was curious, and so when his eyes passed over our table, I snagged his gaze with one of my own—a direct look that caught and held his eyes for a moment. I let my lips curl ever so slightly to let him know my pleasure at the encounter, then I turned my eyes to the empty chair at our table. I raised a cake to my mouth and took a small bite, not daring to look back up.

A moment later, he was standing before us and gave a small bow. "Chevaliere d'Éon," he said, his tone a little sarcastic, as if something in her title was a joke. "I would be most honored if you would introduce me to your friend."

"But of course," she said. "Monsieur Langley, may I present Mademoiselle Claudie Durand, newly arrived from France."

He bowed at the introduction, and I gave a little nod of my head.

"Ladies, you are both without something to drink. May I get you a cup of tea? A glass of lemonade perhaps?"

We both requested lemonade, and he strode across the room to get it for us.

"Not bad," the chevaliere said when he was gone. "With a little training, you could be the most popular girl in the room."

I did not think that was true, but I didn't wish to argue it with her. I was enjoying the flattery of a young gentleman and looking forward to my first taste of lemonade.

The gentleman, as it turned out when he returned with our lemonade and took a seat beside us, had no more stimulating conversation than the silly, dull girls he so despised. What he really wanted was a good listener—and one who was willing to shower him with admiration as he spoke of his most banal accomplishments. I was relieved when Yannig appeared in the doorway to the supper room. I could see several girls trying to catch his eye, and it was easy to see why. Gone was the rough, bushy man who had offended me in my father's innyard. This Yannig was the nobleman's son, well-muscled and well-groomed, his attire elegantly understated, his manner smooth. He looked perfectly at ease in his fine clothes among these highborn people.

"Do you know that man?" Monsieur Langley, who'd proceeded to tell me of his fine country acreage and extensive holdings in the West Indies, had noticed my attention wander and was now looking at Yannig as well.

I pulled my eyes back to my companion, eager to be rid of him but not wanting to insult him. "Indeed I do, sir. That's my cousin. It was his idea that I come to England. I believe he is looking for me. He is a devoted chaperone." I gave a little wave toward Yannig, who, upon seeing me, began making his way among the crowded tables to reach me, the relief plain on his face.

"Your chaperone?" he repeated, sounding a little unsure. Perhaps he was noticing Yannig's size, or the slight frown that had come over his features as he took in the sight of me in conversation with this stranger.

I smiled sweetly at my new friend to add credence to my deceit. "Yes, monsieur. Of course, our parents intended us for each other, and I have had a hard time convincing him it should be otherwise. But I don't believe cousins should be required to marry, do you?"

The gentleman looked alarmed now. I was struggling to keep a straight face, but somehow, I managed. Yannig was still two tables away. "Intended? Mademoiselle, you did not say."

"Because we are not!" I insisted. "At least, I do not regard it to be so."

He scrambled to his feet. "Good day, mademoiselle. Chevaliere." He gave a hasty bow and retreated, just as Yannig arrived at the table.

I glanced at the Chevaliere d'Éon. Her lips were pursed together in a tight line, which I thought was disapproval until a little squeak slipped out and I realized she was suppressing a laugh.

"Where is he going in such a hurry?" Yannig asked, his eyes following the retreating gentleman, who did not look back.

"He just remembered other plans he had to attend to," I said, taking a sip of my lemonade, which was quite delicious.

The chevaliere gave up at that and let out a bark of impolite laughter that turned several nearby heads toward us.

"Oh, *mon ami*! Where did you find this one?" she said, speaking to Yannig as if I wasn't there. "She shows real promise."

Yannig beamed with pride, and a warmth of pleasure washed through me. "Indeed she does, madame," he agreed. "But she promised me a dance, and I have come to claim it. Perhaps you could come to tea tomorrow if you would care to strengthen your acquaintance."

She accepted the invitation, and we returned to the ballroom,

Yannig in high spirits. "You have made an excellent connection in the chevaliere, Claudie. Well done!" he said as we moved out onto the dance floor.

"Tell me more about her and how you know her," I said. "I find her to be a most unusual woman."

He laughed. "More than you know." We performed an intricate turn that required all my attention for a moment.

"I am not surprised that she took a liking to you," he said when we could speak again. "She likes clever people. And she could open doors high up in court for us. She's a personal friend of the prince."

"Could she get us an audience?" I asked.

"We shall see," he said. "She can be . . ." He searched for a word for a moment before settling on "unpredictable."

"Tell me, how do you know her so well?" I asked.

"I do not know her well, but the revolution has given us the occasion to work together from time to time. The title *chevalier* was earned for service as an accomplished spy for the king."

"And was that title given to her husband or her father?" I asked.

"Neither, *ma poule*," he said, his eyes crinkling with amusement. "It was given to her."

I stared at him, trying to understand. "Her?"

"When she was believed to be a man," he said.

I stared at him, confused

He pulled his shoulders back and let out a long breath. "She served France in war and politics for many years as a man, reportedly having been forced by her father to live as his son and heir, then was exiled for revealing Louis XV's secrets. Upon the king's death, she requested permission to return, professing to be a good Christian woman. The new king granted her recognition and gave her permission to return, but required she dress appropriately. She has lived as a woman ever since, raising much speculation among the gossips as to what lies beneath her skirts."

I stared at him, shocked by his story and by the callousness of his last remark. "What lies beneath any woman's skirts is no one's business but her own," I said.

"True enough," he replied. "And of little consequence to us in this case. All that matters is whether she can get us an audience with the prince."

We danced on, me trying to imagine what the chevaliere's life must have been like. Yannig was right—she was an excellent connection, and I vowed in my heart that I would somehow make the best of it when she came to tea.

CHAPTER 22

The Chevaliere d'Éon arrived on our doorstep at precisely four o'clock
the next afternoon, which, I was informed, was the socially correct
time for tea. Yannig, Mathilde, and I met her in the parlor. The family had gone to tea elsewhere so that we might speak in private.
What, exactly, we would speak of, I wasn't sure—Yannig's judgment would have to guide the conversation. I was far too unversed in
the ways of society in general, and London society in particular, to
do more than charm with a smile or witty comment. Come to think
of it, I was unversed in charming as well, but that, at least, was a
challenge without fatal consequences.

The chevaliere had been elegantly, if somewhat austerely, dressed
in black silk the night before. Now, for an afternoon tea, she wore a
cheery dress of pale pink muslin sprigged with tiny rosebuds and a
large bonnet festooned with an enormous spray of wax roses and long
pink ribbons, which tied under her chin, bunching up her aging jowls.

"Allow me to pour out," she said once pleasantries had been ex-
changed. She took up the teapot and, with exquisite grace, poured
and passed around cups of tea, then spread thick Devonshire cream
on scones and handed those out too. The precision with which her
hands moved was mesmerizing, and I found myself watching in fasci-
nation, which seemed ridiculous for a girl who had grown up serving
food in an inn. That had been rough and hurried, however. This was
as artful as a dance.

Once we were all served, she raised her teacup to her lips, sipped delicately, then fixed a steely look on Yannig.

"Now, monsieur, tell me everything," she said.

"Everything?" Yannig said, widening his eyes incredulously. The courtly gentleman of last night had once again retreated, replaced by the roguish, sarcastic rebel. The Yannig I loved. "Everything is quite a lot. I don't think we have that much tea."

"Very well," she said. "Then tell me of your latest scheme. And please don't expect me to believe that you thought that pretty peasant girl would be enough enticement for the prince," she added with a glance toward Mathilde, who blushed to demonstrate her pretty peasantness.

Yannig showed no reaction to this, holding her gaze steadily, but I withered a little inside. It was exactly what I had thought, but on her lips, I could hear it for the naive and foolish plan it was.

"I think you will find, madame," he said, "that our enticement is equal to our need this time."

"And what, exactly, do you need, so I will know how impressed to be with your enticement?" she replied dryly.

"We need what we have always needed," Yannig said. "The strength of the English forces—by sea and on land."

"Ah." She took a long sip of her tea. "Well, then, this enticement of yours better be—"

Her words stopped abruptly, though, for Yannig had reached out his hand over the table and unfolded his fingers. There, in his palm, sat the sparkling blue diamond.

Even I, who had seen the diamond before, who had knowingly

carried it all this way, was struck dumb. Like a fierce and glorious creature that had too long been forced to hide and now stepped out into the sun, the stone blazed and flashed. For a long moment, no one breathed. No one moved.

Mathilde was the first to recover. She had not seen the stone until now. While the rest of us still gaped at the shining stone, she rose from her seat and stepped forward to look down upon it. She stretched out one tentative finger and touched the smooth, hard surface.

"This is it?" she said in a quavering voice. "This is what Jacques died for?"

"Jacques died for Brittany," Yannig said gently. "For the hope of a peaceful life with you, Mathilde."

She shook her head, her eyes still on the diamond. "It is so small."

"I beg your pardon," the Chevaliere d'Éon said, reaching out and plucking the stone from Yannig's hand. "As gems go, it is any-thing but." She turned it in her fingers, then held it up to the light. "Is this what I think it is?" she said, her eyes still devouring the glo-rious stone.

"The Blue of the Crown," Yannig confirmed. "Tell me, madame, what price would Prince George pay to add the Sun King's greatest jewel to his collection of fineries?"

The chevaliere hadn't taken her eyes off the stone. She turned it so that it caught the candlelight and threw azure drops of light against the walls, and her face shone with admiration. "Well, Rooster, you have outdone yourself this time."

Yannig sat back in his chair. "Will it work, do you think?" he asked.

Slowly, she nodded. "I do not think our extravagant little prince will be able to resist an enticement such as this," she said, reluctantly returning the stone to Yannig.

"And will the prince persuade his father to send troops to our aid?" I asked excitedly.

"Oh, much of the responsibility in matters of war lies with the prince now," she explained, "as the English king is not well." She looked back at Yannig and peaked her eyebrows. "Now all you have to do is find a way into the prince's good graces."

Yannig relaxed his shoulders. "Surely you could arrange such a thing, madame."

Her eyebrows lifted in what I suspected was mock surprise. "Me? I couldn't possibly."

Yannig's jaw tightened. "But you move in his circle. One word from you—"

"We émigrés are not well loved by the English, and you rabble-rousers even less so," she said, helping herself to another biscuit from the plate on the table. "There are those who grumble that we are imposing too much upon English hospitality. Why would I want to ally myself with the very people who validate their views?"

"To support our efforts to liberate France," Yannig said, his jaw tight. "To make it safe for the émigrés to return home."

She sighed and spoke as if she were explaining the obvious to a child. "The thing is, *mon ami*, I have made a pleasing life for myself here. I enjoy friendship, a measure of fame, and all the comforts of a civilized life, except, perhaps, a ready supply of good wine. You would have me risk all that for your cause? For a country that has been less kind to me than this one?"

"I ask you only to get me an audience with the prince," Yannig said. "I know you are friendly with him. Your escapades at his most lavish parties have reached our ears even in France."

I looked at the chevaliere with new eyes at this and could see from the little smirk forming on her lips that she enjoyed such a notorious reputation.

"And I have said I will not get involved." The chevaliere glanced at Mathilde and then at me. "You have brought more enticements than just that shiny bauble. Use them to get an invitation to Carlton House. This is the London season; His Royal Highness will be hosting parties almost every week."

Yannig followed her glance to Mathilde and me, and his expression darkened. "It is not as simple as that, and you know it," he said. "They are not titled, as you pointed out. I used them to get your attention, but that is different from getting the prince's."

"We could pose as ladies," Mathilde said, eager to help. "We did well last night, didn't we?"

"Almack's is hardly the prince's palace," Yannig said.

The chevaliere smoothed her skirts. "It's a start. There will be more invitations now that you've been seen. Still, it will take wit and cunning to navigate the infested lagoon of the British aristocracy," she said.

"Teach me how," I demanded, more fiercely than I had meant to.

She tipped her head back, appraising me down the length of her aristocratic nose. I did not flinch but met her appraisal with bold assurance to live up to my daring demand.

"I have an idea of how you might manipulate your way to an invitation from the prince," she said slowly.

"I will do it!" I said without hesitation.

"Me too!" Mathilde chimed in.

Our haste amused the chevaliere. "Excellent," she said. "Now let me tell you what I am thinking." She glanced from Mathilde's pretty face to my eager one. "It can be an attack on two fronts, I think. Wit and beauty. Let us see which is more irresistible to these English gentry, shall we?"

Yannig was shaking his head. "You mean for them to seduce their way into an audience with Prince George? I won't allow it."

"You think I am not clever enough?" I said, my hands going to my hips.

"Oh, you are clever enough," Yannig said, scowling. "But it is as the chevaliere says, these are infested waters. Not all of these English gentlemen are . . . are gentlemen!"

Mathilde gave a most unladylike snort. "Have you forgotten that we are innkeeper's daughters? If there's one thing we know how to deal with, it's men who are not gentlemen!"

This earned a laugh from the chevaliere, and I nodded in agreement.

"But here, you must deal with men who both are and are not gentlemen," the chevaliere said, a twinkle of mischief in her eyes. "Are you prepared for that?"

"They are not," Yannig said.

"We are," Mathilde and I said in unison.

The twinkle of mischief brightened. "You are overruled, my dear Rooster," the chevaliere said as she rose to her feet.

"Come to my house this evening at seven o'clock, dressed for a formal event. Both of you. I will get you through the first door. Then it is up to you to do the rest. Do not be late," she said, and she strode from the room.

Yannig glared after her, while Mathilde bubbled over with excitement.

I watched Yannig after the chevaliere left, while Mathilde chattered on and on about how she would charm the prince, every detail fully imagined, right down to the color of her gown and the dance they would do when he asked her. Through it all, Yannig glowered silently into his now-cold cup of tea, gripping it so hard I expected the fine china to shatter in his fingers.

"Don't be angry with me, Yannig," I said after Mathilde finally ran off to tell Marie-Louise of her dreams, leaving us alone beside the parlor fire.

He looked up at me, grinding his teeth. "I brought you to England to keep you safe, Claudie. That was the deal."

"That was the deal before I joined your cause," I protested. "Things are different now."

He shook his head. "They aren't different for me. I wanted to keep you safe then; I want to keep you safe now. That's why I made that deal."

"You made the deal so that you could get your hands on the diamond," I reminded him.

"True," he said. He patted the seat of the sofa next to him, and I gladly sat down, resting my head on his shoulder as he swung an arm around me.

"But you see," he added in a whisper once I was pressed against him, "I could have just seduced you and saved us the trouble of bringing you to England."

"Too late. I'm here now."

He let out a good-humored huff, but I could tell he was trying to be serious now.

"The prince's parties are . . ." His brow formed a heavy storm cloud over his eyes as he searched for the right word.

"Extravagant?" I suggested.

"Raucous," he answered. "He may be a prince, but he is not respectable. Anything could happen to you there."

"You mean—I might be seduced?"

He didn't laugh at my jest.

"You said yourself, you wanted me to be useful," I said. "This is how I can be useful. Let me at least try."

He lifted my face to his so that he could look me in the eye. "Do I have a choice?" he asked.

I smiled. "I don't think so."

He leaned down and gave me a long, slow kiss. A kiss that left me breathless.

"What was that for?" I asked.

"In case they seduce you. I want to give you something to return home for."

CHAPTER 23

Mathilde was fluttery with excitement as I knocked on the door of the chevaliere's mansion. I, on the other hand, was knotted up with nerves. I had been bold in our meeting, and in my reassurances to Yannig, but now that I was here, the thought of my sister and me ingratiating ourselves to lecherous nobles was making my knees weak.

A butler, formally attired in knee breeches, tails, and a powdered wig, admitted us into the house and led us to a parlor that was at least as big as the common room in Papa's inn. Thick carpets stretched across much of the floor, and the walls were covered in a patterned red silk that made the room feel both warm and decadent all at once.

I sat on the settee to await our hostess, but Mathilde, overflowing with curiosity, flitted around the room admiring the little china figurines, the blown glass inkwells on the desk, and the alabaster vases filled with fresh roses, though December was upon us.

"Does it meet with your approval?" the chevaliere asked in a dry voice as she entered.

Mathilde, in her usual boisterous, enthusiastic way, either missed or disregarded the sarcastic tone. "Oh, yes!" she cried. "It is all so wonderful!"

Our austere hostess arched an eyebrow.

I bit my lip to try to suppress my amusement. This also was not lost on the grand dame. "Life is a comedy, is it not?" she said to me as she worked her hands into a pair of kid gloves. Tonight, she wore a gown of midnight blue silk, swaths of creamy lace billowing along the neckline, throwing her exposed décolletage into shadow. The effect was both dignified and daring, and made me feel rather unsophisticated in my own gown of green brocade, borrowed from Marie-Louise and hastily altered.

"Come, girls. We mustn't be late," she said, turning to leave and not looking back to see if we followed—which we did, very obediently. Her carriage was waiting outside the door, a fine conveyance with gold-painted trim inside and out, drawn by a handsome pair of black horses, plumed with bright white feathers. We climbed inside and sat opposite her, our own skirts crowded and wrinkling, while hers were spread smoothly across the seat around her.

The carriage, as it turned out, was hardly necessary, as it carried us to an elegant house scarcely more than two blocks away, an easy walk.

"A lady *never* arrives on foot," our mentor said, when Mathilde pointed this out. "You wouldn't want to be taken for a simpleton, would you?"

"The carriage is much grander," Mathilde agreed.

"And who is our host this evening?" I asked. The facade was so elegant, I thought it might be the prince himself.

"That is a worthy question," the chevaliere said. "This is the home of one Francis Seymour-Conway, the Third Marquess of Hertford."

Mathilde's brow bunched. "Third Marquess? He doesn't sound very important if there are two others before him."

"How quickly an innkeeper's daughter learns the art of snobbery," the chevaliere said. "He is important, at least to you, as he advises the prince in art purchases. Shall we see what entices him, my dears? Beauty or wit?"

Mathilde fluttered her fan, her eyes sparkling with anticipation over its rim. I could muster only a weak grimace in the face of such odds.

"You have two opportunities here," the chevaliere explained. "If you should happen to impress the lowly Third Marquess of Hertford himself, you could find yourself moving directly into the prince's circle. If not, then perhaps there are others here whom you can charm at least enough to get invited to another party."

"What must I do to impress the marquess?" I asked, twisting my handkerchief in my hands. I was not ready for this. I had thought she would train us first.

"My dear, it is a party. You must enjoy yourself!"

And with that advice, we were disgorged from our carriage before the steps of Lord Seymour-Conway's home, along with scores of other finely dressed ladies and gentlemen. I watched them ascend to the front door, their chins held high and their gaits smooth and graceful, the gentlemen holding out a hand and the ladies gently draping their fingers over it. I wished I had Yannig at my side. I would have gripped his hand far more firmly, and maybe that could have quelled my nerves. As it was, I climbed the steps holding no one's hand and praying I would not trip on my skirts as I went.

Inside, we were greeted with cool courtesy by the mistress of the house, the Marchioness of Hertford, a refined lady with a light Italian accent, a gray wig, and a gown cut in a continental style. Upon hearing my stumbling English, she switched easily into French. Having paid our respects to our hostess, we continued into a long, open gallery glowing with candles. In one corner a group of musicians was playing cheerful tunes, while down the center of the hall, lines of couples were already engaged in a dance.

We had not been long in the room when we were approached by a bland but well-dressed gentleman eager to meet Mathilde. His most striking feature was his ginger hair, which was not to be found on his crown but rather in bushy curls on his temples and cheeks, and even disappearing under his high collar and cravat.

The Chevaliere d'Éon cheerfully introduced him as our host, with a wry glance at me, and Mathilde and I both effected our most artful curtsies, which I feared were barely adequate in this company. Still, our host, the Lord Francis Seymour-Conway, Third Marquess of Hertford, bent and kissed Mathilde's hand and eagerly engaged her in conversation. Within moments, he offered her an elbow, and the two moved into the room to meet his friends.

"It would seem beauty has taken the lead already," the chevaliere said, looping her arm through mine and leading me deeper into the party.

"I didn't even get a chance to speak with him," I said, trying unsuccessfully to keep the defeat from my voice.

"Not to worry. Your sister will no doubt charm him with her good looks. He is, after all, a well-known letch of the first order."

I tried to turn back. "I should keep an eye on her," I said.

"Nonsense," she retorted. "Let the girl have her chance. You have work of your own to do if you want to win this little contest."

I wanted to protest that my sister was only fifteen, and a naive fifteen at that, and that we weren't in competition but working for the same goal. But the chevaliere was leading me away, Mathilde and her new acquaintance had already disappeared into the crowd, and the spirit of competition was awake within me, despite my best intentions.

"Young lords and ladies often find themselves eager to begin the evening on the dance floor, but I much prefer to begin with supper," the chevaliere said as we entered the dining room. "The food is best while still hot, and if there is one thing we French understand that the English do not, it is the importance of food at its very best."

The dining room was as extravagant as, and even more crowded than, the ballroom had been. Here, scores of people sat at a long table, carrying on dozens of loud conversations, shouting over each other, even with food in their mouths. And to think, I had been worried about my manners. A sideboard ran along the longest wall, laden with whole hams, bowls of pickled beetroot, plates of smoked fish, a pile of roasted chestnuts, and tall puddings smelling of brandy.

The chevaliere thrust a china plate into my hands, took one of her own, and released my arm. I followed her along the sideboard, taking bits of this and that, wanting to try all the elegant dishes but afraid my nervous stomach might take none of them.

"What is the occasion of this feast?" I asked the chevaliere.

"There is no occasion other than the London season. Life is dull without the company of friends, is it not? Little gatherings like this, they break the monotony."

"Little gathering?" I said, looking around again. There must have been a hundred guests that I had seen already, and the party stretched on into another room beyond.

"These are hard times, mademoiselle," the chevaliere spoke into my ear. "The aristocracy needs cheering up."

I looked again at the sideboard overflowing with lavish foods and at the crowds of laughing, flirting ladies and gentleman in their powdered wigs, lace cuffs, and jeweled hair ornaments, and I felt a surge of anger. "What does anyone here know of hard times?" I said.

The chevaliere's jaw tightened, and her eyes took on a look of warning. "Do be careful how you judge, *ma chérie*," she said. "You see that lady in the corner?" She pointed to a powdered girl of no more than eighteen, her head thrown back and her pale décolletage heaving with laughter as a gentleman whispered something in her ear. "Lady Marguerite saw her parents, two brothers, and three sisters all guillotined last year. And that one"—she pointed to a young man with dark eyes and a haughty carriage—"escaped his prison through the privy hole and waded neck-deep through the sewer for three miles. And lovely young Adelaide there feigned death and lay among the rotting corpses of her family in a wagon for two days to escape Paris." She paused for a moment, watching my reaction with a shrewd eye. "But you look pale, child. Please, sit down. Eat. Be merry. Life goes on, and we must make of it what we will."

Chagrined, I took the seat at the table where she directed me. The room felt too hot and too crowded, and I faltered, wondering why I was here, why I had ever thought I could do this. I ached to be back in Brittany in a quiet, remote country inn.

"Mademoiselle, you take it hard, I see. Perhaps this is all too much for you just yet," the chevaliere said, a mocking challenge in her eyes. "Perhaps I was wrong about you."

I straightened my shoulders. If she thought I was so easily cowed, she could think again. I forced a smile. "No, you have not misjudged me. But what am I supposed to do? I don't know where to begin in a crowd such as this."

"You are meant to seek out opportunities. Or, when there are none to be found, to create them."

I nodded and waited for her to say more, but she was suddenly more interested in her thick slice of ham than in any lesson I was sup-posed to be learning from her, so I too turned to my food. All around us the noise of conversation ebbed and flowed, and we were but a tiny island of silence, chewing the fine food our host's chef had prepared, saying nothing to each other or to those around us. What could I say? They all spoke English, and I could make out next to nothing of their conversation. If she meant for me to be making my own opportunity by eavesdropping, she would be sorely disappointed.

When she had finished her ham and was starting in on the herring, I leaned in and whispered, "Are we waiting for opportunity to find us?"

She looked up, the expression on her face suggesting she had for-gotten all about me. She wiped a speck of fish from her lips, then looked around her. "Here? Opportunity?" A little snort of laughter burst from her nose, and she glanced around the room. "Look at them all. Silly, shallow creatures. They are not clever enough to make op-portunities. You must do that for yourself."

"But how, if they are all silly and shallow, as you say?" I was start-ing to suspect that I had been brought here only as a joke.

"They may be both of those things, but they also hear a lot. And one thing you can always count on silly, shallow people to do is repeat what they have heard."

"You mean for me to gossip about the diamond?" The thought of it terrified and exhilarated me all at once.

"Of course not! Where is the mystery if you simply blurt it out?" she said, rolling her eyes. "The secret to giving away a secret is to do it by accident. Let them think they are the clever ones who learned something they weren't meant to hear," she said. "The more clandestine the information seems to be, the more eager they will be to betray it to all their friends and family."

I nodded, beginning to understand what she meant. If the nobility was buzzing with curiosity . . . "How many people have to hear the secret for it to reach the prince?" I asked.

"That depends," she said. "If you tell them all the same story, it will circulate for a week or two before people lose interest. It has a small chance of getting to the prince and a much greater chance of getting your house burgled."

"But if we tell people different stories, it will be more interesting," I said, seeing where she was going. "If more than one story is circulating about the diamond, that will pique everyone's interest and the rumors will grow instead of dying away."

"Not *we, ma chérie*. You. I am only here to get you started."

"But how do I start divergent rumors?" I asked, suddenly nervous again. "I should have made these plans before coming—determined what to say."

She shook her head. "Plans are too constraining. When you accidentally let slip something you shouldn't, it should be spontaneous."

"But—"

"Think of your sister, how words bubble up without her thinking."

I knew exactly what she meant. Nearly every hurtful thing Mathilde had ever said to me had been an offhand comment without thought to how it might sting.

"But I thought you wanted me to use my wit," I pointed out.

"Of course you use your wit," she said, suddenly impatient. "You just make it sound like it bubbled up from nowhere."

Her words were rushed because a young man was approaching us, and she wanted to give her final advice before he stood before us. As soon as the last words rolled from her lips, she rose from her seat, reaching both hands to his and gracing each cheek with a kiss.

"Ah, Sir Anthony! How good of you to cross the room to see me."

He bowed slightly, his powdered wig slipping a little as he did so. When he straightened, he glanced at me pointedly.

"Oh, how rude of me. Sir Anthony," the chevaliere said, turning to introduce me. "This is my niece, Claudie Durand, newly arrived from France. Claudie, Sir Anthony of Norfolk. He has been an outspoken critic of the revolution."

I gave a small curtsy before looking up into his face. He had a weak chin but intelligent eyes. "A critic of the revolution is a friend to me," I said.

The chevaliere excused herself with a quirk of her eyebrow that told me I was to make the most of this opportunity.

"Mademoiselle, welcome to England. How do you find our fair isle?" he asked in French far more cultured than my own.

I took the arm he offered me, and we began walking through the

crowded room. With my free hand, I fluttered my fan before my face
as if to cool my overwrought nerves. "London is so grand, sir. You
must excuse me; I am not from Paris. My father preferred to stay on
our estate in the country, and until now, the largest city I had visited
was Rennes. But London! I never knew there to be so many people in
all the world!"

I took a glass of champagne from a passing servant as an excuse to
lapse into silence. I had no idea where I was going with my rambling
words; they certainly weren't turning into an opportunity.

My companion scarcely noticed my discomfort, or if he did, he
took it as a part of my confessed naivete. He quickly filled the silence
between us by telling me of all there was to see in the city—the
Houses of Parliament and the Tower of London.

"Where Anne Boleyn was beheaded," he said.

"Don't speak to me of beheadings!" I said, fluttering my fan before
my face to cool the exaggerated horror that showed on my face.

"Oh, mademoiselle, how insensitive of me. I didn't mean . . . Of
course, being from France . . . I only mentioned it because Anne Boleyn was an ancestor of mine. A great-great-aunt or something like
that. And she was mother to the great Queen Elizabeth, who would
have been a great-great-cousin."

"Do you mean to say that you are in line for the throne?" I asked,
making my eyes as big and round as Mathilde's often appeared and
wondering how this line of conversation would ever turn in my favor.

He laughed. "I am afraid not. Accession to the throne was through
her father's line, not her mother's. But we were speaking of London,"
he said, his expression good-natured and open. "There is London
Bridge and Tower Bridge. You must visit them. And the Tower, as

I was saying. Do you know, there is a menagerie with all manner of exotic beasts? And the crown jewels are there too."

It was by luck that I was taking a sip of my wine at that moment, but it was entirely by design that I choked on it, coughing and spluttering in surprise at the mention of crown jewels.

Sir Anthony gaped in shock before remembering himself and arranging his features in an expression of concern. "Mademoiselle! Are you well? Do you need to sit down?" he asked, very solicitous.

"Forgive me," I said, still flustered. "I only thought . . . You mentioned . . ." I took a few deep breaths, giving him time to remember what he had mentioned that had surprised me.

"Come, mademoiselle, let us find you a seat," he said, directing me across the room toward a chair. I followed meekly, one hand still on his guiding arm. It was only when we reached the chair and he meant to excuse himself from me that I gripped his arm and looked into his face with frightened eyes.

"Please, sir," I implored, "you won't tell anyone of this, will you?"

His brow drew down, and I could see he was trying to work out what there was to tell, but he only assured me that he would not.

"It's just that . . ." I stopped myself, then began again. "I don't know what you've heard about us, sir. It is supposed to be a secret!" I said.

"I . . . mademoiselle, I have heard nothing," he said.

I maintained my beseeching expression, though he was now squirming to get away, as a few people were looking and it threatened to become a scene. "Then you didn't mean anything by mentioning crown jewels?"

"I only meant to tell you about the Tower," he said. Then he cocked his head, and I could see the wheels slowly turning in his mind. I hoped he would put it together—if news of the theft of France's crown jewels made its way to our small village, surely the upper crust of British society must know as well.

I pressed my handkerchief to my lips and looked embarrassed. Or at least what I hoped embarrassed looked like. I might have even managed to blush a little. "Oh! I have said too much! Excuse me, sir. It was very nice to meet you." I rose from my seat and hurried away through the crowd.

Near the doorway into the ballroom, the chevaliere caught up with me. "Well done, if not a little heavy-handed," she said. "Now act like you're telling me a secret."

I wasn't sure whether that was a compliment or not, but it didn't matter. "Why?" I asked. "The deed is done."

"So that you will be seen whispering to me right after making a glaring error," she said. "They will think we are conspirators and will be needling us both to confirm or deny his suspicions now." She laid a gloved hand on my arm.

"I see," I whispered back, wrinkling my brow as if in deep consternation.

"Yes, that will do. Now go off to the ballroom and take a seat among the wallflowers. Let your pounding heart settle a little while you wait your turn to dance. I suspect Sir Anthony's friends will be with you shortly."

I nodded, still doing my best to look concerned, and slipped through the crowd, moving deliberately toward the seats. My heart was racing, not out of consternation but out of excitement. The same pleasure that I had felt sparring with Yannig, that I had felt when I had burst into Yannig's quarters and negotiated with the diamond—it was flowing through me now, the tingle of a dangerous game afoot and me being part of it.

I found an empty chair among the other plain girls and sat down, watching the dance until I found Mathilde smiling brightly and swinging around with a rakish-looking gentleman. Even in this crowd of wealthy, educated, polished women, she managed to shine. I wondered, did Mathilde feel this same excitement? I had always taken her infatuation with Jacques Lambert to be silly, girlish love, but maybe there was more. Maybe she had thrilled at the idea of conspiracy as much as at being admired.

I was still contemplating my sister when a gentleman stepped into my line of sight and asked for the next dance. As I accepted, I could see the chevaliere in the corner of the room, a knowing grin on her face.

By the time the evening ended, I had danced with a handful of young men and given varying answers to many prying questions that edged around the topic of the stolen crown jewels of France. I gave veiled answers, sometimes cagey, sometimes nervous if the question seemed too direct. I neither confirmed nor denied any rumors, which, as the chevaliere said, was the fastest way to ensure that the rumors spread. I was disappointed, however, not to be approached by Lord Seymour-Conway himself. He had flirted shamelessly with my sister and every other pretty girl at the party, right under the nose of his wife, and never seemed to hear a word of the spreading gossip.

The chevaliere only shrugged when I complained of this in the carriage on the way home. "You agreed to a fair contest, beauty versus wit," she said.

"Don't worry, Claudie," Mathilde chirped. "I think he will come visit me after tonight. He asked if he might call." She punctuated her last words with a giggle. She was still swirling across the dance floor in her mind.

"But what good will it do if he knows nothing of the diamond?" I grumbled, my chin in my hand as I gazed out the window. "I doubt you mentioned it to him while you were soaking up all his compliments."

"Of course not," she said. "You said I was to tell no one."

"You've both made a start of it tonight, girls," the chevaliere said. "Now we must wait to see what comes of it." And with that, the carriage stopped before our house, and we bid her good night.

By teatime the next day, what had come of it was a half dozen ladies and their daughters who called to pay their respects—some wanting to size up their new competition from France, others wanting to talk about jewelry. It was clear that the rumors we had started the night before were spreading. We withheld any confirmation of them, or at least I did. Mathilde, in her excitement and eagerness to be liked by these new English associates, tended to prattle on. At first, I thought she was likely to ruin our plans with her careless talk, but gradually, I realized it was not as careless as it seemed. She always came right to the brink of saying too much, then pulled back and said just enough to titillate. Guest after guest came to our parlor, listened to her careless chatter, and came away hungrier than they had started. With every visit, my role seemed to wane while hers grew. She was getting her chance to be useful, just as she wanted. And I was losing mine.

CHAPTER 24

For more than a week, a host of visitors appeared in our parlor, but none of them were the Marquess of Hertford or anyone else close to the prince. It was obvious we would have to do more, so we took every opportunity that presented itself, most in the form of invitations to parties and balls. We went, Mathilde being charming, I witty, the lieutenant and Yannig congenial to the other gentlemen. Still, no one in the prince's circle inquired about the diamond. Somehow, we had to do more, but I did not know what.

I was on the verge of visiting the Chevaliere d'Éon again to beg her help when the butler arrived in the drawing room one gray afternoon to announce a visitor.

"Sir Anthony of Norfolk and a companion, to see Mademoiselle Claudie," he said.

The family de Lavallée had been relaxing with us there, and now they all turned to stare as I got nervously to my feet. Few men had come to call on me. I hoped this was about the diamond but feared it might be an unwanted flirtation.

"You may receive him in the parlor," Lady de Lavallée said graciously.

Yannig rose and accompanied me without comment.

I gave him a pointed look. "What if he wants to see me in private?" I said.

"That is what I'm afraid of," Yannig replied. He pulled me to him and kissed my forehead. "Just think of me as a chaperone—to keep things proper."

Once we were settled in the parlor, me on the settee and Yannig in a stiff horsehair chair in the corner, the butler showed our guests in. Sir Anthony was accompanied by a woman in her midthirties, relatively plain but well dressed and very self-assured. He introduced her as Mrs. Fitzherbert, "a particular friend of the prince's."

I welcomed her cordially, trying to keep my manners and address befitting someone of such high rank, feeling conspicuously coarse.

I needn't have worried. Unlike so many of the aristocrats who had come through our parlor in the last few days, she quickly put me at ease with her comfortable conversation and keen sense of humor.

I was laughing with the lady, completely forgetting myself, when Sir Anthony interrupted us abruptly. "Mademoiselle Claudie, there is a rumor that you have a very fine diamond in your possession." He paused for me to acknowledge the truth of the rumor, but I only sat attentive, waiting for him to continue while my heart thumped against my ribs.

"My dear friend, the Chevaliere d'Éon, says it's a wonder," Mrs. Fitzherbert said, leaning in a little to confide in me. "I should so like to see it myself."

I hesitated, but Yannig, nearly forgotten where he sat in the corner, did not. He rose wordlessly and left the room. Uncertain of what he might be doing, I excused myself and followed. I met him returning to the parlor, the diamond in hand. He grinned and handed it to me.

"Are we sure it's safe to show them? Are they close enough to the prince?" I whispered.

"Oh, she's close enough, all right," Yannig said. "She's the prince's wife."

I stared at him, my mouth open. "She is a princess?"

He shook his head. "She is a commoner and a Catholic. Their marriage is not legal in the eyes of the king, but that hardly matters to how they choose to live. And who better to tell the prince about the diamond than her?"

My heart soaring, I took the diamond from his hands and carried it back into the parlor.

I took a harder look at Mrs. Fitzherbert when I returned to the room, trying to see what about her would tempt a prince into defying his father and the laws of the land he was born to rule. She was nothing special, I thought, but then I realized how well she had put me at ease with her clever conversation. How much she had felt like a kindred spirit.

She did not notice my stare, nor did Sir Anthony. Like everyone who beheld it, they were enraptured by the diamond and saw nothing else in the room for some time. I let them have a good, long look, but not so long that the stone could diminish in their minds. While it still captivated their attention, I politely withdrew it from them and returned it to Yannig to be hidden away once again.

"I will put in a good word for you," Mrs. Fitzherbert said as she departed that afternoon.

We waited anxiously after that for an invitation from the prince, but none came. Instead, Mrs. Fitzherbert returned, first with an earl, then with a duke, and finally with Lord Seymour-Conway, who claimed to have come to see the diamond but seemed more eager to converse with Mathilde again. Her dimples seemed to disarm him as easily as they had the lowborn men of our village. When we showed him the diamond, he examined it with the close and critical eye of an expert. I waited, holding my breath, in case he should say that the stone was in some way flawed or inferior, or that it had sustained damage in the rough handling it had endured since being stolen from Paris, but instead, he nodded with satisfaction as he put away the little set of scales and the series of notes he had scribbled while we looked on.

He tried to wrangle a private dinner with Mathilde, but she demurred, giggling, and agreed that, should she meet him at a dance or a party, she would be happy to have supper with him and to dance as many dances as he wanted.

"That was a nice touch," I told Mathilde as he left. "Surely we will be invited to the palace now."

An invitation did not come the next week, but thieves did. We woke in the night to the sound of shattering glass and someone searching the main floor of the house. Yannig and the lieutenant drove the thieves off, but we were left unnerved. The family retreated to the country for Christmas, leaving the house and its protection in our care. We took extra precautions with the diamond, and Yannig hired guards to patrol the streets around the house day and night.

I could scarcely sleep with the worry of it. I woke from dreams of fire and death, screaming in terror. Yannig rushed into my room, looking for my invisible attackers. Finding none, he held me until the wisps of the dream cleared from the room, but he could not ease all of my fears, and I lay awake, listening for the sounds of thieves on the stairs and wondering if it was all in vain.

We had let the city know we had the diamond, and yet we had heard nothing from the prince. What if he wasn't interested? After all, he was deeply in debt—what if he had decided he couldn't afford such a thing and meant to stay well away from us?

Finally, in the third week of December, an embossed invitation on heavy white paper arrived, requesting our presence at a party at Carlton House, the London residence of the Prince of Wales. The invitation was received with excitement and relief by everyone. It surely meant that Mrs. Fitzherbert and her colleagues had told the prince of the diamond. We were hardly the sort of people to be invited on our own merits. But a party was not what Yannig had hoped for. He had hoped the prince would arrive with an offer to buy as others had or, barring that, would summon us for a private audience.

"Don't be a fool," the chevaliere told him on hearing his displeasure. She had arrived not long after the invitation, already aware we had received it. "The prince can't look too eager on such a subject. He is not going to come as if summoned by your rumor. He has to make it look accidental that he happened upon the opportunity to acquire this stone." She glanced at Mathilde and me. "He is a vain man; if you do not please him at his party, he may decide he does not want your diamond, no matter how fine. It will still come down to either wit or beauty."

I sighed, feeling the dreary weight of my plainness. "More likely, it will be up to you, Mathilde. The prince is said to be a lover of beauty."

Mathilde sat up straighter. "It will be my pleasure," she said, preening at the prospect of charming a prince. Even if he was devoted to Mrs. Fitzherbert, Mathilde was confident she could turn his head long enough for our purposes.

Still, we engaged the help of the chevaliere to prepare her. She agreed and spent the next week guiding Mathilde on what to say to the prince and how to direct him. It was important to please him and let him know that we were interested in selling the diamond to him, but we did not want her negotiating such a sale. No terms, no hint of what we wanted, was to be mentioned until we had arranged a private viewing of the stone. Yannig reasoned, and we all agreed, that seeing the stone made it far harder to resist, and so our job was to get him drawn in adequately to come see the stone, not to engage in any discussion of what we might want in payment.

Mathilde was taking the role she would play very seriously, and by the time the party was upon us, I was reassuring Yannig and Vincent both that she would perform admirably at the task we had set her. I, on the other hand, was feeling a little deflated. I had felt such pleasure in spreading the rumor—in matching wits with the powerful men and women of England and coming out ahead—that the thought of being a spectator now, at the most important event of all, created a dull emptiness inside me, the same feeling I had had all those years watching Mathilde being courted while I was to be left behind in my father's inn. Of course, this wasn't like that. Not really. I had not been pushed aside this time. I had done much of the work to get us to this point. And I had Yannig's love too, so there was nothing to feel jealous about. Still, the old feeling was hard to suppress once it had arisen.

At last, the day of the event arrived. Mathilde and I spent much of the afternoon dressing, powdering, and having our hair twisted and piled in elaborate designs on our heads. We were both quiet, caught up in our thoughts of what the night would hold, or wouldn't hold, for each of us. At seven o'clock, the Chevaliere d'Éon's grand carriage arrived for us, and we were swept away, joining the flow of all the richest, most stylish people of London to Carlton House.

"This is merely a house? Not a palace?" Mathilde whispered to me as we descended the steps of the carriage and looked up at the expanse of white columns that graced the front of the building and stretched the full length of a city block on either side of us.

Yannig's lips curled at her wide-eyed awe. "You did not think the prince would live in less, did you?" he said. "He has extravagant tastes."

The exterior, which had amazed us, was a pauper's hovel compared to the inside. Everything glittered, from the white marble floors up the golden marble columns to the sparkling chandeliers, dripping with crystals, hung from a ceiling painted to mimic the clearest of blue skies.

"It is charming, is it not?" Vincent said with wry understatement.

"Charming. Yes," I stuttered. It hadn't been easy to find my tongue. From somewhere ahead of us, I could hear music and the murmur of many voices, and my knees grew watery. How could I convince anyone accustomed to this kind of opulence that I was a person of any consequence? That I had a glittering marvel beyond comprehension? I glanced at Mathilde. Her eyes were wide. She too was shaken.

I swallowed and found my voice. "But I doubt anything here is as charming as my sister."

She gave me a small, appreciative glance, then took a deep breath, straightened her shoulders, and put a brave smile on her face, bringing out her dimples.

"Come then, lieutenant. Let us meet these dukes and lordlings!" she said.

Her confidence strengthened my own, and my knees grew more solid once again. I nodded, and we proceeded into the great receiving room.

Servants in livery greeted us, taking our cloaks and directing us on into a grand gallery to our right, which I gradually realized was a throne room. Or at least it was a room with a throne, but no one was seated in it, and they certainly weren't holding court. Nor was the scene like any other ball we had attended. Noisy people crowded the room, all laughing and drinking and carrying on shouted conversations. At tables scattered through the room, men and women played lively games of cards or dice, mounds of money changing hands every few minutes amid outbursts of applause and dismayed shouts. In the center of the room, couples were dancing a lively country dance in which the women were holding their skirts scandalously high as they executed the steps and the men were shouting lewd encouragements. In the corner, a group of men sat at a table with large tankards before them, engaged in what appeared to be a drinking game, while laughing girls wearing too much makeup and overly bright dresses sat on their laps.

"I don't like this," Yannig growled. "Perhaps Vincent and I should stay and Claudie and Mathilde go home."

"Nonsense," Mathilde said. "Why, this is nothing worse than what went on in Papa's common room on a nightly basis," she said, relaxing into her old flirtatious, pretty self. "Now, which one is the prince?"

Before Vincent could answer, she was approached by the Third Marquess of Hertford, who seemed very pleased to see her again and was quick to lead her into the crowd. I breathed a sigh of relief. So far, everything was going perfectly. I wasn't sure whether the marquess had sought out my sister so quickly to enjoy her charms or to begin the business of the diamond with the prince, but either way, I was confident Mathilde knew what to do. Now all we had to do was enjoy ourselves and wait to be summoned.

Yannig, Vincent, and I moved farther into the room, but soon, my male companions were pulled off into a loud and boastful conversation among men in military uniform. More people whose support could help our cause. Now it was just me, as alone and useless as I had feared.

I wandered on into the next room, where a banquet of royal proportions and a punch bowl the size of a horse trough greeted me. A fire blazed in the hearth, and bodies crowded around so that the room was overly warm, even for a December evening. I helped myself to a cup of the punch and a delicate slice of cake and retreated to a seat in the corner, where I thought I might pass the evening unnoticed. I picked at the cake with my fork; after all, as long as I had food before me, I would have a reason to be at the table.

A few seats away, a paunchy fellow was engrossed in his meal. His hair swept back from his round-cheeked face in lightly powdered curls, a style that would make most men look roguish, but this man's wide blue eyes and full Cupid's bow lips gave his whole face a soft, silly, childish look. I wondered if he too found the party intimidating and was eating so as not to mingle. He saw me looking and raised his eyes to me. I gave him a small smile.

He finished sucking the meat from a pigeon wing, wiped his greasy fingers on the tablecloth, and moved down the table to sit beside me.

"Mademoiselle, are you not enjoying the party?" he asked in perfect, cultured French.

I gave him another weak twitch of my lips. "I am, sir. I was just overcome by the heat for a moment," I said.

"It is beastly hot in here," he replied. "Beastly hot." He reached up and loosened the elaborate lace-trimmed cravat at his throat. "But nothing a glass of chilled champagne won't cure." He clapped his hands, and a servant appeared with a tray of champagne glasses. The man took one for himself and a second one, which he handed me.

I thanked him and took a sip. The sweet coolness on my tongue was refreshing, and I gave a grateful sigh.

"I have not seen you here before," he said between sips. "Which means my address to you, without an introduction, is quite improper, is it not?" He sipped the champagne and looked at me sidelong with those pale blue eyes in a way that made it clear he had little interest in propriety.

"Allow me, then, to introduce myself and set matters right," I said, finding my courage as I sensed a note of mockery in his manner. "My name is Claudie Durand, and I am newly arrived in England. But I think you knew that, sir, or you would not have addressed me in French."

"I am caught!" he said, smiling and twisting a curl of his hair in his fingers as he regarded me. "It is true, I have heard of you, mademoiselle. You have caused quite a stir in London."

"You have heard of me?" I said innocently. This game of speaking of the diamond without speaking of it had grown natural by now. "Sir, I am flattered."

He leaned in close to me, plucking a cherry off a nearby trifle and holding it before my lips. I obliged him by taking the morsel into my mouth, though the gesture annoyed me, as I suspected he had used it before with a pet dog and thought no more of using it with me now.

"I have heard you and your sister are connoisseurs of fine art," he said.

"Mais oui," I replied, swallowing the cherry. I had no idea who this fop was or what, if any, connection he had to the prince, but though Mathilde was the one we expected to make the important connection here tonight, I saw no point in neglecting any opportunity, so I dabbed at the corners of my mouth with my napkin, then said, "I understand that the prince has a great collection of art," I said.

"Oh, indeed he does!" my companion cried with enthusiasm. "He is said to have the finest taste in all the land. Finish your repast, and I will show you some of it, and you can judge for yourself as to whether or not Carlton House has a collection to rival that of Versailles. You have been to Versailles, have you not?"

For a moment, I considered telling him I had been, but it was too great a lie and one I knew I could not maintain. "I have not, my lord," I said, "nor would I want to be in times like these."

"Right you are, right you are," he said, picking another cherry off the trifle and popping this one into his own mouth. The gesture was shockingly rude, or at least would have been at home, but as I was new to English manners, I made no objection. Instead, I pushed my cake plate away and stood.

"You have piqued my curiosity, sir," I said. "Let us go look at it now."

"You do not wish to eat more?" he said, perhaps surprised that I had not devoured two pigeons and half a goose as he had, judging from the pile of bones on his plate.

"Perhaps later," I said. "I feel I cannot live one moment more without seeing the prince's paintings!"

This response pleased him, though he took a bun from a passing basket and handed it to me. "You can eat this while we walk. To keep your strength up," he said.

"It must be either a very grand or very terrible collection if it is going to require strength," I said.

He laughed, quite delighted by my jest.

"Come," he said, offering his elbow, "we will go take a look, and you can be the judge."

I took his offered arm and we walked together, back through the grand throne room, where I caught a glimpse of Mathilde dancing with a handsome young gentleman and Yannig in earnest conversation with an older man. Neither of them saw us as we crossed. Beyond the entrance to the grand foyer, we passed through another door into a spacious sitting room no less elegantly furnished than where we had been but much less crowded. Here, only a few couples stood or sat in the corners or on settees tucked away behind potted ferns. Faint traces of hushed and urgent conversations hung in the air. I froze, thinking that I had been tricked. He had seen me for the naive country girl that I was and thought he could lead me off into a private corner and seduce me, and I had been fool enough to think he meant to show me art!

"Sir!" I said, but when I looked into his face to confront him, I saw that he was oblivious to the clandestine lovers around us. His face was turned upward, his cheeks a little flushed with excitement, and when I followed his gaze, I saw he was looking at a wall of portraits—four of them, all seemingly of the same sad-eyed man at different ages. His clothes and cap were not fine and fancy, like those of the people around me, but ordinary and drab, and his bulbous nose was a little red, making him look slightly drunk, or perhaps just ill, in some of the pictures.

"What do you think?" he said, as we studied the paintings together. Though the man in the images was ordinary, the light around him seemed to glow in a way that moved me deep inside.

"Who is he?"

"Why, he is the great Rembrandt! These are his self-portraits—four of them, you see? He painted himself many times, and on this wall you can see him as a young man, as a master in his prime, as an aging master, and as an old man. Look at his eyes there—as if he sees his own mortality laid out before him."

He was right—the eyes of the old man did have a certain sad resignation in them. That look made my heart ache, and I felt a tear spring to my eye. I blinked it away.

"Why, I believe you not only have an eye for art but a heart for it too," my companion said in a quiet voice. I swallowed and pulled my eyes from the painting to look at him. He was no longer jesting.

I dabbed at my eye with a lace handkerchief. "It is only a painting, and yet it is like his very soul lives within it."

"Indeed," my companion said. "Let us see more."

We walked on from that room into another, and another, all quiet, private rooms, farther and farther from the grand public spaces where the party carried loudly on. At first, I was hesitant.

"Are you sure we should be here? We don't have the prince's permission to go into his private lodgings."

He smiled reassuringly. "Your discretion does you credit, mademoiselle, but not to worry. The prince would not deny anyone who loved art as you do a look at his collection. He is very proud of it. Too few of the nobility really understand as you and I do."

"It is a collection to be proud of," I agreed, looking up at a huge painting of lords and ladies out for a stroll, dressed in satin and wearing sweeping plumed hats. The colors were glowing and fresh, unspoiled by age.

"You like Gainsborough?" he said, watching me admire the painting.

"What is gainsborough?

He laughed. "Of course you would not know him, newly arrived from France. Thomas Gainsborough is one of our most promising young painters here in England. That is one of the newer acquisitions at Carlton House. What do you think?"

"It is lovely," I said, studying the painting. It was not just the newness of it that made it glow. It was what it portrayed as well, the tranquil, light-filled scene in a well-groomed parkland. Everything was calm and orderly, from the clothes to the landscape. Even the hound that walked beside the lady's hand pranced with grace and good manners. It filled me with longing for such a calm and ordered life.

"And, oh!" I gasped, as I beheld the next painting—a landscape of rolling hills and forests, a village in the background, and common folk harvesting apples. Tears rose again in my eyes.

"Mademoiselle, are you unwell?"

"Forgive me, monsieur," I said, my hand pressed to my aching heart. "It is so much like home—or like my home once was. So . . . so very peaceful."

"You like peace?" he asked.

"Who does not?"

"There are those who foment for war," he said, and I could tell by the sharp edge to his words that he thought he'd caught me in a trap. Of course, he knew who I had arrived with, and he must have known we meant to gain support for the war in France. Still, it hardly seemed fair to say we fomented for war. I felt my face warm at the accusation, not because he had caught me, but because he had angered me.

"The desire to defend your home and all you hold dear is hardly fomenting for war, monsieur. My home was once a place like that," I said, nodding toward the rolling hills and forests that beckoned from the canvas. "Peaceful, quiet, and prosperous. We kept to ourselves, hurting no one, feasting and dancing during the harvests, spending winter by the fire with a cup of cider, warm bread, and toasted cheese. And yet, the armies of the Republic came on a day just as that, with the sun shining and all the good people in the fields, bringing in God's bounty. They demanded we denounce our priests and send our young men off to fight their wars for them. All we wanted, monsieur, was peace. What harm was there in leaving us alone?

"But that is all gone now—all burned, the young men dead, and the old ones too," I continued. "I ask you, is that liberty? Fraternity? Equality? If my companions wage war, it is not because they don't want peace. It is because our peace, our land, our very livelihood has been taken from us. The war we seek to fight is one that was thrust upon us. How I long to simply go back to how things were—how they had been for generations in our little corner of France. But alas, we were cast violently into this war, and war or death are the only ways out of it. So, if there are those among us who want war, it is only in the cause of regaining peace, monsieur." I gestured toward the painting. "They say we fight to restore the king and the church. But for me, it is to restore what you see there. Tranquility. Life."

His expression, which had been keenly amused when he thought he had ensnared me, had gradually grown solemn and sincere. "You are most passionate for your cause, mademoiselle," he said. "You make me quite yearn for this life you once knew."

"I think you would find my country life drab and dull, monsieur. My home was nothing like this. No great parties and elegant styles. And certainly no grand galleries or art to fill them. Where I come from, the mountains and streams and apple blossoms must be our art."

"Grand galleries we have in plenty," he agreed, taking my arm again and leading me out of the parlor we had come to and into the grandest gallery I had ever seen, with gilt edging and scrollwork along its windows and ceilings. The walls were lined with enormous portraits that looked down at the passersby with regal authority. Even their painted gazes unnerved me, so commanding were their poses and their glares. There were great men in royal regalia—past kings of England, no doubt, although I did not know who any of them were. There were young princes and dukes astride their rearing horses, swords drawn to charge into battle, austere kings in flowing robes, beautiful ladies weighed down by loops of pearls and gems.

"She is lovely," I said, stopping before a tall portrait of a lady in a pink dress, a baby on her knee and a second child beside her. But for their noble dress—the children in satin and lace, and enough fabric for ten dresses in her ruffled gown—it might have been Maman, Mathilde, and me, such were the ages of the children. Except, of course, that our mother had not stayed to hold us. I wondered, as I gazed up at the woman, if noble husbands beat their wives like common husbands did.

"That is the Queen Consort Charlotte and the young princes. The boy there," he said, pointing a chubby finger at the standing boy clothed in a long gown of blue lace, "that is Prince George, your host this evening."

I felt a prickle of misgiving again about being in this private gallery without having met the host or gained his permission to wander through his house. "Perhaps we should go back," I said. "I must confess, I hadn't yet met our host when you tempted me away from the table. It was terribly rude of me."

"Don't worry yourself, my dear. We English are not so fastidious about such things, or at least the prince is not. Do you know he is married to a Catholic without his father's consent? I daresay, he is quite a naughty boy," he said, smiling mischievously at this gossip before leading me farther down the gallery.

We came to another portrait of the prince as a young boy in a red satin jacket and trousers. A few steps farther down, and the prince was a young man wearing a stylish gray wig and a green velvet jacket trimmed down the front in gold cord.

"That is another Gainsborough," he said, directing my gaze toward the towering image. "He really is quite good, isn't he? Very promising."

He was right about Gainsborough, I suppose, but I was suddenly in no condition to be discussing artwork. My heart had stopped as I looked up into the face looking down at me, nearly identical to the face that had directed me to look at it. He was, perhaps, ten years younger in the painting and noticeably thinner (or perhaps this Gainsborough fellow knew how to flatter), but there was no mistaking the slope of the forehead or the exaggerated curve of the lips that gave his face its soft, childish look.

I could feel the heat of blood flooding my face, and I was sure there was nothing pretty about my blush. More likely I looked like a pickled beet. My mouth was open, but I couldn't find words to fill it. Should I bow and beg his forgiveness? I pulled my hand from his arm, suddenly aware that I, an illiterate French peasant, was touching the heir to the throne of England.

He was smiling. I could tell even without looking at him. His amusement at his fine joke all but sparkled in the air around me. As for me, I was having a little trouble drawing breath.

Footsteps approached along the marble floor of the corridor. It was probably guards coming to drag me away for my transgression.

"Your Highness," said a voice behind us, and we turned, the prince with smooth grace and me like a child caught thieving from the cider house, to see the Third Marquess of Hertford accompanied by Yannig, Vincent, and Mathilde coming down the galley toward us. The four of them all bowed very low before the prince. I felt I should too, but I was still too mortified to move, and too angry at myself. Why had I been such a fool to go walking off with him without even finding out who he was? What had I been saying—all this nonsense about peace and war as if I knew anything about such great matters of state?

I glanced at my friends. Yannig was staring, wide-eyed. Color was rising in his cheeks, probably anger. I felt a little sick. Had we come all this way only for me to ruin it by making a fool of myself with the prince before our negotiations even had a chance to begin? We had brought Mathilde to charm the prince, but she hadn't gotten a chance because I had somehow pulled him away from the party without even knowing it. I wished I had stayed in France, out of the way of matters so much greater than myself, but it was too late now.

"I have brought the lady and gentlemen you asked for," the marquess said, glancing at me. Perhaps he knew the trick the prince had played on me because he seemed to be fighting to keep the amusement from his face. "But it is as I feared, Your Highness. They mean to draw us into their war. I must advise against it, no matter how fine the prize."

The prince cast an indulgent look at the marquess. "You are a wise advisor, Francis, and I trust you in all matters of art and beauty. But you must leave the subject of war to those who know something of it." He gave a sidelong glance at me before continuing. "I find myself perhaps more persuaded to the merits of this war than I was before."

He turned back to the new arrivals and greeted them in a merry tone. "Welcome, friends! We are all together at last!" He glanced at me, then, his eyes twinkling, gazed up at the picture of himself behind me. "I seem to be doubly here, don't I?"

I turned a little redder, if that was possible, and he giggled before turning back to my associates.

"It has come to my attention that you have brought a great treasure into our fair realm. Or perhaps I should say *several* treasures," he added, taking my hand, lifting it to his lips, and kissing it. Yannig's glare at this gesture added to the heat of my already burning face. He apparently thought I had been clever enough to secure the prince's affections when in truth I hadn't even been clever enough to realize he was the prince.

Yannig opened his mouth, but with a quick, sharp warning glance, the lieutenant spoke over him in a smooth, polite tone. "Yes, Your Highness. When it came into our possession, we knew that there was only one man who could appreciate such a treasure."

"One man other than the King of France, you mean," the prince said.

"I believe that what the King of France would appreciate most right now is his freedom," I said, tagging on a belated, "Your Highness."

The prince chuckled.

"That is true," Vincent said, "and I am sure that he would not begrudge the gift of a fine gem if it were to secure that for him."

"Indeed," the prince said. "When the rabble call for your head, erect the ghastly machine to remove it right outside your window, and demonstrate its use on your friends every day, I suppose a diamond is little comfort."

"So you will help us, then?" Mathilde blurted out, her wide, imploring eyes fixed on the prince.

Such a look from Mathilde had melted strong men before now, but the prince seemed unmoved. He cocked his head, and the corners of his little Cupid's bow mouth curled. "Help you? Mademoiselle, we were talking about me acquiring a fine treasure for my collection."

Mathilde squeezed her lips shut, knowing she spoke out of turn.

"Your Highness, it would be our pleasure to show you the diamond at your earliest convenience," the lieutenant said, giving a formal little bow. "And to discuss the price."

"My earliest convenience would be now," the prince said. "I've grown bored of this party. Only Claudie was good enough to save me from it."

"Alas, Your Highness, we haven't brought it with us," the lieutenant said.

"Then tomorrow." He turned back to me. "You will come tomorrow for tea. You will bring the diamond and whichever of your friends you wish."

"Of course, Your Highness," I said.

"That will be all, Francis," the prince said. "If you will excuse us, we must get back to the artwork. She hasn't yet seen my Titian. You will love it, my dear," he added to me, taking my hand again and draping it on his arm.

I glanced uncertainly at my friends. They were staring with their mouths agape.

Francis, however, was not ready to be dismissed so easily. "Begging your pardon, Your Highness, but your brother has arrived, and he is asking after you."

The prince gave a long-suffering sigh, as if returning to a lavish party was a painful duty, but he released my hand. "Oh, very well. But you must see the rest of my collection when you return tomorrow, Claudie. Promise me?"

"Of course, Your Highness," I said again.

His brow bunched a little, and his delicate mouth turned down, reminding me of a spoiled toddler. "I liked it better when you didn't know who I was."

"I will try to forget by tomorrow, Your Highness," I said.

He laughed at that, and I smiled in response, while my companions all stared at me in disbelief.

The prince extended his elbow to me again, and we walked together back to the celebration, my companions following, slack-jawed, in our wake.

CHAPTER 25

In the carriage on the way home, the lieutenant began laying out a strategic plan for the next day's negotiations, but in truth, I don't think any of us were listening to him. Mathilde's attention was directed out the carriage window—not at anything in particular, just away from us. She was pouting, offended that I had caught the prince's fancy when that had been her presumed role. I wasn't too bothered by that. We were sisters, and I knew she would get over it eventually.

I was more concerned with Yannig and with the expression that had come over his face when he found the prince and me alone and unchaperoned, the prince heaping me with compliments and kissing my hand. I had interrupted Mathilde in her secret tête-à-têtes with Jacques often enough that I knew where such private conversations could lead and what Yannig must now be thinking. I wanted to apologize to him, and yet I didn't. I hadn't done anything wrong. Nothing improper had happened between the prince and me, and I had secured the prince's favor for our cause, even if it had been by accident.

Now, as I sat beside Yannig in the carriage, there was an awkward silence between us. I longed to know what he was thinking, so when the lieutenant addressed a question to Mathilde, I slid my hand into his where it rested on the seat between us. At once, his large fingers closed around it, and he gave a little squeeze. Our eyes met in a gaze that, to my great relief, carried nothing of anger or jealousy. In fact, his face expanded into a huge grin.

"You did it, Claudie," he said quietly, leaning into me.

Relief washed over me. "You're not angry, then?"

He looked a little sheepish. "I was a little worried, that's all. I don't know how I could compete with a prince."

I laughed. "I don't think I could compete with his art collection," I said, returning the squeeze he had given my hand.

"But I have no Titian to show you," he said, a teasing twinkle in his eye.

"I have lived all these years without seeing a Titian," I said with an airy shrug. "I suppose I can live at least this many more without one."

He nodded. "I hope someday to find a way to make up for your loss," he whispered, his lips only a few inches from mine.

The lieutenant cleared his throat, and Yannig and I turned back to him so he could resume the important plans we were making. He soon gave up, seeing the futility of his effort in Yannig's foolish grin, my flushed cheeks, and Mathilde's outthrust lower lip.

After we arrived at home, however, Yannig and Vincent returned their full attention to their plans, with maps and charts and columns of figures spread out across the dining room table. We ladies retired to bed long before they had finished.

Mathilde was subdued as she undressed and slipped under the covers. She did not speak until I had blown out the lantern and tucked myself in beside her.

"The chevaliere will be happy that you won," she said into the darkness. "You are her favorite."

The exhilaration of the party had given way to exhaustion, and I was annoyed by her words now, when sleep beckoned. I opened my eyes and let out an audible sigh. "It wasn't a competition, Mathilde. We were both working for the same cause."

"It's always been a competition," she said matter-of-factly.

"And until now, you've always won," I said, rolling over so my back was to her. "So give me this one victory and let me sleep."

"Just once," she said quietly, as if talking to herself, "just once I would like to be the one who gets listened to. Taken seriously. Just once I would like to be useful."

I opened my eyes again, brought awake by her words. Mathilde wanted what I had? I had never imagined a disadvantage to her beauty. I softened, hearing in her voice the same pain I had felt for myself for so many years. "We are only here now because Jacques trusted that you could complete his mission."

"I didn't even know what it was," she said.

"You knew who we had to look for in Rennes. You saved me from that soldier."

"I did, didn't I?" She snuggled deeper under the covers. "I suppose we all serve as we can. Good night, Claudie." And just like that, the good cheer was back into her voice. We fell off to sleep, warm and comfortable, side by side, as sisters.

We returned to Carlton House early the next day, even as the maids were still clearing away the detritus of the night before—trays of dirty glasses and plates and crumpled linen napkins, ladies' fans and shawls left carelessly behind, a ghastly splash of red wine across an expensive Persian carpet. The butler led us past it all into the private quarters, where Prince George awaited us in a large office, along with Sir Francis Seymour-Conway, Third Marquess of Hertford, and half a dozen other advisors. Yannig and the lieutenant seemed to be known to many of them and were not warmly greeted. I remembered what Yannig had said about doors closed to him, and I bit my lip. Then I remembered what we had to offer, and my fear evaporated.

The prince's face lit when he saw me, and at once he suggested we return to our admiration of his collection, but I reminded him of the business at hand and demurely settled into a chair in the corner where I would not distract. The assembled gentlemen all took their seats at the table, and Yannig set the box before the prince, who eagerly pulled it open. He clapped his hands with delight at the sight of it, then raised it to the light, then held it to his finger, admiring it as if it were already set in a ring that he would flaunt under his father's nose.

"It is glorious!" he declared. "Simply glorious! I must have it, Francis. I must!"

Sir Francis nodded, and the negotiations began.

The day alternated between tense and tedious as Mathilde and I watched from the sidelines, having very little to do. The prince and his advisors were eager to gain the jewel, especially the prince, who had very little self-control and was practically salivating over the great blue diamond. His advisors pressed for Yannig to sell the jewel on credit, but this he flatly refused to do. He had brought the jewel to England to leverage military support, and he was determined to do so. Besides, the prince was famously in debt. There would be a long line of creditors ahead of us before we would see any cash from such a sale.

The prince's enormous debt was a factor we meant to work to our advantage. As soon as the marquess mentioned "the matter of some delicacy regarding the prince's cash flow at the moment," Yannig pressed his case. If the prince could ensure a blockade of French harbors and thirty thousand troops to join the émigré army that would march on Paris, he would not have to raise the money for the gem.

Mathilde and I were quickly bored, having no place in the debate except to offer looks of wordless encouragement to various men in turn. I listened, gaining a better understanding for the art of negotiation. Mathilde, on the other hand, drifted off to sleep in her chair, and when the negotiations extended to a second day, she refused to return with us to the palace.

On the third day, we had a deal, not for the number of ships or troops that we had originally asked for but for enough that Yannig felt victory could be at hand. In high spirits, we returned to our home, but the transaction was not yet complete. The prince had no direct authority over the navy or the army. He had to get his father and the prime minister to agree.

The lieutenant thought this would not be too difficult—the king was already eager to fight the threat to divine monarchy in France, and the prime minister would bow to pressure exerted by the prince and king together. Still, we had a tense week of waiting.

At last, we received a message from the prince—the king and parliament had agreed to send the needed troops, the navy was already on its way across the channel. Papers were signed, hands were shaken, and Mathilde and I, at the prince's request, delivered the diamond to his palace and were given the opportunity to view his Titian, which we did with every admiring word we could think of, though we both blushed at the profusion of naked bodies spread across the enormous canvas before us.

That evening, we celebrated in our London house like we had never celebrated before. Food and wine were in abundance, and we danced, even without an adequate musician, buoyed by our relief and joy.

Late in the evening, when I was considering the merits of my bed, Yannig caught my hand and, with a furtive glance at the others, pulled me out into the back garden. The air was chill, and frost was forming on the bare branches so that they sparkled in the moonlight. I drew the cold air into my lungs, savoring the sensation of being alive.

Yannig wrapped his arms around me, cocooning me in his warmth. I pressed into his embrace.

"What a beautiful night," I said.

"So beautiful," he said, and bending, he put his lips to my neck. My skin prickled eagerly at his touch, and a little hum of pleasure escaped me. I turned and found his lips with my own, and we embraced in a kiss that was deep and long, and much too short.

"I wish we could stay like this forever," I said, my fingers playing in the curls along his neck.

"Forever is a very long time," he said. "Surely you would tire of me before then," he said.

I shook my head and rose on my toes to draw another kiss from

JEANNIE MOBLEY

his lips. He was eager enough to oblige, but after a few seconds he pushed me a little away from him.

"If only I had a forever to spend with you, Claudie Durand, you must know I would."

His words were heartbreaking, and yet I understood. "But you have a war to fight."

"Yes."

We stood like that, locked together in that sparkling garden, and said nothing. What was there to say? He had committed himself to this war before he had ever met me. I could not expect him to abandon it. I had yearned for so long to feel someone's love, and yet I knew it must now be fleeting. Yannig would return to the war in France, and I would either have to find a way to accompany him or say goodbye.

"I have much to do before I leave England, thanks to you," he said. "With the English troops committed, I must raise the émigrés to return. There are thousands of Frenchman in England now. They will be needed."

I nodded into his chest. "Tomorrow," he continued, "I will begin to visit every French noble in London. I will pester every one of them until they have committed to our cause."

"Of that, I have little doubt," I said, mustering a weak smile.

He put a finger under my chin and raised my face to his. There was no humor there. "How it will pain me to leave you," he said.

"I will return with you."

He shook his head. "You will not be safe in France."

"Neither will you," I said, pulling away. "I can help. I can fight for Brittany too."

"I could not bear to lose you," he said. "You must stay here and be safe. Please. For my sake."

"Why must it fall to women to bear the unbearable?" I said breaking his grasp on me. I didn't want to have this conversation. I didn't want to think about him going, let alone the thought of losing him. Of never seeing him again. Of him dying, cold and bloodied in the mud of a battlefield. A sob escaped me as the images of his suffering, like evil omens, blossomed in my mind.

"You know I cannot abandon this cause now. I have sworn my allegiance to the Legion. I have sworn my sword, my strength, the very blood in my body."

I hadn't realized I was crying, but a tear trickled down my cheek, and I wiped it away with the back of my hand, embarrassed. "I can't bear to lose you either."

"Well," he said, a teasing note in his voice, "I'm not planning to get killed."

It was no joking matter. I took a deep breath to steady myself and asked, "When will you be leaving?"

"I can't say for sure. But I hope within the month."

I pressed myself back into his arms. "Then let us make the most of this time we do have."

Time seemed to lose its steady rhythm after that. For the next few weeks, it both dragged and flew by. Yannig went out every day to meet with all the French émigrés in the neighborhood, and then beyond to every neighborhood of London. Some days he returned buoyant, others in a rage, but every day he went out again.

The lieutenant left us after those first few days. As a naval officer, he was taken in by the British navy. We said hasty goodbyes one morning, and we did not see him again after that, but we knew he was engaged in the work that had brought him to England.

For Mathilde and me, the days passed in tedium. We engaged a tutor to learn our letters and to improve our poor English, but I was a poor pupil, worried as I was about matters of war. I bought balls of green wool, remembering the well-camouflaged Chouans, and began knitting socks and caps in the hopes that if I couldn't accompany Yannig back to France, I could at least send with him the things that would keep him warm and safe from the elements. I couldn't do anything to stop bullets or cannon fire, but I could at least keep his toes from freezing in his boots. Mathilde tried to join me in knitting, but she was too distracted and more often spent her time prowling nervously around the house, practicing her English by naming everything she passed until I begged her to be still.

In the evenings, when Yannig would return, the slow, creeping crawl of time would gain speed and propel us toward night. How I longed to slow down the blessed hours I could spend in Yannig's arms each evening, in the narrow span between work and sleep. And yet, those were the hours that turned to minutes and were gone before I could snatch them. Even worse, he sometimes brought gentlemen home with him—men who needed more convincing or who were eager to make plans with him. These men would linger after supper, smoking cigars or playing billiards as they talked, relegating Mathilde and me to the ladies' parlor for more dull loneliness until Yannig was free to be with me. Mathilde did not protest the time I spent with him—in fact, she often gave us privacy, disappearing into the library to practice her reading and writing. But I saw too the secret tears she wiped away at night, and I knew she was still mourning her Jacques. It seemed we Durand sisters were fated to lose the men we loved to this war. I had not lost mine yet, but I could feel my time with him slipping through my fingers.

Gradually, the émigré army became real. The talk had turned into gatherings of men, and the gatherings of men had, with the permission of the English crown, become troops that camped and trained near Portsmouth, just a few miles from the English Channel. As the encampment grew, word spread, and Frenchmen gathered from all corners of England. Yannig no longer had to go house to house to gather support; the support was swelling up from the ground around us and carrying waves of brave, fierce young men with it.

"It is time we left London," Yannig said as we sat by a crackling fire in the parlor one evening three weeks after we had sold the diamond. "I am needed at the camp at Portsmouth. The troops are almost ready. All we await is the signal from Admiral Howe."

My heart twisted, but I tried to speak bravely. "You will go to Portsmouth, then? Before France?"

"We will launch from there," he said. He kissed me, then looked into my eyes. "Will you come with me that far, Claudie? To Portsmouth?"

"Of course!" I said, eager to stay with him every last minute that I could. I was starting to formulate a plan to return to France with him by making myself indispensable to his troops, but I hadn't dared suggest it yet. "Does the encampment need cooks? Washerwomen?"

He grinned. "I doubt there's a soldier anywhere who would turn down a good meal or clean socks."

So the next morning, Mathilde and I put away our fine gowns, dressed in our patched, woolen traveling clothes, and set out with Yannig toward the coast.

The encampment of soldiers spread across a treeless headland from which, if you could withstand the cold and the buffeting wind, you could sometimes see the faint, quivering smudge of France across the slate gray waves. Not that I had time to stand and look out over the ocean. Mathilde and I were busy, along with a small army of cooks, feeding the larger army of men. Our life in an inn, serving food and drink and scrubbing dishes, had prepared us well for the work, and we settled in easily.

Yannig was busy with the troops, and days went by when I saw nothing more of him than a quick glimpse in passing, or a brush of hands when I filled his bowl with soup in the lunch line, but whenever we could, we stole a few moments in the evening just for us, walking away from the camp, hand in hand, seeking out some private grove of trees away from the demands of others, where we could sit together, a blanket spread over us, and whisper our dreams and hopes to each other. He dreamed of restoring a king and a religion, of bringing Brittany through triumphant war to peace. My dreams were more modest—a husband and a quiet home—but these I kept largely to myself, knowing they were beyond my reach in these days of war. And so our tiny snippets of stolen time flew by, and his departure for France loomed before us.

I was carrying a large kettle of fish stew to the lunch line one day, three weeks after our arrival in Portsmouth, when Mathilde came running excitedly toward me.

"Have you heard, Claudie?" she said, breathless. "A party arrived from London an hour ago. The Lieutenant de Tinténiac is among them!" She was flushed with excitement, an excitement that belied more than her passion for the cause, and I remembered all the times the lieutenant had been her escort in London. I had missed it then, but the look on her face was unmistakable. I had seen it many times before, as she had anticipated the arrival of Jacques in our village.

I, however, did not feel the same elation. I knew that Yannig waited only for the signal from the Marquis de la Rouerie, his commander in France, and from Admiral Howe of the British navy. When it came, the coordinated offensive would begin and Yannig would march away from me to his war. Vincent had been working closely with the British navy, and his arrival now surely had to signal great things.

I hurried the kettle to the table and, leaving the other cooks to feed the hungry soldiers, I set out for the commander's tent. Through the open flap, I could see Vincent at the table with Yannig, several commanders from the camp, and two men in British naval uniforms, but a guard at the front of the tent barred my entrance and insisted I return to my duty.

I could barely stand it. They stayed in conference all afternoon, and no information came out, though a variety of men were called to them. Those same men looked grim when they were dismissed, and before long, the camp was astir with uncertainty and discontent.

"What on earth is going on?" Mathilde wondered, but I had no answer for her.

I worked through the day, trying to catch some hint of news from those around us but could learn nothing more than that something had gone wrong. Whole sections of the encampment had dismantled their tents and packed their belongings.

"Maybe they are shipping out to France?" Mathilde said, ever the optimist.

"I don't think so," I replied as I watched one group of men take up their packs and make for the road that led back toward London.

Yannig and the lieutenant did not join the others when we served supper, so when all the men were eating, Mathilde and I took a tray of food and a pitcher of ale to the commander's tent, ready to argue with the guards until they admitted us, only to find the doorway unguarded. Without asking permission, we pulled back the flap and stepped inside. Yannig and Vincent still sat at the table. Alone. Yannig sat hunched, his head in his hands, as if all the world sat on his shoulders. I set down my tray and took the seat beside him, putting my hand on his shoulder.

"What is it? What has happened?"

Yannig shook his head, though he would not take it from his hands. "It is over."

"Over? What is over?" I said, looking in bewilderment from him to the lieutenant and back.

"Everything," Vincent said, his face sagging with the weight of failure.

Though she did not yet know the news, tears were already bright on Mathilde's cheek. She put a gentle hand on Vincent's arm. "Tell us," she said. "Please."

"We have been betrayed," he said. "The Legislative Assembly

may govern from Paris, but they had their fingers in our plans in Brittany, it would seem. They knew everything, all our positions. They raided our command centers in every city and town where we had them. A dozen of our Legion commanders were arrested and taken to Paris, where they were executed. Georges de Fontevieux, Thérèse de Moëlien, Jean Vincent, Madame de la Flonchais. All dead."

My chest tightened until I could scarcely breathe. Mathilde looked so pale I thought she might faint.

"What of the marquis himself?" I asked, fearing the answer but hopeful that his name had not been among those listed. He was the leader; if he had not been captured, there was still hope.

That hope quickly died, however, as Yannig shook his head. "He was spared the guillotine by a putrid fever," he said. "When the Army of the Republic raided the Castle Guyomarch, where he was staying, they found only his cold corpse."

"The Legion is no more," the lieutenant said, "And without it, the English will not sail. Even the Frenchmen we have been training here will not fight without the British at their backs, not when they have already made a safe escape to England. Cowards, the lot of them!"

Yannig's hands came away from his face and slammed hard onto the table in frustrated rage. "Just like that—everything gone!"

"Surely not," I said quickly. "You had ten thousand men in Brittany, did you not?"

"Scattered," Vincent said. "When the raids came, they fled. Some are probably still in the cities and towns, waiting for someone to gather them, but I fear most have returned home or joined the Chouans."

I glanced at Yannig. It had to be a blow to his pride to lose his forces to Jean Chouan after our encounter with him.

"There must be something you can do," I said. "Couldn't you gather them back to you, Yannig? I've seen how they looked up to you in Rennes."

"Yannig can't return," Vincent said. "He was among the leaders that they meant to capture and guillotine. His face and name are known to the Legislative Assembly, and they have posted handbills throughout the region offering a reward for his arrest. Had you not brought the diamond to England, *mon ami*, you would have been lost with the rest of them."

Yannig closed his eyes, his face drawn tight with pain. I could see the guilt he was feeling. He should not have been the one to bring the diamond to England. He should have stayed in France. If he had, the marquis may have survived. I sent a silent prayer of thanks to the heavens for the twist of fate that had spared him. I laid my hand on his arm again, feeling the hard muscle there, taut and ready for action, though there seemed to be no action to take.

"There must be something you can do," I insisted again. It was too impossible that all those months of struggle could come to nothing in just an instant. "Aren't there other countries that will rise against the Republic? What about the Dutch, or the Spanish?"

"And how are we to convince those governments to do more than they do now?" Yannig said. "We've lost our forces that would have helped them. We've lost the diamond with which we might have paid them."

"The prince promised troops in exchange for the diamond. Surely if the British refuse to sail, he must give the diamond back."

The lieutenant laughed bitterly at that. "One thing Prince George does not do is give things back. Ask any of his creditors awaiting their payment."

"But—"

"We knew it was a risk," Yannig said. "We knew he wasn't trustworthy with promised money. We'd only hoped it would be different with a payment in troops, but . . ." He shrugged and turned his eyes to mine. I had never seen such exhaustion there. "It is over."

"Over," Vincent repeated.

We sat in silence then, hearing the hammer of hooves as a single rider approached, undoubtedly bearing a message. Such riders had come and gone on a busy schedule throughout the last month. This one now seemed out of step with the matters around him.

He dismounted outside the tent and called a greeting.

Yannig, ever the commander, straightened his shoulders and bade the messenger enter.

The man walked in and saluted before handing a paper to Yannig. Yannig thanked him and dismissed the messenger to get a meal and a bit of rest.

We all looked hopefully at the paper. Perhaps it carried some news that would save us. Some small victory that would convince the émigrés and the English to keep fighting.

Yannig slid his finger along the edge of the paper, breaking the wax seal. He opened it and read the lines in silence. Then he turned it facedown on the table and looked up at the rest of us. I had never known the full depths of despair until I saw that look in his eyes.

"Louis is dead," he said. "They have guillotined our king."

CHAPTER 26

That was a black night. By noon the next day, half the forces that had gathered in our camp outside Portsmouth had packed their belongings and disappeared, back to wherever they had come from. Those that remained did not go to their daily drills but sat listlessly, waiting for some news that might give them a reason to stay. By afternoon, when none had come and news of the king's execution began to spread, still more of them trickled away. In ordinary times, such action would have been desertion and punishable by death, but as Yannig's army was not sanctioned by any government, there was no authority that would seek them out, and Yannig seemed uninterested or unwilling to force anyone to stay.

When Yannig did not come to eat supper with his men that evening, I once again took his meal to the commander's tent. He was there at the same table in the same seat he had been in the previous night, and I wondered if he had moved at all. He had spread maps and reports out before him, but his eyes did not seem to focus on them, and when I cleared some away to set the plate before him and put a fork in his hand, he did not protest. He looked up at me with bloodshot eyes and sighed.

"It's no use, Claudie. I've been here all day looking for another way—another course of action to move us forward—but there is nothing. Without a force on the ground in France, no nation will send their own troops to meet the same fate as the Duke of Brunswick's."

"What of the Chouans?" I said. "If your forces have joined them, can't we ask them to meet the British when they land?"

Yannig ran a hand through his hair. "The Chouans will never fight beside the English. They don't like foreigners any more than they like the Republicans. And their style of fighting—it will distract the Republic and perhaps keep their priests safe in their local villages, but it is not war. No, I would have to gather men back from the Chouans, and how can I do that when the Republican Army is searching Brittany for me?"

He took a bite of the meat pie I had set before him, then pushed it away. "I am not afraid of them, Claudie. I am not afraid for myself. But I would not have time to rally scattered forces. And I would not trust the Chouan brothers with my safety. If they think I am taking forces away from them, they would not hesitate to betray me to the Army of the Republic. We might fight for the same principles, but their cause is their own."

A treasonous hope rose in my heart as I realized what he was saying. He could not return to France. That fragile dream of home and husband shone before me. I wanted to ask it of him. I could picture an inn here on the coast of England, me in the kitchen making cheese, brewing cider, cooking meals, and Yannig as the good publican, leading a quiet life far from danger.

I wanted nothing more, and it seemed almost in our grasp—but I loved him. I loved him as the man he was—the whole man—complete with ideals and goals and dreams of his own. Because I loved him, I wanted to keep him safe beside me.

Because I loved him, I said, "We will find a way to get the diamond back from the prince. We will take it to the Spanish or the

Dutch. The Americans, if we have to. We'll find someone to help us."

Yannig was shaking his head, but I persisted.

"I will go back to London and talk to him. He liked me. Surely he will see our plight. If not, there must be some legal action we can take. He cannot keep the diamond if he did not come through with his end of the bargain."

"What English court is going to hear your case?" he scoffed. "A French peasant with a stolen diamond versus the heir to their own throne."

I felt the crushing truth of his words. The prince had liked me, but I was nothing to him compared to possessing the diamond of Louis XIV.

"There is really no hope, then?" I asked in a small voice.

He sighed, a long, deep exhale that diminished him from the fierce revolutionary into an ordinary man. "Our war is lost, Claudie. At least for now. Perhaps someday . . ." He trailed off.

Someday was something, but it was something with a wide-open space between me and it, and in that space a bright hope flared. I reached across the table and took his hand, and I held it tightly between my own. "Then stay with me, Yannig. Stay with me, and we will build a new life here."

He shook his head. "But I have failed you. I have failed everyone."

"You have not failed me," I said, drawing him to me and pressing my lips to his—lips I had thought would never know this pleasure. "You have saved me, Yannig."

"By bringing you to England," he said. "I suppose that was what you wanted all along."

"By seeing my worth," I corrected. *By making me see my worth*, I told myself. I held his face in both my hands, looking unflinchingly into his eyes. "You do love me, don't you?"

"I do," he said.

"Then marry me," I said.

He lifted an eyebrow, but he did not pull out of my grasp. "Aren't I supposed to ask that?"

"Then ask it," I told him.

He asked, and I gave him a kiss in answer.

Our wedding was a simple one, as weddings are in times of war. I wore the same worn woolen dress I'd been wearing when we met. I still had the fine dresses I had worn in London, but I did not wish to remind Yannig of our failure there and my role in it. Besides, I wanted to keep the dresses nice. They were well made, in the most current fashion, and I thought that perhaps I might stitch together the price of an inn if I could find the right buyer for them.

Yannig wore his everyday clothes too, but he had shaved and trimmed his hair and tied it back in a neat black ribbon. The sun gleamed behind him as we walked to the tent of a priest-turned-soldier who had not yet left camp, and I was reminded again of the vision I'd beheld that first day Yannig had arrived in our village, looking down from his mount like a knight of old.

He was not a knight; for now, he was not even a soldier, but I knew that it would not always be so. Our wedding and the days that followed were stolen time, a blissful interlude before his ideals called him back into the service of France.

Until that day, he was all mine, bound to me by the priest and the sacrament he bestowed. Bound to me that night on a lumpy straw mattress in a Portsmouth inn, while my sister and our friends celebrated long into the night in the pub below our room, cheering when the creaking of the ancient bedstead became loud enough to carry through the floor below us.

In the morning, Mathilde and Vincent were gone. A note was left behind in the lieutenant's precise hand. They were sailing for France. Vincent too had a price on his head but was not so fiercely sought as Yannig, and they meant to join the Chouan brothers, to fight their scattered skirmishes in the hills. Mathilde had promised herself to the cause long ago in the arms of Jacques, and she meant to honor him by keeping that promise, or so the letter told us, in a passage Vincent had written for her:

> You will want to come after me, Claudie, to take care of me
> like you have always done. But you are a wife now. You must
> take care of Yannig and let me go. You have been the best
> mother to me a girl could have. It is time for me to take care
> of myself. *Au revoir*, dearest Claudie, until we meet again,
> on which shore I cannot say.

Those were the last lines she left me. Of course I wanted to follow her—retrieve her and keep her safe—but Yannig read those lines to me again, and I saw the truth in them. It was time for her to take care of herself. And though I wept to think of her sailing back to France and the wars that raged there, I did not follow. I let her go.

CHAPTER 27

And so here I am, nearly a year later, feeding sailors as they come into Portsmouth, Yannig gathering news from them, always with the hope of returning to the aid of France. So many rumors, each as paper-thin as the last, that this country or that will enter the war. That Louis-Charles, the little heir to the throne, has been spirited out of his prison in Paris, that the Spanish or Italians or Portuguese are promising money or troops or ships, but we have learned not to put too much store in rumors. Time and again, we have been disappointed. Perhaps some of the rumors have an element of truth, but we of all people know that promises might be made and still come to nothing.

We gather money too for the children of Mother France, scattered to the four winds, with nothing but their fragile lives and the hope of a better tomorrow. I take them baskets of food and clothes and a few farthings that might get them to wherever in England they have a friend or relative who can help them rebuild.

Yannig says I do this because I no longer have Mathilde to mother. He says that perhaps he should give me something of my own to mother. The thought fills me with joy, and yet, I cannot let it happen just yet.

Because a new letter has arrived from Mathilde. Vincent has left her with the Army of the Vendée, where the counterrevolution has gained strength more than it ever did in neighboring Brittany. He has at last achieved an agreement with the British navy to bring a fleet to the aid of France if the Vendeans will secure a port city for their landing. My sister writes:

> We have an army twenty-five thousand men strong and
> our eye on Granville. The handsome, young comte de la
> Rochejaquelein, Henri du Vergier, leads our forces. Claudie,
> I never thought to meet a man as wonderful as Jacques, but
> Henri is the best of men. I have joined his forces as one of the
> women who cooks for the troops—my training in Papa's inn
> doing some good after all.
>
> Claudie, I write you now because we need your help.
> Perhaps we can take Granville on our own, but our chances
> would be better, and our losses less severe, if we had aid
> from Brittany. There are men there—hundreds of men—who
> supported the Legion. Every day they trickle in to join us in
> the Vendée. A large number of them are gathering near Rennes,
> but they lack a leader.
>
> I would not take Yannig away from you lightly, Claudie.
> But if you would send him—if he could lead the force from
> Rennes as he was always meant to do—we would be assured
> success. We could at last have the troops and the British
> support that you bought with the diamond. Please consider it.
> I hope to see him in a month's time in Granville.
>
> > Your loving sister,
> > Mathilde

A month's time. November. The hardest time of year, with winter coming. And yet, the time that Yannig had always meant to launch his war, when the farmers can be spared from their work in the fields and food is assured from the harvest.

A month's time. Marching across Brittany once again, to welcome the British, to fight for the ideals of our people. To fight. Perhaps to die. The thought gathers tight in my throat so that I can scarcely breathe.

There is a fire in the kitchen hearth. If I throw the letter into it, Yannig would never know. We could go on here, peacefully. Perhaps we could have that baby—several babies—and raise them as little Cornish lads and lasses knowing nothing of the struggles of France. I close my eyes, breathe in the comfort of that simple, gentle dream.

The dream evaporates when the door opens and Yannig comes in. He has been out, gathering news at the port, unaware that, once again, I have the very thing he wants, right under his nose.

I get up from my seat by the fire and fill him a bowl of the seafood stew I have simmering for him. I cut a slice of bread and pour him a cup of cider. The English, it turns out, grow apples almost as fine as those in Brittany, and the press I put up a few months ago is now crisp and sharp, as a good cider should be.

I take the meal to the table and set it before him. He sits, then sweeps me off my feet and onto his lap, enjoying a nuzzle against my neck before his lunch. I enjoy it too, and I let him linger there, his breath warm against my neck. I close my eyes to savor the moment.

"Claudie? What is it?" he asks, seeing my expression.

I open my eyes. "Good news," I say, though I am choking on it. I hand him the letter.

His eyes are on fire by the time he finishes reading. "I must go, right away."

"You must," I agree.

He cups my face in his big, warm hand. "But I will come back to you, Claudie, I swear."

I shake my head. I cannot bear to look in his eyes, so full of longing and love and sorrow. "You will not."

He frowns. "Do you have so little faith in me?"

"You will not come back to me because I am coming with you," I say, and now I do look in his eyes so he can see my determination and know there is no point in arguing.

His jaw tightens. "Claudie, you must stay here, where it's safe."

"Then so must you."

"You know I cannot . . ."

"Then you know I cannot either. Wheresoever you go, I will follow," I say.

Our gazes lock for a long moment, clashing like the blades of great fencers, but then slowly, he yields.

"It will be dangerous," he says. "Remember, the Republic still has a price on my head."

"Remember how you didn't end up with a bullet in your back before we reached Bon Repos," I reply. If he thinks danger will keep me home, I intend to remind him of how useful I can be at his side.

"You would have to learn to take orders," he says.

"Then you will have to learn to give me orders I want to take," I say.

"You are insufferable," he grumbles.

"I love you too," I say. "Now eat your lunch. We have much to do if we are going to sail in the morning."

The sea is gray as we set out from Plymouth, crossing the channel once again aboard a smuggler's ship, returning a handful of armed émigrés to fight for France. Back to Brittany, to stand, perhaps to die, for what he—what *we*—believe in.

I take his hand in mine as I look out across the water. It is an uncertain future that awaits us on the invisible shore beyond—a future sure to include blood and hardship, but days of joy in each other's arms as well. And after all, what is life without struggle?

"You should have stayed, Claudie," he whispers into my blowing tangles of hair as the wind fills our sails and we are rushed away from the sight of land. "But I am glad you didn't."

I am glad too, whatever the future holds. I turn and press my head against his chest as he wraps his arms around me.

"Promise me one thing, Yannig, whatever happens," I say.

"That I will always love you?" he asks.

"That you will not deny me the chance to be useful, no matter the circumstances," I answer.

His lips curve into a smile, and he squeezes my shoulders. "I promise," he whispers into my ear, and together, we look out at the horizon toward whatever the future holds for us.

HISTORICAL NOTE

The history of the French Blue diamond is a complicated one, some details of which have been preserved, while others have not. We know that the diamond first came from India in 1668, brought by Jean-Baptiste Tavernier, who sold it to Louis XIV as a large raw diamond known as the Tavernier Violet. Louis XIV had the diamond cut by his crown jeweler into the stone that appears in this story, known in France as the Blue of the Crown but to English speakers as the French Blue.

We also know that in 1792, amid the turmoil of the French Revolution, the crown jewels were stolen. Some of the jewels were recovered, but many, including the French Blue, were not. What happened next to the diamond is not known, although a variety of hypotheses have been put forward over the years. It has been suggested that the French Blue was used to bribe the Duke of Brunswick into turning back from his march toward Paris with the Prussian army, thus explaining his inexplicable retreat after the Battle of Valmy in the fall of 1792. Another hypothesis puts the stone in Paris, hidden throughout the revolution and only leaving the country later. Still others have suggested the stone made its way to Austria or to the Netherlands.

The hypothesis that makes the most sense to me, and that I have chosen for this story, is that the stone ended up in England in the collections of Prince George, an extravagant art collector and spender of money. The evidence to support this comes years later, in 1812, when the stone is documented in the possession of a London merchant, Daniel Eliason. The Smithsonian links Eliason to King George IV (Prince George in 1792) and the sale of the diamond in 1830 to the king's death and the need to clear his enormous debts.

In 1787, despite the prince's annual allowance of fifty thousand pounds (a sum equivalent to around six million pounds today), parliament had to extend a grant of 161,000 pounds to clear his debts, which, once cleared, immediately began mounting again. George's penchant for extravagance, art collecting, and overspending, and the documented efforts of the Breton League to gain the support of the British navy, make my fictitious story a possibility.

The diamond's ownership only becomes well documented again in 1839, when it appears in the gem collection of Henry Philip Hope, whose name the diamond has held ever since.

As for why I chose to write about the counterrevolution in Brittany, I wanted to write a French Revolution story that did not center on Paris. There are many excellent stories that focus on the momentous events that took place in that city. I wanted to place my focus elsewhere. I also wanted to find an angle for the story that would cast the thieves as people of principle, not just greedy opportunists out to get rich. When I stumbled upon the counterrevolutions of western France, I knew I had found my story.

The events of 1792 in Paris are some of the most notorious of the French Revolution, with the arrest and imprisonment of the king, the abolishment of the monarchy, the prison massacres, and the outbreak of war between the new government of France and many of the European powers that surrounded it. At the same time, counterrevolution was brewing in western France, in Brittany and the adjacent Vendée region. These areas had not been as devastated by crop failures as other parts of France, the landlord-tenant relationships in the region were not as egregious as elsewhere, and perhaps most importantly, the Catholic faith ran strong in the region. Thus, the people of the region were largely isolated from the factors that drove the revolution elsewhere in France. In Brittany, many saw the revolution as a threat to a long-held, deeply cherished way of life. This threat culminated in the War of the Vendée, from the spring of 1793 to 1796; however, before the War of the Vendée, a number of other counterrevolutionary efforts occurred, including the formation of the *Association Bretonne*, or Breton League, formed by Charles Armond Tuffin, the Marquis of Rouerie, who appears briefly in my novel when he meets with Yannig in Rennes.

This league was one of the better organized attempts at counterrevolution, led by aristocrats and experienced military leaders. It was, however, betrayed before it could come to fruition, and its leaders executed in December of 1792. Simultaneously, peasants and farmers were organizing for a less formal, guerilla-style combat throughout Brittany under the leadership of the Chouan brothers, most notably Jean Chouan. This conflict, known as the Chouannerie, was among the last to be suppressed by the French Republic, with raids, assassinations, and small uprisings persisting until 1800.

In the spring of 1793, these scattered efforts and revolts coalesced into the Army of the Vendée, the most successful of the efforts. The Army of the Vendée experienced a number of military successes in the Loire Valley and advanced across western France, gathering men and gaining control of territory. The naval commander Lieutenant

Vincent de Tinténiac played a role in both the Breton League and, after its collapse, in the Vendean army as a liaison between the British navy and the French forces.

In the fall of 1793, Tinténiac secured the aid of the British, contingent on the Vendean army securing a port. This set up the siege of Granville and the turning point in the Vendean's successful advance. The Vendean forces encountered a strong Republican force around Granville and were unsuccessful in taking the port city, in part because the British fleet never arrived. The failure at Granville set in motion a disastrous retreat in which much of the Vendean army was slaughtered.

If you want a happy ending for Claudie and Yannig, stop reading here because the remaining history of the counterrevolution in western France is a tragic one. In the fall of 1793, the Committee of Public Safety, the governing body of the time, called for a complete "pacification" of the region, a ruthless demand that included the wholesale slaughter of the populace. Farms, villages, and forests were burned, and tens of thousands of people across Brittany and the Vendée were killed—combatants and civilians alike. Historians estimate that between a quarter to a half of the residents of the region were killed in this pacification. Occurring simultaneously with the Reign of Terror in Paris, the War of the Vendée has received less attention. However, historian Reynald Secher has argued that the Republic's response to the War of the Vendée was the first modern genocide in Europe. This claim has been hotly contested by other historians, but whatever side you take, there is no denying that the royalist uprisings of the region met a horrific end. I would like to think Claudie and Yannig survived the atrocities and got their quiet inn in the end, but as they are purely works of fiction, I will let you imagine whatever end for them you please.

I chose to set my story in the early days of this conflict to coordinate with the timing of the theft of the French Blue and to give my characters a more hopeful setting in which to struggle to preserve their way of life. While the main characters of my story—Claudie, Mathilde, Yannig, and Jacques Lambert—are fictional, others are not, as you have no doubt surmised from this historical note. Jean Chouan, Lieutenant Vincent de Tinténiac, Prince George IV of England and his illegal marriage to Maria Fitzherbert, the Chevaliere d'Éon, and Lord Francis Seymour-Conway were all real. I have tried to glean something of their personalities from contemporary accounts and portraiture. My portrayals are, of course, my own imagining, but ones that I hope are mostly accurate. I have taken a few liberties to make my story work, most notably with the Abbey of Bon Repos, which I have made a nunnery when in fact it housed only men of the Cistercian order.

The Chevaliere d'Éon deserves a special note here. Undoubtedly, there are readers who found the presence of an openly transgender individual at the end of the eighteenth century to be surprising or even implausible. She was, however, a real person, well known in London society, and an associate of Prince George IV.

Charles-Geneviève-Louis-Auguste-André-Timothée d'Éon d Beaumont was born in France in 1728 and raised as a boy. D'Éon served as a diplomat for France in England and is supposed to also have spied for Louis XV, infiltrating the Russian court as the lady Lia of Beaumont, although the validity of this story is questionable. D'Éon also served as a military commander during this time.

While serving as an ambassador in England, d'Éon betrayed the French king's secrets and was banished from France for doing so, but continued to receive a monthly pension from the French government, perhaps to keep silent on any remaining secrets. D'Éon was only able to secure a return to France in 1777, after the death of Louis XV, by negotiating a deal with the new king that included the legal recognition of d'Éon as a woman. D'Éon, who stated that she had been assigned female at birth but raised as a boy to secure the family inheritance, was granted recognition and was required to dress in appropriate women's clothing.

In 1785, she returned to England, where she lived openly as a woman, although she still, at times, appeared in public in a man's military garb. She was considered fashionable and moved freely in society, associated with various high governmental and military leaders, and participated in fencing contests and exhibitions. A painting of her fencing at Carlton House before Prince George himself is what inspired me to include her in this novel. She would have been a powerful ally for French émigrés looking to sell a diamond, with her high connections and her history as a spy and diplomat. She is an excellent reminder that our modern lens on the past has often been cleansed by the historians of ensuing years. In fact, the English nobility in the Georgian era enjoyed a somewhat relaxed view of both sexuality and gender, and d'Éon is not the only member of society at the time known to have been transgender or genderfluid. Historians of the subsequent, and more repressed, Victorian era preferred not to remember such individuals, and undoubtedly many have been erased from the history of that time period.

Acknowledgments

Writing this book during the coronavirus pandemic was a challenge, made easier by the family and friends that supported me, albeit from a distance. As always, my Colorado writing community kept me sane, and I am eternally grateful for you (you know who you are!). I look forward to once again sharing dinner, drinks, book launches, laughter, and actual physical space with all of you, but even at a distance, know that you have kept me going. I am grateful, too, for the backing of the remarkable Rocky Mountain Chapter of the SCBWI and the outstanding volunteers who have created so many chances to connect in these isolating times.

At Viking, my editors Dana Leydig and Jenny Bak have been tireless and wonderful. Thank you for your guidance and for involving me in so many key decisions. My agent, Jennifer Weltz, saved me with her critical eye and amazing insight. Val Gryphin provided helpful insights on framing a transgender character in a historical novel. Thank you, too, to all the behind-the-scenes folks at Viking who made my pages of words into the beautiful book it is today. I don't know all your names, but I appreciate your efforts!

My kids and mom remain my lifeline in so many ways, but on this book, I need to offer the hugest debt of gratitude to my husband, Ken, who maintained an infinite supply of patience in the face of my writing woes while stuck in the house with me full time for over a year. Thank you for the space and the quiet and the time to work

house became office, elder care, and classroom. Thank yo
or the companionship in that narrow sliver of the day between
work ended and when I passed out in exhaustion on the couch.
ucky to have you. (Ken, not the couch. Although the couch is
comfy too.)

345